THE
TRUTH
TOGETHER

THE
TRUTH
TOGETHER

KELLY RODGERS

THE TRUTH TOGETHER. Copyright © 2022 Kelly Rodgers

ISBN: 979-8-9860319-0-3

All rights reserved.

Published by Kelly Rodgers 2022

Roswell, GA

No parts of this publication may be reproduced, stored in a retrieval system, or transmitted in any form or by any means, electronic, mechanical, photocopying, recording, or otherwise, without the prior written permission of the copyright owner.

This book is sold subject to the condition that it shall not, by way of trade or otherwise, be lent, resold, hired out, or otherwise circulated without the publisher's prior consent in any form of binding or cover other than that in which it is published and without a similar condition including this condition being imposed on the subsequent purchaser. Under no circumstances may any part of this book be photocopied for resale.

This is a work of fiction. Names, characters, places and incidents either are the product of the author's imagination or are used fictiously. Any resemblance to actual persons, living or dead, events or locales is entirely coincidental.

Cover Photography from Pixabay.
Cover and interior design by Laura Boyle Design.

I'm a history teacher and storytelling is what I do. I have long been fascinated by those whose stories did not end up in the history books. I grew up in Georgia and after a brief stay in other places, I returned some thirty years ago. I am of Georgia. It is my home down deep in my soul. So too are her stories, especially those that have not been shared broadly, outside a small circle of people fortunate to have heard them. This is one of those.

KR

For JBW.
She taught me to cherish family, home,
history, and a good story.

Effie

JUNE, 1922

1

Sweat prickled from her skin and rolled down her spine slow and steady. Early June and already Atlanta was stifling. Her briar-rose colored summer weight suit, a mistake, no longer correctable. Motionless in the middle of Terminal Station, Effie summoned the courage to board the eight o'clock train to Milledgeville. Clutching the one-way first-class ticket purchased days earlier, she drew a breath to calm her jangling nerves. Her light complexion afforded her a possibility. A choice really. *Colored or white?* This choice had never been hers. Her family had always made it for her. *Of all the decisions looming ahead, why should this one matter so much?* By virtue of her purchase, she had already chosen. Now she faced a simple test. Was she bold enough to see it through? *Not for a lifetime*, she reminded herself, but for the simple ease of travel. *Just for today.* She was no Homer Plessy. In fact, Effie hoped to avoid attracting any attention at all, but she had been around enough to know that separate was never equal. The car for Coloreds was tightly packed, there was no place for bags, and the toilet rooms were plain nasty. On her way to something brand new, she was brimming with the untried, a longed-for metamorphosis. All she wanted was that the journey be civilized.

Why didn't I just let Norris drive me? Sometimes, her tenacity was her undoing. After he returned from Harvard the previous year, her brother had stepped right into his Vice President of Atlanta Life shoes like they were custom made. Not only had he taken his place at their father's side, running the family business, he had promoted himself to big boss of Effie's life. Unnecessarily, she mused. Effie reveled in making her own choices, regardless of whether they ended in triumph or defeat. This trip meant everything to her. She wanted to experience every moment of it for herself, not tethered to her brother for safekeeping.

Effie's decision to take a nursing position at the Georgia State Sanitarium was not made on a whim. It was the result of several months' worth of plotting, planning, and sifting through options, since graduating from the Municipal Training School for Colored Nurses at Grady Hospital. The way she saw it, there were three alternatives. Choose one of the beaus Norris offered up and settle into a dull and lifeless marriage, continue as a private duty nurse—which wasn't really nursing at all—or take a leap. So here she was now, leaping.

As her departure had neared, Effie felt like a cat on hot bricks. Did she know enough? Was she strong enough? Could she make it on her own? *Too late to turn back now. Breathe. You are the daughter of Adrienne McNeil Herndon, correction—Anne DuBignon. Get on the damn train.* Effie tipped the porter carrying her mother's slightly worn, but still fashionable, olive-colored traveling bags, and swept rather theatrically across the platform. Arriving at coach number two, she let her eyes linger for a moment on the white metal sign posted near the train door. In bold, black letters, it proclaimed, "Reserved for white ladies and gentlemen." Effie grabbed the handhold and lifted herself onto the train. Once boarded, she slid into the window seat and with trembling fingers, pulled a white linen handkerchief from her purse, dabbed her brow, took a few breaths, and remembered to relax her face. *Composed, tranquil,* she commanded. The stage directions her mother had so often used to correct her behaviors when she was a child remained useful and to some degree, they steadied her. To distract herself from the anticipated encounter with the train's conductor and the potential humiliation of being forced to leave the car, she glanced around to discover who might be there serving witness to her fate.

Across the way, a woman and a young girl with long chestnut curls settled in for the journey. The gentleness that flowed between them as they readied themselves for the trip stirred something inside her. Effie tried not to stare. The woman smoothed her skirts. The girl copied the gesture. The mother laid her hand on the girl's arm. Her daughter smiled, leaning her head on her mother's shoulder.

A longing welled in Effie's throat. Her own mother had died when Effie was eight. It was her mother's voice that played out in her head when she gave herself a good talking to—often as of late.

"Madam, your ticket."

Effie startled. Lost in her reverie, she had failed to notice the conductor's approach. *Meet his gaze, steady your hands,* she directed. Recovering quickly, she handed the ticket over with just the right touch of mundaneness. The conductor raised his eyes to Effie's perfectly composed face. A brief unblinking appraisal and with that the deed was done. The uniformed man turned to the passengers seated on the opposite aisle. The lump in her gut dissolving, Effie pursed her lips and blew out a long breath. Momentarily more confident, she turned to watch the realization of her liberation through the large glass window as they emerged from the dark station into the brilliant sunlit summer morning.

The hours ticked past and the gentle rocking, along with the summer heat, soothed her into a drowsy half-lucid state. She wondered about seeing Sallie Davis again, her mother's old friend. She had no real memories of Sallie, only what she knew from stories told by her nursing school mentor, Ludie Andrews. The women had met at Atlanta University where Effie's mother was a drama and elocution teacher. Dozens of young people had passed through her courses, benefiting from her particular brand of passion and performance. Mrs. Andrews trained to be a nurse and later founded the Municipal School at Grady. She had taken Effie under her wing and encouraged her to take up nursing as a profession. Mrs. Davis became a teacher and returned home to Milledgeville. The two of them had conspired to make this moment possible for Effie.

Everything was coming together. The new position at the sanitarium gave Effie hope that she could indeed take charge of her own future. She understood that the efforts made on her behalf were connected to the feelings the women had for her mother, but she had worked hard to earn this. Effie held fast to that claim. She had skills. She was a smart and diligent student. But more than that, Effie prided herself in keeping her calm in every situation. And she knew how to control her feelings, precisely arrange her features to convey emotions not entirely authentic, but necessary in certain circumstances. This particular skill, she believed, inherited from or taught by her mother, an actress and lover of the stage play.

Having taken inventory of her abilities, Effie fluttered her eyelids open. Not five inches from her stood the young girl who was seated opposite her. Now the two of them were frozen in a stare down.

"Do you have any secrets?" the girl asked.

"Pardon me?" Effie roused herself from her languid state.

"Do *you* have any secrets?" she demanded.

"Plenty," Effie replied.

"Oh, do tell me one of them."

Effie glanced at the girl's sleeping mother. "If I told, they wouldn't be secrets anymore."

"I bet I could guess one," the girl persisted.

"Give it a try," Effie shot back.

Moving closer, she half whispered, "I bet you are black on the inside."

Effie cleared her throat and tugged her suit coat's sleeves over her wrists. "You know how I know?"

Effie glanced out the window. *Middle of nowhere. Would they really put me off here?*

She shook her head and swallowed hard.

"Because I'm black on the inside. Everybody is because there isn't any light in there," the girl said earnestly, pointing to her belly.

Relax. Show your knowledge. Effie smiled. "Hmm. Well actually, people are pretty colorful on the inside."

"How do you know that?"

"I'm a nurse. I've seen the insides of a few people. And every one I've seen is full of colors. Red, brown, yellow, white, practically a rainbow."

"I don't believe that."

"Well you should. It isn't a secret."

"Charlotte, come back to your seat," the girl's mother directed. "I'm so sorry."

"Not to worry," Effie smiled. "She's a perfectly lovely child."

She stepped from the passenger car onto a shade-dappled platform. The magnolia-scented breeze ruffled her clothing. *It's not Auburn Avenue*, Effie observed. Near the small red brick building stood a lovely, statuesque woman in a white dropped-waist dress and a wide-brimmed straw hat, dramatically angled to one side. She raised her hand. Effie moved toward her, unsure how familiar she should be with a woman she did not quite remember meeting so many years ago at her mother's funeral.

"Welcome to Milledgeville, Effie," she said, offering her hand. "Call me Sallie. We might not be contemporaries, but I know we'll have an amicable relationship."

"Thank you. And thank you for inviting me to visit."

Sallie directed the porter to store Effie's large bag at the station for the continuation of her journey. "It's a short walk home. I imagine your legs need a good stretch."

The houses were small and neat. A whiff of frying chicken and baking bread drifted past while children frisked about in the grass-covered yards. Nearing the intersection of Clarke and Washington, Sallie pointed to a pristine white house on the corner lot flanked by myrtle trees and gardenias. "There. Not quite the quarters you're used to, but it's home. My husband passed a few years back. I take on some boarders from time to time, but just now it's you and me. That's my church on the next block. Down the street, The Eddy School. This is where I live and work."

"You'll want to wash up and get out of that suit," Sallie offered as she led Effie to a modest bedroom.

At the window overlooking the backyard, Effie pulled aside the lace curtain. A lush vegetable garden overwhelmed the space. A plum tree, birdhouses, and a couple of cast iron chairs tucked under a matching round table completed the bucolic setting. The flourishing bounty of it tugged at her memory and lifted something cumbersome from her insides. Out of her element in this small, sleepy town, Effie already felt the weight of her life in Atlanta somehow seemed lighter. She wasn't quite sure about Sallie Davis yet. The woman hardly smiled. Not standoffish by any means, on the contrary, she was quite chatty, but somewhat efficient and matter of fact. Perhaps, Effie thought, that was the nature of teachers. They explained things and gave directions, expecting everyone to do as told. "Like Mama," she whispered.

Effie peeled off her traveling clothes and slipped on a light summer shift. After washing her face and combing out her hair, she ventured toward the source of the delightful aroma wafting through the house and found Sallie at the stove.

"I've got tomatoes and okra simmering. Cornbread's in the oven. There's a pitcher of tea on the table. You can get some ice from the icebox."

Effie followed directions.

Sallie cut her eyes at Effie, watching to see how comfortable she was in her kitchen. "The table needs setting, and there's a basket on the counter for some berries."

After supper, Effie and Sallie moved to the front porch with bowls of plump blackberries and fresh cream. They settled into two cane-backed rockers, savored the tart and sweet taste of summer in the South, and tuned into the night music floating across the sultry sweetness of gardenia blossoms. Piano chords hovered above the chirping and clicking of crickets and katydids. Families on other not too distant front porches laughed and talked.

"I expect you remember a good deal of your mother," Sallie offered. "You were young when she passed, but not young enough to forget."

Captivated by fireflies that zigged and zagged through low hanging branches, Effie nodded. "She's been on my mind a lot today."

"She was our teacher, but not much older than us. Almost like sisters instead of students. Don't get me wrong, she expected a lot from us. She knew things we hadn't discovered yet. Handed that knowledge over to us in a way that made us feel like she was giving us something powerful."

Sallie paused for a moment, picking her words with care.

"Our lives were different from yours. Our folks lived through hell and came through on the other side. Most of them went through the Emancipation, but they didn't understand how to be free. The white folks were mostly hostile. They didn't know how to deal with us unfettered. Then all those schools started up, teachers and missionaries poured down from the North. My mama learned to read in the first colored school in our town. Education mattered to her. She made sure I got one. For a minute it looked like things were getting better. But it was hard for folks to get used to things being different. Now, I can't tell if we're moving frontward or backward. I'm afraid I know the answer, but I'm not willing to give up hope just yet."

Effie offered nothing, so Sallie went on.

"I didn't get to see too much of Addy after you were born. She took you and Norris up north for a while. When she came home, she was different, tempered somehow. Went back to the university, dreamed up that house you grew up in, and talked Alonzo into building it for her. And then she was gone."

When someone shared their memories of her mother, Effie tried to drink every drop to quench a thirst that was never going to be satisfied. Sallie's struck a new chord.

"What do you mean, tempered?"

Sallie shrugged. "I'm not sure. Can't quite put my finger on it."

"Did she confide something in you?"

"Nothing she said, just a feeling I had was all. Maybe it was me. She was too young to die. You and Norris no more than babies. There was so much she wanted to do."

Effie didn't feel comfortable pushing for more. She waited, but Sallie steered the conversation to other things.

"I thought we could see a bit of the town tomorrow so you can learn what's what. Come Sunday afternoon, you'll want to catch the train out to the sanitarium."

"That would be nice," Effie answered, promising herself to revisit the topic of her mother on other occasions. "I really appreciate everything you and Mrs. Andrews have done for me."

"Well, I could say I owed it to your mother. But my debt to her isn't one that could be satisfied by doing a few things for you. I know one thing, though. Addy would be pleased about this path you're taking. Leaving Atlanta, coming here, starting a life on your own. She wanted more for you. I 'spect you know that."

Effie nodded and smiled. All day she had felt her mother hovering over her with her arms folded in front, head cocked to one side, nodding her approval.

Effie rose and gathered their dishes. "I'll clean up and head off to bed." At the door, she paused and hesitated before saying, "I'm more than a little bit nervous."

Pale yellow light streaming through the window illuminated an almost imperceptible softening in Sallie's face. "I expect that's normal considering where you're headed. There's a lot of sick people out there. Sick and sad. People who don't have any hope of getting any better. It's hard to find any happiness out there. That'll take some adjusting to."

"I'm sure you're right about that," Effie offered.

Saturday's stroll through town turned into a visitation with friends and neighbors and a history lesson. Sallie introduced her as a new nurse in town and Effie was consulted about numerous ailments and injuries. She tried her best to offer helpful advice and kind words. Everyone had a story to tell or a question for Sallie. What was obvious through their long and winding meander was that Sallie was a pillar of her community, a confidant, a teacher, and a trusted friend to all.

In front of the old Governor's mansion, Effie tried to imagine General Sherman on his March to the Sea, sleeping on the floor for two nights because the house had been emptied of its contents ahead of his arrival. She was so enthralled by Sallie's vivid retelling of Sherman's visit and the

American flag raised by soldiers atop the roof, that Effie almost believed Sallie must have borne witness. The walkabout did more than acquaint Effie with Milledgeville; it bridged a gap that she had imagined might exist between her and her mother's old friend. During the brief time she spent with Sallie, she realized, that no matter what happened at the sanitarium, she had a refuge should one become necessary.

On Sunday afternoon, standing at the depot waiting for the conductor to signal boarding, Effie fidgeted with her handkerchief, working hard to contain her nerves.

Sallie tried to distract her. "Why don't you come into town in a few weeks after you've gotten settled and have supper with me?"

Only half listening, Effie nodded. "I have no idea about my schedule."

Passengers bound for the sanitarium milled around. Most seemed to be headed to their jobs, in their work clothes and uniforms, but some were likely newly arriving patients. They were easy to tell apart. The workers enjoyed their cigarettes, talked among themselves. Others stood anxious and alone. Effie tried to hold on to her inner quietude and prepare herself for what was to come. The only problem was that she was entirely unable to imagine what that might be. A sanitarium was a place for those with long-term illnesses. As Sallie said, people who were sick and sad. Effie clasped her hands to conceal their shaking.

"All aboard!"

Effie met Sallie's eyes. "Thank you," she managed.

Sallie nodded and smiled. "I'll see you soon."

"I'll look forward to that," Effie offered and climbed aboard.

As the train left the depot, Effie realized how little she knew about where she was headed. Originally christened the State Lunatic, Idiot, and Epileptic Asylum, the Georgia State Sanitarium had opened its doors in 1842. Some eighty years later, it was a sprawling two-thousand-acre institution spread over the rolling clay hills south of Milledgeville. With five-thousand residents, it was bigger than many small towns. She felt uneasy heading into the unknown but, in the same instant, powerfully motivated to be there. Effie had barely started the nursing program, when waves of illness hit Atlanta in the wake of the Great War. As the influenza pandemic swept the nation, she, and every other available nurse and nursing student, had been called in to care for the afflicted. Effie worked day and night, barely slept and seldom sat for a meal, as she tended to the needs of hundreds of sick people. Among the suffering and dying, she had never felt so alive.

After the illness subsided, life went back to normal and Effie finished her training. Opportunities for professional nurses, especially colored ones, were limited even in a city like Atlanta. Private duty work was practically the only option. Effie tried that and hated every minute of it. Taking care of well-to-do sick people made her feel like an addition to the household service staff. Not to mention the other obvious motivation to leave Atlanta. Norris kept trying to find her a suitable husband. In her work life Effie felt invisible. In her private life it was as though she were being auctioned off as a prize heifer to the highest bidder.

Her mentor at school, Ludie Andrews, encouraged her to consider the asylum. Despite the institution's growth, there were very few professional nurses on staff and only one who was colored. When the state decided to add a new position for another, the timing was right. Effie wanted out of her Atlanta life. More than that, she wanted to do something that mattered. Her experiences during the pandemic made her realize that more than anything. This one-year assignment was the choice she had made. Her leap. Something entirely new, exactly what she was looking for. And now as the train slowed to a stop inside the sanitarium grounds, her heart pounded, her breaths grew short and shallow.

A young woman in a nursing uniform seated behind her leaned forward and asked, "You new here?"

"I am," Effie answered over her shoulder. "I'm a n-n-nurse," she stammered, so as not to be confused for a patient.

"Well it's Sunday. It's gonna be hard to find anybody to get you situated." Pointing toward a columned white building in the distance, she added, "That's the Powell Building. Start there. I'm sure Mrs. Carroll knows you're coming. She's in charge of nurses. Best of luck."

EFFIE

Effie gathered her things and stepped out on the well-kept lawn of the sanitarium.

I made it, she thought and wondered at how few people who entered those grounds likely felt that same sense of gratification with their first step.

By all accounts it was a sleepy, summer Sunday afternoon in a small southern town. Voices raised in song drifted from some place nearby. People lounged about an impressive fountain in the shade of a large magnolia. Effie climbed the staircase and passed through the wide double doors. In contrast to the bright sunshine outside, the interior was dimly lit and seemingly deserted. Conversation from a hallway radiating off the central lobby led her to an office with a talk through window. Two women inside, dressed similarly in pale gray uniform dresses, were huddled in what seemed like a serious dialogue. Effie paused a moment. *Shoulders back, chin up.* She tapped the glass to call their attention. Reluctantly, the older woman rose, ambled over, and addressed Effie through the porthole opening.

"Yes?"

"I'm reporting for duty. I'm not sure where to go," Effie explained.

"I'm not expecting any new arrivals today," the woman answered, then after pointedly running her eyes over Effie several times, added, "The colored service building is across the west lawn."

Effie straightened and replied, "I'm afraid you misunderstand. I'm a nurse. I was told to report here for my first shift tomorrow."

The woman shared a certain look with her companion, then leaned in closer to the window opening. "No, I certainly don't misunderstand. I understand perfectly. You're a colored gal, right?"

Effie nodded slowly, daring to keep eye contact.

"Speak up. I asked you a question. You trying to fool me?"

"I'm sorry, I don't understand," Effie answered calmly.

"I said, you trying to fool me into thinkin' that you're a white girl?"

"Of course not," Effie responded. "I'm Effie Herndon. I'm a new nurse. I'm reporting for duty."

"You're a colored nurse. And I am Mrs. Ruby Carroll. I'm the head nurse for the regular nurses and the matron of the Powell Building. As I said, the *colored* service building is across the west lawn." She returned to her desk, leaving Effie at the window.

Effie hesitated only a moment, then headed for the exit. Looking across the large expanse of green, she assumed it was the west lawn and chose a large red brick structure in the distance as her next destination. On arrival, Effie circled the building. Rusted wire mesh cages covered the windows. Finding what seemed to be the main entryway, she pushed open a creaking door, badly in need of fresh paint. A breeze ripe with urine and the sweat of unwashed bodies streamed past. In the central hallway a low keening noise was coming from somewhere within the dank building. She wasn't particularly inclined to walk toward it, until a loud crashing and the sound of running called her into the rear corridor. The hallway door stood open. Effie walked with purpose as a woman's scream pierced the air and the muffled voices of others rose, offering comfort. Doors to what she assumed were patient rooms were mostly closed. Those that were open revealed themselves to be empty, practically bare. About halfway down the dreary hallway, two women clad in field work clothes came barreling through a door.

Running toward her, one called, "She's bad off. We need some help in here."

"I'm a nurse," Effie announced, heading toward the room. "What's wrong?"

"Thank the Lord," the younger woman said, "you got your bag?"

"I just arrived," Effie explained as the women cleared the doorway.

In a sweat-soaked nightdress, a young woman in well advanced labor was supported on a chair by two others. Another woman sat opposite, holding the young mother's feet, giving her leverage to aid in the birth of her child.

"She's a nurse," the woman from the hallway reported.

"Something's wrong here," the woman supporting the expectant mother's feet said. "I birthed lots a babies; this one's turned wrong and Nell's bleedin' bad."

"Where's the doctor?" Effie asked. All heads swiveled in her direction.

"It's Sunday," the chorus responded.

"Nobody knows about this here," a frail woman said, glancing at Nell. "Ain't nobody but us know she's got a baby inside."

Effie had not moved from the door. "Is there any morphine?" she asked.

The foot holder said in disgust, "Go find Fern. This here nurse don't know nothin'." A younger woman pushed past Effie, jostling her.

Delirious, sweat poured from Nell's body. Blood began to pool beneath her on the floor.

Effie assessed the primitive surroundings and took charge. "Let's get Nell into bed. I need some scissors and a wash basin. And all the towels you can find. I have to get that baby out."

Effie tugged off her suit coat and rolled up her sleeves. She had never delivered a baby on her own, had only read about it in a textbook. In obstetrics laboratory, a nurse demonstrated childbirth on a medical manikin. None of that prepared her for this moment, birthing a baby in crisis where the mother was bleeding to death. Effie probed the woman's abdomen. The baby was breech, lodged high in the birth canal. Nell lost consciousness.

"She's not big enough to birth that baby. I'll have to help her," Effie explained as she used the scissors to enlarge the opening to the mother's vagina. Having no forceps, with only her hands to deliver the child, she took hold, and slowly wriggled him free. He emerged limp and blue, the cord wrapped tight around his tiny neck.

Fern

JUNE, 1922

2

The door burst open and a young nurse carrying her bag rushed in. "Give him to me," she ordered. She laid the unresponsive infant on the bed and unwound the cord from his neck. Vigorously rubbing the baby's chest, she whispered to him, and listened for a heartbeat with her stethoscope. She picked him up, held him against her, and slapped his back forcefully. She checked his airway, flipped him over and smacked again, harder this time, desperate for a sign of life.

Effie remained at Nell's feet. "I need more packing," she told the women. "Hand me some towels." One of the women began crying, another sang. Despite their efforts, Nell drew one final breath. The blood flow slowed as her heart grew still. Minutes passed as the frantic, fateful room drew in on itself, dim and mournful. The motion and the energy winding down, like an old clock.

A quivering voice asked, "Fern, could you save him?"

She shook her head. "He didn't make it." Cradling him in her arms, Fern brought the baby to his mother, lifeless in a crimson pool on the narrow bed.

"He's beautiful," she breathed softly in the dead woman's ear. Effie watched as the young nurse brushed the baby's hand delicately over Nell's expressionless face.

"Don't worry," Fern told the broken woman, "I'll take care of him."

Fern glared at Effie, wrapped the dead child in a sheet, and carried him out the door.

No one paid Fern any mind when she passed by softly humming, an armful of bedsheets and Nell's dead child tucked protectively within its folds. Back at the laundry, where earlier, an hysterical Esther had burst in and summoned her to Nell's bedside, Fern was thankful that it was Sunday, and hardly anyone was around. They were at church services or Sunday picnic, in the big hall at choir practice or listening to a famous lady singer from Atlanta. The day had its own particular rhythm, the laundry mostly empty for most of the day. Sunday was Fern's favorite, the separateness, like a tonic. A brief respite from the cramped quarters she shared with two roommates in the women's convalescent building. On those solitary days she could sing, read out loud, scream at the top of her lungs, whatever she pleased as long as she kept moving the laundry through. Besides being medicinal, the work was useful for Fern's habits. Fern was a master of disguise. She could pass for a nurse, a gardener, a visitor, whatever was necessary to the predicament of the moment. At first it was how she entertained herself. Then, to see what she could get away with. And later, it was all about moving clandestinely around the grounds in order to unearth the secrets of the sanitarium. She marveled at the clothing that came through the laundry, as new patients arrived and the remnants of their identities were stripped away and replaced with locally made hospital garb. She made the most of what was available and stashed the best of it for her changing needs. On Sundays she took care of staff uniforms. Today for instance, she had no problem donning a freshly laundered gray dress, snatching a nurse's bag she had stowed in the closet, and running across the lawn to the colored women's dormitory. The only bad part was that she didn't get there in time.

They should have come for me sooner. Fern shook her head in dismay. *I might have been able to do something. One of them might have lived. Maybe even both.*

Fern placed the woeful bundle in a basket. She slipped out of the dress and tossed it in the laundry bin. Later, she would deliver the cleaned and pressed uniforms to the nurses' rooms. She made a mental note to take a set to that new nurse who attended Nell at what was supposed to be a birthing but turned into a double murder. At least that was Fern's opinion of what had happened. Neglect was a killer and she figured the sanitarium was probably the most neglectful place on earth. *How is it I know more about what's going on with those women than the people that work here?* she wondered.

After Fern made her deliveries, she pulled the baby from the wicker basket. "I promised your mama I would take care of you," she told him, holding his tiny, wrinkled hand in her own. Fern brought him to the table and laid him out on clean towels. Soaking a soft, white cloth in a wash basin, she held it over the boy's tiny head and watched the water trickle down his forehead while she whispered, "Suffer little children, and forbid them not to come unto me for of such is the kingdom of heaven." She deliberately washed his cool skin and swaddled him in a clean sheet. She held him close, then reluctantly returned him to his resting place so that she could begin preparations for what came next.

From the closet, Fern pulled a heavy, gray-colored work shirt and an oversized men's coat. Reaching high to the top shelf, her fingers skimmed along, seeking something to complete the look. She tugged a dark-colored floppy cap out from under some boxes, dusted it off, adjusted it on her head, and tucked her unruly auburn hair up inside it. In the mechanical room that served the laundry, she rummaged around for a toolbox just big enough to hold the delicate package. Fern arranged the bundled baby inside the box and made her way through the darkness to the carpentry workshop through a light rain. Through the window in the shimmering light, she could see the old man cleaning up at the end of his workday. Fern wasn't concerned. She had played this role before too.

"Hey Mr. Strickland. I got an order for a small pine box," Fern told the apron-shrouded man as she showed him an order for a casket. He never once looked at her face.

"We don't got much use for them small ones round here. I don't make them much. Let me see what I got," he answered and headed to the back room. He returned with a box too large and unwieldy for Fern's mission.

"How 'bout more like the size of this toolbox?" Fern asked, lifting the box for inspection.

He nodded, grudgingly resumed the noisy search, and returned carrying a hinged wooden box roughly the size required. "It's all I've got."

"That'll do," she told him.

Fern passed over the south lawn and made her way to the brick wall that surrounded the sanitarium grounds. Depending on the light from the half-moon and hoping that a hard rain would hold off, she skirted along the wall to where it turned into a split rail fence, the scent of pine trees in the rain, like perfume. She set the toolbox down on the slick, wet grass and opened the tiny box. She lifted the poor infant and held him close, kissed him on the forehead, then delicately lay him down inside the makeshift casket for the last time. Fern pulled a Case three blade gunstock Whittaker knife from her pants pocket and carefully carved into the wooden top, *Loved and Remembered*.

Fern crossed the fence and walked across the field to the dirt road where she came to a white wooden frame house next to a small chapel just as the skies opened up. The house clothed in darkness, familiar. She climbed the front steps, soundlessly lowered the tiny box to the weathered floorboards. For a moment she considered its contents, then knocked loudly on the door, turned and ran across the front lawn. She disappeared down the road, well out of sight when the door opened. A young couple, with a lantern, timidly stepped onto the porch. Clad in their nightclothes, the woman looked down and reached for her husband's arm.

"Oh no, Jim, I think it's another one."

Her husband bent down to inspect the offering. The flickering light cast a golden luster on the stillborn child's somber face.

The woman brought a trembling hand to her mouth. Her husband turned to comfort her. "I'll take care of it," he told her. "Don't you worry."

FERN

With slow, sloshing strides, Fern navigated her way back across the grounds of the asylum in the drenching downpour. Her route led to the boundary of the large cemetery called Cedar Lane. At the edge of the field, Fern dropped to her knees and reached out to trace the outline of an embossed iron grave marker that bore only a number. She whispered to no one who could hear, "I won't let one more little baby be put into this wretched ground if I can help it."

By Monday morning wake-up call the rain had stopped, the sky colored robin's-egg blue. Fern, in her fieldwork clothes, headed for the dining hall, ready to get on with the day. Roselyn, her across-the-hall neighbor, sidled up beside her, half whispering over her shoulder.

"Most everybody was already asleep when you came in last night. Lucky for you, nobody noticed but me."

"Yep, lucky, that's me," Fern answered.

"What kind of trouble are you into now?" Roselyn asked out of sheer nosiness, not a drop of concern for Fern.

"No trouble. Late laundry work is all."

"I know what you were up to. I saw you playing nurse again. Running around in that uniform, carrying a bag, acting like you needed to get somewhere quick. I saw you with a colored girl." Venom dripped from every word that fell from Roselyn's mouth.

"You might be having delusions." Fern's green eyes flashed as she moved in close to Roselyn's face. "Reckon I ought to tell somebody, maybe somebody like Mrs. Carroll, so you can get some help."

Roselyn glared, then backed off. But having found what she thought was a great comeback, swung around. "You better look out, hanging around that colored building. Somebody might get a mind to take an axe handle to your head, just like they did Miss Jackie."

Fern kept eye contact with Roselyn until she turned and walked away. At the service line, she grabbed a slice of bread, stuffed a peach into her pocket, guzzled a cup of milk, wiped her mouth with a backhand swipe, and went outside.

She was headed for the colony farm and a day's worth of work. Those assigned to fieldwork waited in front of the Powell building for wagon transport to the farm three miles up the road. Although their methods relied on manpower rather than machines, more and more the sanitarium was able to provide much of their own food. Rather than sitting around all day, those that were able, worked the farm. For the patients, idleness was not considered a pathway to recovery. Normal, everyday routines that included work, socializing and entertainment were thought to provide a sense of stability for all. Residents and staff worked alongside each other—planting, tending, and harvesting crops. Fern figured it was field peas and okra that she would be picking today. She tied her hair up in a red bandana and climbed aboard the wagon. Arriving at the fields, the sun already climbing the sky, the all-female picking crew grabbed bushel baskets and headed to the crop rows to pick peas. Fern knew Esther and Ruth were there somewhere. She took her basket and began walking to the rows of peas toward the back, where she thought she could see them working. Although the dormitories and the medical facilities were segregated by gender and by race, the field bosses didn't usually mind mixing, as long as the work got done. Fern slid in between the two women, squatted down, and started picking peas.

Before Fern could ask a question, Esther was shaking her head and mumbling to herself. "That poor dead woman is still lying in that bed. Nobody even come to check on her until daylight this morning. And there she was lying in her dried-up blood. Nobody asked nothin'. Nobody said nothin'. Them other girls slept on the floor in the hallway last night. Too afraid to go in there."

"That ain't nothin' new," Ruth chimed in.

"What about that nurse?" Fern asked.

"That city girl was more scared than we was. She kept asking where was the doctor, where was the morphine, where was this and that. She didn't know nothin.'"

"She didn't have her bag?" Fern asked.

"Nothin'," Ruth said. "She didn't have nothin'. Nell just laid there and bled like a stuck pig."

"That girl stood there and watched," Esther added. "I ain't surprised it happened. And I ain't surprised they just left Nell lying there. It makes me sick, is all."

Their pea picking verged on violence as they took their anger out on the vegetables. Fern finally spoke, "I was hoping having a new colored nurse would change things. I guess I was wrong."

Ruth shook her head and turned to Fern. "How you think one colored nurse is gonna make any difference at this nuthouse? No colored girl is gonna make a difference on the outside. No way one can make a difference in here."

"When she decided that Nell was dead, she just left, went on down the hallway and out the front door. We didn't see her again last night. I think she left," Esther concluded.

"And what about the baby, did anybody ask about him?" Fern asked just to be sure.

"Nobody said nothin'," Ruth ended it.

"Somebody might get to nosing around. And that nurse. I'm not sure what she might say. Somebody somewhere might want to know what happened in that room. Anybody can tell by looking at her that Nell gave birth to a baby and died from it," Fern explained.

"What are you worryin'?" Ruth asked Fern.

She replied, "Not worrying, just want to be ready is all, if it comes back that I was there and that when I left, the baby was gone."

Fern wiped the sweat from her brow and went back to pea picking. She wasn't worried exactly. That pesky old Roselyn had riled her up. She didn't think that too many people would be worried about a missing, dead colored baby that wasn't even supposed to be. Nell had kept that baby a secret. The fact that Nell had lived there for three years meant she didn't come there with it—it got planted in her since. That wasn't a new development either. Fern knew well that things went on at the sanitarium, just like they went on everywhere else. The wild card was that new nurse. The fact that she was new meant that she didn't know what all went on there. If she was a proper brought-up lady and educated, too, she might think somebody around here pays attention to what goes on and even gives a damn.

Fern knew more about the Georgia State Sanitarium than almost anybody. She was born there, and for all those years now, she had been raised within its confines. Though she wasn't the only person who could lay claim to the asylum as their place of birth, she thought that she was probably the only one born there that chose to stay even after her mama died. Fern's mother, Nora, had been committed by her husband during an unusually cold December, right after she had told him that she was expecting. Nora had her baby and found life on the inside was somewhat an improvement over life on the outside. By claiming she talked to dead people and saying she sometimes thought about doing harm to others, especially her husband, she had a place to live and food to eat for her and her baby. As long as Fern stayed out of the way and didn't cause any problems, she and Nora even got to spend a good bit of time together. Nora taught her girl how to answer questions, not call attention to herself, and be quiet for long periods of time, all as a means to survive.

Nora was put to work keeping things clean and caring for the little ones in one of the children's wards. Fern was often at her side. Most often the children she met were in much worse circumstances. Many were mentally unfit, suffered from epilepsy or some type of contagious disease. Most had been abandoned by their families and had very little human contact outside of rudimentary hygiene care, which wasn't much to speak of anyway. For some, Fern's little fingers reaching through the bars of their cages were all the human kindness they ever had.

When Fern was eight, Nora developed a hacking cough, then a fever, and then she started coughing up blood. She died a year later from pulmonary tuberculosis. Fern was devastated by the loss of her mother. But even though she was young, her survival instinct was well honed. Because Fern didn't act much like a child, she was able to pass relatively unnoticed among the rest of the sanitarium's population. She was expert at being invisible. At a young age, she made herself useful to attendants and nurses. She took in everything that happened, saw things no child had any business seeing, and learned more about nursing and doctoring and caring for the feeble and insane than many trained professionals. Because the place was overcrowded, understaffed, and neglect really was the daily routine, Fern blended into the chaos. That, along with the help of a nurse and a few patients, meant the sanitarium had become her home. And, then that other business happened. By the time she was sixteen, everything she had ever loved was buried somewhere deep in the soil of Baldwin County. And now she really did talk to dead people sometimes. After what had happened to her, she did think about committing violence, but not on herself. She stored that anger up and kept it for when she needed it most.

Fieldwork did in most everybody, especially on a clear, hot, sticky day like today. Fern gathered strength out in the sun-soaked fields. At quitting time when everybody else walked away, wrung out and peevish, Fern was untroubled, if not quite content. The wagon ride back was quiet.

As soon as Fern stepped foot on the ground, Roselyn was in her face.

"Told on you," she snarled, "and I can't wait to see what they do to you."

Fern reached out and locked a grip of steel around her wrist.

"Oh Roselyn, Roselyn. We'll see who gets what in this deal," Fern said through gritted teeth.

Roselyn lost her composure, while fear transformed her face. Then her snarl came back. "I'm not afraid of you, Fern Walker. And what's coming for you, well, let's just say, it's what you see in your nightmares."

Fern let go of her arm but kept her clear-eyed focus on Roselyn's face. *What did that girl know?* Fern wondered.

In the washroom off the dining hall, Fern ran a sink full of cool water and lifted handful after handful to her face to wash away her anger. She couldn't remember why she and Roselyn started hating each other but thought it had been on first sight. Sneaky and maybe even dangerous, Roselyn was on a mission to do harm to Fern and any person Fern cared about. From the first time she could remember seeing Roselyn, it was as though she held a grudge against Fern for some long-ago insult or injury. Fern kept her guard up, regularly on the lookout for Roselyn, who could be counted on to find out about absolutely everything she did. After scrubbing down her arms and hands, Fern untied her hair and finger combed her auburn curls back into something reasonable.

From the supper line she took a tray of pork and beans and a hunk of cornbread. Her roommates Shirley and Lizbeth had saved a spot between them at their usual table. Fern plopped down and started eating without a word. Both girls watched her, ignoring their own food.

Lizbeth went first. "Why on earth have you mixed it up again with that spiteful, awful girl? She spent the day telling all kinds of stories about you. No telling what truth there is to any of it, but she got word passed right up to Ruby Carroll that you were up to something with the colored girls."

Fern concentrated on eating.

"I was in the office mopping up when they brought in that new nurse that was with you in the colored building yesterday."

Fern looked up. "What was she wearing?"

"What was who wearing?" Lizbeth asked.

"The nurse."

"Her uniform of course," Lizbeth replied, unsure of Fern's interest in that detail.

Fern continued her inquisition. "How did she look?"

"Like a nurse," Lizbeth said, growing impatient.

"I mean was she all put together, or did she look like she was upset or scared or anything?"

"I really didn't spend too much time looking her over. I was surprised that a colored nurse was there to see Mrs. Carroll. She's not in charge of colored nurses. You know how she treats the colored women."

"Did Mrs. Carroll send for her, or did she come on her own?"

"Oh, she sent for her all right," Shirley chimed in, having already heard the story. "And they had a time finding her. You know where they finally did? In the big hall. She was standing right in the middle of the stage. The strangest thing," she recounted, slowly shaking her head. "Standing there on the stage in her uniform."

Lizbeth added with a smirk, "She'd better be careful, or she'll find herself called for intake and end up answering all those questions for crazy people."

"What else happened?" Fern asked, suddenly more interested.

"Don't know," Lizbeth said. "When I left, she hadn't come out yet. I didn't hear anything else about it."

Fern took a bite of cornbread and thought about how she could find a way to see that nurse again and find out what she had told Mrs. Carroll. While Lizbeth and Shirley continued to talk, Fern began to form a plan about Roselyn too. Something Roselyn said had caused a cold shiver to run up Fern's back. She wondered what Roselyn knew about her and just how she came by knowing. *Either somebody's been telling her my business*, she thought, *or she found something somewhere that spelled out my truths.* Her private truths that nobody had any right knowing. Fern aimed to figure that out.

At dusk, Fern waited along the tree line just outside the colored women's dormitory. She had passed word by Esther to that new nurse that she would be waiting outside after dark to talk to her. Esther said the nurse's name was Effie and that she came from Atlanta. Fern figured something must be wrong with her to decide to leave there for here. *But I guess I choose to live here, too*, she thought. *Maybe we're both in the right place.* After a while Effie came out the side door and walked over into the grass. Fern watched her for a few minutes to see if she was jumpy, but the woman stood there, straight and still, looking up at the treetops. Fern had chosen to put on a nurse's uniform without the requisite apron, giving the appearance of a nurse whose shift had ended but hadn't had time to change yet.

"Hey. Come on over here where it's not so obvious," Fern called, in as loud a voice as she could risk.

Effie was dressed in full uniform. "You all right?" Fern asked.

"I'm all right," she replied tersely.

"I heard you got called up to see Mrs. Carroll."

"I did."

"What did she want?"

Effie was slow to reply. "She wanted to know how I was involved in the situation with Nell."

"What did you tell her?"

"Why are you asking me all of these questions? I thought you had already spoken with her," Effie replied.

"No. I haven't been asked yet," she replied, although Fern didn't think there was any reason she would be unless Effie had said something. "I wanted to make sure everything was all right."

"What you mean is that you wanted to find out what I said about who was there and what they did. Like what happened to Nell's baby."

Fern knew better than to try and make up something. "That's right. That's what I want to know."

"I told them that Nell's baby was strangled by his cord and born dead, that I tried to revive him, and save his mother who was hemorrhaging uncontrollably. I told them I didn't have any tools to work with, that I had merely stumbled upon the horrendous scene in that room, and tried to help as best I could." Effie's voice grew more adamant. "And I asked them how a young woman could go through a pregnancy unattended in a medical center. I asked why there wasn't any medical help available for the women in that dormitory."

"You actually said all that to Mrs. Carroll?" Fern asked, with a bit more respect for Effie than she had two minutes before.

Effie, riled up, calmed herself before answering. "I did. I said exactly that."

"I can't imagine how she must have reacted," Fern offered.

"Oh yes you can. You know exactly how. She told me I was out of line speaking to her in that manner and that she would be determining some disciplinary action suitable to my behavior. She told me not to ever address her in that way again, or I would find myself back on the streets of Atlanta with my nursing credentials revoked."

"You didn't say anything about me?" Fern asked.

"No. Why would I?"

"Because I was there. You saw me take that baby. You didn't have to take the blame."

Effie composed herself and said more pointedly, "Yes, I did. Nurses' code."

Fern waited for whatever Effie had to say next.

"Always be accountable for what happens. Never put blame on anyone else, especially another nurse. We are the lowest of the low inside a hospital, barely more than maids really. We have to stick together."

"I'm impressed," Fern responded.

"Impressed about what? That I would speak my mind to a white woman?"

"Yeah, but not really. I meant that you didn't tell about me being there. You could have gotten out of it pretty easy if you had."

"You can't really believe that," Effie replied sharply. "I don't think you're that naïve. Nurses are the lowest of the low. But there is that little difference between you and me. In case you didn't realize it, you are a white nurse and I am colored. It was obvious the first minute I stepped into this place how much that matters. There's not a way in the world that I could ever blame anything on you and think that anyone would listen."

Fern knew the harsh truth in what Effie said. "So how did it end up? What did you say about the baby?"

"I said when they finally came and got Nell this afternoon, the orderlies took the baby too."

"Nobody asked them about it?"

"No, and I doubt that they will. One seemed drunk, and the other one probably didn't have the sense to remember he hauled away a dead woman today. From what I have already seen in the barely twenty-four hours that I have been here, not many people know or care anything about what's going on around here."

"Well we certainly understand that the same way," Fern replied. "One more thing and I've got to get back. You planning on staying?"

Effie paused and thought about it. Since Fern was the only person who had asked her about how she was feeling after the devastating events of the last day, she opened up. "Last night I wanted to get on the next train back to Atlanta. The only thing that stopped me was that there wasn't one." Effie hung her head and crossed her arms, holding herself tight. "This afternoon the longer I waited for somebody to come for Nell, the madder I got. I guess that's why I said what I did to Mrs. Carroll. I remembered why I came here in the first place."

"I was wondering about that myself, for you I mean."

"I've said all I intend to say about what happened in that room. And like I said, I doubt anybody else will care enough to ask anymore. But I do have to ask, where did you take that baby?"

Fern wasn't sure how much she wanted to reveal. She reached in her pocket, pulled out a peach, and held it out in offering. Effie was surprised by the gesture, but shook it off.

"I know you're new here, so you probably haven't seen much yet."

"I think I've seen enough," Effie proclaimed.

"Ever heard of Cedar Lane Cemetery?"

Effie shook her head.

"Ask somebody to show you sometime. Cedar Lane. That's a real pretty name for a pretty ugly place. It's where they bury their dead here. Big green field, seems to stretch on for miles. Lots of people are buried there, but you won't be able to figure out where. No names or nothing. I can tell you one thing, he's not there. I made sure of that."

Fern headed back to Powell. For a minute she considered the fact that Effie thought she was a real nurse and that she had not told her any different. She didn't think it mattered too much. She doubted they would have much cause to see each other.

Fern had one more stop before she could call it a day. She was hoping that she could be invisible as usual. Powell was the intake building. All the new patients came through there. The patients' records were there too. She had asked Lizbeth about them. Lizbeth said she didn't know for sure, but there were two big rooms full of file drawers and stacks of boxes down the hall in the back corner on the first floor behind Mrs. Carroll's office. Fern had decided it was time to see if there was a record there with her name on it and if there was, just exactly what it said. If she could find it, she was pretty sure that other people probably could too. She had a feeling that one of the people that had found it was Roselyn. When she got to Powell and discovered the door to the offices locked, she knew she would have to head over to her laundry closet to get what she needed to do the job. She was satisfied to see that all was quiet. Everything was perfect for a nighttime raid.

Alonzo

DECEMBER, 1902

3

The very circumstances of his parentage, propagation between a white slave owner and a Black slave mother, set in motion the fractured nature of Alonzo Herndon's existence. Was he Black? Was he white? Was he slave? Was he free? Could he rise? Would he be beat down? The simplest answer to all of these questions was yes. But where he was and what he had accomplished mattered most to him in this moment. It was Monday morning of Christmas week. A wintry chill rustled the air, yet Alonzo was overly warm in his bowler hat and coal-black cashmere overcoat with the velvet lapels. He chuckled to himself as he made his way up Atlanta's Peachtree Street in the early gray dawn. It wasn't the weather that left him practically giddy. A bizarre twist of fate had led him here. He had been chased by a firestorm. Six years back his shop alongside the Markham House Hotel was consumed by a fire that burned down the whole block. And just a few weeks past, his Marietta Street store disappeared in a blaze. Not one to stand around wringing his hands, Alonzo had taken action. Little more than ten days ago, his longtime dream to open for business on Peachtree had finally come to fruition.

The street was shaking off sleep in preparation for several days of commerce and camaraderie before the holiday. Alonzo inhaled the scintillating aroma of the city struggling back to life after a languorous Sunday. He had hardly slept the night before, desperate to get back to it. He stopped across the street from his new shop to savor the moment, having purposefully left the crystal chandelier glowing behind the floor to ceiling plate glass window to draw the attention of passersby on the sidewalk. He could not help but swell with pride as he took in the view. The mahogany and glass double doors opened on to an elegant and seemingly endless parlor with light from the chandelier reflecting brilliantly off the French beveled mirrors. This wasn't the first of Herndon's Barbershops in Atlanta but it was certainly the finest. Alonzo had heard whispers that it was possibly the finest in the South. With sixteen barber chairs upholstered with dark green Spanish leather, outfitted in brass and nickel, Alonzo could offer his discriminating clientele an experience well beyond a shave and a haircut.

After lingering a moment longer, he crossed the street, dug into the pocket of his worsted wool trousers, and retrieved the key to unlock the door to his future. The tang of fine leather mingled pleasantly with wood polish and expensive aftershaves. Alonzo had planned every inch of this space with a singular purpose: to entice Atlanta's most prominent and wealthy to enter his door. While he was open for business, the shop was still a work in progress. His vision for it, unfolding and inspired by what he had seen on the streets of Paris when he and Adrienne had traveled there two years back. For Alonzo, this was more than a barbershop, it was his classroom and his boardroom. It was where he honed his business skills and developed relationships, which—if all went according to plan—would one day make him one of the richest men in Atlanta. He aimed high and hardly ever missed his mark.

Alonzo climbed the stairs to his second-floor office. His staff would not arrive for two more hours. There was plenty of time to plan his day, check over accounts, and grab a quick bite to eat on Auburn Avenue before the first customers arrived. He opened the half glass door, never failing to appreciate what his hard work had earned him. A large, polished oak rolltop desk was situated just so, beneath the window that overlooked the city's main thoroughfare. Though he still accepted appointments with several carefully selected clients, he was a businessman with business to attend to.

Alonzo hung his overcoat in the large closet he had built into his office space. In his line of work, appearance was everything. He kept his suit coats and dress shirts at the shop so that he would never look wrinkled or dirty. He insisted that all of his barbers do the same. They employed a full-time laundress who made this possible. To cover her cost, she cleaned and pressed clothes for customers who needed tidying up too.

He pulled out the swivel desk chair, adjusted the height, rolled up his sleeves, and rolled up to his desk. While Alonzo loved his wife and children, this was his passion. He appreciated the good life he was able to provide for his family, but he remained a man of simple tastes. He was at the very core of his being, a money man. He understood the power of money. He knew how to make it, and he was exceptionally shrewd about what to do with it when he got it. Alonzo's driving ambition was to remain forever the master of his own money and, thereby, of his freedom to make more.

The approach of the holiday ensured that it was an especially busy Monday. He pulled his appointment log from the top right-hand drawer and scanned the list. Some regulars and a few dailies. His first appointment at nine o'clock was old Mayor Livingston Mims, who would no longer be mayor come January but ranked as one of the Atlanta elite, worthy of Alonzo's time. At nine-thirty, Mr. Evan Howell, the owner of *The Atlanta Constitution* newspaper and incoming mayor. Alonzo wondered how they had scheduled the two old Confederates, turned leaders of the city, back to back. He intended to get Mims out the door before Howell showed up, or he and his staff would have to endure the exaggerated retelling of their dazzling deeds on the battlefield. And the list went on. Henry Atkinson, the owner of the electric company, Ivan Allen, a purveyor of business products and Eugene Mitchell, a prominent Atlanta attorney. All were counted among Atlanta's most distinguished residents, all valuable for their political and economic connections. Despite the number of patrons he would be serving that day, Alonzo was more interested in the revenues he anticipated from his other stores and rent money due from the tenants who lived in the houses he owned in the south side neighborhoods. Even with the tragedy of the fire on Marietta Street, this year had proven his most successful yet, and he could not wait to calculate the final tally as it drew to a close. While others were planning to toast in the new year, Alonzo would be popping the cork on some fine French champagne to celebrate the cold, hard cash he had accumulated this past year and the real estate he now owned across the city.

Satisfied that he could take care of business, keep his appointments, and make it home in time to get dressed for Adrienne's dinner party, Alonzo grabbed an old tweed jacket from the coat tree and headed for the door.

First stop was Ma Sutton's Boarding House. Alonzo's only business there was fresh hot biscuits and pear preserves served with piping hot coffee and the morning paper. Alonzo's timing was perfect as usual. When he opened the door to her kitchen, Ma was pulling the biscuits from the oven.

"Good morning, Ma," Alonzo tipped his hat and favored Atlanta's best cook with a kiss on the cheek.

"Good morning, Mr. Herndon, I was wondering if I would see you today or not, seeing how it's Christmastime."

"I wouldn't miss your biscuits for anything. I'll be stuck eating in my own kitchen come Christmas morning."

"You want me to teach your wife to cook?" she asked, playing along with the same old ruse.

"She doesn't make time for the kitchen, Ma. She's too busy. I was thinking about bringing Norris with me tomorrow. Think you'll have room for us?"

"You know I do. And that sweet boy of yours likes my biscuits 'bout as much as you do."

"He likes to deliver Christmas presents. We'll be coming by here first thing."

"I'll be lookin' for you," she answered as Alonzo turned and headed for the dining room.

He savored being the morning's first diner. Before long, the small room would be packed wall to wall with other Atlanta early birds out looking for the juiciest worms but stopping by Ma's first for a tastier breakfast. Alonzo would be long gone by then.

ALONZO

The city had come to life when he turned back onto Peachtree. Men hurried to their places of work. Women bustled past, desperate to secure their Christmas treasures. Streetcars clamored through the streets, a symphony to Alonzo's ears. Once through the doors, the sight of his men all making ready for the day ahead soothed him. Wiping down their barbering chairs, sharpening razors, taking care of their own personal grooming, all forged a festive atmosphere made more so by the approaching holiday.

Near the front window, Ollie Johnson, the resident laundress, settled hand-cut decorations onto a medium-sized white pine.

"Now that's a nice touch," Alonzo said to her in greeting. "I really appreciate that, Miss Ollie."

"I thought you might like it," she answered.

"Miss Ollie, how busy are you today?"

"Not too much yet," she replied. "You need me for something?"

"I do. I was hoping that you and Miss Sarah could pick up a package for my wife on Decatur Street around noon and take it over to the house. A pretty new dress for her party tonight."

"Yes, sir. We could do that."

"I thought you might help her out with getting ready too. Maybe Miss Sarah can fix her hair. You might tend to that new dress if it needs something done to it."

"I sure will, Mr. Herndon. I'd be pleased to help out."

"I'll check on Miss Sarah and fix it so she can go too," Alonzo offered.

"All right then. We'll get your Mrs. fixed up real nice."

"I know you will, Miss Ollie. I really appreciate it."

As he did every day, Alonzo walked the chair line, taking note of preparations. "Morning, Mr. Herndon" was offered in greeting from each and every station. He was a fair and considerate boss. The respect the men paid him was genuine. Each one had been handpicked from among Atlanta's best trained and most elegant looking barbers. Some of his fellow shop owners were still a bit irritated that he had poached their best workers. The barbers themselves appreciated the fact that they had been chosen by Alonzo Herndon to work in his exclusive new store with the enviable address. With hard work and the right attitude, they knew their financial futures had taken a considerable upward tick by signing on at Herndon's.

Alonzo selected chair fifteen for his morning spruce up. He took a seat, as a delighted young man snapped his pure white barbering cloth around his distinguished customer.

"You know what I like, Charlie," Alonzo said as the chair reclined and he closed his eyes.

"Yes, sir, I certainly do," the young man responded with a brilliant smile.

Just as the mayor's driver opened the front door, Alonzo in his perfectly starched and pressed white barbering coat, smelling of the sandalwood scented aftershave he favored, stepped forward at chair number seven. Mayor Mims nodded once in his direction. The porter took the man's hat and coat and he headed for the chair.

"Good morning, Alonzo."

"Good morning, Mr. Mayor."

"This is one fine shop. You've done pretty well for yourself," the mayor said curtly. He took his seat and used the mirrors to look around the room as Alonzo prepared him for a trim and a hot shave.

"Looks like you've given a job to every colored boy on Decatur Street," Mayor Mims said, disdain creeping into his words.

"These are the finest barbers in Atlanta, Mr. Mayor," Alonzo replied.

"If you trained them, I reckon they might be," he granted. "You doing your part for that uplift for your race?"

Alonzo answered in a steady voice, "No, sir. I am operating the best barbershop in Atlanta, and I need the best barbers I can find."

"So, what you're saying is that there are no good white barbers in the city?" he persisted.

Alonzo paused only long enough to show he was considering the mayor's statement with all due respect and then replied, "Well, sir, seeing that I am the owner of this establishment and I am a colored man, I doubt that any self-respecting white man would agree to me being his boss."

Mims chuckled. "Well, I reckon you're right about that too. You're pretty smart, considering," he answered, knowing he didn't need to finish the thought for Alonzo to understand what was being considered.

Alonzo reclined the chair and applied a fresh, hot towel to the man's fleshy white face, relieved when he no longer had to look at it.

Business was brisk as the morning hours passed. Shoes were shined, nails were cleaned, hair was trimmed, beards were shorn, and the money of white, wealthy Atlantans flowed into the cash register of Alonzo Herndon's new shop. By midafternoon the constant current of customers slowed to a trickle. It was a holiday week, and most everybody had a reason to get home early.

Around four, a butcher's wagon pulled up to the curb in front of the store. Alonzo saw it through the window and headed for the door.

"Fred, Woodrow, come help me out front," Alonzo called to his men.

Outside, the wagon driver stepped up on the curb. "We've got your order here, Mr. Herndon. Where do you want it?"

"We'll take it inside," Alonzo answered as he motioned to the two men to help with the packages.

"Good lord," Fred exclaimed when he looked into the wagon's interior. "What's all this?"

The driver laughed. "That's what thirty cold smoked hams look like, wrapped and ready for Christmas dinner."

"I didn't want you boys goin' hungry on Christmas," Alonzo replied as he hoisted a box of the hams up to his shoulder. "Get that door propped open, Woodrow. We've got some haulin' to do."

When the last of the hams was unloaded, Alonzo asked the driver, "Will you be coming in the morning with the rest of them?"

"Yes, sir," he answered. We'll come pick you up to make deliveries like you asked. Ned dropped off the oranges and the yams this morning. We'll have it all loaded and ready to go first thing."

"My son will be coming along."

"We've got room. He can sit in back with the packages."

"He'll like that," Alonzo answered and headed back inside.

THE TRUTH TOGETHER

The customers had all been tended to, his barbers, finishing their cleanup as he entered. They stood and faced him, quietly regarding the man. Alonzo was not a man of many words. When he realized that they were allowing him an opportunity to address them if he wanted to, he shuffled around for a minute and stuck his hands into his trouser pockets. He let his eyes linger on each and every one of the men in front of him.

"I'm a proud man today. What could have been my ruin a few weeks back has birthed a revival. You know, I wasn't born a free man. Like Fred and some of your own, we were born somebody's property, hardly considered a person at all. When I left that hellhole where I was raised, I could not have imagined this life I have now. I've been working at the barbering trade for more than twenty years. And in this place with you men, I feel like this is what it was all about. All the hard work, all the times I was told no and showed the door. Now here we are, on Peachtree Street in Atlanta, Georgia, inside what I have dreamed about my whole life, a place of work that I own in the heart of the finest city in the South. A place of work that is a good place with good men doing a good day's work and earning good pay. I'm proud to be here with you."

Not a man moved. The moment was one to relish and so they did.

"Now pick up one of those hams and take 'em home to your families." And with that Alonzo walked through the shop and up the back stairs to his office, taking them two at a time. No matter what he had to accomplish that day, if he didn't get home by the appointed time there would be hell to pay.

At five thirty sharp, Alonzo dashed out the door and jumped into the back of the Hunter Street trolley bound for Diamond Hill. Adrienne's holiday dinner party was an annual event that grew larger and more lavish every year. He couldn't wait to see what kind of transformation had taken place since he had left for work in the predawn darkness. By nightfall the house would be operating at a fevered pitch. The forty invited guests were expected at eight. For weeks, Adrienne had planned every detail. Her experiences with the theater meant that she knew precisely how to set the scene for the greatest dramatic effect. She had enlisted all kinds of help. The Kimball upright piano Alonzo had given her for a wedding present had been fine-tuned. A crew had been out cutting pine boughs and mistletoe, all the while on the lookout for the perfect tree for the big parlor. Adrienne's mother, Mattie, was running the kitchen staff, which had been considerably beefed up from its daily operations. The grocer had made deliveries to the house every day now for a week. Adrienne's elocution students from the university would assist with décor and would most certainly perform. A nanny had been called in to care for five-year-old Norris and baby Effie, who was only two. This was Adrienne's big night, and no expense had been spared. Tonight's guest list read like an accounting of Atlanta's south side literati from the colleges and universities on Diamond Hill to the business district flowering along Auburn Avenue. University colleagues Nina and Will DuBois, Lugenia and John Hope, Nellie and George Towns, would all be there. The university quartet, as well as Adrienne's friends from her early teaching days, Ludie Andrews and Sallie Davis would grace the Herndon's dining room that night. Business associates of Alonzo's were also expected to celebrate the holidays with the Herndons, as this event was the most desirable invite of the season.

Alonzo hopped off the trolley at Ashby and made his way to 169 Vine Street. In the twilight of early evening, the huge house was humming with activity. Although it wasn't their own, the Herndons had made themselves a home at Bumstead Cottage on the edge of the campus. On a typical day the two-story sprawling cottage was alive with the sounds of their children and assorted relatives and friends who needed a place to stay. It was a world apart from the big rambling farm outside of Social Circle, where he had been born.

As expected, the house dazzled, the front porch decked out in greenery and glowing in lantern light. Passing through the open door, his mouth watered as he inhaled the aromas drifting from within. A delightful melody rose from the piano, and lovely young ladies and handsome young men darted to and fro in their holiday finery. Alonzo made his way through the festively adorned big parlor, where a crowd was decorating a fir tree whose top branches brushed the ceiling. No one seemed to notice as he glided up the stairs until he reached the top, where Norris skittered around a corner and lassoed his legs.

"Did you see, Papa, did you see?" Norris squealed. "There's a giant tree in the house."

Alonzo scooped the boy into his arms.

"I don't think I've ever seen a tree so big, have you?"

"Not inside the house," Norris replied, his eyes dancing with wonder.

"Where's Mama?" Alonzo asked.

"She said to tell you not to find her," Norris answered earnestly. "She's a surprise tonight."

"A surprise you say. Well, I guess I'll just have to wait for that," Alonzo answered. "How 'bout your sister?"

"She's in the room with Miss Tillie. Let's go see." Norris pointed the way.

Adorned in a white satin, lace-covered dress and matching bonnet tied in a bow beneath her chin, Effie sat atop a pile of soft blankets in the middle of the nursery floor. Her lips pouty, her eyes narrow, she looked about to blow. Tillie, the children's nurse, circled around her like a lion tamer at the circus.

"I'm trying everything I know to keep her from gettin' dirty before Miss Adrienne has a chance to show her off to her friends, Mr. Herndon, but I'm not sure I can do it. She likes to get into things, and I do believe she likes to get dirty."

"I think you're right, Tillie. Maybe you should take that frilly dress off until our company gets here. If you don't, from the looks of it, she'll probably rip it off herself."

Tillie nodded, reached down and seemingly in one motion removed Effie's dress and bonnet. She scooped the girl up, turned, and handed a now smiling and mostly naked Effie to her father. Alonzo snuggled into her soft, sweet-smelling neck and planted more than several loud kisses. She giggled and held his face close so he could do it again.

Alonzo had time to clean up, dress, and make it back down the stairs before the first guests arrived. He had not seen Adrienne, but he knew how fond she was of making an entrance.

In the kitchen, Alonzo found Mattie, busy orchestrating culinary miracles alongside the kitchen staff. Delicacies of all varieties lay waiting for their guests. Wine bottles sat open on the countertop, fine china and silver stacked neatly and ready for plating, oysters on the half shell sitting atop ice in galvanized metal buckets, soup tureens steaming on the stove, and in the middle of the worktable, a whole roast pig, crispy and gleaming, surrounded by an array of succulent vegetables. Cheeses, crackers, fruits, breads, and nuts were mounded in silver bowls, and cakes and pies that defied description occupied every square inch of space. Alonzo caught Mattie's eye. They smiled and shook their heads. They were both guilty of indulging every one of Adrienne's wishes. They knew it and would have it no other way.

"You better get dressed, Mattie. She'll expect you down at the foot of the stairs when she makes her appearance."

"I'm heading up now," she answered, removing her apron. "There isn't room for another single thing in this kitchen, including me."

At precisely eight thirty sharp, with the guests milling about the parlor, enjoying oysters and champagne, Adrienne appeared at the top of the stairs. All eyes turned toward her as she descended the staircase, radiant in the lovely sea-green silk dress adorned with thousands of tiny seed pearls on a delicately embroidered lace overlay. The bodice of the dress fit her hourglass shape like a glove and cascaded to the floor in a trumpet skirt that swept the ground. She looked every bit a goddess, descending into the briny deep. The flickering candlelight highlighted her delicate creamy skin and her lustrous black hair. Alonzo came to meet her. He reached for her hand, drew her close, and whispered in her ear. Whatever he said to her was for Adrienne's delight alone.

Well past midnight, when the sated guests had mostly made their way back to their homes, the young people were critiquing their performances as they helped return the big parlor to some state of order. Several of Adrienne's colleagues were lounging with brandy and cigars near the glowing embers of the oak logs that had warmed them from the fireplace all evening.

"Where's Nina, Will?" Adrienne asked.

Will DuBois leaned toward Adrienne who sat at his right. "She went upstairs to see Norris about an hour ago. She's especially fond of him. I expect when she sees Norris, it helps her imagine what our son might be like now, had he lived," he answered.

"Norris is probably sound asleep," Adrienne replied. "Should I go check on her?"

"No, she'll be down when she's ready."

Alonzo stood at the fireplace, enjoying its warmth. Will joined him.

"I heard your new shop on Peachtree is already a great success, Alonzo."

"Things are off to a good start," he answered.

"Do you have any plans to open anymore? Maybe somewhere south of Peachtree?"

Alonzo understood the point he was making. Will could never leave this issue alone even in a social setting in the Herndons' own home. DuBois and Adrienne worked closely together and the two couples socialized with each other on a somewhat regular basis, but the men had differences when it came to the way forward for Atlanta's Black citizens.

"I don't have any plans like that right now," Alonzo answered.

"I'm thinking about bringing up the voting problems again now that the election is over. Do you think you could talk to some of your well-connected friends and see what we might be able to work out?" Will asked pointedly.

"My customers are my customers, not my friends," Alonzo answered. "And as I have said before, I don't mix business and politics."

"I thought that was the point of what you do, Alonzo," Will chided him.

"The point of what I do is earn a living, Will."

"Let's not do this tonight," Adrienne said to them both as she stood, in an attempt to change the subject of the conversation. "This is a celebration, not a debate."

Completely ignoring Adrienne's plea, Will, always serious, asked, "What if that isn't enough? Making money? What if having money doesn't change anything? Then what?"

"I make money. And I vote. Every time there's an election," Alonzo responded.

"That's all well and good, you still have the right. You can afford to pay your taxes. But how many Black men can? How many will choose to vote and risk letting their families go hungry because of it?" Will demanded, his voice rising.

ALONZO

"John, let's call it a night. I'm exhausted," Lugenia Hope told her husband. "Ladies, gentlemen, it's been a pleasure."

Adrienne took her arm as they headed toward the front of the house.

"I think Lugenia just said she had enough for tonight," John said with a sly smile as he rose. But he couldn't resist the opportunity to put in his two cents' worth. He took Will by the elbow and looked earnestly into his eyes.

"Will, how many times have we hashed this out? Alonzo and a few other very fine men are laying the foundation for everything we want to accomplish. Low-wage jobs are not going to lift our people up, but capital invested back into the community by men like them, that's what makes everything else possible."

John released Will's arm and turned to Alonzo. "Thank you for your hospitality. It's been a delightful evening, as always, in your home. Happy Christmas to you all," he said raising his hand in a wave as he left to join his wife.

John Hope's words had quieted Will. Still, neither he nor Alonzo had moved from the fireplace. They were stubborn men, but Alonzo would not let DuBois best him in his own parlor. Will might be the intellectual, but Alonzo had experiences the other man could only read and write about.

"You call this a struggle," he said, fully facing Will, as they alone remained in the parlor. "A struggle is like a war. In our times, wars are fought by foot soldiers, horse soldiers, men who fight on the seas and men who fight in hand-to-hand combat. This struggle, our struggle, requires the same approach. We don't have to pick one way forward. There isn't a single right way to go about it. Let every man use his strengths and talents to do his part."

Alonzo paused but Will didn't interrupt.

"I'm doing my part," Alonzo continued. "I'm building businesses for the colored man, owned and operated by the colored man, and I make a good bit of my money off the white man because it is the white man that has most of the money. You're doing your part by agitating for the vote and working on our communities, making them better. We're both a part of the same struggle. We won't win if we don't approach from all sides at the same time."

Will regarded Alonzo. "I think that's the most I've ever heard you say about it, Alonzo. Seems we want the same things," he offered. "We just have different ideas about how to make them happen."

The men were distracted from their conversation by the appearance of their wives. Adrienne and Nina walked into the parlor, arm in arm, talking softly to each other. "Come out to the porch with us," Adrienne said, smiling and reaching out a hand to Alonzo. "You won't believe it."

The lantern light was pale yellow as they stepped off the porch, into the frosty evening. Adrienne lifted her face to the moonlit sky.

"Look," she breathed. Small white snowflakes drifted and swirled. As the flurry grew more intense, Adrienne and Nina laughed, stretched out their arms and twirled among the glittering ice crystals.

Alonzo's gaze was drawn toward the women. Their enchantment warmed him. Turning to Will and placing a hand on his shoulder, he said, "We don't know what's coming our way in the new year, but I think there's one thing we can agree on. This one just passing has been good to us all."

Nora

DECEMBER 1905

4

Nora first laid eyes on Harry Walker at a barn dance in Social Circle when she was fifteen. With his wavy auburn hair and sparkling green eyes, a smattering of tiny freckles across his cheeks, Harry was decidedly the most handsome thing she had ever seen. She could hardly take her eyes off of him. He had rolled up his white shirt sleeves to his elbows and the way his golden glistening arm draped across the back of everyone he danced with was almost too much to bear. Everywhere she looked, the gaze of every other female present lingered on him. He made quick work of getting next to Nora, easily the prettiest girl in the room, and stood a little too close when he bent down and whispered in her ear that he would be so honored if she would dance with him. She didn't mind the attention or the closeness and answered yes to most everything he asked her to do from that moment forward.

That was little over a year ago. Now standing barefoot on the wood plank front porch, surveying the stalky gray landscape of the just harvested cotton fields, Nora felt as worn out as the Georgia soil. A drenching rain had made the old house an island in a sea of muck, and she contemplated the fact that she was as alone as she might be on a raft in the middle of the Atlantic Ocean. Harry had run off before, but he usually turned up in a day or two. *Where is he?* she wondered. *Is he gone for good?* Half of her hoped so, and the other half thought she might just curl up and die without him. The clouds had finally cleared, coming up on sundown. With night setting in she figured he wasn't coming home and headed back inside to face her demons.

Eight days ago, Nora had told Harry the news. She had hoped for a better reception. Instead he had called her every mean name he could think of, punched her where their little baby was living inside her, and put his hands around her neck. She didn't pass out like last time, but her throat was sore and there was still some heat in the bruises his fingers had left.

Harry had really sold her a bill of goods. When he told her he owned a big farm outside of Eatonton and a pretty little house that they could make their home, she had believed him. They ran off in the night without a word to her family. When she told him she wanted them to be married, he had quickly agreed, and they had taken care of that with the justice of the peace in Putnam County. As it turned out, Harry had been selling off his land piece by piece to keep the bank from taking it over. Cotton farming was about the hardest work a farmer could do, and from the looks of it, Harry didn't have any intention of breaking a sweat while making a go of it. Harry's father might have left him a good-sized farm, but Harry hated hard work and loved corn whiskey.

She realized too late that Harry must have thought her family was well to do and would step in to help her and her hard-luck husband. But she had burned that bridge the night she left town without a word to anybody when her old granddaddy was on his deathbed. Since then, Nora had not looked back, nor had her family looked for her. Nora was the last in a large family with seven siblings, born late in the lives of both her parents. When she left, she thought, they probably just packed up her things and wondered who was going to cook supper now that she was gone.

NORA

Nora lit two kerosene lamps in the kitchen. She had been so sick most of the day that she couldn't eat a thing. Now she was feeling hungry and knew it wasn't good for the baby to go without. In the dim kitchen she lifted the lid on the iron pot atop the wood stove and stirred the ham and bean soup she had made two days ago. She cut a piece of cornbread, took a seat at the small wooden table. She wondered how much longer she might have food to eat and what she would do when she didn't. The Georgia winter wasn't particularly harsh or long, but she had not put up much in the way of vegetables, and the ham was the last of the meat they had on hand. Nora needed to find a way to get to town. Walking was probably the only option since Harry had taken the wagon. She guessed that Harry didn't have any credit with the grocer. A couple of crumpled up dollars in her coat pocket wouldn't go far but at least it was something.

After supper she cleaned up the kitchen and carried one of the lamps with her to the bedroom. There, Nora slipped on her nightdress and climbed into the lumpy bed with the moth-eaten quilt. She had gotten used to sleeping with her coat on top of the covers for extra warmth against the night air that seeped in through the cracks. She pulled the coat up and over her nose and breathed in what she thought was the last lingering scent of home she had left as she drifted off to sleep.

Scared awake in the darkness, Nora sat up in bed, trying to make sense of the noises she heard outside, whinnying and footfalls on the porch steps. She grabbed the lamp left burning on the tall chest, turned up the light as she tiptoed across the room, her mouth suddenly as dry as August clay. Just beyond the corner from the front door, she crouched, trembling and waiting for whatever happened next. The door burst open, and Harry stumbled in, reeking of whiskey and cheap perfume. He staggered past without even looking at her and fell into their bed. Nora followed him into the room, stood over him for a good while. With every deep breath he took, anger and disappointment flooded through her like blood and water. Did he even know he was home? Had he even seen her? His drinking had aged him, but his face was as carefree as the night they had met. Not a worry in the world or so it seemed. Grown weary of the watch, she picked up her coat from the floor and went out to the rocker on the front porch, where for the rest of the moonless night she rocked and listened in on the conversation of at least three wise owls.

When the sky began to lighten, Nora shuffled into the kitchen and started cooking Harry a breakfast he would never forget. Around sunrise she made a trip out to the barn for the secret ingredient she knew Harry kept on hand for controlling the rat population. She planned to put it to its intended use, only the rat she had determined to control was a good-sized one so she needed a good-sized dose. Back in the kitchen she stirred a heaping spoonful of Rough on Rats into the pot of steaming grits. She caught herself right before she licked the spoon. She set the coffee to perk, went to check on Harry. He was right where she had left him. Back in the kitchen, Nora poured herself a steaming cup of coffee and headed back to her rocker.

It was midafternoon when a bleary-eyed Harry finally appeared in the doorway, still dressed in the rumpled, reeking clothes he had slept in.

"Fix me something to eat."

Nora didn't rise or even turn to look at Harry. Lulled by the rocking, she said almost dreamily, "I made you some breakfast."

When the screen door slammed shut, Nora vaulted from the rocker and pushed past Harry on her way to the kitchen.

"Grits are hard as rock by now. I'll make some fresh and cook some eggs," she said, hurrying to the stove. "Why don't you see if there's bacon in the smokehouse and I'll start some biscuits." She offered a weak smile. Harry went outside to look for bacon. Full of guilt and hope, Nora picked up the baneful brew she'd stirred up earlier and shoved it into the larder behind the cornmeal.

Few words passed over breakfast. Mostly Nora hurried back and forth between the stove and the table, refilling Harry's plate and coffee cup. Afterward Harry wandered out to the barn and didn't make an appearance until almost sundown. When he came through the door, Nora saw the wagon standing out front, the old gray mule already hitched up and waiting. Harry held a length of rope.

"You can't run off again, Harry. We're out of food, and we've got this baby to think of," Nora told him, placing her hand on her belly.

"That's not my baby," Harry growled, coming close to Nora.

"It is your baby. How could it be anybody's but yours? I don't see nobody but you," Nora answered, fear rising in her voice.

"You're nothing but a little tramp," he said. "I oughta fix you right."

That was the last thing Nora heard before Harry's hands went around her throat and didn't let go until the world went dark and she slid to the floor.

When Nora came to, it was to the rough rhythm of the wagon and the tops of the pine trees passing in the night sky. She couldn't make sense of it. One eye was swollen shut, and a rag was tied around her mouth, making it hard to breathe. When she tried to get some air, her chest ached and she was pretty sure something was broken. Nora couldn't clear her head enough to figure out what was going on, and so she let the darkness and the rocking take her back under.

White. Everything was white. Nora lay on her back, a white sheet tucked snuggly across her chest. Turning her head to one side and through her one good eye, she could make out the vague outline of someone dressed in white, silhouetted against a window. Through the wall of tall windows, brilliant sunlight streamed in, the white light so intense that Nora could hardly keep her eye open. When she finally could, she had no idea where she was. She tried to bring her hand to her face, but it wouldn't move. Looking down, she discovered that her wrists were bound with thick white straps.

As the room came into focus, Nora knew she was somewhere unfamiliar in a bed, not her own. Other beds stood lined up beside hers in a dormitory room, and she could make out the shapes of what she assumed were other people under other tightly tucked white sheets. Unsure that she wanted to call attention to herself until she knew where she was, or even if this was real, she kept quiet. Her throat parched, her tongue puffy, she wasn't sure she could make a sound even if she wanted to. It took so much effort to keep her eye open that she closed it again, and when she heard someone calling her name from somewhere far away, she struggled to come to her senses.

"Nora. Nora."

It was a woman's voice, gentle and soft. For a moment Nora thought she was home, her mama calling her.

"Nora. Try to open your eyes, Nora."

The room came into focus, not as bright as before. Nora didn't recognize the face, but it was kind, framed in graying hair tucked under a white cap. "Do you think you could take a sip of water?"

Nora swallowed hard and nodded.

"I'll need to sit you up first."

Nora tried to help with righting herself, but she didn't have a bit of strength and the hand ties made it near impossible. The woman knew what she was doing. She untied one of Nora's hands, pulled her up enough so that she was nearly sitting. It made Nora's head spin, but she needed to figure out some things. She pulled herself together while trying not to gag. The cool water soothed her parched throat. She got greedy, began gulping.

"Not too much and not too fast. You haven't had anything for four days now. Don't make yourself sick," the woman told her as she took the cup away.

"Four days," Nora croaked. "It's been four days?"

"You were brought in on Wednesday morning real early. It's Sunday. Four days ago," she answered.

"Where am I?" Nora asked.

"You're at the sanitarium in Milledgeville. I'm Mrs. Carroll, the day nurse for this ward. I've been caring for you since."

"Am I sick?" Nora asked.

"You just rest for now. We'll have time to talk later," the kind woman said as she helped lower Nora back down to the bed.

"Where's Harry?" Nora asked her. "Is he here too?"

The nurse patted Nora's arm and walked away.

Flickering gas lamplight bathed the room when Nora woke next, whispering voices nearby, the faint sound of someone crying. Her hands free now, she was able to open both eyes. Nora turned on her side. In the bed nearest to her lay a small, frail girl with coal-black hair and the palest skin Nora had ever seen. She watched Nora through unblinking eyes. Nora returned her gaze, smiled. The girl smiled back.

"You're both awake. That's a nice change. We might even try some supper tonight. What do you think about that?" A much younger, white-clad nurse came into view and stood between the two beds, her hands on her hips as she looked from one to the other.

"Yes please." Nora answered.

"Good. Let's get you girls upright and I'll get some soup. I'm Louella, the night nurse," she explained as she pulled Nora upright. "Nora, this is Annie. Annie, this is Nora. Now you know each other," she said over her shoulder as she walked away.

Nora looked at Annie. "Are you sick?"

"I have fits sometimes," she answered. "They say it's the epilepsy. Are you sick too?"

"I'm not sure," Nora answered. "My husband must have brought me here."

Annie moved a little closer, spoke in a whisper.

"I heard the nurses talkin' 'bout you that first day. They said you was hurt. You tried to hang yourself with a rope in your barn. Least that's what they said," Annie answered, her eyes darting away from Nora.

Nora brought her hand up to her neck. "I don't remember that," she said, mostly to herself. Her neck was sore, raw, tender to the touch. Nora tried to think back to what happened before she woke up in the hospital but everything was fuzzy.

The nurse arrived with warm broth and a slice of bread on a tray. Nora ate in silence and tried to put the pieces together.

"Miss," Nora said, when Louella returned for the tray, "I don't recollect what I'm doing here. Can you tell me what's wrong with me?"

Louella came to Nora's bedside. "I'm not supposed to talk about those things. I'm just a nurse. You'll see the doctor in a day or two when you're feeling better. He can answer your questions then."

"I can't wait that long. I don't understand why I'm here. If you know somethin', please tell me," Nora pleaded.

The night nurse looked around, found a chair and pulled it up to Nora's bedside. She leaned in close. "I was still on duty when you came in. It was just past daylight on Wednesday. He had you in the back of the wagon on a straw bed. Your husband, I guess. Said he found you hanging in the barn." She reached over to Nora and softly touched the abrasion on her neck. "The rope mark's still there. He said he had some papers from the judge in Putnam County to bring you here before he found you like that. Said you've been hurting yourself for a while now, and he wanted you to get some help before it was too late."

Nora listened but could not make sense of what the nurse was telling her. "I don't remember anything like that," she said, shaking her head. "Why can't I remember?"

"Sometimes you forget when you're sick," Louella said, hoping to soothe Nora.

"I'm not sick," Nora answered. "And I don't remember tryin' to hurt myself." She brought her hand up to her neck. "I didn't do this. A rope didn't do this."

"Shhhhh now, don't get yourself upset," Louella said, looking around nervously. "The doctor will talk to you soon. Some rest will do you good." When she tried to settle her into bed, Nora reached out and took her arm.

"Please listen to me. I didn't try to hurt myself. I wouldn't do that," she said, tears threatening.

"Try to rest now. You're safe right here. Settle down."

Nora lay back, too tired to explain herself. She wondered if there was still a baby. Tears trickled down her face, then pooled in a salty sting around her neck until finally she could fight off sleep no longer.

On Monday morning after breakfast, Mrs. Carroll appeared at Nora's bed with a wheeled chair.

"Doctor Albertson will see you this morning. Let's see if we can clean you up a little."

With a basin of water and a cloth, she cleaned Nora's face. Careful around her bruised eye, she lifted Nora's chin and looked closely at her neck, touching the raw skin lightly with her fingertips.

"Does it hurt?"

"Some," Nora answered.

She offered Nora a worn, but clean, gray cotton dress. "Why don't we get you into some fresh clothes too?"

NORA

Mrs. Carroll helped Nora into the chair, took her through the ward and down a long, white-walled corridor to an office across the hallway. The office held two desks. Through an open door on the far wall, Nora saw what she thought was an examination room. The nurse parked Nora's chair near the larger desk.

"Doctor Albertson will be in directly," Mrs. Carroll assured her before she left.

A stout, dark-haired middle-aged man with a full beard entered from the far room.

"Good morning, I'm Doctor Albertson. I believe you're Nora." He consulted the folder that he carried. "Nora Walker from Putnam County, is that right?" he asked, looking at her over the top of his round eyeglasses.

"Yes, I'm Nora Walker," she answered shyly.

The doctor moved behind his desk, opened the folder, and turned his attention to Nora.

"I understand you've been asking questions about what you're doing here."

Nora, somewhat fearful that he knew this about her answered, "Yes. Yes, I have."

"You don't know why you're here?"

"No. I was told Harry—my husband, Harry Walker—brought me here."

"I examined you on Wednesday morning, Nora. You were in pretty bad shape," he said, consulting his notes again. "Some broken ribs, abrasions around your right eye, a good bit of bruising on your back and stomach, and you had likely come close to death from hanging by a rope around your neck."

He looked over his glasses to judge her reaction.

Nora said nothing.

"Do you remember how you got hurt, Nora?"

She shook her head.

"Do you remember tying a rope around a beam up in the hayloft in the barn and then placing that rope around your neck?"

"No, I don't remember that at all."

"Do you remember stepping off the hayloft with a rope around your neck, Nora?"

"I don't remember because that didn't happen," she answered.

"You didn't try to end your life by hanging yourself in the barn?"

"I would never do that. That would be a sin. I would never hang myself," Nora said firmly, staring directly into his eyes.

"There are abrasions around your neck where a rope was tied. If you don't remember, perhaps you've tried to forget because it's too painful to think about, or maybe you were without oxygen for a period of time. The doctor folded his hands on the desk. "So, what do you think happened that night?" he asked more gently.

Nora took a deep breath, gathered her courage to tell the truth she had never told to anybody. "I would never try to kill myself. I remember what happened that night with Harry. I know what he did. He put his hands around my neck. He choked me. That's what he does when he's mad. He squeezes the air out of me until everything goes black. What I don't remember is how I got here. Why did he bring me here? That's what I want to know."

"There were rope marks on your neck when you came in, Nora, and I would imagine they are still visible. I saw them myself when I examined you."

"Then he must have tied a rope around my neck after I blacked out."

"I have a court order here from a judge in Putnam County," the doctor said as he shuffled through the papers. "Here it is. Signed last week after a court hearing. Do you know about this?"

Nora was dumbstruck.

"Did you know about the hearing? You weren't there but your husband was. He gave testimony about your illness." The doctor looked over the court paper in the file. "It says here that you've been experiencing blackouts and memory loss. It says you've tried to do harm to yourself on several occasions." He watched Nora to gauge her reaction.

But she was no longer looking at Doctor Albertson. She was staring through the window behind him and thinking about everything that had happened over the past months. Nora remembered all the mean things that Harry had done and all the terrible names he had called her. She thought about how he had punched her in the stomach after she told him she was expecting. She counted the days she had spent alone in that wretched shack, wondering where he had gone. *That must have been what he was up to all that time,* she thought. *He was making plans to send me off.* She remembered how easy it had been for them to get married at the courthouse in Putnam County because a friend of Harry's daddy was the judge there. Harry told her that old judge was always good for taking care of business. Now she suspected that same judge had taken care of her and their baby too. He had taken good care of them, real good.

"I should have let him eat those grits," she said, looking past the doctor and letting her eyes linger on the filtered sunlight and the puffy white clouds in the clear blue sky.

"What was that? Nora, are you feeling all right?" Doctor Albertson asked as he rose from his chair and came around to the front of the desk. "Maybe we've talked enough for today. Let me get the nurse."

Once she was back in the ward and settled into bed, Nora fell fast asleep. She dreamed of being back home, sitting on the back porch in a rocking chair, shelling peas with her mama. In the dream, Nora watched the work-hardened hands of her mother, splitting open the sun-ripened purple hulls and scraping the small green peas into the old metal basin. They fell with a plinking sound as they filled the bowl.

Sometime in the late afternoon Nora woke from a deep sleep. She sat up in bed, just as Mrs. Carroll wheeled Annie in after her treatment. Annie looked worn out. She closed her eyes as soon as she was in bed and tucked under the covers.

Nora could hardly contain herself. "Mrs. Carroll, can I write a letter? Would you be able to send a letter for me?"

"Yes, I could. I'll bring you some writing paper when I bring your supper," she answered.

Nora eased out of bed and crossed the room to the windows that lined the wall. A warm, pink-tinted light bathed the green branches of the tall pines, while a light breeze stirred the treetops, and Nora wished she were out among them. For the first time in months, a thin thread of hopefulness unspooled in her head. She wasn't yet sure about what she would say to her mother in the letter, but she couldn't wait to write it. She knew that once she started, the words would come one by one, just like the peas dropping into the basin filling the empty space.

The next morning Nora was ushered to the reception office to go through what Mrs. Carroll called intake. She wasn't sure what that meant but hoped that it wasn't something painful. She had not yet told anybody about the baby, and she intended to hold on to that bit of news a little while longer.

As it turned out, intake meant a lot of questions. Nora answered them the best she could, telling as much of the truth as she thought necessary. The blank-faced woman behind the desk barely looked at her as she read from the paper that lay on the desk between them.

"Have you ever had convulsions?"

"No."

"Have you ever had an injury to the head?"

"No."

"Have you ever had a serious illness?"

"No."

"Have you ever been suicidal?"

"No."

"Have you ever been homicidal?"

"What does that mean?"

"Have you ever wanted to kill somebody?"

"Maybe once."

"Is that a yes?"

"Yes."

The sour-faced woman taking notes paused to write something down, looked up at Nora before she started asking questions again.

"Have you ever been addicted to the use of liquor or tobacco?"

"No."

"Have you ever been addicted to the use of morphine, cocaine, or chloral?"

"No."

"Have you ever been violent?"

"What do you mean by violent?"

"Have you ever been violent?" the woman asked again.

"Well if you mean, have I ever got mad enough to yell and break stuff and beat on Harry's chest when he chokes me, then yes, I have been violent."

The woman stared at Nora again but responded to nothing and went on to the next question.

"Have you ever been destructive?"

"Same answer I just said. When he leaves me for days on end, I tear stuff up. Wouldn't you?"

"Have you ever done mischief with fire?"

"No, but I thought about it when Harry left the last time and stayed gone so long."

"Have you ever been treated for insanity?"

"No."

Finally, the questions ended. The mean-looking woman wrote and wrote. Then without saying anything, she stood and left the room.

When Nora got back to her bed, Annie was gone. All of her things were gone, too, the bed stripped of its sheets. Even though she and Annie had not shared much more than a few words, Nora felt sad.

Mrs. Carroll came by later with a ham sandwich and some milk.

"Where's Annie?"

"She went home," the nurse replied.

"She's well now?"

"I don't think I would say she's well, but we done all we could do, like always."

"She's been here before?" Nora asked.

"Been comin' since she was a little girl. When she's bad off and her family can't do anything for her, they bring her here to see if we can help. Then they come get her. We'll see her again, I'm pretty sure."

"I've got that letter you said you would send off for me." Nora reached over to the small wooden table next to the bed. "You sure you don't mind?"

"I'm happy to do it. It's good to keep in touch with your family."

Nora handed over the letter. "I appreciate it."

Before she left for the day, Mrs. Carroll stopped by Doctor Albertson's office. The doctor, seated at his desk, was taking care of paperwork when she approached, Nora's letter in her hands.

"Nora Walker asked me to mail a letter for her," she told him.

"To her husband?"

"No. That's why I came to see you. It's addressed to her mother."

"That's odd," Doctor Albertson replied, picking up a file from the corner of his desk. "I recollect that her parents are both deceased, according to the court filing I read." He looked through the papers to find it. "Yes. That's what it says."

"What should I do about the letter then?" she asked.

"I'll put it in her file," he answered, taking it from her.

"See you tomorrow, Doctor."

"Good night, Mrs. Carroll."

On the flat, white surface of the envelope in Nora's precise penmanship the letter was addressed to Mrs. Elisha Herndon. Doctor Albertson glanced at it briefly, placed it in the file, and turned off his desk lamp. It had been a long day.

Effie

SEPTEMBER, 1922

5

More than anything, Effie craved order. Order and cleanliness.

"How on earth did I end up here?" she asked no one in particular as she made her way to the infirmary from the tiny dormitory room. In a place brimming with humanity, in buildings overflowing with people and their problems, Effie felt entirely alone.

Three months had slipped past since she left Atlanta. She could hardly believe it had been that long. The stretch of time, one of those curious experiences when hours passed so quickly and yet every day stretched into the longest day of her life. At least she had established a daily routine. It lacked variety, but it was one step in the right direction. Up well before dawn, work until she could hardly put one foot in front of the other, fall into bed, sleep fitfully and repeat. Three months and already she was that kind of tired that couldn't be cured by a good night's sleep.

Tasked to work in the infirmary for colored female patients, Effie put in a sixteen-hour shift, five days a week, eight hours on Sundays. Most of her time spent in what was meant to be a twenty-five-bed ward that presently held fifty-two patients, the sick and the dying, her only companions. Two women, recovering from their most recent bouts of illness themselves, were kept on the ward to assist her with the care of the others.

Effie diagnosed the situation immediately. No one really cared about these women. They were the pushed aside, the left alone, the forgotten. Before she arrived, the attention they were allotted was decidedly void of much medical knowledge or compassion. Neglect and hunger a staple of their daily lives. The infirmary served mostly as an isolation ward for patients who had some type of illness in addition to whatever else had brought them to Milledgeville. Pellagra and tuberculosis were the most common complaints. Effie advocated for separating the tubercular patients from the others, in an attempt to prevent the spread of the dreaded disease, as was the practice in the white wards. But space was a luxury unavailable. She settled for relocating their beds to the windowed outer wall of the long room and a daily regimen of fresh air on the portico. Many of her patients were ambulatory, able to sit up for a good part of the day and attend to their own feeding. Hopefully, most would recover and return to their more regular lives inside the grounds of the sanitarium. Some were confined to bed due to their poor conditions, and more than a few were restrained for their own safety and that of the others. They were women waiting to die, and their care was purely custodial. Regardless of their conditions, fifty patients in need of succor and support were still fifty patients. And more than nurse, Effie was housekeeper, counselor, confidant, priest, mother, and companion to them all.

Well before dawn, Effie climbed the stairs to the third-floor ward and paused outside the double doors, smoothed her freshly laundered gray nursing uniform and sucked in a deep breath to steel herself against the anticipated chaos beyond. Already she was looking forward to tomorrow. Sallie Davis had invited her for a visit with a promise of home-cooked food and quiet time.

Effie unlocked the door and pushed it open. The silence struck her first. With a few hesitant steps, her eyes adjusted to the half-light. At the front desk where the night attendant usually sat, the chair stood empty. She lifted the kerosene lamp from the table and treaded lightly into the room. The white-sheeted emptiness of so many vacant beds in the open floor patient room made the bottom drop out of her stomach. *Where could they be?* Effie wondered and quickened her pace, with each step tallying the seriously ill patients confined to bed. All seventeen accounted for, but thirty-some missing. The gauzy drapery covering the glass portico doors flapped eerily in the breeze, squeezing through the narrow opening. *Those doors should have been locked.* Hushed voices whispered in the darkness beyond. Stepping through, she paused to listen. Snickering and giggling floated across the damp air, muted voices, low and indistinct. Effie took in the long expanse of porch. A white shrouded crowd in the far corner pressed against the barred opening, their attention riveted on something below. Bright moonlight reflected off their gowns, their black limbs lost in the darkness, the gathering enveloped in an ethereal glow. Stepping forward, Effie felt her foot upset several mostly empty brown pint bottles. The distinct smell of whiskey rose from the liquid as it trickled onto the floorboards. Cora, the night attendant, snoring, slept soundly on a wooden lounge chair near the puddle. All of a sudden, a flurry of barefooted patients fluttered past her like a flock of birds heading for their nests. Some giggled, others whispered. Effie let them pass, then headed to where they had gathered at the edge of the enclosure. She peered through the bars, searching for what had attracted their attention and amused them so. It didn't take long. Out in the opening, what she first thought were three, but like a kaleidoscope slowly revealed themselves to be six human forms—animated by the light of the moon, and enjoying each other's naked flesh in the late summer's lush green grass. Though not a prude, Effie pondered why the gathering hadn't searched out a more intimate setting, but quickly wrote it off to the pervasive desperation of the place. Effie watched for a moment, wondering whether they were patients or staff or both. After pausing to sniff Cora's rancid whiskey breath to confirm her suspicion, she left her where she had found her and closed the portico door. With the patient room now full of deep breathing pretend sleepers, Effie returned the lamp to the desk, paused for a moment and went about her morning duties.

First, a head count and a wellness check to assure that her charges survived the night, more urgent this morning under the circumstances. At bed twenty-two the bedcovers remained turned back and empty. She consulted her room chart. Pearl was missing. Effie perused the room. Maybe she was using the toilet. She made a mental note to check on Pearl on her next pass. All patients had survived the night. At this moment, with all patients alive and accounted for, Effie always felt a huge sense of relief. On mornings where she had to deal with a death, it took an emotional toll on her and the women in the ward. Reaching the last bed, she roused Bertie, a five-year resident of the sanitarium and now Effie's most trusted assistant. Bertie's family had brought her there the year after she lost her husband and son to typhoid fever. She had recovered from the fever herself, but suffered from melancholia and had since contracted pellagra.

"I really need your help this morning. Get yourself together quick as you can. And check the lavatory for Pearl," Effie directed.

Rising slowly, Bertie sighed as she stood and stretched. She glanced at Pearl's bed, hesitated. "She ain't here. She's gone."

"What do you mean gone?"

"They came and got her last night."

"Who did?" Effie asked, hands on hips.

"Two men showed up. She left with 'em."

"What two men, and how did they get in here?"

"They was shoutin' from outside to Cora out on the porch. They came up, and she let 'em in."

"Were they attendants?"

"I don't know. I never seen 'em before."

"Did Pearl know them?"

"I don't rightly know, Miss Effie. I don't think so. She looked scared."

"Why did Cora let them in? Did she know them?"

"Seemed like it." She added sheepishly, "They brung her them whiskey bottles."

Effie shook her head. "I don't have time to deal with that right now. Get dressed, and let's start morning rounds."

Effie went to the missing woman's bed for a look around. Pearl's one pair of long worn-out cloth shoes were missing from her bedside chest. A patient had never disappeared overnight. There was nothing she could do at the moment. She couldn't spare Bertie, and Cora was still sleeping off her nighttime activities. It would have to wait until after breakfast.

Bertie returned, pushing a cart with two large water basins, stacks of cotton washcloths, and fresh bed linens. She handed it off to Effie as they began waking the women, helping them through the morning routine. Those who could got out of their beds on their own, turned back their bed covers to let them air while they went to the lavatory to use the toilet and wash their faces.

Effie took charge of those who could not manage alone. Usually a two-person job, she had to help some relieve themselves in their bedpans, clean them up afterwards, change bed linens that had been soiled in the night, wash those who had been lying in their own filth, and reassure those who awoke frightened and disoriented that they were safe.

Though the work was physical and challenging, as Effie moved from patient to patient, her touch remained gentle, her voice soothing. For whatever reasons, these women had been brought here, and now she was in charge of their care at a time when they were most vulnerable. Effie understood that she was the first trained professional nurse that ever cared for most of these patients. Many had never visited a doctor, and most had been sent to the sanitarium by loved ones who could no longer care for them. More than a few had spent time in jail for petty offenses or simply to await the court order that would send them to Milledgeville because there was nowhere left for them to go. Now they had Effie. And she had them. She had never known hunger or loneliness, seldom felt fear. She had never seen such deprivation as that experienced by the women on her ward. She was cared for and cherished by her family. From her very first day at the sanitarium and every day since, Effie came to understand what a privileged life she had led. Despite her exhaustion and the overwhelming sadness of the place, this was exactly what she had craved—to be needed, to matter.

More than half the patients had pellagra. An awful disease, its victims were marked by a disfiguring rash and the flux. In the advanced stages, they drifted into dementia and wasted away. While some had come to the sanitarium suffering from it, others had developed it during their confinement. In all of Effie's time at the nurses' training school at Grady Hospital, and even during the influenza epidemic, she had never encountered a case of it. The extent of her knowledge, what she had read in a textbook. And that hadn't helped much either. Confusion about its cause and treatment persisted. It didn't seem to be contagious like tuberculosis, but it was most certainly an epidemic. From what she had heard, not too long ago, hundreds of sanitarium patients suffered from it and more than two hundred died in just a year's time. There was some talk among the patients about a couple of doctors trying to figure out what caused it, but the details were vague. Effie wanted to find out more about that, but she just didn't have the time, and she wasn't quite sure how to go about it. Nurses, even professionally trained ones, were considered custodial staff members, their medical skills and training hardly acknowledged. More than that, she had found, the fact that she was colored, meant the possibility for interaction or any professional association with others at the sanitarium was nonexistent.

"Mabel. Good morning, Mabel. Time to wake up," Effie called in her rich and soothing voice. She reached for Mabel's shoulder, careful not to make contact with the crusty red rash covering her neck and face. The old woman's wrists were secured to the bed with cuffs. Effie hated the practice. She was told it insured patients' safety, but she could not understand what possible harm a seventy-year-old woman could do to herself or anyone else, especially in such a weakened state. Effie didn't know what had brought Mabel to the hospital ten years ago, only that she suffered from progressively destructive pellagra outbreaks. And if Effie were to guess, she thought Mabel was down to about ninety pounds, her body wasting away. Due to worsening dementia, she recognized hardly anyone, and for long stretches of time thought that she was being held against her will in a dungeon full of wild animals. From day to day, Effie was unsure of what to expect from Mabel.

"Time to wake up, Mabel," Effie said with a firmer shake of the woman's shoulder. Mabel moaned.

Effie moistened a washcloth, gently wiping Mabel's parched lips. The cool dampness revived her a bit.

"Let's get you cleaned up. Maybe you can eat a little breakfast this morning," she added hopefully, knowing that Mabel had not eaten for the past three days and that it was becoming more difficult to get her to take any liquids.

Mabel's eyes fluttered open. A weak smile creased her lips.

"Good morning, Mabel," Effie tried again.

"Good morning," Mabel answered, confused. "And who are you?" she asked, as she did on most days she awoke lucid.

"I'm Effie. Your nurse. How'd you sleep last night?" she inquired patiently, unwrapping Mabel's wrist restraints as they talked.

"Effie, that's a nice name," Mabel replied. "I hardly slept a wink. Some folks was laughin' and singin' all night long."

Though Mabel claimed to barely sleep a wink every night, Effie wondered at the truth of what she claimed this morning.

"I'm sorry to hear that, Mabel. Maybe you can get a little nap after breakfast," Effie reassured her.

"That sounds good," Mabel answered in her frail voice. "I've got some washin' to do. I always have a full day on wash day."

Effie nodded. Mabel had been confined to her bed for the better part of six months, and the laundry day she remembered likely, more than a decade past.

Effie and Bertie were finishing their morning rounds when the kitchen attendant called "breakfast" and wheeled in the tray carts.

With all those who could be brought upright or put in chairs, several patients, familiar with the daily routine, began handing out food so that they could enjoy these few moments of familiar communal ritual as much as possible. Trays with grits, biscuits, and syrup along with cups of weak, lukewarm coffee were passed around. No one complained about the food, though the quality and quantity left much to be desired.

The porch door opened, and a still woozy Cora headed through the long room. She didn't bother to look at Effie, who followed her every step with a long, cool glare.

When Cora returned from the lavatory, Effie immediately overtook her and gently pulled her back to the desk.

"What in God's name happened here last night, Cora?" she asked.

Cora stared at the floor as if an answer might appear on the floorboards.

"And where on earth is Pearl?"

Cora looked up. "What do you mean, she ain't here?"

"She's not. And who were those men you let in here last night?" Effie asked. Holding Cora's arm, she gave it a little shake.

Cora's mouth opened but nothing came out.

"Cora, what happened?"

Tears welled in Cora's big eyes. "I don't know, Miss Effie. It's all kind a cloudy. I don't remember much."

"Pearl's missing. You were passed out drunk on the porch when I got here this morning. Everybody who could get out of bed was out there with you. I imagine several shared your whiskey bottles. Do you remember any of that?" Effie demanded.

Cora continued to cry and shake her head. "I don't know. I don't remember."

"Well you best be tryin' to," Effie snarled. "And get yourself together. We have work to do. I had to change beds all by myself this morning. I couldn't even do medical rounds because of you."

Effie headed back to the floor to attend to her patients and cool down. She didn't like speaking harshly to anyone, especially these poor women who could hardly take care of themselves. But she needed Cora and Bertie to take on some of the responsibilities or any sense of order would disappear. That would mean chaos. Effie shuddered at the thought.

By the end of Effie's shift, Pearl had not returned. Her disappearance had been reported to the central office, though Effie doubted much was being done to find her. Mabel had taken her nap that afternoon and never woke up. Off duty at nine, Effie sat with Mabel until the attendants came and took her to the morgue. Following them out of the building, she watched them wheel Mabel away and then headed toward the Big Hall. Since her first days at the sanitarium, Effie had established a habit of taking refuge in the auditorium. She had no idea why she was drawn to the cavernous building. Standing on the stage in the middle of the dark, quiet emptiness of the place, she could somehow let loose the emotions she kept locked in a vault inside and restore some sense of inner calm. Thinking about poor, frail and now dead Mabel, she cried and made her peace with the events of the day. One foot in front of the other, Effie sought the refuge of her room, fell into bed, and summoned sleep.

On Saturday morning, an overnight case in hand, Effie waited at the sanitarium depot to take the Milledgeville bound train into town. Her first outing since June. As soon as the train pulled to a stop and the inbound passengers got off, Effie rushed inside, claiming a seat. She exhaled and closed her eyes, the tension in her neck easing. The memory of the train trip from Atlanta to Milledgeville filled her thoughts, then just as suddenly, a remembrance of another train trip overtook it. One she had taken as a child with her mother and her brother Norris and her grandmother too. Though not as clear, it was powerful. How tightly her mother held her hand, the scent she breathed in from her mother's tweed, traveling suit as she rested her head against her shoulder. And then, that her mother was crying. Effie's eyes flew open. The realization, startling. Her mother had been sad. And for the rest of the journey to Milledgeville, Effie wondered why.

Expecting Sallie to greet her at the station, Effie stepped down to the platform, sorting through the waiting faces. To her surprise, her brother Norris, smiling and as handsome as ever, closed the distance between them, his arms flung open. She hesitated for only the briefest moment, then rushed right into them.

"I was thinking about you just now," she whispered into his ear as they stood in a long embrace. Effie pulled back. "Is everything okay?"

"I think I should be asking you that."

"Papa?" she asked anxiously.

"He's fine," Norris answered. "We missed you is all. He's waiting for us back at Sallie's."

"He's here?"

"He's here. And he's anxious to see you." Norris took her bag and her arm, moving her toward the sidewalk that would lead them to Sallie's.

"He insisted I drive him down here to see you. He's been asking since June. I could only hold him off for so long."

Effie held tight to his arm as they walked along. "I wrote him after I arrived. I told him not to worry."

Norris nodded and chuckled. "Right. You ran off to work in the state asylum for the insane, and you expected a letter to make that right with our father?"

"He knew I was going. It wasn't a surprise," Effie answered somewhat uncomfortably.

"I think you're stretching the truth a little bit, sister," Norris replied with a friendly nudge.

Coming up on Sallie's house, Effie spotted her father in his finest, on the porch, hat in hand, waiting for her. She could hardly keep from breaking into a run. She lifted her hand in a wave. He waved back.

Alonzo Herndon folded his daughter into his arms, held tight for as long as she would let him. Stepping back, he grasped her shoulders, lifted his chin and looked through his gold-framed pince-nez glasses to appraise her.

"You look a little worn down and your hair is a mess, but otherwise…" his voice trailed off as he embraced her again. This time she let him hold her as long as he needed to.

When they parted, she spoke lovingly, "I told you I would be okay, Papa. I am. You don't have to worry so much."

"Oh, I do have to worry. You're my only daughter. You can't deny me that. I was more than a little bit surprised when you up and left town without even telling me you were going."

"You were in Florida, Papa. And we had talked about the possibility."

"Possibility. That was what I thought it was. You made it a reality without letting me know."

"I was afraid you would try to stop me," Effie answered, straightaway.

Sallie, carrying a tea tray, appeared at the screen door, and Norris opened it to let her pass.

"Look who showed up uninvited," she indicated the men with her sly eye. "I had no idea they were coming."

"How did you know I'd be here?" Effie asked. "I haven't had a chance since June."

"That's my fault," Sallie answered. "I wrote to tell him not to worry about you and let slip that you were coming today. I never knew he would just show up like this," she said, putting the tray down on the table.

"I needed to see Effie," Alonzo explained, "I didn't mean to intrude."

"I'm happy to see you," Effie replied.

"And I need to find something to feed some hungry men," Sallie answered, walking back into the house.

"Don't put yourself out, Sallie," Alonzo called after her.

"I remember your appetite, Alonzo," she called back.

"Come sit by me," Alonzo said, taking a seat in the porch swing. "Norris, you go see if Miss Sallie needs some help."

Norris grabbed a glass of tea and followed Sallie into the house. Alonzo's children always obeyed his orders, at least while in his sight.

"Tell me about your work, daughter. Is it what you wanted?"

Effie sat down next to her father. He reached over and took her hand.

"I don't quite know how to answer that, Papa," she said, looking into his eyes. "It's hard. I mean physically hard. Not to mention just dealing with everything that's going on with the patients. They're more than just sick. They're poor and sad and helpless."

Alonzo picked up a glass and passed it to Effie, then took one for himself. They both sipped their tea to let their feelings settle.

"Is it what you wanted?" Alonzo asked again.

"I haven't had time to even know. I work long shifts. I don't have much time for anything other than just reacting to what's happening. I see and do things I never imagined doing or seeing. I cry myself to sleep a lot."

She glanced at her father to make sure he was okay hearing what she had to say.

"I don't think anyone can understand what a situation will be like if they've never experienced anything like it before," she continued. "You can imagine all you want, but you're really just guessing about it. I remember feeling that way, nursing for the Red Cross. Exhausted and heartsick. But it was different somehow. I got to come home at the end of the day, for one thing."

"I miss you at home," Alonzo admitted.

"I miss being there," Effie replied. "But I think this is what I needed. I want to work hard. I like working hard. I'm a lot like you when it comes to that."

Alonzo smiled. "Yes, you are. And you're a lot like me some other ways too. You're stubborn. And you're bossy."

"Now hold on a minute. Don't start calling me all those bad things," she teased.

"I don't consider those bad traits, girl. I'm proud of being like that. I'm proud of you being like that too." He leaned in a little closer and lowered his voice. "I wish your brother was more like us." They shared a quick laugh.

"I'm glad you're proud of me, Papa. But I work because I want to. I went to nursing school because I want to help people. I took this job for that same reason. The circumstances at the sanitarium are difficult in the extreme. I'm not completely sure I'll want to stay there any longer than the one year I signed on for, but I'm learning so much from my experiences. Those women need me. I want to help them as much as I can."

Alonzo relaxed back into the swing and gave a big push with his foot. "Do you need anything? Is there anything I can do for you? That's really what I came down here to find out. And just to set the record straight, I would never have kept you from following your dream."

Tears welled up in Effie's eyes. She worked to keep them from sliding out. "I can't think of anything right now, Papa. I appreciate you asking, though. And I'm happy you came."

"Luncheon is served in the backyard," Norris said from the doorway with a tea towel draped over his arm. "May I escort you, young lady?"

"I'm starved," Alonzo said as they walked through the house to the back door.

"I knew you would be," Sallie called from the backyard.

"That woman hears everything," Alonzo said.

"I heard that," Sallie called back.

After a delicious lunch of thick-sliced baked ham sandwiches with potato salad, followed by hugs and hopes to see each other soon, the Herndon men left for Atlanta.

Effie helped Sallie in the kitchen. They cleaned up and put the ham bone to good use in a pot of split pea soup they planned to share for supper. A bit later, they found themselves once again in Sallie's backyard garden, relaxing in the shade on a peaceful afternoon.

"I appreciate you not asking me about my work at the sanitarium," Effie offered.

"I figure if you wanted to talk about it, you would," Sallie said matter of factly.

"I need a break from it, at least a mental break from it. I haven't even processed everything that's happened since I got there, and so much has happened."

"Maybe you don't need to process it. Maybe just getting through it is all you can do. There've been lots of things in my life that I decided that was just the way it was. Get to it. Live through it. Move on."

After a comfortable silence, Effie said, "This morning on the train, I remembered something about a train trip I took with Mama. I don't even know where we were going or really even how old I was."

"What was it?" Sallie asked, holding up her hand, shading her eyes from the sun.

"I remember what she was wearing and how she smelled. She always smelled so nice. Sometimes I think I can still smell her. I loved to burrow into that magnificent hair of hers."

Sallie nodded. "Scent memory. She fell in love with some French perfume when she and Alonzo were in Paris. From then on, he always bought it for her. I can't remember the name. It just smelled like Addie."

"She was crying. Crying hard, body shaking hard," Effie said, still wrapped up in the memory. "I have no idea what could have upset her so."

"I don't know either. But I know you all went on several trips up north.

You might not remember, but your mama went to school in New York and Boston when you were little. I think I remember that you all took her up there on the train. You and Norris and Alonzo. She stayed, and you all came back home to Atlanta. Maybe that was the trip you remember. She would have been sad to be leaving you even if she was the one who insisted on finishing her studies up north."

"I don't remember that Papa was with us. Big Mama was, though."

"Well, maybe it was another time. Maybe after all those troubles in Atlanta, those riots. I reckon you know about that."

"I know some. I was little. Norris told me that she wanted to leave Atlanta and never come back. Maybe that was the trip I remember," Effie said, not trusting that she remembered well enough to figure it out.

Thoughtful, Sallie added, "Your mama had some struggles. I guess you know that."

Effie nodded. "You mentioned that the first time I was here. I think you used the word "tempered" to describe her. I think she was sad. That's what I remembered about that train trip today. And I know she had struggles. I'm not sure that I really understand what they were about, though. Did you?"

Sallie nodded. "Some. It's hard to talk about."

"I'm an adult, Sallie. I think I can hear truths about my mother who died over ten years ago and be all right with knowing."

Sallie regarded Effie for a minute. "I expect that's so." Sallie settled back in her chair and closed her eyes. She let out a long sigh. Then, as was her nature, she went right to the heart of the matter.

"Your mama had a hard time trying to decide if she wanted to live as a white person or as a colored." She paused and waited for Effie's reaction, then added, "Her father was a very light-skinned man."

"My grandfather was Archie McNeil. He wasn't particularly light-skinned," Effie replied, confused.

Sallie sighed. "I'm a little surprised your daddy hasn't told you about this. Archie wasn't Adrienne's father. Her father was a man named George Stephens. He came from South Carolina. He and your grandmother never married. He went to Philadelphia after Addy was born and never came back."

"Why didn't I know that?" Effie asked. "Does Papa?"

Sallie just nodded. "I expect you were too young to ever have been told. And then your mama died." She paused, making sure to speak plainly, genuinely, so Effie could take things in. "There was a little more to it than that. He went north and lived his life as a white man, passing, you know," Sallie told her. "It was a choice, more than a few people made. Life was hard in the South. Hard anywhere for colored people."

"Did my mother ever talk about this?"

"She did. Your grandmother Martha never hid it from her. But something about that story haunted Addy. We talked about it often. She was curious about his life. She wondered if maybe he had made the right decision, considering how bad things got. The riots in Atlanta, her experiences up north, she grieved about that."

"So how is all of this connected to my memory of that train trip, Sallie?" Effie asked earnestly.

"Have you ever heard the name Anne Du Bignon?" Sallie asked.

"Of course. That was Mama's stage name. I always loved it. I call her that when I want to tap into some of her strength," Effie said proudly.

"It was more than a stage name for Adrienne. That was who she was when she went up north," Sallie answered.

"What do you mean it was who she was?" Effie asked.

"She worried she could never make a stage career for herself as a colored woman. Not even in Boston or New York. So, she came up with Anne Du Bignon. Claimed she was from an old South Carolina family. A French and Creole family. Like what her daddy had done. And while she was there, she lived that life."

Effie was silent.

"Can you make sense of that?" Sallie asked gently.

Effie sifted through the revelation. "It's not that unusual. I know people who live that way. I just never understood that Mama did. What did my father think about that?"

"You would have to ask him. I tried not to get into the middle of their relationship. They were both so strongheaded, and they wanted so much." Sallie added, "I do know one thing, they loved each other fiercely."

Despite what Sallie had advised about not having to process everything, this was definitely something Effie would have to process. Her mother lived as a white woman in the North and a colored woman in the South. *Why didn't Papa tell us? Did this come between them in some way?* This secret had to have troubled both of her parents. She wanted answers but wasn't sure how to go about finding them. Asking her father would certainly be a place to start. It was still on her mind the next morning when she caught the early train back to the sanitarium.

Effie barely had time to run to her room and change into her uniform before reporting for duty at two o'clock. One look into the ward and she knew something was wrong. Cora and Bertie were huddled together at the front desk, whispering. Patients were sitting on their beds, comforting each other, their arms draped around shoulders, and she could hear crying.

"What's wrong, Cora?" Effie asked.

Cora turned a tearful face to Effie, her voice wavering as she spoke. "They just found Pearl. In her old room, where she lived, before she got sick. She hung herself on them window bars."

Stunned, Effie glanced around the mournful room, her broken women shattered by the news. She turned back to Cora and Bertie.

"Are they sure it's Pearl?"

"I seen her myself," Bertie whispered.

Effie ran for Pearl's old room on the floor beneath the infirmary. A crowd of the curious had gathered around the door. Effie pushed her way to the front in time to see Pearl's tiny frame being lifted down from her self-made gallows as her thin, white cotton nightgown that served as her hanging rope was cut loose.

"How could I have let this happen?" Effie murmured.

Fern

SEPTEMBER, 1922

6

Beneath the low-hanging branches of a magnolia, Fern waited. In worn gray work clothes that gave off a distinct odor of fieldwork and old sweat, she sat, knees bent, arms wrapped around them. Though it hung on her like a scarecrow, the disguise concealed her well on a cloudy night that sometimes gave way to a patchy pale glow from a partially hidden full moon. She pulled a pear and a three-blade knife from her pocket, cut off slices of the juicy, sweet fruit, and savored each one as she slid them into her mouth. Fern bided time while all the curious gawkers stopped near her hiding spot, passing whispers about Pearl, what she had done to herself and why. Word traveled fast, but the truth would require some sorting out.

Fern had her own suspicions. She wasn't ready to believe that Pearl had taken her own life. There was something about two men coming for Pearl two nights before that was disturbingly familiar. Fern needed to know more.

THE TRUTH TOGETHER

A little after midnight a side door opened and Effie stepped out. Fern was surprised that the new nurse hadn't run back to Atlanta by now. She had heard that she worked hard and seemed to care about the women she took care of in the third-floor ward.

Fern eased out from under her shelter, brushed off the debris, and walked quietly until she caught up her prey.

"Hey," Fern said almost in Effie's ear.

Effie rounded on her, poised to throw a punch. "You. My God, you scared me. What are you doing over here?" she asked indignantly.

Fern, palms forward, said coolly, "Whoa now. Just calm down a minute. I didn't mean to scare you."

"And why are you slinking around over here dressed like that?"

"I didn't want anybody to recognize me," Fern answered, looking down at herself.

"I didn't. And you stink," Effie offered.

"That's fair," Fern agreed.

They stepped back and took each other in.

"I heard about Pearl. What happened?" Fern laid out her agenda.

Effie looked away to calm her edgy nerves. "I wish I knew."

"You were there, right? I heard you were there when they found her."

"No. I came on duty right after. I was there when they brought her down from the bars," she answered, subconsciously moving a hand to her throat.

"You saw the room, then. You saw her hanging there?"

Effie could only nod.

"What do you think happened?"

"She hung herself," Effie answered. "With her gown."

"I mean, how did she do it? Was she standing on something? Where was the gown?" Fern fired off questions like a feisty lawyer.

"I didn't pay a lot of attention to all that. All I saw was her naked, lifeless little body slumping to the floor," Effie's voice trailed off with each word.

"Did you get to see her up close? Was there any blood?"

"Only from the doorway. They wouldn't let anybody in."

"Who was in there? Who found her?" Fern was relentless.

"I don't know. Nobody shared any of that information with me," Effie answered.

Fern went quiet for a minute, planning her next line of inquiry. "Go change out of that uniform," she ordered.

"What?" Effie asked.

"Don't you want to find out what happened?" Fern asked her.

"Pearl's dead. She hung herself. That's what happened."

"You believe that? Really? Do you know anything about Pearl? She had two kids waitin' for her back home. Do you really think she would have killed herself?" Fern asked.

"What are you saying? You think she didn't?"

"That's exactly what I'm saying. Go change. We're about to get a closer look."

"Change into what? I don't own any clothes that look like that," she said, nodding toward Fern.

"Come on then," Fern directed.

After crossing the green, following the gravel path to the service buildings, Fern indicated the dark laundry. She opened the door and motioned for Effie to follow. Once inside, Fern struck a match and by the quivering light led Effie into a back hallway.

"Where are we?" Effie asked.

"The laundry," Fern answered as she opened her closet. She disappeared inside, then reemerged holding a pair of denim pants and a gray work shirt. "Here, these should fit about right."

Effie took the clothes, holding them like they were something dead she found along the roadside.

"What, not fancy enough for you? Where we're headed, nobody cares what you look like." Fern moved to the door and waited for Effie to change.

Fern and Effie headed across the grounds, past the colored chapel. Fern motioned for Effie to follow her around back to a smaller wooden building tucked behind a stand of pines. Fern knocked softly on the door. A tall man opened it, raised a lantern to see who was calling, and let them pass through.

"Hey, Mr. Ingram. I appreciate you helping us out. She's the nurse I told you about that took care of Pearl."

"Hello," Effie offered.

"She's back here." Mr. Ingram led the way.

In the back room, lit by old gas lights, Pearl's small body lay exposed on the table. Her skin pale, but for the dark bruises that circled her eyes.

Fern heard Effie's sharp intake of breath and hoped she hadn't made a mistake bringing her there.

"What do you think happened to her?" Fern asked the old undertaker. He looked up and glanced at each of the two women through round eyeglasses that did not mask his red-rimmed, tired eyes.

"Somebody abused this poor child," he said sadly. "She's covered in bruises. Took a hard blow to the back of her head. Her skull is cracked. She was violated, and then somebody used a knife on her." He was unable to look at the women as he explained Pearl's fate. "I'm guessing that she was already dead before they hung her up on them window bars. She couldn't have done that to herself."

Stunned, Effie half whispered, "I remember now, there wasn't any blood on the floor. But I was told she hung herself. Why would they say that if she was murdered? Are you sure about this?"

"I'm afraid I am, young lady," Mr. Ingram answered softly. Taking off his glasses, he pinched the corners of his eyes. "I've seen some bad things done to people. Around here, suicide is a simple explanation. Especially when colored folks are the victims."

"How can that be? If someone is taken from my infirmary and murdered, I need to know about that. What about an investigation? Have the authorities been notified?"

"Suicide. That's what they told me. That's what I wrote down in my report."

"In your official capacity as what, I might ask?" Effie couldn't leave it alone.

"I bury our people around here. In cases like these, I just do what I'm told."

Mr. Ingram, a lifelong Milledgeville resident and an employee of the sanitarium for most of that time, took it upon himself to explain to Effie.

"You're a young woman. I suspect you didn't grow up around here."

"Not meaning any disrespect, Mr. Ingram, but I'm not sure what one thing has to do with the other," Effie countered.

"What I mean is, we have a different perspective on things. Based on age and circumstances, I would imagine," he continued. "Colored folks around here never expect they have the right to know. We get told what happened and whether or not that's the truth, well, that remains unaccounted for."

"And you accept that?" Effie questioned.

"We have to," the old man answered. "It's a matter of survival."

"Miss," Effie stopped, fumbling for what she wanted to say, "I can't remember your name."

"Fern."

"Your circumstances are more different than mine. Why are you involved in any of this?"

Fern didn't want to have this discussion in front of an audience and so simply answered, "I've been here for a while. I know how things work."

With that, Fern determined to end the discussion and make an exit. "Let's head back. Thank you again for letting us stop by. I wanted to know what happened to Pearl. And Nurse Effie is right about one thing. Everybody has a right to know what happened. Especially Pearl's family."

"Won't do no good," Mr. Ingram said. "It would just cause more pain for her loved ones to know the truth."

"Thank you, sir," Fern said, sensing that any further discussion was pointless.

They walked in silence back to their point of divergence where they would part ways. Effie stopped and turned to Fern.

"I'm not sure what to do about this now."

"Oh, there's nothing for you to do," Fern answered firmly. "I didn't take you there for you to do something about it. I thought you wanted to know about Pearl, like I did."

"I don't understand why you involved yourself in this. You're the only white person who has even spoken to me since I got here. And now, twice, when something happened to one of the colored women, you showed up. Why is that? Don't you have enough white patients to take care of?"

Fern nodded. "I have plenty to take care of. But why does what color they are make any difference as to whether I can care about them or not?"

"And how long have you been here?" Effie continued. "You're probably younger than me by a good five years or more. Where did you get your nurse's training?"

"You do have a lot of questions," Fern deflected. "And whoever said I went to nursing school?"

"You did. On that first day."

"I don't remember saying that."

"Yes, you did. Out under the trees."

Fern lifted her chin, looked skyward to give the impression of trying to remember.

She settled on her response and answered, "Around here you don't really need all that schooling to be a nurse. A lot of nurses are trained here at the sanitarium. My training was working here, and besides, I'm older than I look."

With that, she turned and loped away into the darkness.

Relieved to see the porch light on outside her new living quarters, Fern shook herself free from her worries about Pearl and bounded up the steps. Over the summer ten additional two-bedroom frame houses, intended to shelter four patients each, had been completed and made ready to help relieve some of the overcrowding in the wards. Fern and her roommates, Shirley and Lizbeth, had moved into one. Their lives had seemed much improved ever since. For Fern, it marked the beginning of life outside the patient buildings. She savored the newfound freedom and security she felt with her own four walls and roof overhead. Two houses down, Fern's nemesis, Roselyn, had moved in shortly afterward. Fern supposed the only good news was that she had not been assigned to their cottage. From the looks of things tonight, the coast was clear. No Roselyn on the prowl. Fern opened the door, then closed it behind her without a sound so as not to wake her sleeping roommates. She turned the lock, pulling on the handle to check that it held.

On the side table in the small living room, sat a paper-wrapped package she desperately hoped was food. She could always count on Shirley and Lizbeth to take care of all the things she simply forgot about like eating. She held the package to her nose, then tore the paper free. Two fried chicken legs and a biscuit in all their savory goodness. She plopped down on a cane-back chair and turned off the table lamp. Cloaked in darkness, Fern devoured what she realized was the first thing she had eaten all day.

Footsteps on the front stoop roused her from sleep on the small two-seater sofa. Fern froze. The door handle was being tested from the outside. She slid to the floor, making her way across the room on hands and knees. Desperate to get out of her foul clothes, for she had stripped to her underwear before lying down on the sofa. Exposed and not prepared to defend herself, she pressed against the wall as the would-be intruder lingered at the door. When the handle released and footsteps retreated, Fern stood and peered through the paper-thin window covering. A ghostly figure moved away from the door. She could almost swear before a judge that it was Roselyn. On any other night, Fern would have chased her down. Too tired to care much, she flipped on the light in the bathroom and drew a bath, testing it with a toe before climbing in. Fern slid into the steaming water and lay back against the porcelain tub. She could spend an hour but knew if her eyes closed, she would most certainly fall asleep. After a quick scrub to rid herself of the reminder of her latest disguise, she toweled off, headed to her room, gave thanks for the solitude it gave her, and slipped into bed.

Around dawn the sky let loose. Rain thrummed against the roof over Fern's head. On her back, arms and legs flung wide, Fern imagined floating across an endless, turquoise-colored sea, while raindrops flattened and bounced.

"Better get a move on, girl, you're on laundry duty," Lizbeth called through the door, ending Fern's reverie. "Want to grab some breakfast first?"

"Give me two minutes," Fern replied, bounding from bed.

Fern plodded through the routine of her day. She couldn't get Pearl out of her head. After work, she headed back over to the old morgue to see that Pearl had been properly cared for.

"Hello. Is anybody here?" She entered the small building, still dreary in the light of day.

"In the back," a familiar voice called.

Fern found Mr. Ingram sitting near a white pine casket.

"No one came for her?" Fern asked.

"Her family is on the way. Should be here in the morning," Mr. Ingram replied. "I didn't want to leave her all alone."

"Mind if I sit for a while?"

"Not at all, Miss Fern. I appreciate your respect for her."

Fern brought a wooden stool nearer to the casket. Watching her, Mr. Ingram could guess what was on her mind.

"I reckon you find all this a little too familiar, Miss Fern."

She swallowed hard and closed her eyes to stop her tears.

"There does seem to be a pattern. This makes what, seven that I count, excepting you, in three years' time," Mr. Ingram observed somberly.

"Why don't you count me?" Fern asked in a quiet voice.

"Because you lived," was all he answered.

When night settled in, Mr. Ingram placed a candle in a wooden candlestick atop Pearl's casket. "It's getting late, and you need to get your supper. Let me see you out," he offered.

At the door Fern remembered that Mr. Ingram had been away for much of the summer. She looked for him back in June and was told he was ill.

"You were gone for a time this past summer. I heard you were sick."

"Sick in the heart. My wife passed."

"I'm sorry to hear that," Fern answered.

"It's hard to get used to being alone."

"Yes, it is," she said as she reached up to give him a kiss on the cheek. "I almost forgot to ask you. I'm looking for some old patients' records to see if I can learn anything about my mother." She told the white lie, knowing he wouldn't think it wise for her to be looking into those other matters. "Do you know where they're kept?"

"Let me think. Miss Nora came here in about '06. Them old files is upstairs in the attic of the Center Building if I remember right. That attic is kept locked up. Not sure you can get in there without a key."

With a cunning smile Fern asked, "You happen to know anybody who might have a key for that room?"

"Well I reckon I do. I imagine he's a damn fool if he gives it to you, and pestered to death if he don't. You wait here."

A few minutes later Mr. Ingram reappeared, head shaking and muttering, with a key on a worn strap of leather. "Don't you lose this now. And don't you tell nobody I gave it to you, you hear me?"

"Yes sir," she said, taking the key, holding his hand for a moment. "I promise."

With the key sizzling in her pocket, Fern had a hard time sitting though the idle chatter at the supper table. The only thing that held her, the chicken and dumplings and the other quest she was on. She had seconds and begged off heading back to the cottage with Shirley, claiming she still had work to do at the laundry.

Finally alone in the dining hall except for two women wiping down tables and Roselyn, Fern rose. She walked over to where Roselyn was sitting, approaching her from the back, catching her unaware.

Fern leaned down, snarled in the most menacing tone she could manage. "You were on my porch in the middle of the night. Did you have some business with me?"

"Not that I can recall," Roselyn replied coyly.

"Don't come messin' around my house. And you best stay away from Lizbeth and Shirley. You understand?"

Roslyn didn't answer.

"Do you understand me?" Fern asked again.

Roselyn nodded slowly. Fern straightened. The two women had stopped what they were doing to watch. She stared them down, casually walked past, and left by the front door.

Outside the Center Building Fern waited in the shadows for the traffic to die down and made her way to the front entrance. One of the glass-fronted doors was unlocked. With a noisy shove, it opened, and she found herself inside a darkened corridor. The old four-story building, once the center of operations, was mostly used for storage now. There were a few office spaces on the main floor, but no one was likely to be working this late at night. Satisfied that she had not been discovered, Fern climbed the stairs to the attic. The higher she climbed, the darker it got. Fern pulled a flashlight from her coat pocket, careful not to use it near any windows but wanting to have it in her hand, in case she had to rely on it as a weapon.

Reaching the top floor, Fern looked for the door that Mr. Ingram told her would lead to the attic. Finding it, she inserted the key and worked it open. She swept the light across the room. Old file cabinets, wooden crates and boxes covered the space, papers lay scattered across the floor. The sights and smells assaulting her senses made it clear that rats had been making this their home for years. She hated rats and realized they were probably hiding in all the darkest corners. Not one to be daunted, she walked around the room and mapped out a plan of attack.

Near midnight she decided to call it a day, locked the room behind her, tucked the key into a pocket, and headed out into the nighttime air. She paused outside to catch a fresh breeze on her face. Based on her progress, or lack thereof, she estimated it to be about a hundred-hour job to get through the papers in the room. Unconvinced she would find her own file, or that one even existed, she was still encouraged by what she had found. There were patients' records there. Records that revealed the private details of patients' lives. Fern wondered how much she could bear, uncovering the tragic details of those wretched people who ended up here. That was a mistake, she realized. She couldn't read the files, only sort through them. That might save some time. For the first time in a long while, she thought about all the misery this place brought and wondered about walking away. But where could she go? An inventory of unanswerable questions looped through her head.

As she drew near the cottage, lamplight flooded from the windows, and the prospect of companionship with her roommates lightened her step.

"Well look what the cat dragged in," Lizbeth needled from the sofa, thumbing through a magazine, holding it up for Fern to see. "Look what Thelma brought me. Makes me want to get out of here and go shopping again."

"Maybe you can do that soon enough," Shirley offered.

"Not if Daddy has anything to with it," Lizbeth answered. "He thinks I'm a rummy for life. And who knows, he might be right."

Fern walked past Shirley at the table, who was busy writing a letter to her husband, sharing the good news about her hope for returning home in December. It had been a little over two years since she had lost her parents in a house fire. There were days when she couldn't get out of bed, but she was getting better. Fern leaned down to see what she had written, and Shirley wrinkled her nose. "You stink, Fern. What have you been up to?"

"You're not the first person to tell me that." She tousled Shirley's hair, leaning in closer.

"I was in the attic at the old Center Building. That's where all those old files are kept."

"What are you trying to find in old files?"

"I'm not sure. I've always wondered if there was a file on me. I'm not a regular patient, but I have been through intake and treated. I just wonder what all it might say, if there is such a thing," Fern answered.

"Did you find anything up there?" Lizbeth asked her.

"More files than you can imagine. Stuffed in boxes and crates, papers everywhere, covered in rat pee."

"That sounds awful. No wonder you stink."

"Sounds kind of interesting," Shirley said from across the room. "Kind of like a mystery to solve. Maybe like Sherlock Holmes."

"Who's that?" Fern asked.

"He's a character in a book, a detective. You never heard of him?"

"No, I haven't," Fern answered.

"You really need to get out more," Shirley added, drawing a laugh from the others. "Sherlock Holmes, he's a detective who solves crimes. The stories are pretty popular."

She thought for a minute and then asked, "Do you want some help? Looking for that file?"

"I don't know if it's worth it," Fern answered. "There may not be one."

"You won't know unless you look, Sherlock." Shirley added, "And besides, he had a partner who helped him. What was his name?"

"I don't know," Fern answered. "I never even heard of him until just now."

"Doctor Somebody. He was a doctor. I think he was a doctor," Shirley answered, flapping her hand.

"I need a bath," Fern said, rising from the sofa.

"You do," Lizbeth and Shirley confirmed.

The next night, Fern, Lizbeth, and Shirley made their way to the attic of the Center Building under the cover of darkness. Braving rats and insects of all varieties, they combed through the crates and boxes every night for the next week until late Friday, when Shirley found something.

"Fern"— Shirley flashed the light on a brown folder—"here's something with your name on it."

Fern stood. "Okay then," she said. "Let's get out of here."

They walked back in silence. Once inside Fern hugged both her friends, took the folder to her room, and shut the door.

Two days later Fern had not shared anything from the file with Lizbeth or Shirley. That night she waited under the magnolia tree for Effie to finish her shift. Around midnight Effie appeared. Rather than wait for her to get ahead, Fern came out from under the tree limbs, dusting herself off and faced Effie straight on.

"I watch for you now, you know," Effie told her. "I was wondering when I would see you again."

"Here I am," Fern said. They stood in awkward silence.

Fern pulled a pomegranate from her pocket and offered it to Effie. "No thank you," she said.

Fern nodded and put the sun-ripened fruit away.

"Pearl's family came and got her. But I guess you knew that," Fern told her.

"No, I didn't. I'm glad to hear that, though. I remember you telling me about that cemetery. I went to see it. Nobody should end up there. It's awful."

Fern nodded again, looked around, uneasily.

"I wanted to ask you something," Fern watched Effie closely. "Do you know lots of medical words?"

"What kinds of words?"

"Words for operations and things. You know, the medical words for them."

"I know some, why?"

Fern pulled a slip of paper from her pocket and handed it to Effie, then flicked on her flashlight to illuminate the one word written on it.

"How about that word right there. You know what it means?'

Effie looked at the paper and then at Fern. "I do," she answered.

"What is it?" Fern asked anxiously.

"Salpingectomy. That's how you say it. It's a procedure. An operation."

"What kind of operation?"

"To remove a woman's fallopian tubes," Effie replied, wondering why this was of interest to Fern. "Do you know what those are, fallopian tubes?"

Fern shook her head slowly.

In that moment Effie understood fully that the girl standing before her was not a nurse after all.

"Fallopian tubes are what carry a woman's eggs to her uterus."

"Why would somebody remove those?" Fern asked, in a voice grown small and hesitant.

Effie's own voice gentled. "Well, most often it's a procedure performed to keep a woman from having children. Why are you asking about that?"

Fern looked down, no longer able to look into Effie's eyes.

Before Effie could question her further, Fern turned and disappeared into the night.

Adrienne

OCTOBER, 1905

7

Adrienne inspected the crowd over the top of her menu at Durand's on Alabama Street and scrutinized the white-aproned young man standing tableside with his hands behind his back.

"We'll start with some Norfolk oysters."

She turned to her dining companion Amina. "Does that suit you?"

"Yes, of course," Amina answered.

"And the green turtle soup with the roast quail to follow."

Adrienne had asked to be seated in the rear of the mahogany-paneled room at a table tucked behind some rather large potted ferns, under the guise that the space nearer the kitchen was warmer and away from any possible draft from the entrance doors. Although she hoped to pass unnoticed, she was dressed for an evening on the town in an aqua silk and satin floor-length dress trimmed with cream-colored embroidery and topped with a sheer black, calf-length jacket edged in black velvet. A stylish black beret adorned with a black satin bow completed the look.

"It's been months since we've been able to get out like this," Adrienne murmured as she scanned the room again and ran her hands across the white linen cloth covering the table in front of her. She was more interested in the staff than the other patrons as they likely posed the greater threat. Several of her former students had worked at Durand's from time to time. If one of them recognized her and against better judgement was inclined to speak or even smile in her direction, she stood to miss out on the scrumptious meal soon to be prepared for her in the kitchen.

"It's been a year since you moved back from Boston, and we've hardly had time to talk. Have you really been that busy?" Amina asked.

Satisfied that the threat level was low, Adrienne turned her attention to her friend. "With my teaching schedule, the performances, and the trip to Ontario, I haven't been very thoughtful. I'm sorry I've neglected you. I hope that will change with you and Howard staying with us for a while."

Amina reached across the table and placed her hand atop Adrienne's. "Oh no, I wasn't complaining. I just missed you is all. You and Alonzo are so generous, making room for us."

Her friend's warm palm soothed Adrienne. "Thank you for that. You never ask anything of me. And you're forever willing to join in my great misadventures, regardless of how they might turn out. That house is so big. I love to fill it up with friends and family."

"I'm sure you realize that your misadventures are the most exciting part of my life," Amina admitted. "And how on earth did you get Alonzo to Ontario?" She had been more than a bit surprised that the Herndons had attended a political gathering in July to promote the founding of a new civil rights organization.

Adrienne shook her head and chuckled, relaxing into sharing the tales of her latest exploits with her friend.

"It took some persuading. I told him to think of it as a family vacation rather than something political and possibly controversial."

"You mean you played him," Amina accurately interpreted her friend's often used ploy when it came to getting what she wanted from her husband.

"You probably added a big dose of 'poor little me, I'm just desperate to get out of town this summer,' too, didn't you?"

Adrienne smiled again. "You think you know all my tricks."

"Don't I?" Amina admonished.

"Mostly. And yes, I may have been just a little pitiful. But I thought it was a good opportunity for Alonzo to take part in something important. He understood the value of it too. It wasn't all my doing."

"I thought he avoided being political, as you call it," Amina chided.

"Generally, he does. But being that it was in Ontario and not Atlanta helped a little. And Will DuBois has always been so supportive of me and my career. We did it out of our gratitude to him as much as anything."

"Now tell me all about Boston and that performance I read about in that newspaper clipping Alonzo showed me. *Antony and Cleopatra*. All twenty-two roles. How thrilling for you."

Adrienne's conflicted emotions played out across her face like a summer storm. "Well, the performance was exhilarating. I'll never forget being on that stage alone without a costume to hide behind. It was just me and my love for Shakespeare. The only sound in the theater, my own voice," she recounted, recalling the moment for Amina as she had in her dreams most every day for the past many months. "Being Cleopatra on that stage was most certainly the pinnacle of my dramatic career. I realize that now more than I did at the moment."

"There's so much more to come," Amina consoled her. "Your production of *The Merchant of Venice* at the university was brilliant. I was spellbound."

Adrienne's eyes begin to fill with tears.

"I'm so sorry, Adrienne. I never meant to upset you," Amina offered.

"Here are our oysters." Adrienne nodded in the direction of the young waiter heading toward them. "I'm famished."

What Adrienne did not share with Amina, but her friend already understood, was that although she and everyone present in Steinhart Hall that day had declared her one-woman dramatic performance nothing short of a theatrical triumph, she had since lost her allure for the northern theater establishment. The promise of untold engagements made by her newly hired representative at the George Britt Company never materialized. More than that, though, Adrienne had always believed that she was born to the stage, but there was something hollow at the center of the fame she had chased once she held it in her hand. As the curtain fell that evening, the woman standing center stage had not been Adrienne but Anne. Anne du Bignon. Of her own creation. Anne was what Adrienne was not. What Adrienne was not was white. Though her outward appearance might allow her to sit in a crowded restaurant in Atlanta on a Tuesday evening with her equally light-skinned and stylishly dressed friend, there was another truth that mattered more. She was the daughter of a woman born in slavery. After all of the years she had lived as though that did not matter, in that moment of reckoning, according to society in the South and in the North, it mattered most. It mattered more than her talent. It mattered more than her training. After working for so long and having made so many sacrifices, the attainment of what she thought had mattered to her most could not have mattered less. And for that reason alone, the memory of it brought her to tears. She had expected to be changed by the experience of her stage debut. She expected she would think about her life as it existed before that moment and after that moment as some kind of momentous transformation. She had not expected this great conflict would be the heart of that change. *Adrienne or Anne? Who was she really at the core? Did she have to choose? Couldn't she be both?* The entire experience left her unmoored.

Adrienne returned to Atlanta somewhat hopeful that the opportunity for a stage career still existed, but as the weeks and months passed, that dream faded. There were no offers. There were no invitations to return to Boston or New York. She was left to wonder, *had the northern theater establishment learned her truth? And if so, had that truth derailed her life dreams?* She threw herself into her classes at Atlanta University. She worked the drama students relentlessly. The senior class had staged the first Shakespeare production at the university during the senior night exercises in June. It was a rousing success. The children, Norris and Effie, were thriving. Her mother, Mattie, had seen to that. Alonzo was consumed by his new business. Adrienne's life was full but that empty place that had opened up inside her on that stage in Boston remained. She was unable to imagine how she would fill it up.

ADRIENNE

Adrienne looked around the crowded restaurant, full of well-to-do patrons on a Tuesday night. "Life is different in the North, Amina. But not as different as you might think. I've come to believe that there is something about strength in numbers in the South that provides a sort of buffer, perhaps even a layer of protection. Why just looking around this room, I can pick out at least three other parties just like us, not to mention the service staff."

Amina risked a quick look around the room. "But not in Boston?"

"I felt so isolated there, uncomfortable even. I'm not sure why any of us would choose to live there," Adrienne added.

"I haven't been to Boston, but I don't know that I agree about any protection here. I always feel exposed, even when no one takes any notice." Amina's eyes darted around the room again. "Except when I'm with you, Addy. You're always so confident that I feel that way too."

Having finished their dinner with pistachio ice cream and Turkish coffee, Adrienne and Amina walked arm in arm down Marietta Street, the evening air, pleasantly cool on the last night of October. They hurried, keeping pace with the growing crowd of theater patrons, in order to be seated before the lights went down at the Grand Opera House.

"So, what does Alonzo think you're doing this evening?" Amina asked slyly.

Adrienne smiled. "I told mother to tell him I went to the theater with you. I didn't say which or what performance."

Amid the bustling crowd, they came to a stop outside the three-story, granite-fronted theater. The marquee read *"The Clansman*, dramatized by Thomas Dixon, Jr."

"Would he mind if he knew?" Amina asked.

"He would mind. But he wouldn't stop me," Adrienne said, trying to reassure herself that what she said was true. She and Alonzo had read in the newspaper what had happened in other cities across the South where audiences had reacted to Dixon's stage play, an ode to white supremacy. She knew that some towns had banned the production because of the potential for violence in its wake.

"Besides, Mr. Dixon once offered me the leading role in his drama. Or, rather, he offered it to Anne du Bignon. My curiosity must be satisfied based on that alone."

They giggled like schoolgirls at the absurdity.

Adrienne studied the glittering lights. "This won't be just another distraction at the theater, Amina. Are you sure you want to do this?"

Amina tightened her grip on Adrienne's arm. "Let's go inside before I change my mind."

As they waited in the coat check line, Amina stood aloof, her eyes darting everywhere, never falling on another person. Adrienne took in everything about everyone around them—their jewelry, their hairstyles, the way they held themselves. She noted with a little concern the larger than usual presence of a number of Atlanta policemen.

Inside, the magnificent interior of the theater was alive with the excited chatter of women straining to see what others were wearing. Adrienne had secured orchestra center seats in row six. As they made their way there, she allowed herself a glance at the uppermost rear balcony, surprised to see it packed full of colored patrons. Settled in her damask cushioned seat, Adrienne admired the beauty of the theater. The majesty of the arched ceiling, the delicately carved woodwork and the gold-trimmed green velvet curtains tightly drawn across the stage made it one of the most luxurious in Georgia. Behind the curtains, a flurry of final preparations was underway. The theater buzzed with the energy of the crowd and the anticipation of the night's entertainment.

Five minutes before curtains were set to rise, the play's author, the stern faced, dark-haired Thomas Dixon walked to the stage to loud applause. He basked in the adoration for a few moments, then raised his hands, silencing the crowd.

"Thank you, my friends. And welcome to all of you this evening. I want to especially welcome Mr. Joseph Terrell."

The author bowed deeply toward the governor who stood and waved from the opulently outfitted second-level box seat to the left of the stage. The audience clapped politely. A chorus of rebel yells echoed across the theater. Amina moved her hand to Adrienne's, this time for reassurance rather than to offer comfort.

Mr. Dixon continued. "A few years back I attended a stage play purported to expose the realities of life in the South before the bloodiest war in history savagely lay waste to our precious homeland. That play, *Uncle Tom's Cabin*, changed the course of my life. As I left the theater that night, I swore to expose the bitter lies of that abomination. Tonight, you will serve witness to the true story of the South. Many of you can recall the horrible suffering of that dreadful period of reconstruction visited on us by the conquerors after our defeat in the war."

Mr. Dixon stopped briefly, allowing his words to settle into the hearts of the audience. He slowly surveyed the entirety of the theater, his piercing dark eyes pausing on each patron and penetrating their very souls. Adrienne watched the skillful former minister command the playgoers, his new congregation.

"My play is a love story. It is a love story set in the historic South. Yes, it is a traditional story about love between a man and a woman, but it is much more than that. It is my story of love for those saviors of the South who arose to combat the intolerable conditions during a reign of terror under Negro rule. I have been faithful to the real emotions of the people of that time and to the historic truth about the victory of organized manhood over organized crime masquerading under the forms of government. These white-shrouded warriors were our saviors, and they alone were responsible for our salvation."

The spectators roared their enthusiasm for the fiery introduction. Adrienne risked a glance at Amina. Amina turned to face her with eyes wide, and Adrienne glimpsed a red droplet of blood on Amina's lower lip where she had bitten herself. She handed Amina a handkerchief and touched her own lip to communicate her meaning. Mr. Dixon exited the stage with a flourish, and the house lights dimmed. The curtains parted to reveal the pastoral setting of a southern plantation home. As the patrons adjusted to the scene, their understanding of what might unfold was upended as the stage filled with crowds of black-faced actors representing the new-world order where white society had been overturned by a Black mob.

Adrienne and Amina sat mesmerized as the first dialogue was uttered by a black-faced preacher. "Ain't I done tole ye dat de Lawd call de cullud men ter come up on high…de judgment day done come fur de white Man!"

The theater erupted with loud hissing and boos from the floor, and applause and cheering from above. Adrienne reflexively looked to the upper balcony brimming with colored spectators and saw it filling quickly with policemen armed with clubs, making their way through the crowd. She quietly turned back to the stage, while the actors maintained their places and the audience gradually regained its composure.

As the drama unfolded, the crowd exalted in the glorious mission undertaken by the Ku Klux Klan. Each scene revealed Mr. Dixon's "truth" about how those white knights saved the South from complete destruction, protecting the virtue of white women against the ravaging and lustful black savages all around them. Through it all, Adrienne worked to calm her own breathing as she gently rubbed Amina's hand. She hoped her friend would understand, as she did, that the safest option was to stay seated and call no attention to their distress at the chaos on the stage and the larger chaos surrounding them in the theater. Through a rape scene, a suicide, and a lynching, they remained silent observers. Burning crosses and live horses added to the spectacle. Many times over, Adrienne wondered what she had been thinking when she had arranged to bring Amina to the theater tonight. Perhaps she thought she was somehow immune to the message of hate because of her own recent experiences. But this had been so much more than she had bargained for. She wanted nothing more than to leap from her seat and run for the exit, but refrained from taking such drastic action because Amina was at her side. Amina needed her, and Adrienne would not let her down.

When Mr. Dixon took to the stage to deliver yet another message of vitriolic racial hatred and white supremacy, the crowd could hardly be quieted so that the play could continue. Adrienne heard Amina quietly repeating the words, "I'm going to hold steady on you, and you've got to see me through." She recognized the affirmation they had been taught in school that Harriett Tubman had used to help herself through trying times. Adrienne picked up the chant and continued until the lights went up and an ovation of avid believers rose in praise, their accolades almost deafening. She pulled Amina to her feet and stood alongside them, careful yet to avoid calling any attention to their fearfulness and unease so that they might reach the safety of the street.

Adrienne and Amina emerged amid the jostling throngs of agitated theatergoers. Their excitement unabated, the shouting continued as they pushed and shoved and dispersed in different directions. As the colored audience made their way through the exit doors, several were grabbed by burly white men, throwing punches and kicking as the innocent victims were knocked to the ground. It was unclear if the policemen outside were defending those hurt or assisting those who were waging violence against them.

Desperate to gather their wits and recover from the experiences of the evening, the two women stood clutching each other at the edge of the street, unsure which way to proceed. Just as she was about to step forward and make a dash across the street, out of the corner of her eye, Adrienne caught sight of two men running toward her, calling her name. Frightened, she pulled at Amina's arm to urge her forward.

"Addy, look." Amina pointed. "It's Alonzo and Howard."

If Adrienne had ever felt more relief seeing Alonzo heading her way through the departing crowd she could not remember. She reached out to him, he gathered her protectively in his arm and draped his coat around her shoulders.

Howard comforted Amina as they walked away from the theater and the remnants of the rowdy crowd.

"Let's go, ladies. We've a carriage waiting two blocks back."

Wordlessly, they made their way up the street to the waiting car. Safely seated inside, Alonzo gave directions to his man Fred from the Peachtree Street shop, to head for Diamond Hill.

"How did you know where to find us?" Adrienne asked, still clutching his arm.

"I went home for supper to see the children before bedtime. Mattie told me you went out. On my way back to the office, I saw all the commotion. I asked what was going on. Somebody said half the police in town had been called to the Opera House for the opening of *The Clansman*. I figured that was where you had to be. I was able to track down Howard. He borrowed the car from Doctor Butler and Fred drove us down here," Alonzo reached forward and patted the driver's shoulder. "You know how to handle a car, man."

"Thank goodness for that," Adrienne replied.

Alonzo finally ventured a look at his tiny, headstrong wife. "I can't even imagine what you were thinking, Addy."

"I've been asking myself that for the past two hours." She turned to Amina behind her. "I'm so sorry, Amina. I didn't mean to put you in harm's way. I don't know what I expected."

Amina huddled close to Howard, her head on his shoulder, tears coursing down her cheeks.

"Thanks, Fred. Since I came to Atlanta all those years ago, you've always had my back. I can always count on you in a tight spot. See you tomorrow," Alonzo called as they got the women out of the car and headed up the walkway to the house.

Mattie met them at the door. "Well, I didn't know you were all out together. Come to the kitchen. I made an apple cake and a fresh pot of coffee."

"Thank you, Miss Mattie, but I want to get Amina into bed, she's worn out," Howard explained and followed his wife up the stairs.

Alonzo watched them go as Adrienne headed for the kitchen. He hung up their coats and steeled himself to confront his wife about her reckless behavior. He found her seated at the table, Mattie pouring her a glass of whiskey instead of the previously offered coffee. She held the bottle up in offer to Alonzo, but he shook it off. He slid into a chair opposite Adrienne and folded his hands on the table.

She swallowed her whiskey in two quick gulps. "Mama, why don't you head on up to bed yourself? It's late, and I would appreciate a minute alone with Alonzo."

"I wanted to check on the children anyway," Mattie said, drying her hands on a towel. "See you in the morning."

For several long minutes they simply looked at each other across the table.

"The hatred and anger in that theater, Lonzo, I never felt anything like it. It was as if the devil himself reached out his long, bony fingers and wrapped them around my neck. I could hardly breathe." She shivered recalling the feeling.

Alonzo let her get it all out.

"I kept thinking about Mr. Dixon offering me the lead role in that loathsome spectacle. Thank goodness I had the sense to turn him down. I wonder how anyone would think to bring something so hateful to the stage."

Alonzo could no longer contain himself. "Why did you go, Addy? What did you imagine you would gain by going?"

"I don't know. I don't think I can explain it," she answered.

"Give it a try. I want to understand why you would risk your well-being and Amina's in the bargain. What was worth that risk?"

"I didn't think of it as a risk. I wanted to see it for myself."

"See what for yourself? A hate-filled abomination? What exactly did you want to see?" Alonzo asked, his voice rising in a way that Adrienne had seldom heard.

"I don't know if I can make you understand. I guess I wanted to see what the only role I have been offered in the past year was all about and know what I had turned down. That was at least a part of it."

She stood, walked to the cupboard where Mattie had put away the whiskey, got another glass for Alonzo, and returned to the table where she poured them both a drink. She cupped her hands around the glass and peeked at her husband. "It was all Will and John Hope could talk about the past few weeks. The opening of this play tonight. Who might be there, what might happen. I got curious."

"Did they go too?"

"No. No, they were concerned something would be made of their being there. They're easily recognizable in the theatergoing community."

"And you don't think you are, Addy?"

"Not so much. Hardly anybody gives much notice to two women at the theater. Especially if you know how to keep from bringing attention to yourself."

"Did you even think about the kind of people who might be there tonight? Did you think about what kind of trouble might get stirred up and what could happen to you if things got out of hand?"

Adrienne watched Alonzo closely. She thought at first that he was angry. While it dawned on her that he was not so much angry at her as he was frightened for her, the great tumult inside her broke loose. She put her head down on the table.

Alonzo stood, came around to stand beside her, waiting for the storm to pass.

Finally, she turned her tear-ravaged face to Alonzo. "I was scared tonight," she admitted.

He nodded.

"I don't think I understood until tonight how angry people are. I've been living in a way that made me think that everything was okay. I thought I could keep doing all the things that I do. I thought I could keep on going where I wanted to go. I was wrong, Alonzo. I was wrong thinking that things were getting better. How could I have been so naive? Why didn't you tell me? Why didn't you tell me how bad things have gotten? You knew that already. I see it in your face. And I see something else, too, that frightens me even more."

Alonzo pulled a chair closer, sat near.

"You're scared." Adrienne placed her hands on either side of his face.

Alonzo took one of her hands, held the inside of her wrist to his mouth, and kissed it gently. "I was scared tonight. I was scared something had happened to you. I was afraid I wouldn't be able to find you."

"It's more than that, Lonzo. I see it in your eyes. You're worried."

"I am worried, Addy. I'm worried about you and the children. Things have to change now. We've been able to have a good life. But the way we live is different from how most Black folk do."

"Change how?"

"I don't think it's safe for you to run all over town anymore. And you're wrong when you think that people don't notice you. You're a beautiful woman. Everybody looks at you. I know because I watch them watching you."

"What you're saying is that I need to stay in my place," Adrienne replied.

"You can't even bring yourself to say it, Adrienne. Let's be honest about this with each other. Let's face what we're really talking about here. What I'm saying is you're going to have to live one life here. You can't be white in one part of town and colored in another. It's that simple."

Adrienne started to speak, but he put his finger to her lips to quiet her.

"Listen to me for a minute. I know that you've lived a different life from most. The world you've grown up in and work in at the university, well, let's just say it's a special place. What you have there is not common in the rest of the city. I think you've found out it isn't even common in other cities. You work in a place where the color of somebody's skin isn't the first thing everybody sees—where that isn't what's used as the measuring stick of who you are and what you can be. But that's not the world we live in. That's not our world."

Tears filled Adrienne's eyes again.

"You have to make that choice now, Addy. Once and for all. It can't be both anymore. Not here. Not anymore. It's just not safe."

When she spoke, her voice was quiet. "I saw him, Alonzo. In Boston. He came there to see me."

It took Alonzo a moment to understand.

"My father. George Stephens. I saw him."

"Where?"

"I wrote him a letter. I told him about you and the children. I told him I was in Boston and that I was going to perform at Steinhart Hall."

"He was there?"

"Yes. He took the train from Philadelphia, came to see me. After rehearsal one night, I was walking back to my room. He stopped me on the street, introduced himself."

"What did he say?"

"Not much, really. He told me to never contact him again. He said he didn't want to know anything about my life. He said he had a family who knew nothing about me or my mother, and he planned to keep it that way. That was it. That was all he said. Then he walked away."

"I'm sorry, Addy."

"I'm not," she replied quickly. "I'm glad to know what he is and what he's not."

"Why didn't you tell me sooner?"

"I don't know. I regretted that I had written him. I don't know what I thought would come of it. It was just another part of my humiliation."

"What humiliation?" Alonzo asked her.

"That's how I feel about Boston. Humiliated. I don't know what I was thinking. I don't know what I'm doing still."

She put her hands over her eyes and shook her head. Alonzo stood, reached out to her. He lifted her by her elbows and, when she was standing, took her in his arms, towering over her five-foot frame.

Adrienne stepped back and looked up at him. "You're right. I do have to choose. I think that's the answer. And the choice is not as difficult as you might think. Not as difficult as I might have led you to believe."

She braced herself by taking hold of his arms. "What I choose is you, Alonzo. I choose our children and our life together."

Even as she said it, she wasn't sure what it meant.

Nora

OCTOBER, 1908

8

Nora waited near the bottom of the stone steps outside the Center Building in the early morning darkness, wishing she had anything else to wear but the old handed down summer print dress with the button front and large collar. The borrowed shoes didn't fit quite right and she was sure to rub her feet raw with the walking she expected to do that day. At least the rain had held off and the air was just a little on the cool side.

She half hoped James Robert, Louella's brother who had agreed to give her a ride, didn't show. Her jitters were getting the best of her when the Elmore Delivery Wagon made the turn up the gravel drive. As she followed the glow of the headlamp while the truck wended its way toward her, Nora was distracted from her worries by the thought that this was about to be her first ever ride in an automobile. Considering her plans for the day ahead, this was probably the best part. Not only had Louella helped her get a day pass and promised to take care of Fern while she was gone, she had asked James Robert to provide transportation. He had a delivery to make to the Imperial Mill over in Eatonton and said he could drop her off on his way and pick her up on his way back. With all of the logistics to work through, she hadn't really given much thought to what she was planning to do during the in-between.

It had been almost three years since Harry had left her at the Georgia State Sanitarium in Milledgeville. She hadn't heard a peep out of him since. She had written letters every week for the first year but never got a single one in reply. She had written her mama too. Not as often but with the same result. Nora needed to know what was what. She would be willing to call an end to it if Harry or her mama would just write back once and tell her to stop. Because she was at the sanitarium under court order, there wasn't anything to be done about it. That was what Mrs. Carroll told her. If nobody came for her then the sanitarium would be her home as far into the future as she could see. So today was all about finding out and putting an end to the not knowing.

"Hey. You must be Nora." James Robert jumped out of the wagon and jogged around the front to greet her. He reached out to help Nora up to the bench seat. Nora stared at his hand until it dawned on her that he was offering his help and not asking for something.

"I'm Nora. Thank you for your help, sir. I mean, mister," she bumbled.

James Robert laughed a little and then realized she was uncomfortable in his presence and tried to set her at ease. "You can call me James Robert. Everybody does. Louella says you're a real nice person and needed some help today. I'm headed where you're headed," he said, helping her into the car. "So that works out real fine."

James Robert bounded back around the front of the vehicle and climbed in. The wagon lurched forward, and Nora grabbed hold of his arm to keep herself from flying out of the front.

"Sorry about that, Miss Nora. I'm still new to this drivin'." Realizing that revelation might frighten her even more, he added, "But don't worry. There ain't been no rain in days, so the roads are good. I can get us there and back safe." He turned onto the roadway and headed north toward Eatonton.

The flicker of the acetylene headlamp barely pierced the murky predawn darkness. Nora sat mesmerized by the motion. She held tight to the edge of the seat and had to remind herself to breathe. James Robert cut his eyes over a time or two, but the number of deer standing in the road brought his attention back to the job at hand. After daybreak lightened the landscape, Nora settled down and enjoyed the scenery that middle Georgia had to offer in mid-October. Most of the land had been turned over to cotton but here and there a stand of trees showed signs of autumn color, fiery red and sunlit orange. For a while Nora forgot about where she was headed and why she was going there. The wind in her face and the sense of adventure she felt perched up on the bench seat beside a nice-looking man tempted her to daydream about a life she had all but given up on.

"Louella said you're going to see your husband," James Robert said, bringing her back to the disagreeable reality.

With an audible sigh she replied, "I am. But I don't know what to expect. I haven't seen him in a while. I haven't even heard from him in almost three years. I'm not sure what I'll find when I get there."

He nodded slowly.

Suddenly nervous, Nora added. "We have a baby girl he hasn't even seen. Fern. Fern is her name. He thought she wasn't his baby. I guess that's why he took me there. I don't know. If he could see her, he would know right quick. She's got his red hair and green eyes. I never did know how I ended up in Milledgeville. He had a judge do it. A judge signed a paper that said I tried to kill myself and that I needed to go to the nut house."

Nora turned to James Robert. "What are you smiling at?"

"You called it a nuthouse. That's what Louella calls it," he said. Realizing that she was possibly one of the nuts Louella was talking about, he added, "I think she just calls all those real crazy people that, not the ones like you. She likes you. You don't seem crazy to me."

Nora watched him while he talked. "I'm not. The only crazy thing I ever did was run off with Harry. That was just plain stupid."

They shared a smile.

"And most of those people there at the sanitarium are just poor people that need somebody to care about them. They don't have nobody. They got problems, and the people they love just can't help them. So, they bring them there. I think most of them are more sad than sick," Nora answered, looking off into the tall Georgia pines that lined the road.

Lost in their own thoughts, they continued in silence for the rest of the trip. Nearing the crossroad where Nora needed to be dropped off, James Robert fretted.

"You sure this is what you want to do Miss Nora? You need me to go with you? I could, you know. I could drive right up to the house."

"I don't think so. If I show up with a man, that would probably be the worst that could happen."

"Why don't I stay out here at the road, wait for you? Then you could come with me to the mill."

She reached over, lay a hand on his arm. "That's real kind of you. I appreciate that you're worrying for me. Let's just do what we planned all along. You drop me off. I'll walk back to the farm. It's only about a mile. It'll give me time to think about what I aim to say to Harry. You go on and take care of your business. Wait right here for me on your way back," Nora said with more fortitude than she felt.

"It'll be a couple of hours." James Robert shook his head and started to speak again.

"It's all right. I promise. I can take care of myself," Nora told him, flashing the prettiest smile he had seen in days.

"I don't feel right about it," he replied as he pulled over.

"Well, this is mine to take care of," Nora insisted as she climbed down from the wagon before she changed her mind.

Nora started down the road without looking back. James Robert sat and watched until she disappeared over the low rise of the first hill.

The first thing she noticed was that a crop hadn't been put in the summer just past. The fields were plowed under from the last season, and no new cotton had been set in since. She walked along the rutted road and rounded the bend. The gray frame house came into view. The sight of it made Nora queasy. With each step she was more certain that the house was empty, maybe even deserted. At the front porch, she stopped and listened. It was quiet, no clothes on the line, no wagon, no signs of animals.

Nora headed toward the barn. The side door stood open. As she stepped across the threshold, her eyes were drawn to the tiny filaments of cotton lint caught in the old wooden door—pure white and shimmering in the morning light. She ran her hand across them.

The familiar scent of old hay and animal sweat filled her nose. A rusted one-horse turn plow lay near the door. A fifty-pound burlap bag of cotton seed, ripped open by rodents, lay spilled at the foot of the hayloft ladder. Nora looked up and tried to imagine the scene of her supposed suicide that Harry had described to who knows how many people. Try as she might, she couldn't understand where she was supposed to have tied a rope to hang herself from.

She pulled the door closed as she left the barn and headed back to the old house. Having climbed the front steps, she paused, looking out over the fields. As far as she could see, the Walker farm showed no signs of life. She wondered for a minute if Harry had picked up and moved. This land was his. She couldn't imagine that he would leave it. Fearful that she might be walking into a trap laid by Harry for just such a day that she might come calling, she knocked on the weather-worn wooden door.

"Harry! Harry Walker. Is anybody there? Hello!" Satisfied that the house was empty, she tried the door. With a little push it swung open with a bang, and two mourning doves fluttered out, causing Nora to stumble back down the steps and wait in the yard to see what happened next. Nothing did, and so she ventured into the cold, musty emptiness of the house she had last seen on a gray December night three years past.

The house was deserted but not empty. The timeworn table stood in the corner of the kitchen, the wood stove against the back wall, the oven door resting on the floor nearby. Nora made her way to the doorway of the bedroom, unwilling to enter its space. She braced herself on the doorframe. Dust floated in the sunlight filtering in through the single window. The rusted iron bedstead lay broken, the filthy mattress a nest for all kinds of critters. The most precious thing in her life, her baby girl, Fern, had been made right there. Lost in her memory, she suddenly heard the sound of footfalls on the porch steps, sending shock waves through her.

"Hello, who's there?" a small voice called out.

Nora bolted to the front room, figuring that getting outside would give her a better chance to run if she needed to. She pushed open the screen door and stepped onto the porch.

A young girl, her hair the color of corn silk stood at the bottom of the steps with her hands on her hips. She was barefoot in the cool October air and rail-thin except for the huge bulge of her pregnant belly.

"Hey."

"Hello," Nora answered.

"What you doin' inside this house?" the girl asked.

"I'm just lookin'. I thought it was empty."

"That's Harry Walker's house. You know him?" she asked, cocking her head to the side.

"I used to," Nora replied.

"What's your name?" The inquisitive girl continued her interrogation.

"Nora," she answered.

"I'm Lizzie. He ain't here right now. You lookin' for him?"

"No. I just came by to check on his house is all," Nora lied easily.

"He's comin' back next week. Tuesday or thereabouts, when he's done his time in the Jasper jail."

"That's right. I forgot it was next week," Nora said, stepping down from the porch slowly. "So how long has Harry been locked up?"

"Seven months. Second time in Jasper. He just can't help fightin' when he's liquored up."

Nora swallowed hard and didn't trust that her voice wouldn't sound shaky, but she had to ask anyway. "When's your baby coming?"

The girl smiled and wrapped her arms around her protruding belly. "Real soon. Harry's gonna be so happy."

"I'm sure he can't wait to get back to you and the baby, Lizzie. I bet he's real happy about that."

"He will be. I ain't seen him to tell him." She smiled again, hopeful.

"You aren't stayin' here at Harry's, are you? It don't seem fit for livin'." Nora turned back and looked at the house.

"No. I stay over at my Ma and Pa's house. I didn't like being here by myself after Harry got took off to jail."

"I'm sure that's better for you and your baby." Nora looked around, still nodding her head. "So how long have you and Harry been living together?"

"Been married 'bout eight months, right before the law got him," the girl answered. "I knowed him for a while before that. But he was so sad and all about his first wife. She died. Harry was broke up about it."

Nora continued to nod. "Is that right? I mean, that's right. She died. I remember."

"You know her? You said you used to know Harry. Did you know his wife?"

"No. I never met her. I knew Harry a long time ago." Nora knew she was feeding her own anger, but she had to get through it. "I don't recollect what she died from, though, do you?"

"I don't rightly know. She's buried right back yonder in the family plot," she said, pointing past the barn.

"Is she now? I didn't know that." Nora took a deep breath and looked around again, finally resting her gaze on Harry's young wife. "I think I would like to pay my respects. Would you mind showin' me?"

"C'mon then," the girl answered.

They made their way around the far side of the barn and out to the tree line. Under a stand of ancient oaks stood an iron gated family burial site. Nora passed through the opening and looked over the gravestones of Harry's parents and the two infant children they had lost before Harry came along.

"It's this one over here. There ain't no stone. A wood marker is all," she said, pointing down at a half-rotted board standing half buried in the soil with Nora's name etched crudely into it with a knife.

"Her name was Nora." Puzzled, Lizzie asked, "What'd you say your name was?"

"Nora. My name is Nora too. I forgot. That was strange. Harry married a girl named Nora. It's a common name," she said reassuringly.

"Not that common. I ain't ever knowed anybody named that before," the young girl answered, suspicion clouding her blue eyes.

"Well, thank you for bringing me back here."

"I remember now," the girl said, looking squarely at Nora. "I remember that she died havin' her baby. Baby died too. That's what Harry said. They's both buried there together."

Nora nodded again.

"You got any babies?"

"I do. I have a little girl. Her name is Fern. She's two years old now. Maybe you'll have a little girl too."

"I don't want no girl. I want a boy baby. Harry, he'll want a boy baby too," she said defiantly.

"You're probably right about that," Nora agreed, turning to walk back toward the house. "You might want to get home before you catch a chill. You need to think about taking care of your baby, you know."

"I'm goin'." The girl pointed out past the back field. "Our house is over yonder in them trees. That's why I seen you walk up the road. You done in that house?"

"I am," Nora answered.

"Could you close that door good?"

"Sure will. You take care of yourself, Lizzie. And that baby. Take care of him too."

She watched the girl go, and after she slipped through the trees, Nora headed back to the little cemetery. She stood above the crude grave marker with her name etched into it, beneath her name the words "Died December 1905." Nora reached down and took it by the rough edges. She worked it back and forth, wrenched it free from the dry Georgia clay. She tucked it under one arm and walked back to the house, laid the wooden marker on the porch, and went back inside. She looked through the kitchen drawer and found a dull but serviceable knife. Out on the porch, Nora picked up the marker and sat down in the old rocker where she had spent so many hours waiting for Harry to come back home from wherever he went. She fell into an old familiar rhythm. She watched a round of robins skirting along the edge of the field, searching for mealworms and listened to the roar of the wind through the tops of the towering pines. The sky was that perfect October blue that you just wanted to look at until it disappeared or changed somehow. Nora rocked for a long while with the marker on her lap, the knife clutched in her fist. When the sun had started its descent in the western sky, she roused herself from the past. She scratched deep into the soft rotting wood with the dull blade. Satisfied with her work, Nora took the flimsy memorial into the bedroom and laid it down on the stinking mattress. Back in the kitchen she pushed aside a few jars of pickled peppers in the old cupboard to find a half-filled canister of kerosene. She screwed off the top, sniffed to make certain the liquid was what she needed. On tiptoes, she ran her hand across the shelf above the wood stove, landing on a box of wooden matches, stuck them in her pocket, and padded back to the bedroom. Standing over the mattress, Nora eyed the grave marker one last time. Satisfied with its message, she poured the contents of the canister right where she had scuffed out the word "Died" and scratched above it the word "Born." With one quick strike, Nora dropped the flame to the fuel and walked from the room. She exited by the front door and left it standing wide open.

Nora headed down the long drive, not once turning back to see the smoke rise and the flames burst through the front of the house. She reached the main road in the gloaming. James Robert stood by his truck, his hands buried deep in his pockets. Before he saw her, she could tell he was watching the smoke beginning to curl through the tops of the trees.

"Something's on fire back yonder. Did you see it?"

She nodded. Nora walked around the delivery wagon. James Robert followed and helped her up to the seat. He glanced back at the smoke rising as he walked to the other side and climbed in.

"I was startin' to get worried," he said.

Nora turned to face him. "I 'spect you ought to take me to the sheriff's office."

James Robert couldn't take his eyes off Nora as he fumbled around, trying to crank the engine. Without words, he turned the truck around and headed back toward town. He pulled his delivery wagon up to the front of the sheriff's office in the tiny one-street downtown of Eatonton, Nora unblinking beside him.

"You want to tell me what we're doing here, Nora?"

She didn't hesitate. "I have to report a crime, James Robert."

"What crime are you reportin' on?" he asked, alarm rising.

"Arson. I did arson back at Harry's house. And before you start yappin' about it, you need to head on back to Milledgeville and tell Louella what happened."

She lowered herself from the car. "I need somebody to take care of Fern. Could be for more than a few days. Now go on. I told you already that this is mine to take care of and I mean it."

Nora made her way to the door of the sheriff's office, looked back once, and shushed James Robert away with her hand.

When the door closed behind her, James Robert slapped his hand hard against the steering wheel, muttered "damn girl" under his breath and headed for home.

The Eatonton sheriff couldn't remember if anybody had ever walked in off the street and reported that they had committed a crime. He locked Nora in a holding cell because she asked him to and went out to check on the truth of what she told him she had done. He came back three hours later, satisfied that Nora Walker had indeed run off from the state sanitarium and set fire to her husband's house. It burned to the ground. Nora smiled when he told her the news.

Two days later Nora appeared before the Putnam County magistrate judge who just happened to be the same one who married Harry and Nora and had drawn up the papers to send her off to Milledgeville. When she was brought into the courtroom, she was relieved to see Doctor Albertson sitting in the front row. He came to stand beside her before the judge.

"Nora Walker, you are guilty of the crime of arson and destruction of property. I am remanding you back to confinement at the Georgia State Sanitarium with the understanding that you will no longer have the privilege of a day pass or any other means to leave the institution. Do you understand?" he asked, refusing to make eye contact with Nora or Doctor Albertson.

"Yes, I do," she answered.

The judge gaveled Nora's case closed.

"Sir, may I ask you one question?" Nora spoke in her most solicitous voice. The judge lifted his eyes and glared at her, while Doctor Albertson shook his head. "Just one thing, sir?"

The judge nodded his assent.

"You married me to Harry Walker a few years back. Then you signed a paper that sent me to Milledgeville. A couple days ago I met a girl who said she's Harry's wife. I was just wondering if you married them too? Because what I'm thinking is that one man can't be married to two women at the same time. I never divorced Harry. And I'm not buried in that family plot behind his shack. So, before the law and before God, he's still my husband. Is that right?"

After the judge gathered his thoughts, he answered, "You were found to be incompetent by this court, young lady. That means that you were unable to be party to a divorce. Your incompetence meant that the court no longer recognized your rights as a spouse. Mr. Walker's signature was the only one necessary for a divorce to be granted. We took care of that. This case is closed." The judge used the gavel again with a bit more force and rose from his desk.

"I just wanted to make sure I was done with Harry for good is all," she said to the judge, who had already turned his back on her. "You be sure to tell him I hope he burns in hell just like that old shack of his. I wish he'd been in it."

Doctor Albertson gave Nora's arm a shake. "Don't, Nora. Leave it be."

When the judge had left the courtroom, the doctor took Nora's arm more gently. "I don't know what made you do this, Nora. You've never shown any signs of this type of behavior."

"Thank you for coming for me."

"It's my job," he replied wearily.

For the second time in her life, Nora found herself traveling the Eatonton to Milledgeville Road in the dark. This time the means of transport was a little fancier. Doctor Albertson's driver, Buck, was behind the wheel and Nora rode in the back with the doctor in his 1907 Pierce Great Arrow. Despite the luxury, the mood in the car was sour. Not a word was spoken nor a glance exchanged. At the sanitarium, Buck helped Nora out of the car.

111

Still seated in the back Doctor Albertson told her, "You know we'll have to put you under observation for the next ten days now, Nora. It's the law. Louella's up on the second floor. Head on up there and get checked in. Don't cause any more trouble now. I stuck my neck out for you when that baby was born. I broke all the rules by letting you keep her. Don't put me in this position again, you hear me? I would hate for you to lose that baby because of all of this."

Nora stepped back as the car moved. She had not considered any such outcome that included losing Fern. She had done all this for Fern. She wanted to know if Harry might come for them one day. She wanted to find out if he might show up sometime and want her. That was really what this was all about. Now she knew he wouldn't. He had a new wife and another baby on the way. Nora wasn't sure Harry would be the happy Daddy his young bride was hoping for, but she was reasonably sure he wouldn't be coming for Fern.

In the second-floor ward, Nora waited like a new patient at the front desk. With the bustling of the night staff surrounding her, she thought how strange it was that she felt so peaceful in such a place. She lived in the nuthouse. And she and her daughter were safe and, yes, happy there. Nora thought about how she could ever make anybody on the outside understand that she had found a home at a mental institution. And then it hit her that she likely would never have to explain it to anyone on the outside anyway. This was her home. It was her home as far as she could see into the future. She wasn't quite sure what that meant for Fern or Fern's future. But for now, they had a place to live and food to eat. Nora had a job helping people. She worried for a minute that she might not have that job anymore but then resolved to fix it somehow if she had to. She was finally done with Harry Walker. But she wondered about her mother and the rest of her family. Why hadn't they come for her or at least written to ask how she was? She had told her mama about the baby in a letter. Nora knew there was nothing she could do about that right now. She would have to save that for another day.

Finally, she saw Louella heading toward her. Nora stood, not sure she could deal with Louella's anger if she was mad at her too. Louella walked up, put her arms around her. Nora lowered her head to her shoulder.

"Fern's with my mama. She'll keep her for the next few days."

Hearing the news that her girl was safe, Nora slumped in Louella's arms.

"It's all right now. Just let it go. Let's get you into a bath and then into something clean."

Nora let her lead the way, suddenly unable to make sense of anything else. Louella cared for Nora like she had through those very first nights she had spent in the hospital. She gave her a warm bath, scrubbed the dirt from her legs, bandaged the raw places on her feet. She put her in a soft gown and combed out her hair.

After she was tucked into a bed, with a bowl of soup and piece of cornbread on a tray in front of her, Nora finally spoke.

"He had me dead and buried in his family plot. I burned that old shack down. I struck a match and lit it up. He had me dead and buried. But I'm not. I'm not dead and I'm not buried," she said, now looking at Louella. "I've got my Fern. And I've got a friend like you. I was born on that night he brought me here. I won't ever think nothin' different."

Effie

DECEMBER, 1922

9

Effie cupped her hands around her eyes to get a better view beyond the dust-covered window. The room appeared to be a laboratory of some type. This could be the place she was looking for. For several weeks now, Effie had been trying to find the doctors who were doing the pellagra research at the sanitarium. If someone was working to find the cause or the cure, she wanted to know. There could be help for the women on her ward, and if that were so, she intended to find it and bring it to them. Effie pulled her coat closed against the winter chill, and still wondering about the mysterious building, turned and found herself face to face with a tall, bearded gentleman. A look of panic immediately lay claim to her face.

"So sorry, miss, I didn't mean to startle you."

"You did." Effie noted the kind and rather handsome face. "Startle me, that is."

Offering his hand, he added, "I'm William."

"Effie Herndon, nurse," she said, still recovering from her fright. "This is your laboratory?"

"Yes, it is. For the past five years or so."

"Are you employed by the sanitarium?"

"I work for the Public Health Service."

"I've been looking for you, Doctor Tanner," Effie said, taking his hand since it was hanging between them, still offered. "No one seems to know where you do your work."

He nodded, smiled, and raised his eyebrows. "Some people would rather forget that I'm here."

"Why would you say that?"

"My work isn't very popular. I believe that pellagra is linked to a poor diet. And I hope to prove it. It riles people up to be told the reason so many people are sick is because they're starving."

"Whatever the cause, I understand you're trying to find a cure. I would think that would give your work credibility."

"If you're a nurse here at the sanitarium, I would guess you've seen the ravages of pellagra up close. It's not pretty."

"I had no idea until just a few weeks ago that your research was ongoing here," she said, motioning toward the doctor's lab. "Why are my patients suffering if you know how to help them?"

"Our work is in progress. We've gathered a lot of data from patients here, but we won't be able to make widespread changes until we have verifiable conclusions. Research is a complicated process, Miss Herndon."

"I understand that, Doctor, but I heard that you were able to help quite a few patients, even those who had advanced cases of the disease. I was told you were helping the colored women. That's why I'm here."

"Why don't you come in, if you have the time?"

"I'm not on duty today, but I don't want to intrude if you're busy."

"I wouldn't have asked if I didn't have the time. I like to show off my work. Come on in," he answered kindly, opening the door.

Effie was surprised to see the workspace more closely resembled a large kitchen rather than a laboratory. Food choppers, knives, large ladles, huge metal pots were all neatly organized. "I haven't been in many laboratories, but this doesn't look like any that I've seen," she said, making her way around the room, looking into the copper and tin pots lining the surface of the table, while others simmered on the massive stove top.

"This is a diet laboratory, so it is primarily a kitchen," the doctor explained. "My research is based on the premise that pellagra is caused by some dietary deficiency. We believe we've linked the occurrence of the disease to the lack of protein and a specific amino acid. Now we have to establish proof, and hopefully others will do similar work with the same result."

"So, what kind of proof are you looking for?"

"In our early work we simply changed the diet of a group of patients to include more protein and restricted the protein in another group and measured the outbreak and progression of the disease in the patients."

"You used the patients for your experiments?" Effie asked, puzzled.

"I understand how that sounds, but this is the only way to determine the cause and find a cure. If it's as simple as changing what people eat to keep them from developing pellagra, isn't that a greater good?" Tanner asked optimistically.

Effie considered that argument as she looked around. "So, you actually cook food for patients here in your kitchen and then see what happens when they eat it?"

The doctor laughed. "That sounds about right."

The door opened and a man entered, took off his coat, and got an apron. He was surprised to see Effie in the room. He took her in, head to toe, then wordlessly turned his gaze to the doctor.

"This is Albert," Tanner said, introducing the stocky, sour-faced man who wore a black patch over his left eye. "He helps me out in the kitchen." Albert offered a quick nod, then headed to the long sink and began shuffling though the pots and pans.

"What's different about this food from the food my patients get?"

"At this stage, instead of so much corn meal and cane syrup, the patients get more eggs and milk."

"And how did you choose the colored women for your experiments?"

"There are others in our study as well, but the colored women are the most neglected patients, sadly, and at the highest risk for developing the disease. I'm sure you understand that better than most. And frankly, they stand to gain the most through the process."

"That's all there is to it? There's no medicine or anything?"

"No medicine, but we have supplemented with some amino acids, like tryptophan. That's shown our most impressive improvement so far. Dietary change is the only significant difference."

Effie took a step forward. "So how do I get this food for my women?"

Effie wanted to know more about Tanner and the work he was doing. He treated her as a professional, he was kind and he had offered her a chance to work in his lab. *He must not be from the South*, she mused. She was still considering what Doctor Tanner had proposed as she passed the construction site of the new nurses' home where work had finally started up again. The work was being done in fits and starts due to funding problems with the state. Effie doubted anyone of her persuasion would ever be allowed to live there. The roof was finished, and the sashes were in place to hold the windows. If she had been paying closer attention, she would have remembered to avoid the area.

"Hey, girl! Hey, pretty girl! Why don't you come over here, tell me what ails you, and see if I can fix it!" a man yelled down from an opening in the upper floor.

Effie quickened her pace.

"Hey, I'm talkin' to you. Ow! What the... who did that?"

She turned enough to see the man holding one hand over his forehead, looking angrily in both directions. Just at that moment Fern snatched at her arm.

"What are you doing walking around over here? Don't you have a lick of good sense?" Fern asked, as she hurried Effie past the unfinished building.

Effie noticed the slingshot tucked into the front of her work pants. "Did you hit that man?"

Fern opened her palm to reveal two hard, round stones. "He earned it."

"Are you still following me?" Effie asked her half-jokingly.

Fern wasn't offended. "Sometimes. Not today, though. I've been watching what's going on around this new building."

"You're watching the construction?"

"No. I'm watching the work crew. You know where they come from?" Fern asked her, eyes scanning back and forth as they walked.

"I don't know anything about it. I'm hardly ever over here," Effie said.

"They're a work gang from the prison farm. You know when they were here last? September. The week Pearl was killed."

They continued in silence, then came to a stop where they often parted ways.

Still agitated, Fern asked, "You got something you have to do right now?"

"No, I don't."

With her head Fern indicated that they should keep walking.

When they reached the cottage colony, Effie hesitated. "Where are we going?"

"My place," Fern answered.

At the white-washed cottage, Fern unlocked the door and called to her roommates. Effie waited off to the side, next to the porch.

"Nobody's here," Fern motioned for Effie to come inside.

Effie took in the details of the tidy room. A round table with a yellow cloth and three cane back chairs, a sofa, and a wooden crate that held a lamp. There was a small icebox and a sink in the kitchen but no stove for cooking. She was surprised to see a compact pine tree standing in the corner, covered with cut-out snowflake decorations.

"You're ready for Christmas," she said with a smile.

"My first Christmas tree. It's not much, but we had fun doing it. Take your shoes off. They get mad when I track in dirt. Come back here."

Fern directed Effie down the short hallway. She opened the door to a room that held a small cot and, from first count, about fifteen crates full of file folders and papers. There was hardly room for the two of them.

"Let me get a chair," Fern said.

"What's all this?" Effie asked when Fern returned.

Fern wedged the chair next to the bed and motioned for Effie to sit. "My research. I've been trying to put some things together."

"What are these papers?"

"Files on patients and stuff about this place."

"How did you get a hold of all this?" Effie asked.

Fern shook her head. "From the attic in the Center Building. Not really locked up or anything. Rats had got at some of it, tore it to bits. This is what I'm looking through right now."

"Are you searching for something specific?" Effie asked.

"I'm trying to figure out what's been going on around here for the last couple of years for one thing. Pearl wasn't the only one to be murdered and called a suicide. This has been going on for a while. I'm beginning to think it has something to do with the men they bring in from the prison for labor."

"How have you made that connection, other than Pearl?"

Fern hesitated. "I haven't yet. I haven't found what I'm looking for in these papers anyway. All I know is from personal experience," she said, looking squarely at Effie. "I think the men that attacked Pearl are the same ones who ambushed me two years ago. Only difference was, I lived."

Fern sat down on the bed, pulled her knees up to her chest, and leaned back against the wall. She looked small and mournful. Effie hadn't seen her like that before. Fern was constantly in motion, as if driven by some deep innate energy. Since the first time Effie met her, she had forever seemed to be on a mission of some kind.

"What happened to you, Fern?" Effie asked quietly.

"I never had to tell all of this before. Never thought I would have to." She risked a glance at Effie. "This here doesn't need to go out of this room."

Effie nodded. Fern's focus was on the blank wall as she told her story.

"Almost two years ago now. It was in the spring. We were getting the fields ready for planting. They were building a new feed shed over at the farm. Back then I did a lot more fieldwork than I do now. It wasn't much of a building but it was big. Prison labor was brought over to do it. Every day when we went to the fields, those men would be hootin' and hollerin' at us. I didn't pay much mind to it. I was in a funk."

Effie could see that these were painful things Fern was dredging up. She wasn't sure if she should ask questions or simply listen. She could tell Fern was scrolling through some images in her mind, but she was anxious to learn more.

"Was that when your mother died?"

"How do you know about my mama?"

"I asked Bertie if she knew you. She told me that your mother was a patient here and that she died."

Fern nodded. "Mama died when I was eight. This was after Tom died. Tom Ennis. I guess you can say he was my boyfriend. But that sounds kind of dumb. He was in the war. He came here to get better after he got back home. His family was from Milledgeville. I met him that summer before he got sick with the influenza."

Effie nodded, recalling the epidemic. "I worked in a Red Cross influenza ward that summer. It was heartbreaking."

"Tom wasn't sick when he got here. At least not with the influenza. To look at him you wouldn't even know anything was wrong. He couldn't get the war out of his head. Things he saw. He was a kindhearted person. Not fit for soldier's work. He was heartsick. I think he just needed something good in his life."

Fern smiled, remembering that too short, sweetest summer. "Back during the war and right after, this place was kind of quiet. Lots of men went off to fight. Girls too. They went off to be nurses. Doctors left. That summer and fall it was like that. Almost peaceful. Tom got sick in November. Died in December."

"I'm so sorry, Fern," Effie offered.

With a single shake of her head, Fern cut off Effie's sympathy.

"That part's not what I wanted to talk about. It's what happened after. I was young. I grew up here and didn't have any real sense of danger. I'd always been quiet and knew how to stay out of the way, hide in the shadows."

"You do have a talent for that," Effie couldn't help adding.

"I kept to myself a lot back then. Especially after Tom died. I wasn't watching out like I should have been. One afternoon, it was later than usual when we were finishing. Sun was almost down. They called for us to head to the wagon. I went over to the well for some water. I reached in for the bucket and got grabbed from behind. Before I could scream, he had his hand clamped over my mouth. He picked me up, took me into the trees next to the field. I was squirming and fighting, so he held me down until the wagon was loaded and left. When he went to take his pants down, I started swinging. I wasn't about to let him rape me. Not with the baby and all. I fought him hard. He knocked me around pretty good. While we were tussling, another man came up on us. He took a knife to my throat and held it there. "

Fern pulled her shirt from around her neck and ran her hand across a long, welted scar that ran just beneath her collarbone.

"I don't know much that happened then. I guess I passed out. I came to in the ditch where they left me. It was late. I tried to get myself together best I could. I was bleeding pretty bad, walked up to the road. That's where they found me that night when they came looking. A nurse that cared for my mama and me. We were supposed to meet for supper. When she couldn't find me, she sent Mr. Ingram out to look."

Effie, though spellbound by Fern's story, had so many questions she didn't know where to begin.

"I can't believe all you've been through. I don't know how you survived all of that. You said there was a baby. You had a baby?"

Fern let out a huge whoosh of air. She moved back to the center of the small bed, picked up the pillow and held it tight.

"I was pregnant when those men attacked me. I hadn't told anybody. The doctor that took care of me figured it out of course. I lost so much blood that they had mostly given up any hope for me or the baby. While I was in the hospital, they took the baby out. I didn't get to see him. The doctor told me later that he died the next day. He was buried somewhere in that cemetery before I got well enough to get out of bed."

"So, he was born by caesarean birth. Is that when you had that other surgery?" Effie asked gently.

"That file I found, the only thing in it was something about them doing that to me." Fern had a hard time naming what had happened. "That paper said the baby was born on May 7th. The same day they did that surgery. What it said on the paper was *"undertaken to control promiscuity and fertility,"* she recited from memory.

"I need some air. You want to go out on the porch?" Fern practically jumped from the bed. She flung the door open and was halfway down the hallway before Effie rose from her chair. She was standing in the small kitchen when Effie walked into the room.

"You want a pear?" Fern asked, holding one up for Effie to see.

Effie nodded and took the fruit from Fern's hand as they stood face to face, quiet after all that had been shared.

"If it's not too cold for you, it's nice on the porch. We've got two rocking chairs out there."

They pulled on their shoes. Effie grabbed her coat and slipped into it as they walked out on the porch. Fern sat down in one of the rockers.

Effie pulled her coat together, sliding the pear into her pocket, still shaken by Fern's story. "You think it was men in the work gang that did that to you?"

Before Fern could answer, a door slam and hardy laughter caught their attention. A few doors down, a burly man in an unbuttoned steel-gray coverall stood on a nearby porch, towering over a woman clad only in a dressing gown that was busy sliding off her shoulder. He pulled it even lower and licked his tongue across her exposed breast. Roselyn giggled, pulled him close, and started fastening his buttons while he rubbed up against her. Effie stepped soundlessly back inside the door to Fern's cottage.

The man turned up the collar on his jacket as he backed down the stairs, still leering at Roselyn. He stuffed his hands in his pockets and walked right past Fern. When her rocker squeaked against the floorboards, he turned toward her, and she recognized the red lump on his forehead as the wound she had inflicted earlier.

"You better keep your mouth shut," Roselyn said to her from where she stood on her porch. "You start messin' with me, bad things will land right in your lap, Fern Walker."

Fern rose from the rocker, walked to the edge of her porch, then made a show of stretching as she kept her eyes on Roselyn.

"You running a cathouse now, Roselyn?"

"Why don't you try to figure that out, detective," Roselyn snarked back.

Fern walked back inside, ending the showdown.

Effie stood waiting in the kitchen.

"I better walk you back," Fern told her as she went to grab her coat.

"I don't need you to do that. I just didn't want to cause you any other problems with me being here. I was afraid if they saw me--"

Fern cut her off. "Anybody I want to come into my house can come. And with what I've just seen, I doubt very much that Roselyn would want to stir up any trouble with me today."

Effie put her hand on the doorknob. "You stay here. I'm fine. And I wanted to tell you. I'm going home for a few days next week. Back to Atlanta for Christmas. So, if I don't see you, Merry Christmas."

Fern nodded. "And no. Not the prisoners. The men that did that to me. They weren't prisoners; they were the men with the guns, the ones that were the work-crew guards. Dressed like that man that we saw outside. That one I beaned in the head with the rock."

"They didn't find out who did that to you?" Effie asked.

"I don't think anybody even tried. You see anybody trying to find out what happened to Pearl? If you haven't figured it out yet, the people that run this place don't like to draw much attention to what goes on here."

"It could be dangerous, you know. If you keep looking," Effie said earnestly.

"I'm smarter than I was when that happened," Fern answered confidently.

As she walked back to her room, Effie couldn't get Fern's story out of her mind. Fern had been through a lot. And if her suspicions were correct, that someone was attacking and killing women at the sanitarium. Something needed to be done about that.

When Effie woke on Sunday morning, she bounded out of bed. She felt a new invigorated sense of purpose. She tried to put a finger on it and realized it was a combination of things that led to her improved state of mind. As she pulled on her clothes, she listed them for herself, forever desperate to keep things in order, even inside her own head. First, she had finagled her way into William Tanner's laboratory. She couldn't believe she had the nerve to suggest it. This morning she was headed there to assist with his work. She wasn't sure yet quite how that would work out, but she had gotten his guarantee that they could include the pellagra patients in her infirmary ward in his study, maybe even conduct some new investigations under her care there. That alone gave her a glimmer of hope about somehow doing something that really mattered. Next, the time she had spent with Fern yesterday had been a kind of turning point in their relationship. Until yesterday, Effie had become resigned to the loneliness she endured every day. Though the two of them had very little in common, for some reason, since the first day she arrived in Milledgeville, they had been thrown together in all sorts of situations. Now Fern had confided some of her deepest and darkest secrets. She wanted to help Fern figure out the answers to all the questions she had about what had happened to her and to Pearl and maybe to others too. Perhaps they could unravel some of those mysteries together. And she simply liked being around her. Fern was a lot like Effie. No nonsense. Strong-willed. Effie was attracted by her energy. Despite all that had happened in Fern's life, there was a lightness about her that Effie was drawn to. And finally, in five days her brother Norris was coming to pick her up and take her home to spend Christmas with her family. She had been so sure when she left Atlanta in June that she had closed a chapter in her life. Now she couldn't wait to see it all dressed up for Christmas. Her good mood went with her as she made her way to Tanner's kitchen lab. She knocked on the door and waited to be asked in.

Opening the door, Doctor Tanner said, "You don't have to knock. Just come on in. And would you please call me William."

"Good morning to you, too, William," Effie replied. Something about how she had walked past him and replied so smartly reminded her of her mother, and it made her laugh.

"My, my, you seem to be in wonderful spirits today. That's kind of rare around here. You can hang your coat there." He pointed to the coat rack in the corner. "You may want to put on an apron; it seems more appropriate than a lab coat."

Effie picked out an apron from those hanging on the rack and, as she tied it, walked over to the steaming row of pots.

"I hope you show up in this mood every day. It certainly brightens the place up. Old Albert's not much for talking," he said, lifting the lid on one of the pots. "Now this is really exciting stuff here. You should take a look," he added, motioning Effie over. "I'm boiling six dozen eggs."

THE TRUTH TOGETHER

Having established a friendly camaraderie, Effie paid close attention while William Tanner patiently explained what had happened during the course of his research into pellagra over the past years. As she listened, they worked in the kitchen, and he taught her how to record the specific food items and the exact amounts they would be serving to the patients who were part of the study. He explained that her most important role would be back in the ward. Not only did she have to distribute the food they prepared, she would have to actually see that the patients ate it. One of the biggest problems he had faced in his work was that the high protein food he prepared was often taken by staff members or other patients, and those who were supposed to eat it never had the chance. If the patients under observation never got the required treatment, the results of the study were not valid.

When their work was finished, Effie got ready to leave and head back to change for her Sunday afternoon shift. "I still don't understand why we aren't able to provide a more nutritious meal for all the patients here. If better food makes people healthier, then why can't we serve better food?"

"You forget this is a government institution. The money to run this place comes from the state. Unfortunately, the patients at this hospital are a low priority. The board takes great pride in lowering their per person operation cost every year."

"It's about money?" Effie asked.

"Mostly, money and indifference, I would guess."

"Can I ask you something else?" Effie ventured.

"Of course."

"Why don't you care that I'm colored?" Effie asked in a steady voice.

William hesitated for a moment. "If I may be so bold, I could ask the same of you. Why don't you care that I'm white?"

"It's just that everybody else here does," Effie answered.

William considered for a moment and replied. "I guess I would answer that I am a man of science. Human beings are human beings."

"So you don't think we're different, colored people I mean?"

William crossed his arms, "Because of the color of your skin?"

Effie nodded.

"No, I don't. I don't think the color of someone's skin is what sets human beings apart from each other, Effie. Take you and me. I'm a man. My parents came to America from Prussia. I was born and raised in New York. I'm Jewish. All of those things make me different from you. The color of my skin, that came from my parents. My skin happens to be white. In all of those ways, you are different from me. That's really the best I can do, Effie."

Effie nodded again. They were quiet while she removed her apron and put on her coat.

"I can't wait to see what happens with the women in my ward." At the door she added, "I won't be here next Saturday or Sunday. I'm going home for Christmas."

"Lucky girl. Happy Christmas, Effie," William said as he saw her out. "I'll look forward to seeing you when you return then."

The melodious sound of female voices joyfully singing "Oh Come, All Ye Faithful!" greeted Effie at the doors to the third-floor infirmary. Since her women were patients who were ill, they did not enjoy the same Sunday experience that others had. There were no church services or afternoon amusements for them. But today was different. A small group of choir members had come for a visit. Effie took off her coat, lay it across the chair at the front desk, and headed into the room. The carolers filled the corridor between the rows of patient beds, the room overflowing. The women raised their voices in celebration of the season. Effie stood quietly, looking from one to the next, saying their names in her head as she watched them experiencing this brief moment of joy. As she passed by each one, she took special note of their eyes. She wondered had she ever seen them in such a state, free from their worries and their pain, forgetting their loneliness and fears. Lost in her reverie, she had not noticed the rather impressive Christmas tree that stood in the corner of the room. Some gathered around it, looking through boxes that contained decorations. They added them to the tree as they continued singing. As she watched the celebration, she became aware of two women she had not seen before. Curious, she began making her way toward them. As she drew near, Fern appeared from behind the tree, a burlap bag thrown over her shoulder. She walked by Effie and passed through the throngs of women, handing each of them a ripe green pear and wishing them a happy Christmas.

Effie watched from where she was, a catch in her throat. Struggling to maintain her poise, she made her way through the singing women who were now on "Silent Night." By this time Fern had seen Effie. They met near the tree.

"I'm guessing you did all of this," Effie said, leaning into Fern's ear in order to be heard.

"With a little help from my friends." Turning toward her roommates who had joined in her Christmas scheme, Fern held out her hand. "Shirley and Lizbeth, this is Effie."

Effie looked from one to the other. Pointing at Shirley, she asked Fern, "Is this your sister?"

Shirley and Lizbeth both answered, "It's just the hair."

Late Friday afternoon found an exhausted Effie waiting near the train depot at the sanitarium with a suitcase in her hand, watching the driveway for Norris. Despite her elevated mood on Sunday, Effie now showed the ravages of a typical workweek at the sanitarium. Two of her patients had died. Another would probably be gone by the time she returned. The women on her ward had experienced a sweet respite, singing songs and decorating a tree, but then settled into a week leading up to Christmas without their loved ones. They made the most of their shared sisterhood in the ward, but there was something sorrowful threaded through it. Maybe the memories of times past or the fear that life's moments of celebration in the future would be empty as well.

A shaft of late afternoon sunlight reflected off the front of Norris's car when he made the turn into the drive. It sparked like a shining star and brought a surge of happiness to Effie as she grabbed the car door before Norris could exit to greet her.

"I can't tell you how good it is to see you," Effie said as she threw her bag into the back and clamored into the seat beside Norris. She practically jumped in his lap.

Laughing and hugging her he said, "I couldn't wait to see you, Sister."

Effie settled in, and Norris pulled the car back onto the road and headed for home.

She looked back once as they pulled past the gates and then turned to her brother.

"So just how much money do we have?" Effie asked.

Norris almost had to pull off the road to get control of himself. He was still laughing when he replied, "Plenty, Effie. We have plenty of money."

"Good. That's good to hear, Norris. Because I need some. You'll have to help me convince Papa it's a good idea, so let me tell you what I want it for, and you tell me how much I can have."

And with that Effie spelled out to Norris just exactly how she thought they should spend some of their family's hard-earned fortune to change the lives of the women on her ward.

Fern

DECEMBER, 1922

10

For all of the years she could remember, this was how Fern had spent Christmas Eve, in the company of the residents of the Georgia State Sanitarium, dressed in the finest of what they had and on the best behavior they could summon. From the rear of the auditorium, Fern surveyed the cavernous room. Though not quite full, the turnout was respectable. The Christmas Eve festivities were not always well attended. So much depended on the relative health of the residents and whether or not any special care had been taken by the staff to make the holiday memorable. Pine boughs and sprigs of holly with crimson-colored berries adorned the top of an old upright Lester piano perched on the stage. A towering red cedar dressed in colorful electric lights and wrapped in foil tinsel stood to one side of the risers, soon to be filled with enthusiastic singers who for the last two months had been perfecting their performances for the annual Christmas Cantata. A companionable hum rose from the assembly as they waited.

When she first arrived, Fern had made a point of slowly walking through the room as if looking for someone in particular so that she would be remembered that evening as being dressed in a wraparound wool velour check skirt and a tuxedo style sweater coat. More than a few heads turned. Mostly of those unaccustomed to seeing her dressed as a respectable young woman instead of in a variety of men's work clothes that she favored. She was sure to make eye contact, smile, and wave at most everyone who gave her the chance. Just as she had hoped, Roselyn seated at the front near the stage, could hardly take her eyes off her. Even now as Fern stood in the back, pretending to wait for her friends, Roselyn was watching.

Fern took a seat on the end of the next to the last row nearest the rear doors. She tugged the uncomfortable skirt up above her knees and slipped the silly shoes from her feet. The surrounding seats were yet to be filled. She hoped they stayed that way since her plans to leave early and without notice were critical to the night's errand. Unable to simply sit and wait, Fern checked her pockets. The colony farm and the surrounding pecan grove provided an endless supply of treats. Since she was a child, Fern could not resist gathering what was ripe for the picking and stuffing her pockets anytime she walked across the grounds. But she was disappointed just now. She had never worn these clothes before and her jacket pockets were empty.

The floor lights dimmed, and the performers filled the stage. The pianist entered carrying her music, waving enthusiastically to the crowd. Everyone began waving and calling out "Merry Christmas!" Fern smiled at the familiarity of it all.

Before the first chords rang out, Lizbeth slid in next to her. She smiled and leaned over to whisper in Fern's ear.

Fern nodded. They listened to a couple of the holiday songs, and when satisfied that most of their fellow residents, their attention riveted to the stage, were content to spend the evening inside together, they made their getaway undetected.

Surrounded by December darkness, they hustled back to their cottage.

"Did you put that hand truck and barrel up against the house, like I asked you?" Fern asked.

"Sure did, right at the back corner," Lizbeth answered breathlessly, trying to keep up with Fern. "Are you sure all of this is necessary?"

"No, I'm not. But anytime we have the chance to outsmart Roselyn, I'd say it's worth it."

Lizbeth giggled. "That's good enough for me."

Shirley was waiting for them just inside the door. As soon as she entered, Fern slipped out of the skirt and sweater and just as quickly Shirley put them on.

"Let me see," Lizbeth said to them. She took Shirley's chin in one hand and Fern's in the other and turned them from side to side. "I did a pretty good job. You practically look like twins."

"It's the hair," Shirley and Fern said together.

"Be sure and sit in the exact same spot." Fern pushed them out the door. "And don't forget, as soon as the lights come up and Roselyn gets a chance to see you, head for the door. Shirley, you go to the circle drive. Lizbeth, you come straight back here. Lock the door when you come in and keep the lights on."

"Don't forget to take my bag out," Shirley reminded her.

"John knows where you'll meet him?" Fern asked.

"He knows. I told him to look for the bag under the big magnolia and wait right there with the lights off. I almost forgot," Shirley said, turning back, throwing her arms around Fern's neck. "I won't see you again. Merry Christmas. I'll come visit. I promise."

Fern watched them go, then headed to her room. She slid into the smelly, but comfortable, old work clothes and patted the pockets of her coat to make sure she had all the essentials—flashlight, knife, and a pocket full of pecans. She gathered the laundry bags they had earlier crammed full of the files and records. Fern's research into her own past and her hunch about who might be responsible for the attacks on the women at the sanitarium wasn't finished, but her suspicions about Roselyn spying on her activities had gotten under her skin. Tonight, she was relocating the evidence that she was pretty sure Roselyn knew she had taken from the Center Building storage room. Though she couldn't quite figure out what Roselyn planned to do with that information, Fern knew she didn't want to be caught with all those files in her room. And more than that, Fern knew what the papers revealed about past and present patients, and those particulars in the hands of someone like Roselyn meant trouble.

Tonight's job was all about getting the files out of Fern's room and depositing them somewhere safe without Roselyn watching. It had taken some time to figure out where to stash the contents of the crates so that she would still have access to them, but Roselyn would not follow and snoop around. She had decided on the old colored chapel. She doubted seriously that Roselyn would venture inside there.

Fern lugged the big bags out to the barrel in four trips. She was used to heavy lifting and hard work, but pushing that loaded barrel over the uneven ground was more strenuous than she had imagined and took longer than she had planned. Once she got to the chapel, she unloaded the bags again and coaxed the barrel up two steps and into the side door. She dragged it to where the back staircase led to the attic, then toted the bags up, hefted the barrel up the stairs, and repacked it.

Satisfied that she had secured the documents for the time being, Fern walked silently into the nave. She stood for a few moments to soak in the stillness of the hallowed place. Since Fern was little, she had used it as a quiet space when she was sad or a hiding place if she'd been bad. In all the time she had spent there, no one had ever found her. The peeling white-washed slat wood interior and floor made the space seem unassailable and protected. Though it was deserted, it was pristine. Someone must have cared for it, someone who cherished it. Fern thought it was probably Mr. Ingram. Fern stepped out the side door, silently closing it behind her. She headed toward home, but stopped short when she remembered the hand truck she meant to return to the cold storage shed. Reaching the side entrance to the chapel where the hand truck had fallen into the shrubs, she stooped down to grab it. The sound of crunching gravel stopped her cold. Not three feet from where she crouched between the chapel and the bushes, two figures walked past. Undetected, Fern rose quietly and caught the unmistakable sound of Roselyn's coy laughter. Fern skirted into the shadows and tailed the couple to the back side of the Center Building. There, they opened the door to the basement and disappeared inside.

Grateful that Roselyn was otherwise occupied tonight and not prowling around spying on her, Fern decided to wait a while and see what else she might be up to. She settled into the cover of a stand of pines, reached into her pocket and pulled out two pecans. She crushed them together between her hands hard enough to crack both shells. Fern turned her attention to picking through the chipped apart shell to find the musty, buttery pieces of nut that she promptly popped into her mouth, the darkness making it a challenge. Glancing back at the basement door, Fern caught sight of another shadowy figure slipping inside the building. The hairs on the back of Fern's neck prickled. She scouted out another hiding place where she could more closely keep watch on the door.

Fern knew the secrets of the buildings on the sanitarium grounds. She had played in them, hidden in them, and learned everything she knew about life tucked away in the myriad of clandestine spaces they contained. She knew about the old tunnels under the Center Building that spread out in all directions. When the sanitarium had expanded, some of the pathways were connected to other buildings, providing for underground passage. She wasn't sure about their originally intended purpose, but she had heard stories about how the tunnels had been used. Sometime back when the colored patients' building had burned, mattresses and blankets were moved into the tunnels and some six hundred unfortunate souls had lived inside them until other arrangements could be made. Some tales claimed there were rooms with shackles and cages, but she had never been able to confirm that. The tunnels were creepy, and she had avoided them. Now, they mostly served as storage for the broken and discarded debris that accumulated in places like this. That, and a secluded hideaway for carnal encounters. Fern was certain that was what Roselyn was up to.

An hour or more had passed when the door opened and a man emerged. He looked in all directions, then darted across the open green into the tree line.

Fern waited, her apprehension growing until she could contain herself no longer. She rose, walked briskly to the door, yanked it open, and disappeared inside. She knew it was risky to use her flashlight, but she counted on her ability to move quickly if necessary more than she was willing to go blindly into the unknown. The shaft of light revealed crates, broken bed frames, wastewater pipes, and rusted metal tools.

Fern listened for some clue as to where Roselyn and her companion might be holed up, but the silence clung to her like the darkness. She ventured through the tunnel, her flashlight out front, her other hand concealing her open knife just inside her coat sleeve. Where the tunnel made an abrupt turn to the right, there was a definite narrowing of the walkway, and the height of the tunnel dropped about two feet. Fern figured that was where the pathway led toward some other building. She paused, trying to make up her mind about going deeper into the tunnel or heading home. In the stillness rustling and whimpering sounds were faint. Fern tucked back around the corner, turning off the light. Barely breathing, she strained to make sense of distant noises. Whoever it was, they were headed her way.

Fern shifted to the entrance of the narrow pathway, flicked on her light, and held her knife at the ready. Roselyn, bracing herself against the wall, gasped, "Please help me," and slid to the ground.

Fern rushed over, knelt down, and ran the beam of light over her to see what was the matter. "Where did this blood come from? Where are you hurt? Roselyn, be quiet. I know you're scared and hurt. But be quiet. Whoever did this could still be in here."

Roselyn grabbed Fern's wrist. "He hurt Eddie. He stabbed him with a knife. It was bad. He's hurt real bad," she managed between sobs.

"Who was it, did you see him?"

"No, I couldn't. I don't know. I've never seen him before. He came up on us fast. He started in on Eddie with his knife, slashing." She covered her face with her hands still sobbing. "I'm scared. He kept fighting. He's probably dead." She looked up at Fern. "He told me to run."

Fern saw that Roselyn's feet were bare. "Where are your shoes?"

"I lost them." She held up one foot. "I twisted my ankle on the stones and fell. I can't walk on it."

Fern slipped her hand gently around Roselyn's ankle. It was swollen, her foot lifeless and bruised. "We need to get you out of here."

Roselyn was shaking. Fern realized she was barely dressed. "Where is your coat? Is that all you were wearing?" she asked, taking in the thin, lacy chemise.

"I left my dress. It's with Eddie," she said, pulling her arms across her chest against the chill.

"Here. Take this." Fern took off her coat and put it on Roselyn.

"Why are you being nice to me?" Roselyn asked suspiciously. "You hate me."

"You asked me for help." She guided Roselyn's arm into the coat. "We need to wrap up that foot so we can get you out of here." Fern looked around for something to use. "Maybe your stockings would do. Do you mind? Here. You hold the light." She reached up to take the stockings from Roselyn's thin quivering legs.

Fern braced Roselyn's foot while she looked more closely at her injured ankle. "I think it might be broken. Maybe I can wrap it up tight so you can at least put a little weight on it. I can do the rest."

She wrapped Roselyn's ankle in the silky fabric. "Why do you hate me, Roselyn? I really never understood that. I don't even remember when you came here. I really don't know anything about you."

Roselyn watched as Fern handled her foot carefully and then shifted her attention to Fern's face. "You wouldn't remember that. When I came, you were in pretty bad shape. It was two years ago."

Fern looked up from her work.

"I was in the hospital. Two beds down. You know what those ward rooms are like. Everybody knows everything about everybody. No such thing as keeping anything private."

Fern went back to wrapping.

"From the minute they brought you in, everything was all about you. The nurses, even a doctor or two. They was pretty sure you wouldn't make it. Those first couple of days. That nurse. Was she a friend of yours?"

Fern looked up. "She used to take care of me when I was little. She was friends with my mama."

"She read to you from the Bible, held your hand, cried a time or two."

"I think I'd better use the other one too. Give you a little more support." Fern wrapped the other stocking around Roslyn's useless foot.

"Her brother was an old friend of mine, but that night he acted like he'd never seen me before. Somehow, I wasn't worth his time no more. That nurse was his sister I'm guessing," Roselyn rambled on.

"You know James Robert?" Fern asked, surprised.

"Yeah. Known him a long time. He brought me over from the Baldwin County jail a couple of days before you ended up in the hospital."

"What were you doing in jail?"

"Prostitution, they said," she answered with a smirk. "Fourth time I was in for it. Not sure why they called it that. Not like I was gettin' paid."

"Let's see if you can stand up," Fern said, realizing it was the first time they had been this close to each other without hateful words spewing from their mouths.

"I was jealous. When I saw how you got treated. I wanted somebody to care about me that way. That's all. Purely jealous."

"Let's see if we can get you out of here," Fern said, worried that the attacker might return. She reached to button up the jacket. "Let's close this up to keep you warm."

"I'm not a bad person," Roselyn said as they stood face to face. "Just mean, I guess."

"Let me check that pocket." Fern reached across Roselyn and found her knife. "I might need that." She opened it skillfully and slipped it into her sleeve, testing to make sure it wouldn't fall out. She took the flashlight from Roselyn's hand.

"I think Eddie's probably dead," Roselyn said again, shaking her head.

"We don't know that yet." Fern tried to make some progress toward the exit. Roselyn couldn't put any weight on her right foot. Fern had to bear it all.

"I need to stop a minute." Roselyn pulled away from Fern and lowered herself to the ground. "This thing is killing me. I feel like I might be sick." Roselyn put a hand to her stomach. She rolled to her side and retched. When it was over, she wiped her hand across her mouth and looked closely at Fern.

"I know something I think I oughta tell you. At least I think I know something you don't know. It's about your baby."

Fern felt her throat tightening.

"I know you've been looking for something in those files you stole. You ain't gonna find it there. They didn't write none of that down."

"What are you talking about?" Fern asked, trying to keep her emotions in check.

"That nurse took him."

Roselyn looked up and screamed. Fern saw motion with her side vision and swung her light around just in time to see two raised arms coming down. Pain then darkness.

Searing pain throbbed across her head. Slowly, Fern coaxed herself back to consciousness.

Willing her eyes open, Fern tried to lift her hands to touch her head, but her arms were tied behind her back, her legs bound together. The air was frigid and wet and smelled like something dead. She listened, hoping that the person that did this had gone.

Hearing only silence and sensing no movement, Fern risked one raspy word.

"Roselyn."

No answer.

In the darkness, fighting for clarity, Fern thought through what had happened. A man had knocked her senseless. That part she remembered well. Beyond that nothing. Before that, though, there was something. Something Roselyn said. Fern swallowed the bile rising up her throat. She wiggled her numb and tingly fingers, moving her wrists to test for slackness in the binding. Something slipped inside her sleeve. The knife if she could reach it. Adrenaline pushed her past the pain and fear. In due time she worked the open blade through her shirt sleeve. Careful not to drop it, she sawed through the twine that held her hands. Free from her bonds, Fern stood, dizzy headed, and once again risked calling quietly for Roselyn. She remembered the flashlight she was holding when the attacker struck. She dropped to her knees and crawled across the brick floor, sweeping ahead for the light that would lead her from her prison. Relief flooded through her when she brushed its metal surface.

Fern stood, shaky, but ready with her knife if the situation turned ugly. She switched on the light and scanned the darkness. No attacker. No Roselyn.

But to her great dismay, she noticed a pool of coagulating dark red blood where she had last seen Roselyn's terrified face before the lights went out.

Fern moved swiftly through the tunnel, desperate for the open space and freedom beyond. Reaching the door, she hesitated briefly, ready for a confrontation. She shoved it open, burst free and ran for her life. Once in sight of home, she doubled her speed. On the porch, she fumbled in her pants pocket for the key, drove it home, stepped inside, turned the lock, and slid to the floor.

"Fern?" Lizbeth called from the back room.

"It's me," Fern called weakly.

"What on earth?" Lizbeth asked, dropping to the floor in front of her, eyeing the huge red welt that ran along Fern's hairline. She gently lifted Fern's chin and saw the bruises already forming below her eyes.

"What happened to you? Who did this?"

Tears seeped through Fern's closed eyes and poured down her face.

"You need a doctor," Lizbeth said, clutching her friend's arms. "Let me help you get up."

"Put me in the water, hot as you can make it," Fern pleaded.

Lizbeth pulled Fern to her feet and walked her to the bathroom where she helped her out of her clothes and into the tub. Lizbeth gently lay a cold cloth against Fern's head while she soaked in the steaming water. She brought a chair into the tiny room to sit next to Fern, worried about the blow that must have caused her face to look like it did.

"Can you tell me what happened?" she asked.

"Somebody got us in the tunnel." Fern answered, groggy.

"Who got you? And why were you in the tunnel? You hate the tunnel."

Fern risked opening her eyes to look at Lizbeth.

"Roselyn. I was with Roselyn."

"Okay. Now I'm not sure you even know what you're saying. What were you doing with Roselyn?"

"I saw her go in there with somebody. I waited for her to come back out. When she didn't, I got worried. There was a man. Another man who went in there after them. I had a bad feeling about it."

Lizbeth shook her head. "That was a stupid thing to do, Fern. You know what happens to women in dark places around here."

Fern turned to look at Lizbeth. "I don't know what happened to Roselyn."

"I thought you were together."

"We were. I mean I found her in there. She was hurt. I think her ankle's broken. I was trying to get her out of there when this happened." Fern brought her hand to her head and winced when she touched the cloth on her forehead.

"And then she was gone. I got knocked out. Tied up. When I woke up, she was gone."

"Oh my God, Fern. This is terrible. We need a doctor and we need the police."

Fern started to speak but wasn't sure how to answer. She closed her eyes and nodded.

"I need to lay down for a little while first. Let's wait for daylight before we go out again. I don't want anything to happen to you," Fern said, reaching for Lizbeth's hand.

"Give me a few minutes, then help me get to bed."

A tear drifted down Lizbeth's cheek. "Okay. Whatever you think is best."

A hard rain was falling when Fern next opened her eyes. She had no idea what time it was. The rain pounded on the roof and against the windowpanes as the wind blew. The door to her room stood open.

"Lizbeth," she mumbled, not sure she could stand by herself. "Lizbeth," she called, louder this time.

Nothing. It was daylight but a gloomy one to be sure. Fern didn't know what to think about first. So much had happened since yesterday. What had happened in that tunnel? Where was Roselyn? And what about that man she had been with in there? Eddie was the name Roselyn said. And there was more. What kind of connection did Roselyn have to James Robert and Louella? Fern couldn't remember when exactly she last saw either of them. Even before her mother died, James Robert had wanted Fern to come live with him and his family. She was young when that happened, but she still remembered wailing how she didn't want to go and she didn't want to live with anybody but Nora. After Nora died, Fern saw Louella pretty regularly, though Louella left the children's ward and went to work somewhere else at the sanitarium. And James Robert, he had come around to visit Fern. Sometimes he brought her presents. Candy and a book or two and always some kind of fruit. He knew how much she liked fruit. He brought it all. Pears, apples, oranges, peaches. He would come and get her from the children's ward, where she still lived in the little closet room. They would go outside and sit under a tree on a blanket, just like she had with Nora. Sometimes they would read and other times just talk. He didn't ask her anymore if she wanted to come live with him. That had ended before her mama died. On those days when he came to visit and they went outside together, she wanted more than anything for him to ask her again. She was ready to say yes. But he never did.

And then everything changed. The war started, and little by little the sanitarium emptied out. And Fern had grown up some by then. She had to move out of the children's ward. She remembered that Louella had something to say about that. Nobody really knew why Fern was still there. But nobody really knew what to do with her either. Like so many others who came to the sanitarium, she stayed, simply because there was nowhere else for her to go.

And besides all that, what did Roselyn know about the baby? She couldn't even think about that right now. Fern eased herself up to the edge of the bed. She needed the toilet and some water to ease the dryness in her throat. Standing up, the room spinning, she realized she needed to hold on to something in order to walk across the room without falling and so made her way to the wall and moved along it until she reached the doorway. The house was definitely empty. Lizbeth had gone out for something. Fern cupped her hand under the water faucet and drank, her head throbbing in protest. She returned to her room in the same slow fashion and found some reasonably clean clothes on the floor. She sat down on the bed and pulled them on, fighting waves of nausea, trying to stop the room from whirling. After navigating the short hallway, Fern sat down on the sofa, surprised when she saw the Christmas tree in the corner and remembered what day it was.

Too much work to hold herself upright, she slid down on the sofa and bunched up her knees to fit on its small surface.

Fern jolted awake, annoyed that she had fallen back asleep. She tried to work the kinks out and looked beyond the gauzy window covering. The rain had stopped. The setting sun cast a soft pink hue in long, wavy shadows across the room. Recalling the closeness of the tunnel from the night before, she wanted nothing more than some fresh air and to feel some sun on her face before it disappeared again. Fern moved across the room, still groggy from sleep and the lump on her head. At the door, she slipped on a pair of Shirley's old shoes left behind in her rush to go home and smiled when she thought about how happy she must be to be back with her husband on Christmas. The house would be empty without her, but it was time for Shirley to get back to her life in the real world. Fern wondered what that must be like. She opened the door slowly, searching for the sunlight as she stepped out to the porch. Out of habit, she turned in the direction where she always looked first for Roselyn, two doors down to the right.

But what Fern saw on her own front porch sent a cold dagger through her chest. There in her rocker—where Fern had spent hours talking with her friends, thinking about her mother, remembering Tom, wondering what the future held for her—was Roselyn. Fern's old work coat hung limply on her small frame. The buttons Fern had closed against the chill of the tunnel just hours before had been ripped off. An ugly red gash ran from her neck in a straight line between her exposed breasts down to her belly. Roselyn's lifeless eyes stared straight through Fern as she stepped forward to close them.

With darkness fast approaching, Lizbeth and two Milledgeville policemen, along with a nurse carrying her medical bag walked up the steps to the porch. The gruesome guest greeted them. Seeing Roselyn, Lizbeth screamed and collapsed. One of the policemen walked through the open front door calling, "Police, police. Come out where I can see you."

It didn't matter. The house was empty. The nurse helped Lizbeth inside. A crowd gathered.

Under the cover of the pecan trees stretching along the front drive that circled through the center of the sanitarium, Fern stood silently. At her feet, a laundry bag, stuffed with what she thought she needed to survive on the outside. The sanitarium guards fanned out across the grounds. Their flashlights glinted against the night sky like oversized fireflies. Her name echoed through the bare branches of the trees as they called out for her.

"Fern Walker, this is the police. Show yourself."

Fern grabbed the bag and hefted it across her shoulder. She turned and headed across the landscape that she had known forever as home.

Alonzo

SEPTEMBER, 1906

11

Alonzo pulled an already damp handkerchief from his jacket front pocket and wiped his brow. The last day of summer had only brought more heat and humidity to the streets of Atlanta. It was mid-afternoon and after spending the morning at his Atlanta Mutual offices on Auburn Avenue, Alonzo was making the rounds. He loved this Saturday ritual, the weekly stroll, stopping by to speak to some of his tenants and check on his properties. The satisfaction he felt when he learned that all was well was hard to match. Headed for his shop, he was already thinking about a bath, a shave, and a fresh change of clothing. As he made the turn onto Peachtree from Auburn, he slowed his pace to take in the sights. On Saturdays the thoroughfare was jam-packed with throngs of people, enjoying a day off work, in the company of family and friends partaking in the various amusements the bustling city offered. Usually, their excitement was a source of joy for Alonzo. Today, the crowd set him on edge. The sweat pooling under his arms and around his collar was made worse by the sultry air, but he had no doubt the source was the sense of unease that hovered over the streets like a thick wool blanket. The summer months had been filled with angry and hateful rhetoric as the August Democratic primary for the Georgia governor's office drew to a close. Candidate Hoke Smith had campaigned on ending voting rights for Black men and claimed a victory based entirely on stoking racial fears. Lurid stories of wild-eyed colored criminals attacking defenseless white women dominated conversations and headlined newspapers across the city. Atlanta was wound up tight, and Alonzo could see in the faces of the people he passed that tensions were running as high as the heat.

As he approached his destination, the familiar sound of newsboys calling the *Atlanta Evening News* headlines brought Alonzo to a standstill.

"*Insulting Negro Badly Beaten at Terminal Station!*"

"*Bold Negro Kisses White Girl's Hand!*"

"*Cops Tear Nude Photos of White Women from Decatur Street Dives!*"

Alonzo watched as people scurried across the street and clustered around the rowdy hucksters to grab a copy. If the tension in the streets and the weather didn't cool down soon, he thought, there would be hell to pay.

Up ahead at Herndon's Barbershop, two of his white-clad barbers leaned up against the entryway watching the Saturday afternoon street traffic. When Alonzo reached them, they stood a little straighter and took their hands out of their pockets.

"Woodrow, Charlie, business must be on the slow side for you to be out here gawkin'," Alonzo ribbed them.

"We had a run early on, but it's been the slows since around noon," Woodrow answered.

Two men that Alonzo recognized as Atlanta plainclothes policemen came up beside them.

"You boys head on back inside," Alonzo told his young barbers before he turned to greet them.

"Could we have a word with you, Alonzo?" one of the men asked.

"Let's go up to my office," Alonzo offered, opening the door for the men to pass.

ALONZO

As he walked through the alley that ran through the center, separating the long rows of barber chairs, Alonzo nodded to his workers, trying to calm their fears at seeing the white officers following him through the shop.

"Miss Ollie, could you bring us some ice tea?"

"Why yes sir, Mr. Herndon, I'll be right up," she answered, heading into the back room.

"What can I do for you gentlemen?" Alonzo asked after they got settled in his office.

"We stopped by as a courtesy to you, Alonzo. Word on the street is that there's trouble coming tonight. You might want to send everybody home early and close up."

"What kind of trouble?" Alonzo asked.

"There's a bunch of boys want to go into Decatur Street and tear them joints up."

"You mean the police want to do that," Alonzo clarified.

"Them and some others," the man answered solemnly. "It's them others I can't promise what they will and won't do."

Alonzo understood exactly who the others were, mobs of hate-filled men who didn't wait for the law to handle trouble, but took it on themselves to do violence and call it justice.

"You know those dives need to be shut down. Your colored preachers have been calling for it too," the younger officer said defiantly.

"I know there are many legitimate businesses on Decatur Street. It's them I'm concerned about. The mob you're talking about won't make any distinction between them," Alonzo answered calmly.

The officers stood. "That's why we're here, Alonzo. I can't protect you in this. I wanted you to know, so you could get ready. Send your people home. Close up and get home yourself."

Miss Ollie slipped through the office door with a tea tray.

Back on the main floor, Alonzo saw the two men out. Glancing outside as they left, he watched the newsboys flooding through the street with *The*

Atlanta Journal extra. Woodrow walked up behind him. Alonzo flipped him a nickel.

"Go get me a paper, Woodrow."

Alonzo waited at the large plate glass window that fronted his store, arms crossed. Woodrow returned with the paper and held it up for Alonzo to see. The headline screamed, "Negro Attempts to Assault Mrs. Mary Chafin!"

"It's tense out there, boss," he said to Alonzo. "What's up with the coppers?"

"This thing might break open tonight." Alonzo clapped the man on the back. "We need to get ready. Let's close up."

Woodrow stood watching as Alonzo walked through the shop, speaking to each of the workers. Placing his hand on their backs, calming them at the same time, he was telling them to finish up and get ready to close early. That was something that had never happened before.

"Fred, you reckon you can borrow a car from Doc Butler and drive me home?"

"Sure can, Mr. Herndon. I'll go get it."

"Pull up the back alley when you get here. Don't wait out front. Take your time. I've got some things to take care of first," he said, watching as the old bootblack limped toward the door.

"Woodrow, you walk Miss Ollie home," Alonzo ordered.

"Will do. But then I'm coming back and I'm staying put," he said, puffing out his chest. "They don't scare me."

Alonzo answered so that all could hear, "It's not about being scared. It's about being safe. I've been in this city a long time. There's something different brewing here. Let's be smart about it."

Alonzo looked around the large, luxurious establishment that he had dreamed up and made come true through good luck, hard work, and wise decisions.

"Put your tools away, men. What you can't lock up at your stations, take to the back room. Let's pack it up and close it down right."

Alonzo headed downstairs and took a quick shower to wash off the day's grime. Back in his top-floor office, he changed into some clean clothes. He sat down at his desk and pulled together some things he wanted to keep close. His ledger book, his bank box, and the insurance papers. He rolled his chair around to the small safe on the floor beneath the table, dialed in the combination, and opened it up. He took the cash he had stored inside and put it in his bank box along with the other papers. He lifted a strong box from the bottom of the safe and carefully removed two Colt automatic 45-caliber pistols and placed them on his desk.

With a light knock on the door, Woodrow stuck his head in. "Can I come in?"

"Come on," Alonzo answered.

Woodrow's eyes went wide at the sight of the guns on Alonzo's desk.

"These are legal and registered to me," Alonzo said, his eyes on the guns. "I don't get much practice, but I know how to handle them. How 'bout you, Woodrow?"

"Yes, sir, I do," he answered.

"I don't know what might happen tonight, but if you plan to stay here in the shop, I want you to have some protection," he said, standing so that they could look eye to eye. "When I leave, I don't want you going back out."

"No. I don't want to. That's what I wanted to tell you. I think it's 'bout to blow up out there. I came though the alleyway to get back just now. Packs of men are roving along Decatur, chasing any Coloreds they see, waving clubs, beatin' them they catch. News is some other white woman says she was attacked," he relayed, shaking his head.

The office door opened again. Charlie stuck his head in. "Fred's back with that car, Mr. Herndon."

"Thank you, Charlie. Why don't you come with me over to my place for the night?"

"I'm staying here with Woodrow, Mr. Herndon. We'll be all right," he said, coming into the room. "A couple of the boys are going with you. They'll help you out if you need 'em."

"All right then," Alonzo answered. He picked up one of the pistols and handed it to Woodrow.

"Use this to protect yourself. Nothing in this shop matters. You boys are all that does." He nodded his head toward the windows. "Best view of the street is right through here. Make yourselves comfortable. Stay away from the main floor. Keep out of sight and keep the lights out."

"We'll be all right, boss. Don't worry 'bout us. You get home," Woodrow answered with Charlie nodding beside him.

Alonzo picked up the other pistol and tucked it into the front of his pants, grabbed the bank box, and headed down the stairs.

"Get the lights, Archer," Alonzo told his cousin, a porter in the shop who lived with the Herndons. In the dim interior, Alonzo walked to the front of the store and looked out onto the wide street that he loved. A quick downpour had caused a foggy haze to rise from the cobblestones. In both directions clutches of men were gathering, some carrying clubs and others with makeshift weapons. The eerie sight made a shiver run up his back.

"Me and Early's comin' with you, Mr. Herndon, a tall dark-skinned barber named Talmadge said as Alonzo headed for the back door.

Alonzo nodded. "Lock up, Archer, and let's go."

In the alleyway Fred sat waiting behind the wheel with the motor idling. "Take us home, Fred," Alonzo told him as he swung in beside him.

They kept to the alleyways and back roads. Passing over the cross streets, gangs of men—some running, some armed—streamed by. Where they made the turn to cross the southside and head up to Diamond Hill, a Black man who had been beaten bloody lay on the street corner and was being tended to by some passersby. The men in the car kept silent.

They arrived without incident at Bumstead Cottage. "Come on, Fred, let's get something to eat," Alonzo said, climbing from the car.

"Told Doc Butler I'd get his car right back."

"All right then. Get home yourself after that. No telling what's going down tonight."

"See you Monday, Mr. Herndon."

"Thanks for getting us home safe, Fred. See you later."

Alonzo led the men up the front walk. The front door opened before they got there, and Norris, wide-eyed, darted out.

"Can we go for a ride, Papa?" he called out as Fred pulled away from the curb. "Mr. Fred always gives us a ride."

"Not today son." Alonzo bent down to scoop up his son, careful to balance his load.

"What are you doing with that gun?" Norris asked, not missing a thing. "Can we shoot something?"

"Not today, Norris," Alonzo said again.

"Miss Mattie, we've got some hungry boys here," Alonzo called as he entered the house, knowing his mother-in-law would be in the kitchen working on supper and Sunday dinner on a Saturday afternoon. He put Norris down and saw Adrienne and Effie coming down the stairs. Their progress was slow since Effie was just mastering the art of stair walking.

"What are you doing home at this time of day?" Adrienne asked. Reaching the bottom of the staircase, her eyes dropped to the gun tucked into Alonzo's waistband, then lifted back to his face, questioning. "Is everything okay?"

Alonzo nodded but Adrienne wasn't convinced.

"We closed up early."

Those words told Adrienne all she needed to know. Alonzo Herndon had never closed up early. Not once. Wasn't in his nature. He always said, if he wasn't making money, it meant somebody else was.

"Something's brewing down on Decatur. I got some friendly advice to go home."

"You've been told to go home lots of times."

"This one felt different."

Mattie walked in, wiping her hands on a dish towel and counted heads. "I'll cut up a couple more chickens. Norrie, you and Effie come on and get your supper before bath time."

The children didn't have to be told twice.

Turning back to the kitchen, she added, "You boys take them shoes off in my house and leave them on the front porch."

"Fried chicken, Miss Mattie?" Archer asked.

"For them that takes off their shoes," she answered over her shoulder.

"More might be coming," Alonzo told her as he slipped out of his shoes. "It could be a long night."

"Get some rest if you can. I'll be back down for supper," Alonzo told the room full of men as he and Adrienne went upstairs.

THE TRUTH TOGETHER

He closed their door for privacy. Adrienne sat down on the corner of the bed. Alonzo walked to the wardrobe that he kept locked. Knowing what was inside, Adrienne sighed.

"Is this something bad?"

Alonzo turned, holding two Winchester 22-long rifles. "If it is, I want to be ready." He placed them on the bed where he normally slept in warmth and comfort next to his wife. He lay the pistol next to the long guns. He returned to the cabinet for some ammunition and another pistol.

"That's quite an arsenal. Are we safe here?"

He paused, then nodded slowly. "I think so, Addy. I promise I'll take care of you and the children no matter what."

He took the bank box to the wardrobe and squatted down in front, reaching in to turn the combination on the safe. "You remember how to get into this safe, don't you?"

"*A* for Adrienne, *N* for Norris and *E* for Effie. 1, two turns to the left, 15, turn to the right, and 5."

"There's a little over two-thousand dollars in here now. If anything should happen, that should be enough to get you and the children safely out of here, keep you for a while," Alonzo said, returning to sit beside her.

"Now I'm worried, Lonzo. What do you think could happen that we would have to leave? And if we did, I'm not going without you." She reached over and took his hand.

"Whatever this is that's going on, I could be a target. We've talked about this already."

"I don't understand what you mean by that. Why would you be a target?"

"Because of who I am and what I've done. I'm a Black man in a white man's city, and I'm richer than most of them. I'm one that has a lot to lose."

"And that's what you think this is about?"

"Some. That's what we've heard all summer. Hoke Smith will be our governor, and he wants to take everything we've gained away from us. He's brought this city to a fever pitch. Those men in the streets believe that most Black men are thieves, rapists, and murderers, and they've decided to take matters into their own hands. It would be a convenient time to get rid of those that prove them wrong in their thinking."

ALONZO

"What do you think could happen?"
"I don't know. I really don't know."

Mattie had fed and bathed the children, when Alonzo and Adrienne came back downstairs.

"Up, Papa," Effie said to Alonzo, her arms held toward him. He bent down, gathered his little girl into his arms, and held her close. Norris took advantage and scrambled onto Alonzo's back. Effie snuggled into his neck, as she had done since she was a baby. Norris wrapped his legs around Alonzo as the tall man stood up. "I'll put them to bed," he told Mattie.

"Don't be long. Your supper's getting cold," she answered, while she watched him effortlessly climb the stairs draped with the children.

Having tucked the children in for the night, Alonzo returned to the parlor with the firearms and placed them on top of the upright piano. In the kitchen, the men were seated around the table—white napkins hanging around their necks—making quick work of the platters of chicken, mashed potatoes, and field peas Mattie had prepared. Alonzo sat down and helped himself. Having eaten their fill, the men cleared their plates from the table, thanked Mattie for the kindness, and left the kitchen to wash up.

When they returned to the parlor, Alonzo was waiting for them.

"I don't know what we might be facing tonight, but I don't want anybody getting inside my house or anywhere near my family."

He passed around the weapons, and the men headed out the front door.

"Let's cover from the porches. Two men in the front, two in the rear," Alonzo directed.

The house on Diamond Hill perched above the city on the west side of Atlanta. It was the only house on the block and adjacent to the campus of the college where Adrienne taught. It had always seemed apart and protected from everything ugly and dangerous. A safe haven for his family. They could go to school, to work, to church, play in the yard, sit out on the porch in the evenings without any fear. Tonight, it felt dark and isolated.

THE TRUTH TOGETHER

Alonzo took a seat in one of the porch chairs and lay the Winchester across his lap. Talmadge leaned up against the porch rail and looked out over the city lights.

"What you reckon is happenin' down there?" he asked Alonzo.

"Something vile" was his simple reply.

As night settled in, the sound of gunfire could be heard sporadically in the distance. From their posts, they could see that the entire southside of the city had gone dark. Around eleven o'clock, the sound of an approaching automobile caught the attention of the drowsy sentries. A black Paxon delivery van made its way slowly up the street and pulled to a stop in front of the Herndon house. Talmadge and Alonzo stood, their weapons at the ready. Charlie, the young barber he had left with Woodrow back at the shop, made his way across the street and ran up the walk to the porch. Realizing who it was, the men lowered their weapons.

"Son, what are you doing over here?" Alonzo asked the visibly shaken young man.

"Mr. White wanted us to get word to you, Mr. Herndon." He shook his head and bent over, placing his hands on his thighs. "It's real bad news. They got Fred. They killed Fred out on the street."

"What? Who? Who killed Fred?" Alonzo asked, unable to make sense of what Charlie told him.

"A gang of white men. They got him. He couldn't outrun em' with that bad leg. They beat him to death with clubs and rocks, left him lying there in the gutter. Mr. White and his son saw it happen. They couldn't do nothin' but hide."

Talmadge put his hand on Charlie's shoulder. "How bad is it down there?

"It's bad. There's people lying in the street everywhere. Don't know who's dead or who's hurt. Must be thousands of people. And they got guns. Broke into the hardware stores and stole 'em, some did. Mr. White wanted you to know about Fred. He came to the shop through the alley in this car, banged on the door calling for Woodrow, told me to get over here with the news."

Alonzo stared at Charlie for a minute, put down his rifle, and walked out to the street and down to a spot where he could look out over the city.

He stood there alone with his hands in his pockets. He had known Fred for more than half of his life. He was nothing but good.

Charlie and Talmadge watched him quietly.

The two men talked about what Charlie had seen and didn't notice that Alonzo had come back until he stepped up on the porch.

"Go inside and get something to eat, Charlie. You're not going out again tonight."

"I'm real sorry, Mr. Herndon," the young man said with a quiver in his voice. "Fred never hurt nobody. He treated me like I mattered."

"Fred was the best of us," Alonzo answered. "Go on inside now."

A little after midnight, they could make out the distinct sound of the tolling of the big bell at the fire department. Alonzo closed his eyes while he counted. It sounded fifteen times.

"Fifteen?" Talmadge questioned.

Alonzo didn't move from his seat on the porch. "They're calling up the state militia. That's what fifteen strokes means."

"Good God," Talmadge muttered. "I wonder if anything will be left of it."

Around two in the morning, a hard rain began to fall. When it was falling harder at three, Alonzo called off the night watch. Weary, the men headed inside.

"There's a room with some clean-made beds down the hallway behind the stairs. Get some shut eye," he said before he headed up.

By the time Alonzo came down the next morning, Mattie was in the kitchen stirring up a big breakfast. Adrienne was at the table with Woodrow, drinking coffee. She stood when she saw him.

"I'm so sorry about Fred. Woodrow told me," she said softly, touching his arm.

Woodrow stood too. He started shaking his head before he could get the words out. "The shop's still standing, but it's torn up, boss. Front window's gone, chairs and mirrors, some of them too. All smashed up."

Alonzo reached out and shook Woodrow's hand. "I don't know how to thank you for being there last night."

"Couldn't do nothin' when they decided they was coming in. Hid in the attic."

"Glad you did. Probably saved your life," Alonzo answered.

"Me and some of the boys got the front boarded up after daylight. Don't know what might happen next," Woodrow offered, still shaking his head. "Word was this morning most every barbershop in town got hit, least ways Black-owned ones. Some boys over on Marietta Street got killed right inside the shop. Took the bodies out, stripped 'em naked, and left 'em in the street. At Leland's, too, they shot Will Marion dead."

Adrienne covered her face with her hand.

"Over at Durand's and the Union Depot, they came inside after the Coloreds."

"What happened on Auburn? Did you hear anything about that?"

"Decatur is mostly wiped out. Auburn hardly got touched. Folks down there shot out the streetlights and locked up tight. Streets was dark and empty when the mob got there."

Alonzo nodded, relieved and hopeful that some of his people and his properties might have made it through the night.

"There's soldiers in the streets now. Guns ready. Coloreds what was hidin' somewhere last night, comin' out, goin' home. That's what I did. Walked right down Peachtree. Got checked to see if I was carryin' a gun. I weren't, though. Found a bicycle just layin' there, grabbed it, and hauled it over here."

Charlie shuffled in, bleary-eyed. "Thought I heard you."

"Glad to see you safe, man," Woodrow told him, throwing a good-natured jab to his ribs.

"You want us to head back over to the shop this morning, boss?" Woodrow asked.

"No, I don't." Alonzo did not hesitate to answer. "We're safe. We're staying put. Get yourself some breakfast and get some sleep. Your shift's over. We'll see what the day brings."

The Herndons were regulars at First Congregational Church and it was Sunday. The family stayed home. Alonzo headed over to the chapel on the university campus to see if he could learn anything else about the situation in the city. There was a large gathering but not any preaching. There was more anger than fear, though fear ran a close second. Them that knew said that the newspapers and the white churches had placed most of the blame on lawlessness and alcohol found in great abundance along Decatur Street. The morning editions' editorials called for deputizing more white men to protect their women against depraved Negroes. Few spoke harshly about the criminality and horrors of white vigilante justice. Some said that only a complete segregation of the city would calm the furor. The hunt was still on to find yesterday's attackers, and the public was called out to help. The city that had until recently prided itself on racial cooperation had become the epicenter of racial hatred and a call for the reorganization of the Ku Klux Klan.

Among those that gathered at the chapel, some voiced their concerns about Black retaliation against whites. Some supported that idea, and others thought it would bring a death sentence to the whole community. Many believed that the violence wasn't ended, and as they left for home, there were exchanges about who had what weapons and how much ammunition.

Alonzo walked home in the afternoon drizzle, his heart heavy but his mind made up. On arrival he discovered that his front porch and parlor had become the gathering spot for a potluck Sunday dinner. He said some hellos, listened to some rehashing of the past night's events, wandered inside, and walked down to the basement.

When Adrienne started looking for him a little while later, she found him in their bedroom, where he had deposited the family's suitcases and was now sitting on the bed.

"Now what's all this?" she asked him, coming around the far side so she could see his face.

He met her gaze and held it before he spoke.

"After all these people leave, I want you to start packing," he said with no emotion.

"And just what do you want me to pack?" she asked in the very same tone.

"Your things. The children's things. I left a case for Mattie in her room."

"And what about your things? What should I do with them?"

"I'm not going' anywhere."

Adrienne raised her chin. "The children, Mama, and I." She raised her eyebrows. "Where is it you would have us go?"

"Tomorrow morning I'll send a telegram to Rachel in Philadelphia," he told her calmly. "She has room for all of you. Norris can go to school with Clara. Mattie will be there to help you with Effie."

"So, you've decided all this. Already. You made all these plans without a single word to me. And what makes you think Philadelphia is any better off than Atlanta? They've got their own problems."

"Everywhere has its own problems. But what we've got in Atlanta right now is the greater danger. I have decided, Addy. I warned you this might happen."

"And what if I refuse?"

"You won't. This is how I keep you safe."

Alonzo stood without looking at her and left the room, closing the door softly behind him.

By early evening, word came that the state militia was keeping Blacks from coming into downtown. Skirmishes had broken out throughout the afternoon. Fears were mounting about what the night might bring.

Those of Alonzo's men who had made their way out to Diamond Hill hunkered down for another night of guard duty. Some helped Mattie in the kitchen, keeping hungry bellies full, and cleaning up after them. The tension that filled the air was due largely to the situation in and around Atlanta, but not entirely. Alonzo and Adrienne were uncharacteristically cold toward each other and remained aloof from most everyone except the children. Too young to really understand what was happening, Norris and Effie made the most of having a host of playmates tucked into every nook and cranny of the house. Their squeals and laughter from piggyback rides and hide-and-seek provided a playful diversion for everyone, as uncertainty settled in with the darkness.

There were enough men to take shifts on guard duty outside, but hardly anyone was thinking about sleep. For hours, the men kept track of an unnatural glow that hovered above Darktown. They speculated it came from the torches of white marauders who roamed the streets, looking for trouble and wondered who was suffering from what in their own neighborhoods. Sporadic gunshots rang out and occasionally roused the men from their half slumbers on the porches surrounding the Herndon home, but the night passed without incident.

At daybreak Monday morning, coffee and biscuits were passed around and plans were made for Woodrow and Charlie to drive Alonzo to the shop to assess the damage. Talmadge and Early would wait at the house until Alonzo made it home, just in case the family needed their help. After he secured his firearms, Alonzo waited on the front porch for the men to gather and then left without a word to Adrienne.

"Drive down Decatur," Alonzo told Woodrow as they neared the site of the violence.

When they approached the cross street, armed militia were standing in the road, waving the few automobiles that ventured out, away.

"Militia boys won't let us. We'll have to walk down there later," Woodrow offered.

The men quietly observed the damage to the city as they drove up Peachtree. Burned-out storefronts, smashed windows, the furnishings from businesses piled in charred heaps along the roadside. Other than the armed guards, few pedestrians were visible.

"They hit the Black-owned businesses," Alonzo pointed out what all could see.

Woodrow turned into the alleyway behind Herndon's Barbershop and parked the car. They let themselves in through the rear door to Alonzo's once opulent establishment that had catered to the whims of white men and earned him a small fortune. The glittering chandelier lay in ruins on the floor. The Spanish leather barber chairs had been sliced with knives, and it seemed that one of them had been lifted from the floor and used to smash the massive mirrors.

Alonzo wasn't surprised to see that several of his barbers were already busy inside, sweeping glass, removing broken mirrors, returning things to their rightful places. He watched for a few minutes, then headed to the back room. He returned in an apron Fred had worn when he cleaned up his bootblack stand most every evening. Alonzo grabbed a broom and joined the men on the floor.

"Let's open up that front door, and let some air in here, Charlie," Alonzo called over his shoulder.

"Yes sir, boss, I'll take care of it."

Eddie

AUGUST, 1919

12

Eddie left the truck to idle and climbed out to open the padlocked gate that led to what remained of his inheritance. Though his daddy and his granddaddy before him were life-long cotton farmers, most folks in Baldwin County knew the Johnson family's real talent was cultivating another cash crop, corn whiskey. The boll weevil decimated the cotton trade when Eddie was a boy and when the state of Georgia banned alcohol in 1907, the Johnson men figured out early that passing laws to make whiskey illegal was one thing— stopping people from making it or drinking it was entirely another. They might not have been good for much else, but they knew how to cook corn. Eddie had come of age with the secrets of his forefathers' moonshine making business burned hot in his brain. That was all they left him, besides a bad temper and a mean streak. And while it was a side gig for Eddie, bootlegging meant moneymaking and he aimed to keep at it for as long as he could.

The road down to the river's edge was deep rutted from days of hard rain. He eased the truck slow and easy, down to the bank of the Oconee, squeezed it into a stand of spindly, green pines just after five o'clock on Thursday. Eddie had ten gallons of mash worked off and ready to run through. Counting on a twelve-hour run to cook and finish deliveries right before sunup, he grabbed his dinner pail and a crate full of fruit jars from the truck bed, hoisted it to his shoulder, and weaved his way through the trees to the wood slat shed. His day job at the State Prison Farm left him dog-tired and hankering for a good supper. Since his wife had run out on him two months back, nobody much cared where he was or what he was up to. It was times like these that for a minute, he wished he had a partner in the business, but he knew how risky that could be. Whiskey making was best a solitary undertaking, and he reckoned that suited him just fine.

Eddie yanked the tarp off his still and ran his hand along the copper tubing that coiled through the inside of the oak barrel and ended in a spout on the outside. He strained the mash into the cooker, snatched up two five-gallon pails and headed to the river. Four runs to the water's edge and back, and he had the barrel topped off with cool water. Eddie lit the two-burner kerosene stove, adjusted the heat, took his metal camp chair, and headed back to the shoreline to keep watch and have some smokes. He remembered his Lugar pistol shoved up under the front seat of his truck but shook off the thought that he might need it on the airless summer evening. Eddie set his chair on the bank and walked down a way to get a look around the bend. The only real danger to starting a run before sundown came from the river. The clay-colored water was running high and fast after the heavy rains. Tied to a branch on a half-submerged tree fifty yards upstream, an old wooden rowboat bumped and tottered. Eddie took a long drag on his cigarette and combed the shoreline for whoever might have climbed out. He sensed no movement in the thick tree cover but determined to keep an eye on it. He figured it was probably somebody just like him, taking care of business ahead of Friday night.

Eddie headed back to his lookout spot, stopped along the way and picked up rocks good for skipping. He checked to see that his run wasn't dripping yet and ambled back down to the water. He pulled a gray stone from his pocket and savored the cool smoothness of its triangular shape. Gripping the rock between his middle finger and thumb, he hooked his index finger along the edge, with a quick flip released it into a spin. Six skips. Not bad. He pulled another, thinner stone from his pocket, adjusted his angle to the water and threw out and down, harder this time. Eight skips. Better. As he got into his rhythm, Eddie got lost in the past and the days he had spent along the Oconee as a kid. Him and Jimmy Little. They spent more time on the river than they had on dry land. And like a lot of local boys, they had gone together to the Georgia Military Prep School. It was there that they met Furman Lee. They'd played football, chased girls at the Georgia Normal and Industrial College up the road, and drank a little too much of their daddy's shine. The other boys called them the three musketeers. Eddie's football playing ended with a broken leg. His daddy's whiskey making ended with a bullet in his back. And when the war broke out in 1914, he and his buddies waited and hoped they'd get the chance to serve, not so much for the patriotic duty but to relive the glory days that ended too soon for backwoods boys like them. They had headed to Fort Gordon together, 82nd division, crossed the Atlantic in May, 1918, on the same ship, and got split up before they reached the action in France. Of the three, he was the only one to make it home. In the front lines in the Toul Sector in August, Jimmy got gassed and died two days later. In October, Furman Lee was on board the Otranto, a transport ship off the coast of Scotland with 700 other American soldiers when the boat got rammed by a British vessel in the convoy. In high winds and sixty-foot waves, the ship stood dead in the water. A rescue attempt by another boat fed the tragedy when men leapt from the stranded craft into the sea. Furman disappeared under the raging waves that day. Eddie still didn't understand how he could have drowned. They were river rats, and that wasn't supposed to be how it ended for them. Some others he knew from school were lost too—Billy Morris and Tom Huff. It got his blood up thinking about it. A couple of the younger boys made it home, but Eddie didn't have much to do with them. He had no use for hardship tales or war stories. He might have come home without any physical signs of what he'd been through, but his anger was on a hair trigger, and his bloodlust sizzled right under his skin.

When he ran out of rocks, Eddie walked along the bank to check on the tied-up boat. Bobbing on its rope and not a soul in sight, he headed back to his still. He poured off the first cut and unwrapped a pork sandwich that he gulped down in four bites. After dark settled in, he lit a lantern, put together a new mash for the next week, took inventory of his supplies, and tidied up the shed to the sound of frog music.

A little after midnight, he was measuring his run into pint jars when the sharp snap of a branch cracking brought him to full alert. He eased the bottle down to the table, lowered the wick in his lamp, and lay his hand over the top of the chimney to put out the flame. Eddie drew his flashlight from where it sat on the table and waited. When another unmistakable pop gave away the location of the intruder, he shot the beam out through the trees.

"Stop right there. My weapon's aimed right at your head and my finger's itchy," Eddie bluffed.

The man held his hands up. "Whoa now. I ain't carryin' nothin'."

"I'm in my rights to protect what's mine. You go on back to where you come from."

"You Eddie Johnson? I know you from the brick company. You used to work there."

"Who's askin'?"

"Carl Watson. We was there 'round the same time. We both got laid off when old man McMillian hired all them colored boys on the cheap."

"What 'chu want?"

"Somethin' to drink."

"How'd you get back here?"

He pointed toward the water. "My boat's right down yonder."

"Don't come messin' in these woods. This here is private owned. You're likely to get your head blowed off as not."

"Word is you've got some of the best hooch on the river. Come to get me some."

"I don't sell back here in the woods. I'm a wholesale man."

"That's what I heard," the man said, taking a slow step forward. "Said you was kind of slow on production, you bein' a one-man shop."

"Don't come any closer," Eddie ordered. "I don't know you from Adam."

EDDIE

"Why don't you give me a taste, and then I've got a business proposition. I work over at the sanitarium now, and I tell you what, that place could be a gold mine for the right man."

Eddie stood quiet for a minute. He kept his light on the man while he picked up the gallon jug, poured a thimble full in a copper mug, and set it down on the table. He took a step back as the man approached.

Carl Watson kept his eyes on Eddie. He picked up the cup, drew it to his nose and sniffed, swirled, and swallowed it down.

"Got a nice little burn to it, pretty smooth for just run," he nodded, clanking the mug back on the table and looking at Eddie straight on.

"I hear tell you been hustlin' them colored gals on your chain gang in a meat rack out on the highway."

Eddie pointed the light at the man's eyes. "Where you gettin' all your information?"

"Just admirin' your resourcefulness is all. I could set you up easy if you're lookin' to expand. That place I work now—tail traders, shady ladies. You can find 'em or make 'em. Customers already lined up. Plenty of space, hardly nobody watchin'. Perfect setup, man. Hide a gin joint down in them tunnels. We'd be rollin' in the dough."

"I'm doin' just fine doin' what I can. Don't need no help. 'Specially from one as yappy as you."

He chuckled. "All right then. Just sayin'." He looked over Eddie's setup. "You want some help out here?"

"Don't need it. Why don't you take your leave? I've got work to finish."

The man stepped slowly backward, taking in the wide view of the place. "You doin' all right for yourself. Take care out here in the dark now. Just about anybody could sneak up on you, if they had a mind to."

He watched Carl slip out of sight, the darkness swallowed him quickly. Eddie made his way through the woods down to the water, crouched and waited, listened for the sound of the boat pushing off, and an oar hitting the water. Mostly certain the man had gone, he headed to the truck, felt around for his Lugar in the floor. He cursed his foolishness for not having it earlier and buckled on his gun belt. He finished up his work with his ears perked up, his lantern turned so low he could hardly see his hands in front of him.

Eddie made it back to the two-room board and batten shed on the edge of the prison farm right before sunup. He fried up a half-dozen eggs on the wood stove, wolfed them down on some white bread, and lay out across his bed with his clothes on. There was no time for sleep, but he had to get the kinks out of his back before standing guard duty for the next twelve hours.

Since his springtime homecoming, Eddie had gone through three jobs, two houses, and one wife. The coca cola bottling company, the brickworks, and the mill jobs hadn't worked out. His temper and the labor situation after the war didn't add up to any kind of job security. Then the prison farm job came along with the benefit of a roof over his head, and as he had found out, a few other perks too. Turned out that the job suited his temperament just right. Eddie ran one of the chain gang crews, one of the most productive to ever come from the place. What it amounted to was gangs of prison laborers, mostly poor Black men and women, locked up for being poor and Black, doing backbreaking labor, building roads under the most foul conditions from sunup to sundown, six days a week. With a rifle and a lash, he drove the half-starved, washed-out, worn down souls into the ground, mile after mile, and reveled in every minute of it.

Eddie stood with his shotgun at the ready while they loaded the work crew into the back of the old Packard truck. Five females, specially chosen in a gang of thirty he had picked that morning. While the others were clearing brush, crushing rocks, and spreading stones on the roadbed, they'd be keeping busy inside the old tumbledown shanty down the dirt road off Highway 22. He climbed up on the running board and gave the signal to pull out. After the dusty, five-mile ride to their work site, the truck glided off the road under a big oak and stopped. If he was lucky and he didn't have to chase anybody down or wear out his lash, Eddie hoped to spend most of the day kicked back in the truck, snoozing while his men kept the work moving. He tramped around to the back of the truck, and sorted the workers into brushers, crushers, spreaders, and hooks. He had four guards to handle the crew.

It was Frank's turn to run the bawdy house. He was eyeing the women when Eddie came up beside him.

"Frank, you know a fella named Carl Watson?"

Frank nodded his head. "He's a big mouth drunk. What you want with him?"

"I don't want nothin' with him. He dropped by to see me last night. Seemed to know all about my business."

Frank's eyes narrowed, and he turned his attention to the road crew.

"You been talkin' too much, man. That could cause all kinds of trouble. Especially for you, if you get where I'm headin'." Eddie put his hand on the man's shoulder and squeezed. "You need to shut the hell up. You understand?"

"He just wanted to get the lay of the land. Didn't know it was no secret. How you do any business if nobody knows where to find some action?"

"I do all right," Eddie said curtly.

"Carl works at the sanitarium."

"He told me."

"Says there's money to be made there."

"That's what he said. Just don't want no yapper gettin' mixed up in it. Too much talk is what brings a man down."

"You don't want to check it out? See for yourself?"

The problem was, Eddie did want to see for himself. He just wasn't sure that Carl Watson was a man to trust. Their conversation had made him curious.

"You know anything about him? Where's he from?"

"Nah. He showed up last spring. Seen him around in some joints. Started talkin'."

Eddie glanced over at the women waiting under the shade of the tree. They needed to get out of those prison dresses and into their workin' clothes before customers showed up.

"You think we could find him tonight?" Eddie asked.

"Sure 'nuf. He's a regular over at Bud's place."

Eddie decided. "See you there around ten. Get them girls ready now." Eddie waved toward the vacant house barely visible in the weed-filled yard.

He watched them walk away and told himself he was just checkin' out the situation. He didn't need a partner. Didn't want one. But the idea of making more green had some appeal.

He walked back to the truck, pulled the red flag out from under the driver's seat, and tied it around the headlamp. The signal alerted potential customers that the game was on and walk-ins were welcome. Fridays were always busy days.

It was almost midnight when Eddie passed over the bridge on Route 24, pulled his truck off the road, and headed through the woods. Bud's shanty boat was tied up about a quarter mile downriver. Bud had served up home brews and bootleg whiskey off the rickety raft for as long as Eddie could remember. The local boys got to know him well during their school days and now he was one of Eddie's best customers. The old man was sitting dockside, counting his till, his bluetick hound keeping a lookout.

"Hey, Bud. You had a good night?"

Bud looked up. "Not bad. You drinkin' or sellin'?"

"Meetin' some boys, havin' a beer," he said, handing over a quarter and heading across the plankway to the screen door. Beer barrel tables and wooden stools crowded the close-packed space. Low light lanterns wobbled from the ceiling. Eddie had waited until the crowd thinned out. He drew a beer into a river water washed mug and headed over to where he spotted Frank and Carl. He slid onto a stool and ignored Carl's shaky hand offered across the table.

"Frank. I heard your wife was lookin' for you," Eddie muttered, not taking his eyes off Carl.

Frank stood without hesitating, clapping his hand on Eddie's back as he moved past him. "See you later."

Carl fumbled around with his cigarettes, took his time lighting a smoke. Eddie sipped his beer. The place had mostly emptied out when he finally spoke.

"You ain't been around here long. Where you from?"

"Alabama, born and raised. Needed to get out a town. Heard there might be work here."

EDDIE

"You on the lam?"

"Might be some boys lookin' for me," he answered with a smirk.

Eddie nodded. Sipped some more.

"Sounded like you been in the business."

"Worked a barrel house, a couple of juice joints."

"You get soused like this pretty regular?"

Carl snorted. "You ask as many questions as a copper."

"Want to know what I'm gettin' mixed up with. Where you stay?"

Carl blew out smoke, rolled his eyes.

"Boardin' house over in Midway."

"So, what is it you know about the sanitarium that makes you think it's good for a setup?"

"Like I said. Thirsty people. Ladybirds. Tunnels. Hardly any law dogs. Money for jam, man."

The man was too slick for Eddie's tastes, but it sounded like he might be on to something.

"I want to get a look around."

Carl grinned. "The sanitarium? I'm workin' tomorrow. Come after dark."

Eddie stood, gave a quick nod.

Late Saturday night, Eddie sat in his truck under the pines near the river. Passing clouds cast moonlit shadows beneath the trees and scattered diamond sparkles across the water. He ran through his mind what he had seen that day that had brought him to this moment. With some patience and some planning, that place might be his ticket. He wouldn't be anybody's middleman anymore. He could cook. He could go directly to the customer. He could run some whores. And all the cash would come to him.

He pulled his Luger from under the seat, climbed out, snugged the gun into the front of his pants, and lit a cigarette. He walked down to the river and passed his light along the shoreline. Carl was coming in by boat, but it didn't look like he was there yet. His eyes got heavy while he waited, the night sounds gentling him to sleep. He startled awake in the dark and eased out of his chair. Eddie stepped soundlessly to a wide tree for cover and hoped the clouds would part long enough to let some light through so he could see what was coming. He didn't have to wait long. Carl's careless footfalls gave him away. Eddie slipped the gun out of the front of his pants and held it low by his side.

"Hey, man. Turn your torch on so I can see what I'm doin," Carl called.

Eddie picked up his flashlight and waved the beam out to find him.

"You start without me?" Carl called again.

"No. I waited. Wanted you to see it from start to finish."

Carl stumbled his way forward. "You got a stash I could wet my whistle?"

Eddie pulled a stoneware gallon jug from under the table and set it down. He put the copper mug next to it, removed the cork, and poured, all with one hand.

"That's mighty generous, my friend," Carl said as he stumbled up to the table.

Eddie pushed the cup across to him. He could smell the sweat and liquor stink rising up off the man.

"Ain't you gonna pour one for yourself?"

"I don't drink when I'm workin."

"That's probably a good thing. Keep your wits about 'cha." Carl picked up the mug. "Here's to partners."

Eddie nodded. Carl lifted the mug to his mouth and tilted his head back to slug it down.

Eddie brought his gun up fast and fired.

A five-day drencher put a damper on the roadwork. Stir crazy and feeling like a prisoner, Eddie shuffled into the cellblock Saturday morning for his shift. On rainy days he had to do day guard duty at the female building. He was desperate to get back out on the road where he could breathe. Walking through the holding area, he swore that if he was ever about to be locked up, he would put a bullet in his head and end it. A sullen-faced Frank stood behind the table in the guard room.

"Sorry I'm late," Eddie lied.

"You usually are on rainy days."

Eddie shrugged.

Frank kept his voice low. "Thought I might see you last night at Bud's."

"Nah. Had things to take care of. Not much for socializin'."

"Some boys was talkin'. Heard something 'bout Carl Watson." Frank's eyes never left Eddie's face.

"Yeah. What's that?"

"Some boys out fishin' yesterday mornin' found him floatin' 'bout half a mile from the bridge. Bullet through his throat. Skull bashed in. Looked like he'd been there awhile."

"That right?"

"Yep."

"Talker like him, ain't no wonder," Eddie offered, turning his back on Frank's steady gaze.

"You seen him this week?" Frank asked.

"Nope. You?"

Frank shook his head. "Last I saw him was downtown Saturday night. He was tellin' a bunch of boys he would bring 'em his first batch of hooch. Said he was gettin' into the business and headin' out to make his first run. Got a fist full of cash before he left."

"Maybe somebody robbed him."

"Could be."

Eddie turned back to face him and moved in closer to Frank so his size would impress the man. "That's what happens to them drunk yappers. They don't know when to shut up. Somebody takes care of it for 'em."

Frank stared at him for a few seconds, gave a quick nod. "Probably them boys from Alabama he was runnin' from caught up with him." He looked away, then picked up his mug from the table. "I need some joe. Want some?"

"Sure. Bring me a couple of them biscuits too." Eddie followed Frank to the door and watched him as he walked through the cellblock.

At the end of his shift, Eddie headed to the warden's office. The old man, the father of one of his classmates from school, was rising from his nap on the sofa when Eddie walked in.

"What can I do for you, son?" he asked, pulling up his suspenders.

"I been wonderin' if maybe I could try somethin' different. Maybe somethin' else instead of chain gang work."

"You got something in mind?"

"I heard you send building crews over to the sanitarium. I was thinkin' maybe I could give that a try. I did some work like that during the war. Liked it."

"Is that so? I reckon we could do that. Got a couple of things going on over there right now."

"I would really appreciate that, sir. I need to branch out a little bit, relieve the boredom."

"I understand that, son." He walked over to Eddie, put his hand on his shoulder. "You're a hard worker. We'll put you on the crew come Monday. You know your way around over there?"

Eddie smiled. "Some. I'm sure I'll figure things out pretty quick."

Effie

MARCH, 1923

13

On the day after Christmas when Effie returned to the sanitarium, the world she had grown accustomed to there had turned upside down. Another woman was dead. Roselyn, Fern's antagonist, had been found on the porch of Fern's cottage no less. Both of Fern's roommates had been discharged. From what Effie could gather from the gossip on the ward, Fern had been involved in a confrontation with the dead woman in the cafeteria and, on more than one occasion, numerous people had overheard threats they had lobbed at each other, an ongoing feud, months in the making. There was some speculation that Fern had done the murder and run off. Those that knew her didn't buy that. For the better part of two weeks, guards with dogs roamed the grounds at night. Effie first thought they were there to protect against another attack but quickly realized they were looking for a suspect. A suspect that the authorities assumed was Fern. Though she was exhausted, Effie had barely slept those first few weeks. The bleak, cold days hardened into colder, darker nights. Until finally, a book and a pear gave her hope that somehow the mystery of what had happened could be unraveled, the guilty parties would be caught and the wrongly accused freed from the accusation. Just inside the frame of her door, a red-and-green colored pear sat atop a hymnal. Nothing more. The meaning crystal clear. Fern was waiting for her in the old colored chapel. Relieved that Fern was okay but concerned for her safety, Effie convinced her to seek refuge until they could figure out what to do next. Fern objected that she had nowhere to go. Effie convinced her she did and after it was arranged, she was comforted by the knowledge that Fern was safe.

Effie stood at William's elbow, watching as he measured dose after dose of brewer's yeast into glass medicine cups.

"The precise quantity of yeast must be used to treat every patient or our results will be meaningless. If others can't replicate our findings, then our work is all for naught," he explained for what seemed like the tenth time.

She nodded, thinking she hadn't fully realized how high-strung he was, "Would you like me to measure?"

"I prefer to do that myself for now. Just to be sure," he responded matter-of-factly.

Effie stepped back and crossed her arms, thinking, *he's fussy, more than anything.* "I'm a trained medical professional. I understand the necessity of precision, Doctor."

William glanced at Effie. "Yes. Of course. I know that. It's just that we've spent so much time looking for a pellagra preventative. I'm always nervous when we start a new protocol. This is different from the work we've been doing. Until now it was all about the protein—more eggs, more milk, more meat. With the yeast, a new level of control in administering the treatment is necessary."

"Well, it certainly makes more sense for me to do this part in the ward. Now we'll have to take these cups to the infirmary. They could spill or get broken. Why don't you let me show you that I know what to do, so you'll feel more comfortable?"

Reluctantly, William handed the measuring spoon to Effie. He watched intently as she demonstrated the exactness of her skills several times over. "Well, did I pass the test?" she asked with a note of sarcasm, methodically returning all of the measured doses of yeast to the container from which he had drawn them.

"And there's the measuring of the milk too. Exactly eight ounces. All of the test subjects must be dosed three times each day. You'll have to watch them drink the entire contents of the glass before you indicate on the chart that the yeast was administered. Do you think that you can handle that?"

"I've been responsible for the care and medicating of fifty women in my ward every day for the past nine months, William. I think I can handle this."

"All the same, for the first few days I'll be there as well." Then noting her expression added, "Just to observe, Effie. That's all I'll do. I'll watch you. And help if you need it." He stopped talking but continued nodding.

Effie was somewhat charmed by the doctor's nervousness around her. It was a new development. She wasn't quite sure what brought it about, but it made her strangely more comfortable in his presence.

"You'll just watch. I'll hold you to that, Doctor."

"I'm sorry. It's just that Dr. Goldberger believes this might be the answer this time. The brewer's yeast might be the cure and the preventative. This could be the breakthrough we've been working for all these years."

Effie smiled as he rambled. "I understand. And I won't let you or Dr. Goldberger down. Far be it from me to disappoint the Public Health Service. I'm hoping for the best outcome, too, William."

"I'll have Albert bring everything over on Monday morning. Your shift begins at five, right? And breakfast is the first order of business?"

"Breakfast is at seven. And Rudy and George usually deliver to us."

"Rudy went home. George can't work just now. I've only got Albert Monday morning. We'll be there at six? If that's okay with you?" William asked more than told.

"Why is Albert a patient here?" Effie asked.

"Victim of the Great War, I think. Shell shock when he first came back. Depression, alcoholism. He couldn't hold a job long. Got thrown in jail a time or two. He's been declared cured and sent home twice, but he came back both times."

"There are so many sorrowful stories."

"It's the nature of the place, Effie."

"Let me grab my jacket and I'll walk you," William said before he disappeared into the back. This was their new Saturday night routine. Saturday was Effie's off duty day from nursing, but it had become her research kitchen day instead. She and William worked through the afternoon, had supper together in the lab, and worked a couple more hours before calling it quits. Then he walked her back to her room. She enjoyed the work and believed she was doing something that had already made a difference in the lives of the women on her ward. But she had to admit, she enjoyed the walk more and more. It was the one time they put aside their professional relationship and talked about things other than the research or the problems of the sanitarium. They discussed everything—books, music, Atlanta, William's three sisters, Effie's brother. Everything except what occupied most of Effie's thoughts. Fern and their fears about someone doing harm to the women of the sanitarium. Even now, walking with William on an early spring evening, the air still warm from the daytime heat, a cooling breeze rippling through it, Effie looked carefully under the low hanging branches of every tree they passed. In all the places where she had been surprised by Fern, or overtaken by her on her path from the infirmary to her room, Effie looked expectantly, wondering when and where Fern might materialize or startle her with a touch on the shoulder. Or when she was overcome by a more sinister feeling, she kept her guard up and plotted what she might do if someone attacked her. She had no idea how she might react. She had never thought of herself as particularly brave. She had certainly never been in a perilous situation with her own safety in question. Once again tonight, all was quiet.

"Thank you, William," Effie offered at the entrance to her building. "I'll see you Monday morning then."

He watched until she disappeared inside.

Effie got off to an early start on Monday morning. By 4:30, she was on the ward at the front desk, looking through the new lab journal she had carefully prepared the day before. Already, with the better-quality food they were all getting, her women were healthier than they had been since she arrived last June. Few were experiencing pellagra outbreaks, and when they did, they weren't as debilitating as before. Several had put on a little healthy weight. Especially Bertie. She was the picture of health. Her eyes alert, her energy level improved, and she seemed stronger emotionally. Effie hoped Bertie would continue to progress through the spring when pellagra usually made a comeback. Of course, good food could not save those suffering from cancer or yellow fever or tuberculosis, but at least her women weren't tormented by hunger. Regardless of the outcome of the yeast experiment, that she was able to make their lives better in that one, not insignificant way gave her a sense of triumph in a place mostly known for despair. She knew she had William to thank for agreeing to add her ward to his nutrition experiments. And just as important, Norris and her father to thank for funding the extension of the nutritional therapy so that all the women on her ward could be included. But she took some satisfaction that she had been the conduit between William's work, her women, and her family's money that made their better health possible. She mattered. She wanted to hold on to that thought.

At five, she roused Bertie and Cora. Rising from her bed, Cora scratched her head and yawned as she shambled toward the washroom. Bertie turned back her covers to air her bed, changed into her work dress and apron, and walked the ward to do a first well check on the patients.

"You said something new is startin' up today, Miss Effie?' Bertie asked.

"Yes. We have to mix a special drink for the pellagra patients. I'll take care of that part, and you can help me give 'em out. We have to watch 'em drink it so we can write down that they actually did. I included you in the count. You're getting stronger every day. The new drink might help even more. You haven't had an outbreak in months. Dr. Tanner will be here soon to see how we do this morning," she said, looking up from her work.

"Uh huh, I 'spect he will be," Bertie responded all sassy, putting her hands on her hips.

"What do you mean by that, Bertie?"

She nodded and raised her eyebrow. "He comes 'round here to watch you. That's what I'm sayin'."

Effie rolled her eyes. "He's fussy about his work. Wants to make sure we're following directions is all."

"You say so," Bertie answered. "I better go clean up a little before he gets here," she sassed again. "I know I'm lookin' good. It might be me he's watchin'."

Effie watched Bertie walk away and rolled her eyes again.

"Cora, let's get ready for breakfast," she directed when the still yawning and scratching woman reappeared.

"Let me throw my clothes on first."

A short time later a knock on the ward doors signaled the arrival of breakfast. Effie unlocked them, and Albert, William's assistant, rolled in a large food service cart. William followed close behind with another one.

"Right over here, Albert," Effie ordered. "I don't think you've been on my ward before."

The man kept his head down, his cap pulled low, as he placed the cart where directed.

"You can hand those to my helpers," she told him, indicating the food trays.

"Not yet," William corrected. "Let's take care of the milk first. It should be the first thing so they don't fill up on food and can't take all the milk."

Effie nodded and started assembling the necessary items.

When the first glasses were ready, Effie and Bertie pushed the drink cart down the row of beds where the women waited for their breakfasts.

Distracted by the task and nervous about William watching every move, Effie had not noticed Cora standing at the far end beyond the beds, unmoving and staring at the men.

"Cora, we've got to get these out to everyone, and when they've finished drinking, please pick up the empties and bring their food trays."

Cora didn't acknowledge anything Effie had said.

"Cora," Effie said again loudly, "we got work to do."

Cora raised an arm and pointed. "It's that creeper," she whispered.

Effie turned and looked where Cora was pointing. Bertie, now at Cora's side, looked, too, and then quickly stepped in front of Cora, reached out, and lowered the other woman's arm. The two of them nodded at each other.

Cora said in a low voice, "It's him, ain't it?"

Without turning to look again, Bertie nodded.

"What is it?" Effie asked.

"It's that creeper. That one that took Pearl. He had that patch on his eye, I remember," Cora said, leaning to look past Bertie for another peek at the man.

Effie turned to Bertie, questioning with her look.

Bertie nodded. "I think it's him, Miss Effie. I think he was one of them men that night."

Effie smoothed her apron, turned and walked back toward the table where William was preparing the rest of the milk.

With her eyes on Albert, she said, "Dr. Tanner, I think we can handle things from here. We won't need Albert to help with the trays. Bertie and Cora can manage."

William looked up and noted the intent look on Effie's face. "Albert, why don't you head on back to the kitchen."

Albert gave a quick nod and without a word or a glance hurriedly headed for the door.

"Is something wrong?" William asked her.

"Might be," she answered. "We'll talk about it later."

She gathered up her lab book and walked back to check on her patients.

With the yeast drink administered and the appropriate notes recorded and verified, breakfast trays were passed out, and then Effie saw William to the door.

"That went well. You really don't need me to check up on you," he admitted.

"Can you send somebody else from now on?" Effie asked. "I don't want Albert in my ward again."

"Yes. But I want to know what's going on. Is there something about Albert I should know?"

"I don't want to accuse someone without more evidence, but both Bertie and Cora think he was one of the men that took a patient from our ward last fall. I told you about her, remember? Pearl?"

He nodded slowly, remembering the gruesome details. "She was found later, murdered, you said, but identified as a suicide."

William pursed his lips, considering the gravity of the charge. "This is probably something I should look into, Effie. That's quite disturbing." He turned to go. "I'll see you later."

"I'm not sure when that will be. Maybe later in the week. I'm heading into town on Saturday to visit my friend Sallie Davis."

He nodded.

"William. I want you to know how much I appreciate you doing what you're doing for all of us." She looked over her shoulder, indicating the women of her ward. "It really makes a difference in their lives, no matter the outcome of the protocol. That someone cares enough to help. That means a lot."

He smiled. "Thank you, Effie. You take care of yourself." He lingered a moment, and added, "I don't want you to come back to the kitchen until I find out what I need to about Albert." He nodded one last time, then headed through the doors.

Effie wouldn't have admitted it to William, but the simple addition of the yeast milk protocol to her workload took more time than she had anticipated. Fitting it in three times a day, the measuring, the mixing, the monitoring and the recording of information, pushed her to her limits. She found herself coming earlier and staying late. By Thursday afternoon, she was exhausted and wondering how long the experiment might take.

After the noontime meal, the weather had taken such a pleasant turn, that she had Cora open up the porch door and let the women out to enjoy some fresh air. She was recording data in her logbook when a student nurse appeared at her desk. Effie looked up, surprised to see the young woman in her ward.

"May I help you with something?" Effie asked.

The nurse looked around, her blue eyes transfixed by the mostly empty room.

"I have a message for the nurse." She looked down at the slip of paper she held. "Effie Herndon."

"I'm Effie Herndon."

"You're wanted at the main office. I'm supposed to take over for you while you're gone." She looked around the mostly empty room. "I thought there were a lot of patients here."

"Out on the porch, just through those doors," Effie explained.

"They sent me here to get you and stay until you get back."

"Bertie and Cora are on the porch. They're my aides. They'll help you with anything you need. There's nothing pressing right now. My bed patients are sleeping. No one is in any kind of crisis," Effie instructed. "Will you be all right here?"

The girl turned. "I suppose sick women are sick women no matter what color they are."

Effie replied, "I would imagine that's so." She turned to go but couldn't resist saying while she took off her apron, "I don't think they'll hold it against you. That you're white. I think you'll be okay. I'll be back as soon as I can."

Effie hadn't been in the administrative building since her arrival in June. As she pushed the door open, her hands trembled. A uniformed police officer rose from the wooden bench just outside the front office and stood in her path. She held her breath and came to a stop, then hesitantly raised her eyes to meet his.

"Miss Herndon?"

"I'm Effie Herndon."

He started to offer his hand, but thought better of it and pulled it back.

"I'm Sheriff Guthrie. Don't be scared. I'm not really here on official business. I wanted to talk with you for a minute, if that's okay. I knew I had to wear my uniform to get past those gatekeepers in there." He cut his eyes over toward the offices. "I think we have a friend who might be in some trouble."

Effie had never had a conversation with a police officer before, much less a sheriff. She wasn't sure what to say or do.

"I'm not here to cause you any problems. I just want to talk with you. Outside. Could you give me a few minutes of your time?"

Effie nodded and headed for the door, keeping her eyes on the tall man beside her. He wasn't frightening looking. In fact, his face was kind. It was the uniform that made her nervous.

"How about over there on that bench. It's not too chilly for you, is it?" he asked.

Effie hadn't found her voice yet.

"Lizbeth Harris told me you and Fern Walker were acquainted. She said you and Fern were friends. Would you describe it that way, Miss Herndon?"

Effie finally found the courage to speak. "I would say we are."

"I don't suppose you would mind me asking, not in an official capacity, but just because I'm worried about her, when you might have seen Fern last?"

Effie realized he was almost as nervous as she was, though she wasn't sure what was behind it.

"It's been a while," Effie answered vaguely.

"Could you be a little more specific about that?"

Effie shook her head and looked around.

"I don't know how much you know about Fern, but if you count her as a friend, I'm gonna guess you don't believe that she was somehow involved in what happened here on Christmas."

Effie shook her head again. "No, sir, I don't."

"Let me tell you a few things that might help you understand why I'm here. Then maybe we can talk."

Effie turned her attention to him. "All right."

"I've known Fern since she was a baby. I was a friend of her mama's, Nora. My sister, Louella, was a nurse here back then. She and Miss Nora were good friends. She took care of Fern a lot when she was a baby. And then after Fern's mama died, I wanted her to come live with me and my family but my wife, she wouldn't have it. So, Fern stayed here," he said, looking around. "On a day like this, outside on a bench in the sunshine, it don't seem like such a bad place. But I reckon you and me know different."

Still leery, Effie listened, though she was softening toward him as he told the tale.

"Things went bad for my sister here. She got mixed up with some stuff. A doctor. Nothing I could do about it, even from the sheriff's office. And those things that happened to Fern. She was just a child really. It was a lot to sort out."

"What things do you mean?" Effie asked, testing him.

"I thought she might have told you about being attacked a couple of years back. It was bad. Almost lost her. No matter what this place looks like on a good day, ain't enough people or money to take care of all that needs taking care of. You've been here awhile now. You know what's what."

"So, what is it you want with Fern, Sheriff?" Effie asked.

"I'm not sure what she got caught up in, but I know one thing. Ain't no way she killed that woman," he answered.

"No. Fern didn't do that."

He sighed, relieved that the young, frightened nurse beside him had let down her guard enough to say a few words.

"It's been a long time since I've seen Fern or even talked to her. But I'm worried about her," he confessed. "I'm worried that even though it looks like she's gone, she's still here somewhere, hidin' out. Trying to put two and two together. Find the ones that did this. That's what she would do."

He paused for a moment and then asked, "Do I need to be worried about that, Miss Herndon? That's what I want to know about Fern."

Effie had to decide how far to go. She wasn't sure how much to trust this man she just met. He seemed sincere. He knew some of Fern's story. He said he cared about her. But she couldn't risk everything.

"There's more to it than just this most recent murder. Are you aware of that, Mr. Guthrie?"

He nodded. "This is a state-run facility. You've got your own police precinct right here on the grounds. State government controls everything that happens here; they decide if the local police are called in or not. I know that on Christmas night the only reason we got the call was because Lizbeth Harris's daddy is Senator William Harris. She called him and he called us. He sent us here to get her. That dead girl on the porch, that was just what we found when we got here. The governor was fit to be tied. He wanted his boys to handle it. That helps keep what happens out here out of the public eye."

"That explains a lot. We hadn't been able to put that together."

"You mean you and Fern? The two of you couldn't put it together?"

"That's right. She said she'd never seen so many policemen show up here before. No matter what happened, no matter how bad it was, nobody ever came to help."

"So, you have seen Fern."

Effie had to be careful, but she wanted to take it one step further.

"We both know there's really another reason you don't know anything about those other women, Sheriff. The ones being murdered. It's because they were colored. Isn't that right?" Effie said what she couldn't hold back. "And Roselyn, the girl that was killed on Christmas night? She was white but nobody cared about her. She was just a prostitute that ended up here because nobody knew what to do with her. Family didn't want her. Jail didn't want her. So, this is where she ended up and then she ended up murdered."

The truth spoken aloud put a damper on their conversation, until Sheriff Guthrie broke the silence.

"If you have a way to get a message to Fern for me, pass this along. As far as I'm concerned, she's not a suspect in this case. There is no case. The state wants it to end here. There won't be any investigation. Senator Harris got what he wanted. He moved his daughter to another facility outside of Georgia but far enough from Washington that he won't have to explain any embarrassing details about his family to his high and mighty friends."

"And what do you think a message like that would do to stop Fern? She was trying to figure out why women have been disappearing around here, not to mention that sometimes there was evidence they were murdered. That was before what happened with Roselyn. Fern was obsessed with it. She was looking through old records, staking out the construction sites, looking for clues."

He dropped his elbows to his knees, clasped his hands together, and slowly shook his head. "I was afraid of that."

After another awkward silence, he rose. "If you see her, try to convince her to stay away from here. There's nothing but heartache for her if she stays. And worse even."

Effie stood and shielded her eyes with her hand to block the sun and better look him in the eye. "I'll try to convince her of that, Sheriff. I don't know if I'll be able to, though."

He reached in his shirt pocket and pulled out a small piece of paper. "If you should need me for any reason, get a message to Ray Barnes in the precinct office. He'll let me know. And when you see Fern, tell her James Robert's still lookin' out for her, like he told her mama he would."

He walked away, and as Effie watched him go, she thought he looked sadder somehow—his shoulders slumped, his head hanging down—than when she had first seen him.

On Saturday morning, Effie caught the first train into Milledgeville. As she neared Sallie's house, she saw the teacher had made the most of an exceptionally sunny morning and was already on her knees in her front flower bed hard at work.

"What're you planting?" she asked, coming into the yard.

"Some black-eyed-Susans and cornflowers," Sallie answered without looking up. "You're mighty early this morning."

"And so are you. I thought you'd be taking it easy on a Saturday," Effie teased.

"I've been so cold all winter, I took an oath to soak in every minute of sunshine I could this spring. I like a colorful yard, so here I am. Coffee's hot. Cinnamon rolls 'bout ready."

"That's the best news I've heard," Effie said, heading for the door.

The cinnamon and coffee laced air left Effie lightheaded as she walked toward the kitchen, where the cinnamon rolls were sitting on top of the stove. Effie bent down to inhale the aroma.

"Don't you lick my cinnamon rolls. They're the best ones yet," Fern said from outside the kitchen screen door.

Effie stuck her finger in the creamy vanilla topping yet to be applied to the still warm buns.

"So, more than just biology and algebra, she's teaching you up in the kitchen?" she asked before putting her finger in her mouth.

Fern opened the door, removing her hat and gardening gloves as she walked across the room. "Oh yes. I'm becoming quite the cook." She poured a cup of coffee, handed it to Effie and refilled her own. She topped the cinnamon rolls and brought the plate to the table. "See. Perfection, if I do say so myself."

Fern sat down across from Effie, and they gave in to their craving, devouring half the plate before exchanging another word.

"I had a visitor this week," Effie began.

Fern raised her eyebrows. "Oh?"

"He sent his regards to you. Said to tell you that James Robert's still looking out for you."

Fern's mouth dropped open. "I wasn't sure he was still around. Why did he come see you? What did you tell him?" she asked, alarm rising in her voice and on her face.

"It was kind of a strange encounter. And he's more than just around. He's the Baldwin County Sheriff. And he wants you to get away from here. Not here. He doesn't know you're here," she explained, motioning to the kitchen. "He doesn't want you to hang around the sanitarium. He thinks it's dangerous."

"He's the sheriff and he thinks it's dangerous? Then why doesn't he do something about it?"

"He said he can't. Seems that powerful people keep the local police from having anything to do with what goes on at the sanitarium. Speaking of that. Did you know that Lizbeth's father is a US Senator?"

Fern closed her eyes, confounded by all that Effie had said. "Seems like I remember something about that. What does that have to do with anything?"

"That's the reason the police were called on Christmas when everything happened with Roselyn. They weren't there for Roselyn, really, or for you. They came to get Lizbeth out of there. She called her father. Raised the alarm."

Fern sat back in her chair and took a long pull of her coffee.

"And there's more," Effie said, reaching for another roll.

"You've had a busy week," Fern taunted.

"I have actually. But besides that. A man, a patient at the sanitarium who works with William Tanner, came to the ward this week. When Cora saw him, she thought she recognized him. Bertie too. You won't believe this. They both said he was one of the men who took Pearl that night."

"Who is he? He works with Tanner?" Fern tried to sort it all out.

"Albert somebody. I don't know his last name. I've seen him several times. He's definitely a creeper, just like Cora said."

"What did you do?" Fern asked.

"I told William what Cora and Bertie said. He seemed upset. Said he was going to look into it. Whatever that means."

"Do you think he will? Do anything about it?"

"He said he would. He asked me not to come back to the kitchen lab until he had a chance to check him out. I don't know. I trust William. He seemed genuinely concerned."

"What about that guy with Roselyn that night, that construction worker, Eddie, did you say anything about him to James Robert? Roselyn was pretty sure he was dead."

"No, I couldn't remember his name. I wasn't sure how much to tell him. I wanted to talk with you first. He really didn't know much about what goes on there. I'm not sure he even knew about any of those women that have been murdered but reported as suicides."

"He wouldn't. You remember what Mr. Ingram said. He gets told what to write down about deaths at the sanitarium. There's no record of murders being committed."

The front door opened and closed. Sallie walked in, took off her hat and gloves, and looked at the nearly empty plate between them.

"Well, I see you've mastered the cinnamon roll," she said as she headed down the hallway. "I want to wash up, and I hope at least two of those buns with lots of frostin' will be sitting on a plate waiting for me when I get back."

"I'll put on a fresh pot of coffee," Fern offered and told Effie, "I like how feisty she is."

"That's funny. That's just what she says about you," Effie answered.

Fern

MARCH, 1923

14

"You can't remember anything about the person who attacked you in the tunnel?" Effie asked.

"It happened so quick. All I can remember is hands wrapped around a big stone and it coming down too fast for me to move," Fern closed her eyes and replayed the scene again. "I didn't see a face. It was dark, and it hurt like hell. Even now, some of what happened is fuzzy. I keep trying to pull it together."

It was Saturday, nearing sundown. After an early supper, Sallie had left to attend a church meeting to prepare for upcoming Easter services. Fern and Effie had spread a quilt on a patch of green grass near the vegetable garden Fern had been working hard to put in, according to Sallie's instructions. They lounged beside the young sprouts and the backyard azaleas in a sea of pink, purple, and red. Bumble bees buzzed overhead, chickadees absorbed by the process of nest building, darted to and fro—everything tinted a pale raspberry in the fading light.

"I think you had a concussion from that blow," Effie said in her nurse voice. "I just wish you had gotten a glimpse of his face. Then we might know if it was Albert or not."

"I want to know if Eddie, that man with Roselyn, was ever found," Fern added.

"What about your friend the sheriff? Do you think he's trustworthy? Could we ask him what he knows about Eddie? Should I tell him our suspicions about Albert?" She fired off all the questions she'd been holding inside.

"I don't have any reason not to trust him. At least I don't think so. James Robert and Louella kind of disappeared. I hadn't thought about them in a while," Fern replied, feeling suddenly uneasy, like she had forgotten something about them that deserved more careful consideration.

"Do you want to see him? Talk to him yourself?"

Fern thought about that possibility for a moment. "I don't know. I want to think about it some more before I make up my mind."

"For what's it's worth, I got the impression that he really does care about you."

"Did he say anything about Louella?"

"He mentioned something about her getting into trouble. He didn't explain what it was, but it seemed like it was something that he couldn't really do anything about."

Fern searched for snippets that might help her put it together. "I can't quite remember when I saw either of them last."

A pair of chipmunks scampered across the stepping-stone path through the backyard and disappeared beneath the azaleas.

"So how is it, being here with Sallie?" Effie asked.

Fern smiled. "It's comfortable. I know that sounds crazy, considering all the circumstances. I never lived anywhere with a kitchen where I could cook, or a garden I could sit in like this."

"I don't think it's the kitchen or the yard that makes it feel that way," Effie offered, "I think it's Sallie."

"Thanks for bringing me here. And I think it's a pretty good cover. I doubt anyone would come looking for me. I have to admit I wasn't sure what to expect. I was afraid you twisted her arm, but I think she kind of likes it."

"She didn't even hesitate when I asked her to take you in."

"She keeps me busy. Gives me schoolwork every day. She's trying to make up for all the years of schoolin' I've missed."

"Are you finding it hard to stay here at the house all the time?" Effie asked, attempting to cover her interest in finding out if Fern had been up to her old tricks, donning disguises and sneaking around to see what was going on.

"I don't want to call any attention to my being here and make problems for Sallie," Fern answered, avoiding a straight answer.

"So, you haven't been back to the sanitarium?"

Fern didn't hesitate. "Did I mention that Sallie and I have been reading the Constitution together? I asked her if we could take a break from the Bible, and that's what she came up with." She turned to Effie. "You ever read it?"

Effie narrowed her eyes. "What are you getting at?"

"It says in the Constitution that a person doesn't have to give witness against herself."

"So, I'm guessing that means you have been there. Fern, that could be dangerous, not just for Sallie but for you too."

"From what you told me James Robert said about there not being any investigation into Roselyn's death, I think there's even more reason than ever for me to try to find out what happened. Nobody else cares enough to do anything."

"You might not have seen the person that attacked you, but he certainly saw you. Whoever killed Roselyn brought her to your front porch. What kind of a message do you think that was? That should be reason enough for you to stay away from there."

"I know how to be invisible," Fern answered defiantly.

Effie shook her head. "Don't think you're the only one with those skills. That murderer knew right where you lived. He put her on your porch in broad daylight. I'd say he's invisible too."

"Have you seen me at the sanitarium?" Fern asked.

"No. But I look for you almost every day."

"I've seen you. And I can tell you that for sure I'll be getting a better look at that man Albert just as soon as I can." Fern stood up. "I want another piece of that pound cake Sallie made. You want some?"

Effie watched Fern disappear through the back door.

Effie left Sunday morning to make it back in time for her afternoon shift. With Sallie at church all day, Fern worked in the backyard garden. Digging in the dirt had a calming effect. Outside in the sunshine, unburdened by the weight of living at the sanitarium, reminded her of the days she had spent with Tom Ennis. In the few moments when she let her guard down, her mind always returned to that time. Being in Milledgeville left Fern to wonder if she might see Tom's family. Or at least see where he grew up. She craved a connection to him that had nothing to do with the sanitarium. He had talked about his family's big, happy house and the wide yard he had played in as a boy. The fishpond hidden by the trees, Sunday dinners after church, and campfires on summer nights, his father walking through the front door, tired from work. All unfamiliar to Fern. He told her about a beautiful staircase that was magical every day and especially so when adorned with garlands for Christmas. She wanted to see it for herself.

Over the past few months, she had learned more about Milledgeville from Sallie—it's proud, but in many ways, unsavory history. Sallie knew nothing about her connection to the Ennis family and so Fern had no problem asking if she knew of them and if they might still live in Milledgeville.

While Fern worked the garden, she worked out a plan. Starting today she vowed to be on the lookout even more than usual. She felt safe at Sallie's. It was certainly better than hiding out in the woods near the sanitarium, as she had been forced to do for the first weeks after Roselyn's murder, but she wasn't about to hole up there and do nothing. She wanted to find out who killed Roselyn, maybe killed Pearl and the others, and if she was honest about it, had tried to kill her too. Maybe she would stay away from the sanitarium for a while, but nobody had said anything about staying out of Milledgeville. She wanted to find out what James Robert was up to these days. Maybe even track down Louella and find out more about things Fern was having a hard time putting together. And with Tom on her mind and stuck there until she did something about it, she decided that was where she was headed first, the Ennis place.

Early Monday morning, Fern sorted through the cast-off clothes Sallie had brought home from the church collection box to find something suitable to wear. Sallie had left for school before daybreak. A little rattled by things Effie had said during her visit, Fern couldn't stop asking herself. Was she a target? Was she a suspect? Was she being watched? Not knowing who she might meet and where she would have to blend in, she decided to double dress. She pulled on a pair of high waisted wool tweed trousers and a button front shirt, added suspenders to keep the too loose pants in place, rolled on some knee-high socks, and slipped into an olive-green coverall, and turned the collar up to mask her distinctive hair. Back in December, Lizbeth had cut and styled it in a soft curl bob and she had asked Sallie to trim it even shorter. A pair of mahogany oxford walking shoes and a gray felt newsboy cap completed the look. Taking in the view of herself in the bathroom mirror, above the white porcelain pedestal sink, Fern thought she looked like any ordinary somebody headed off to work. For a few minutes she allowed herself to think about a life in the future where she might be one of those somebodies and just what kind of job she might be heading to on a Monday morning.

"Maybe," she uttered, adjusting the shoulder strap of the forest-green canvas Tornister rucksack she had found under the bed. Fern had been using it for a while now to carry the essentials wherever she went. Her knife, a flashlight, a box of matches, and some twine.

As she stepped out the back door, the fading darkness was giving way to what promised to be an exceptionally beautiful early spring day. The air was cool and crisp, and birds tucked into the blooming trees twittered and sang as Fern made her way from Clarke Street to Franklin. She headed south out of town as though on her way to the sanitarium, the roads familiar by now. She kept her head down and one hand in the deep pocket of the coveralls, whistling an old song she remembered from her childhood to keep her company. She figured on about two hours of walking time and wasn't wrong. Except for the occasional truck or another somebody off to work, she didn't meet anyone that showed any interest in her at all.

Fern had gotten enough details from Sallie to know that she should be on the lookout for an impressive cast-iron fence to recognize when she had reached her destination. She had no doubt she had arrived when she found herself walking alongside massive, ornately decorative posts and intricate scrollwork that fronted a magnificent Federal style mansion. The house was situated well off the road at the crest of a hill in the middle of a grove of pecans and magnolias. Fern paused at the gate to take it all in. She had walked the streets of Milledgeville lately, and had become accustomed to the grand old homes that graced its shaded streets, but this was something out of the ordinary. A long, wide staircase ascended to a two-story entrance portico, flanked by pairs of fluted Ionic columns. The pediment that extended beyond the roofline was topped by a fan ventilator. A balcony with an ornamented iron railing overlooked a double door entrance, framed by sidelights and a fanlight transom.

Peeling her eyes away from the grandeur of the house, Fern imagined Tom as a boy, running and tumbling across the front lawn. As she reached for the gate, she thought better of her attire and headed back to the edge of the wooded property. There, she took off the coverall and stuffed it in the rucksack, opting instead for the look that Sallie called "newly fashionable" for young ladies, pants and a button top. She cuffed the baggy trousers as she had seen Lizbeth do, removed the cap, and fluffed her hair, not sure what she was doing or why. She nestled her bag into the brush at the corner of the fence and checked to make sure it was out of sight. Back at the gate, she gathered her resolve, pushed it open, and walked with purpose across the wide grass covered lawn, sidestepping a child's wooden Oak Leaf pull wagon before she bounded up the stairway to the front door.

Giant sago palms in iron pots sat beside the entrance. A pillow-shaped floral arrangement with the words "At Rest" on a silk ribbon was hanging on the door, the flowers fresh and fragrant. Fern pondered the meaning, then reached out and wrapped her fingers around the doorknob, imagining how many times Tom might have done the same. She sucked in a lung full of air, blew it out gently, took her hand from the knob, and knocked. She became more aware of the quietness of the place as she waited. On the porch, rocking chairs were scattered about. Her eyes were drawn to a child-size rocker and a wooden toy next to it, that she gradually recalled was something Tom had once described. It was a large wooden ark, like the one from the story in the Bible about Noah and the flood. Its red-roof paint, cracked and peeling with age. She walked over to it, crouched down for a better look. Two sheep, two zebras, two peacocks, two camels, two giraffes, two bears, and countless others. She picked up the giraffes, smiling, remembering that they were Tom's favorites. The door behind her opened.

"Yes? Can I help you with something?" asked a young woman in a gray uniform dress that Fern recognized from the sanitarium.

Fern stood, still clutching the giraffes in her hands.

"Hello. I'm sorry. I was just looking at these. I heard a story about them once," Fern answered, putting the giraffes back where she had found them.

"Are you a friend of the family?" the timid nurse asked.

Fern hesitated, even though she had practiced what she might say in this moment. "Yes, actually, I was a friend of Tom's," she answered.

"The Ennises' son, Tom? He died of the influenza a few years back."

"Yes, that's right."

"I didn't know him. I've only been here for two weeks now, since Mrs. Ennis passed."

"Oh. I'm sorry to hear that. I didn't know she was ill," Fern elaborated her tale. "And Mr. Ennis, is he home?"

"Not just now. Should be, directly."

"Do you know when he might be back?" Fern asked, hatching a plan as she went along.

"He comes home for his noontime meal most days."

"Maybe I could wait to see him, then. That is, if it's all right with you."

The nurse bit her lip and looked out beyond the front gate. "I guess that would be all right," she answered, still standing in the doorway.

"Might I come in then?" Fern asked, moving to the door. "I'm Effie, by the way, Effie Herndon."

The nurse didn't offer a name, but turned so Fern could pass.

Entering the front hall, Fern's eyes traveled up the oval spiral staircase that hugged the eastern wall and curved toward the upper level of the house. Its beauty had not been exaggerated in the telling. The wide oak plank floors, the mahogany railings and spindles contrasted against the expansive white walls. It was magical, just as Tom had described.

"Could I maybe have a drink of water?" Fern asked, anxious to look around on her own.

"Of course, please make yourself comfortable in the front parlor," the girl directed, somewhat put out that she was expected to wait on the intruder.

As she walked through the entrance to the parlor, Fern was stuck by the sheer size of the space. The doorways were wide, the ceilings so high, she had to lean her head back to appreciate them. The parlor was flooded with light from the massive double windows on two sides of the room. And across the front hall was another matching room just as large and lovely. She wanted nothing more than to run up the staircase and find as many hidden treasures as she could, but before she got the chance, the young nurse returned with her water.

"Thank you," Fern said, taking it and gulping it down.

"So, you were a friend of Tom Ennis?"

Fern knew she needed to avoid too many questions and so answered quickly and redirected, "Yes, he and my brother were school chums. And you. You said you've only been here for two weeks, is that right?"

"Yes, when Mrs. Ennis passed. The nurse who tended them decided to leave, so I was brought over from the nurse's school."

"The one at the sanitarium?"

"Yes, that's right," she answered.

"Is someone else sick so that they need a nurse?" Fern asked, curious.

"No. They're well, thank goodness," she answered.

Fern nodded. "Well, I don't want to keep you from your work. I think I'll just come back another time to see Mr. Ennis," she said as she headed for the door.

After she stepped onto the front porch, Fern turned back for a last look up the staircase. A young boy, trailing a blanket, with his thumb in his mouth and one hand brushing against the wall to steady himself, was making his way down the steps.

"I'll be sure to tell him you came by," the nurse said as she closed the door.

Fern moved to the sidelight and watched as the nurse met the little boy on the stairs and took one of his hands to ensure his safety. Without spending much time to think about it, Fern knocked on the door.

When it opened, the nurse looked puzzled and suspicious.

"I'm sorry to bother you again, but I think I left my bag in the parlor," knowing full well that she hadn't.

Fern made a show of walking back through the lovely rooms and looking for her bag, her eyes more on the boy than the search. "Well, it isn't here. I don't know where I might have left it."

"I don't remember that you had a bag," the girl observed, still holding the hand of the child.

Fern crouched down in front of him and smiled.

"Hey. What's your name?" she asked. With his thumb still firmly lodged in his mouth, the little boy closed his eyes and slid between the folds of the girl's skirt.

"He's bashful," she answered.

"I didn't know the Ennises had another son," Fern prodded, standing.

As she passed through the door, the girl responded, "He's their grandson."

Just as Fern turned to ask more, the door shut and silenced her.

She stood there for as long as she dared, then headed across the yard to her bag, pulled the coverall back on and adjusted the cap on her head. With her eyes fastened on the grand house, but not quite seeing it, she turned toward town.

Due to some determined walking, Fern made it back in half the time. Coming up on Main Street, she stopped to ask for directions to the sheriff's office. After she found it, she sat down on a bench across the street and waited. It was midafternoon and she knew it was best not to go to Sallie's until she could slip down Clarke Street unnoticed in the darkness. She was glad for the wait. She needed some time to think. What she needed to think about was James Robert and Louella. Though that wasn't necessarily what flooded her mind. She needed to put that other thought aside, that wild and crazy one she had looking through the sidelight at that little dark-haired, blue-eyed boy that looked exactly like Tom Ennis. She had to chase that nonsense right out of her head and lock it in a box that when she was brave enough, she might open.

Sitting on that bench on this beautiful spring day, Fern realized she really knew nothing about who she was. She didn't know her own father, or if her mother's name was Walker before she married him or after. She couldn't even be sure they were married, come to think of it. And she didn't know where her mother had lived before she lived at the sanitarium. The longer Fern sat there, the more she realized she didn't know much. And more than that, she didn't think there was anyone else who knew any of it either. If there were records on her mother at the sanitarium, she had never found them. But her search had been cut short by all that happened. While she lived at the sanitarium with other people who were without their families, none of that had really mattered. They were just who they were. People who had been put in an institution for any kind of reason and what they did there most was try to survive. They lived their lives from day to day without too much thought about what happened before or what might happen next.

Now, for the first time in her life, living on the outside, Fern wanted to know. She wanted to know about everything. And she thought that sitting on that bench waiting for James Robert was the best place to start.

A Chevrolet police truck pulled up in front of the sheriff's office. An officer in uniform that Fern recognized immediately as James Robert with about twenty extra pounds around his middle, climbed out of the driver's seat. He took off his hat and looked in both directions before heading inside. About ten minutes had passed when he came out and put his hat back on his head. He looked straight across the street to where Fern was sitting on the bench. He stood there for a moment, shoved his hands in his pockets, and walked across to meet her.

"I'm taking my lunch break. You hungry?" he asked, like he had seen her just yesterday.

"It's late for lunch, but I could eat something," she answered in the same everyday sort of way.

He pointed at a corner diner, and they walked in silence to the front door. Before James Robert could open it, Fern stepped in front, walked in ahead of him, and sat down in a booth in the back corner.

"The usual, Sheriff?" the counter cook asked.

"Make it two," James Robert answered as he slid into the booth across from Fern.

As soon as he sat down, a waitress in a tight-fitting blue-and-white checked dress and white apron—her blond hair piled high on her head—put two ice-filled Coca-Colas on the table in front of them.

"Egg sandwiches will be right up," she said to him with a wink.

"Thanks, Wanda," James Robert answered, smiling.

After she had walked away, James Robert folded his hands on the table.

"I've been looking for you, Fern."

"I heard that, James Robert."

"Tell me you're not still hanging around that nuthouse. That's no place for you."

"What's it to you where I am or what I do? I haven't seen you in years," she answered with more venom than she knew she felt.

She could see him trying to put together an explanation.

"I can't answer to that. And I feel guilty about the bad that's happened to you."

She cut him off. "And how do you know anything about what's happened to me? I'm doin' just fine."

"You know I wanted to take you into my family when your mama was sick. My wife, she didn't like that idea. Somehow she got it in her head that you might be my daughter."

Fern was dumbstruck. Her eyes asked him to answer to that charge.

"I'm not, Fern. I'm not your daddy. Your mama was pregnant with you when she was brought to the asylum. You know that. She told you about Harry. I remember when she did," he said, confused by the look on Fern's face.

"You're right. I do know that." Fern shook her head, then brought a hand to her forehead and held it there. "Things that happened in December. You know about that, right?"

He nodded.

"Sometimes I just can't remember. Things I know or used to know. They just aren't there anymore," Fern admitted.

"Lizbeth Harris told me about what shape you were in. That head injury you had. With that and what you went through, sometimes it takes some time to get over. You oughta be all right after a while," he tried to comfort her.

"So now you're the nurse instead of Louella? Is she the sheriff?"

"I'm sorry about everything, Fern," he answered, and she could tell he meant it.

She sat back and held on to the edge of the table, took in some deep breaths to get a hold of herself.

Wanda put their plates on the table and snuck in a quick once over of the pretty young woman James Robert was having some intense conversation with. "Ya'll need a refill on those Co-Colas?"

"We're fine, Wanda. Thanks."

The waitress walked away with a trailing look at the two of them.

"No, I'm sorry," Fern answered, coming back to herself. "This is not what I meant to say to you and not how I meant to act. I'm not mad at you. Not really."

"You're doing a pretty good imitation of it then," he said and got the first smile from her he had seen.

He picked up his egg sandwich and took a big bite.

Fern watched how much he was enjoying it and followed his lead. For a minute they ate and sipped their Cokes. Looking at each other a time or two, passing a smile.

When they had finished eating, Wanda put two slices of apple pie in front of them. "Ya'll want some coffee?"

Fern nodded. "Make that two," James Robert said, holding up two fingers.

"So, what are you gonna do now?" James Robert asked her. "You gonna keep on wandering around Milledgeville?"

Fern shook her head. "I guess you know something about sheriffing. Keeping a watch on your town?"

"I have to know what's going on around here. Still haven't figured out where you're stayin' though."

Fern laughed. "Well at least I'm able to keep some secrets."

"Coffee with cream," Wanda said as she put the cups on the table. "This on your tab, Sheriff?" she asked more businesslike now.

"Thanks, Wanda," he said again.

Fern had so much to ask but spent a minute trying to decide where to start. She knew what she needed to know most, but still uncertain why it mattered.

"Where's Louella?"

She could tell by the look on his face that she had caught him off guard.

"She's still around. Not at the sanitarium. I guess you already know that," he answered vaguely.

"Is she still nursing?" Fern asked him, watching his eyes dart back and forth a few times before he answered.

"She has been, until recent."

"At a hospital?" Fern persisted.

He pursed his lips, then answered. "No. Mostly she's been private duty nursing here and around."

"You said until recent. Did she quit?"

Fern moved her twitchy hands to her lap and held them there.

"No. She didn't quit. The woman she was taking care of died. Family didn't need her anymore."

Fern nodded slowly, thinking how things fit together. "That's sad."

"Yep," James Robert answered.

When they came back outside into the late afternoon sunshine, neither one was sure how to walk away.

"You need a ride somewhere?" James Robert asked.

Fern chuckled. "It's not gonna be that easy, Sheriff."

"All right then." He turned and looked at her, seriousness made his face more sober than she had ever seen. "You need to stay away from the sanitarium. That place is not the place for you. There's no reason for you to be there. It's time for you to find your life on the outside, Fern."

She nodded. "I know that. I'm not sure how to do that, but I want to try."

She looked around at the last-minute bustle as evening was setting in over the town.

"I want to talk with you some more. I want to find out what's going on out there, even if I'm not going back. Women are dying, and I'm not talking about from sickness. Somebody's killing women out there. Have been for a while. Don't you care about that?"

"There's a lot you don't understand about what goes on out there, Fern. And it's not just a sidewalk conversation that'll explain it. I don't understand it. I just know I'm mostly told to keep my nose out of it."

"Does that seem right to you? You're the sheriff. Shouldn't you be the one to get your nose in it?"

"That place belongs to the state of Georgia. That's what I'm told time and time again when I look into anything going on out there. And more than me, you need to keep out of it, Fern. It's not safe to poke around in dangerous places."

Fern sighed, knowing that it wasn't a quick conversation that they needed to have but frustrated all the same.

"Is this when you usually take your lunch break?" she asked him.

"It's not regular. Depends on what's going on around here."

"I'm coming back," she said and pointed to the bench where she had waited for him earlier. "And I'll be waiting for you right there. We've got a lot to talk about, James Robert."

"All right. But I'm not sure Wanda is gonna be all that happy about seeing us together all the time," he said, trying to lighten the mood.

"Why don't you tell her I'm your long-lost daughter. That ought to make her feel better," Fern said, turning to go.

James Robert kept his smile on as he watched her cross the street.

When she looked back, as he knew she would, he waved and muttered under his breath, "Damn. All hell is 'bout to break loose."

Adrienne

MARCH, 1908

15

Adrienne dashed through the foyer of the New Empire Theater. She opened the door to the auditorium, treaded lightly to Row H, and lowered her bag to the floor. She tugged off her black leather gloves, unbuttoned her marmot-trimmed seal jacket and hung it on the back of the aisle seat while she adjusted to the murky lighting and the mood and then took her place. Dress rehearsal was already under way. The players, the Academy Stock Company, Adrienne's classmates at the American Academy for Dramatic Arts, were in their last week of rehearsals in preparation for what would be their final performance of three one act plays and a comedy before graduation. The comedy, *A Scrap of Paper*, did not appeal to her in the least. For the briefest of moments, she was perfectly accepting of her fate as an observer and not a participant. She felt only the tiniest pinprick of the sting.

Another pair of late comers dropped noisily into their seats a few rows behind her. The two young men offered their less than glowing critique of the casting choices in voices meant to be overheard by Franklin Sargent, president of the Academy, seated as was the custom, in the center of Row E. After a couple of exchanges and some exaggerated snickering from the back-seat critics, Mr. Sargent stood abruptly, glowered at the students and pointed to the exit. He watched them take their leave then his eyes fell on Adrienne. She held his gaze. He offered a polite nod before returning his attention to the stage.

It was their first encounter since he had summoned her to his office a few days before the holiday break in December. She hadn't seen him then, as he was conveniently indisposed when she arrived. Instead, it had fallen to his secretary to give her the news that she would not be graduating with her classmates come March. For some unspecified reason, her enrollment contract had never been formalized by his signature. It had seemed an oversight in the first telling—correctable, forgivable. But as the uncomfortable scene unfolded and the woman made clear that Adrienne had never been considered a fully-fledged student of the academic program, she understood the heart of the matter.

It had taken a couple of months to reconcile herself with the reality revealed to her that day. And though she had not yet shared that news with anyone, not even Alonzo, she knew now, seated in the darkened theater, that she had made her peace with it.

After the riots in Atlanta upended their lives almost two years ago, Adrienne had taken the children and Mattie to Philadelphia for safekeeping. She settled them in as best she could and returned home to begin the school year in the strained confines of her life with Alonzo without them for ballast. Within days of her return, the dismantling of their family life was made complete when a letter from Horace Bumstead arrived. Their home of the past ten years was being sold to the university, and they would need to make other living arrangements as soon as possible. They moved into the men's dormitory on the campus, disheartened and discouraged, longing for the children. As Atlanta fashioned an uneasy truce, the heartsore Herndons muddled through. Adrienne devoted herself to her students, Alonzo to his business enterprises.

When summer came, she fled north again, driven by the dual desires to be nearer the children and the outside chance that she might somehow yet have that breakout moment she had forever longed for on the stage. She took a room in New York's theater district and enrolled as Anne du Bignon at the Academy. The experience of the unrest and violence in Atlanta had changed completely what that meant to her. Her connection to that name was no longer an assumed identity but simply the name under which she had previously performed. She had chosen the Academy purposefully, knowing that several of the board members knew precisely who she was. Adrienne McNeil Herndon, of Savannah and Atlanta, a Black scholar, the recipient of noteworthy praise for her stage work in the North and in the South. She had chosen as she promised Alonzo she would. But as the weeks passed her miscalculation revealed itself. As she was told time and time again that there was no suitable stage role for her in any of the Academy productions, Adrienne grew weary of the poorly cloaked deception. And finally, all pretense was dropped. She had come to realize that New York was the same as Atlanta in matters of race. The only difference was that in Atlanta, bigotry was enshrined in law, out in the open for all to see, while in New York it lay coiled in the corner, vaguely disguised, yet no less devastating when it struck.

A faculty member reminded her that she was there to further her dramatic teaching and production skills and that at her age, it was after all the higher calling. And so, she embraced it. She ran auditions, scheduled rehearsals, helped other students with their techniques and character development. She consulted on script rewrites and costume design, built props, and assisted the stage production teams. Adrienne was confident that she had contributed to a successful season for the senior class and that she had developed skills that would energize her work back home, despite the refusal of the Academy to award her any credential attesting to such. That's what she had told herself anyway, and gradually she acknowledged it as her truth.

Adrienne pulled her sketchbook from her bag and flipped through the collection of drawings and notes she had recorded over the past months. The majority had come not from within the walls of the Academy, but from all the productions she had enjoyed across the magnificent collection of sumptuous theaters mere steps from her rented room. The lush murals and the stained glass octagonals in the ceiling of the Stuyvesant, Ethel Barrymore in costume as Eleanor Alderson in *Her Sister* at the Hudson, the witches cavern in Act Four of *Macbeth* at the Lyric. She reached into her bag to retrieve her colored pencils and turned past the drawings, ready to record the set on the stage. There, stuck between the pages was the photograph her Aunt Rachel insisted be taken of the Herndon family reunited for the Christmas holiday. Adrienne dropped the pencils back in the bag. She brought the picture close, to see more clearly the faces of her beautiful children and adoring husband. The dim lighting obscured their features. She needed to see them. She returned the portrait to the book, grabbed her jacket from the back of her chair and with a final glance at the stage and the back of Franklin Sargent's head, walked up the aisle and made her way to the street.

Adrienne hailed a taxicab. The driver helped her into the compact compartment. She directed him to the St. Regis Hotel before he climbed aboard his bench-seat perch. The taxi moved into street traffic, and Adrienne lifted the photograph from the book for another look in the outside light. The four of them together. Norris had grown. His features had matured but were recognizably those of her sweet boy. His eyes were Alonzo's, soft brown and gentle. The slightest smile at the corner of his lips. He bore the expression of someone much older, composed and content. She wanted to run her hand across his closely shorn head and watch his eyes crinkle, the smile breaking free. Effie, in her father's lap, snuggled into his warmth, mischief dancing across every inch of her. Her face no longer holding any of its baby plumpness, her eyes joyful. She saw herself in Effie, but she saw Alonzo too. How quickly they had grown. Adrienne moved her eyes from one to the other, searching for any hint of heartache or loneliness in their faces. Relieved that she saw none, she turned her attention to Alonzo and marveled at the resemblance between father and son. She hadn't noticed before that Alonzo's tie was pulled to one side. Hadn't she straightened it just after he sat down? She chuckled when she realized that he had probably tugged it loose when her back was turned. He had always hated ties. Too confining, they choked him, he said. She thought about how he always asked her if his appearance met her approval before they went out in public. She wondered if she had been harsh with him. She hoped not. For he had certainly never been harsh with her. She found herself drawn to his eyes. She pulled the picture closer. What did she see there? He seemed to be thinking about something, perhaps far removed from the portrait studio or the nearness of his family. Was it, emptiness she detected? Was it, sadness? Or were those the eyes of a busy man with a lot on his mind? Then she recalled what had happened that night. Maybe, she told herself, those were the eyes of a hopeful man. Hopeful and yet somewhat uncertain that he had made the appropriate calculation. It was later that evening, with the family gathered around the table—Rachel and her mother fussing over them, piling food in front of them—that Alonzo had pulled an envelope from under his dinner plate. Feigning surprise when it was addressed to "The Herndon Family," he passed it to her and when she questioned him with her eyes, he had responded, "Maybe a jolly old elf put it there."

Adrienne had smiled and asked, "Should I open it?" Norris and Effie both shouted, "Yes!" And so, she had. It was a deed of sale made out to Alonzo for a piece of land. Not just any piece of land, but the vacant lot that sat on the rise just beyond the Bumstead cottage. At the bottom of the page, in Alonzo's writing was, "Site of the new Herndon family home. Construction to begin in June. Dreams come true. Love, Alonzo."

Yes, she told herself, determined to look forward and not backward, *that was the faraway look in his eyes, that dream of home*. Not just Alonzo's, but her dream as well.

Adrienne was lost in thought when the taxi driver opened the door and offered his hand. She paid him, gathered her things, and made her way to the Ladies' Restaurant, the grand room alive with chatter, a feast for the eyes. Beneath an arched and glowing gold ceiling festooned with electric lights, Pavanazzo and Serpentine marble graced the walls. Irish linens and Limoges china dressed the table, and within minutes a white-gloved waiter placed a silver teapot in front of her. Adrienne relaxed into the cool comfort of the place.

After a sip of tea, she pulled her sketchbook from her bag, took a few pieces of stationery from the back pocket and found her Waterman fountain pen. Her intention was to write a letter to Alonzo, telling him everything. She started once, then twice, then folded the two pieces of wasted paper and slid them into her bag. After tea and scones, she began again. By then, she had changed her mind about the recipient, but not so much about the message.

Dear Will,

I hope this letter finds you, Nina, and Yolande happy and well. I was pleased to see your work in "The Horizon." Happy that you are expressing yourself poetically again. It's been far too long. Your words strike such a powerful chord, my friend. Do not deny us.

I'm writing to you from the St. Regis, where I linger over tea in such a lovely space, drawing the attention of none. Is that a blessing? Or is it my curse?

My intention was to write my distant husband, but, alas, I am too weak to offer my feelings up to him. So, it is without any explanation or excuses that I am writing to you so that I might speak my heart and mind, and not worry about how they might be received. Pen to paper!

For what have I been searching? The answer is neither complicated nor simple. Value. Worth. Fulfillment. Contribution. Desire. Esteem. Prestige. Belonging. Are these not all expressions of the human spirit? Or are these simply the selfish pursuits of a selfish woman? And yet if they remained unpursued, what then? If I had risked nothing or risked being a fool in the pursuit of my dreams, which would be the greater travesty? And now I feel that I am the fool. But not for the reasons one might suppose. Not a fool because I pursued my dreams. Not a fool because I fell short. Not a fool because I hoped that I might transcend the restrictions of my gender and my race. But a fool for failing to realize that the risks I was taking had grave consequences for the people that I love.

A year ago, your friend, Mr. Washington, asked if I might be included in an article he was working on about colored women. I refused. My excuse was that I wished not to be made an object of scorn for southern white men. In my letter declining his invitation, I wrote quite haughtily that white society refused to acknowledge the sanctity of the Negro home. How arrogant! I have been as guilty as they. While I was busy thinking of myself, my family was scattered to the winds.

My children, my husband, in the care of others. And to what avail?

That is the end of my lament.

And now a few words of celebration! I am Atlanta bound! I leave for Philadelphia tomorrow evening. A weekend with my aunt and to gather mother and the children and we head for home. How liberating the very words, "we head for home." We are to have a home, at last. Alonzo, generous to a fault, has bought for us the property adjacent to the old Bumstead cottage. There, we will make a place for ourselves. There, I will make amends.

And what of our dreams, Will? I have plans for us too. If there is any positive reckoning arising from my northern exile, it is this. You once told me that the stage is my soap box. I want to make the most of that. Let's bring theater to our people in the South. Let's cultivate and curate a southern theater that celebrates our proud heritage and opens a portal to possibilities not yet imagined. Will you join me on this journey?

With gratitude and deep affection, I look forward to seeing you again upon my homecoming,

Adrienne

Adrienne wound her way through the crush of humanity typical of early evening in the city, rejuvenated by the bracing March wind. Once outside the door to her building at 355 West 55th, she came to a standstill and breathed in the briny air laced with fresh bread and coffee and the musty rotten egg smell of spent gasoline. Her eyes drifted upward to the towering skyline and then back down to the street. Snippets of conversation in languages unfamiliar joined the clatter and clank of the world rushing past and seemed almost deafening.

She lifted her hand and whispered, *"Adieu, ancient amant,"* and headed to her room to pack her things.

It was almost midnight when Adrienne arrived at the Cambridge Street brownstone in Philadelphia.

"They're sleeping, I'm sure," Adrienne said to Rachel as she put her bags down and took off her coat.

"They wanted to wait up for you but there's school tomorrow. I told them they would see you first thing."

"I can't wait that long. I'll just have a quick look and be right back down."

She climbed the stairs and opened the door to the room where they slept, the lamp shining on the table between them. Adrienne stood beside the small beds, the rhythm of her children's steady breathing, a sedative. Norris lay flat on his back. His hands laced behind his head. She hovered over him for a moment, then put her hand on his cheek. Her touch woke him. His eyes widened and that smile she missed broke across his face. She put a finger to her lips to quiet him. He latched his arms around her neck.

"I missed you so much, Mama."

"Well, you don't have to anymore," she said quietly in his ear before she kissed him on the forehead. She pulled his covers up and tucked them around him. "Now get some sleep, there's school tomorrow."

Effie was scrunched into a tight ball in the middle of her bed, her thumb in her mouth for comfort. Effie gently pulled it free and kissed her softly on the cheek. The little girl stirred and brought her thumb back to its rightful place.

Adrienne took a deep breath and felt the fretfulness slip from her shoulders. She left the light burning and quietly pulled the door closed when she left.

"I'm making some mint tea," Rachel said from the stove.

"That sounds nice. Is Mother in bed?"

"She said she'd see you in the morning."

Adrienne sat down at the table.

"You're a few days earlier than we thought."

Adrienne stifled a yawn. "I decided not to stay for graduation."

Rachel placed their teacups on the table.

"And frankly, Aunt Rachel, I'm ready to go home."

Rachel spooned sugar into her tea and stirred. "I 'spect it's past time."

Adrienne sighed. "I hope it's not past time for Lonzo."

"You've tried the limits of that man's patience, Addy."

"I have. I was thinking about that today. That lovely portrait you insisted we have made over Christmas. I was looking at that, at Alonzo. He was worried about something. I could see it in his eyes. I think he was worried that I would reject his proposal that we build a new home together."

ADRIENNE

Adrienne put her cup down and closed her eyes.

"He said he wasn't sure what you wanted more, your life here or a life with him. Said he couldn't wait any longer to find out."

"He told you that?"

Rachel nodded.

"He sent us away. Does he not remember that?"

"Oh, he remembers. Said it's the biggest mistake he ever made. That land? That's him trying to fix it."

They were quiet, drinking their tea.

"He's always let you do what you wanted to, Addy. He made you that promise when you got married. He never broke it."

"That's the problem, Rachel. I always wanted so much."

"There's nothing wrong with that."

"There is when what one person wants always requires that the other one makes the sacrifice."

"I think you've supported his dreams too. Look at everything he's accomplished. He couldn't have done that without a lot of hard work and a lot of long hours."

Rachel rose and took their dishes to the sink. "It's late. We'd better get some sleep. Those young'uns will be up in a few hours."

"I don't know how to thank you for all you've done for the children and Mother," Adrienne said, coming to Rachel's side.

"I don't know if I've a mind to let you take them away. It'll be awful quiet without them."

Adrienne picked up a dish towel to dry their cups.

"Some mail came for you. It's out on the front table. I'm off to bed. You get some sleep. You and Lonzo will work things out when you get home."

Adrienne smiled. "Good night, Rachel."

Adrienne walked through the living room to pick up her bags. On the front table were the letters that Rachel had mentioned. She picked up the short stack and shuffled through them. One, addressed to Anne Du Bignon had come from the Academy. She moved to the sofa and turned on the table lamp. The envelope held a graduation announcement and a slip of paper with a handwritten note from Franklin Sargent's secretary.

THE TRUTH TOGETHER

Mr. Sargent and the faculty of the Academy are pleased to inform you that you have been awarded the David Belasco Silver Medal for Technical Excellence. Congratulations and our best wishes for ongoing success in your theater teaching career.

Adrienne read and reread the terse acknowledgement, returned the letter to the table, turned out the lights and headed to bed.

The children stood at the window of their compartment, watching as the train made its way through the outskirts of Atlanta toward Terminal Station.

"Will Papa be waiting?" Norris asked.

"It's Tuesday morning, a workday for Papa. He may have to send someone for us if he's busy," Adrienne responded.

"I want to kiss Papa!" Effie shouted, unable to contain her excitement.

Mattie smiled at Adrienne. "You look a little nervy, Addy. Are you worried?"

Adrienne shook her head. "I don't know why. He's pleased we're coming home. I do feel anxious though."

"It'll take some getting used to. Everybody together again after so long. But it's time," Mattie assured her.

"I can't help but remember how I felt when we took the children to Philadelphia. I thought my heart would break. I was scared and sad and mad at him for sending us away. I didn't know if we would ever call Atlanta home again."

She looked at the children. "This feels so completely different. I don't want to get my hopes up though."

"Hopes about what?" Mattie prodded.

"About Lonzo. About how he feels about me."

Mattie shook her head and chuckled. "You must be the only person on God's green earth who doesn't know the answer to that question."

Adrienne sighed and turned to watch the children.

They stopped on the tracks just outside the station and Norris returned to his seat next to his mother. "When will our new house be ready?"

"Papa said by next summer if all goes well. We'll be living the college life until then," she said her mood brightening.

ADRIENNE

"Will Papa be with us?"

"Of course he will. Where else would he be?"

When the train finally made it into the station, Adrienne and Mattie gathered their things and waited for the doors to open for disembarking.

"I'll need to make arrangements for our luggage," Adrienne told them as they stepped onto the platform. "Wait for me in the lobby."

Making her way toward the baggage car, Adrienne stopped short when she caught sight of Alonzo standing in the middle of the platform with an arm load of bright yellow daffodils, waiting for her. He smiled and waved.

"Welcome home, Addy," he said, walking to her, taking her overnight bag from her arm and handing the flowers over. He kissed her on the cheek.

She buried her face in the flowers. "They're beautiful. Thank you."

"Hand me your claim checks so I can get a porter for your bags."

Adrienne watched him make the arrangements. When he came back to her, he offered his arm. She latched her hand to it and pulled him a little closer, looking up at him to see that he noticed.

"Papa!" Effie squealed when she saw them. The children broke into a run, Norris practically tackling him when he got to him. He scooped Effie up and wrapped his arm around his son.

At the curb outside, Alonzo directed his family to a waiting car—his brand-new, shiny, black Pierce Great Arrow.

Wide-eyed Norris asked, "Who does this belong to?"

Alonzo opened the back door and the children scampered aboard. He helped Mattie into the seat beside them. "Maybe you in a few years, but for right now it's mine."

"Well aren't you full of surprises," Adrienne teased as he walked her around the front and handed her up to the seat.

"This is just the beginning, Mrs. Herndon."

When they pulled up outside the men's dormitory, Alonzo directed, "You wait here, Addy."

He helped the others out and took them inside. A few minutes later he reemerged alone.

"I want to show you something," he told her, climbing behind the wheel again. He slowly wound his way to the back side of the campus and drove along the recently graded road.

"I talked to Rachel yesterday after you left Philadelphia. She told me you left New York before graduation and that you had gotten some kind of award."

"You and Rachel can't keep your mouths shut, can you?" she replied, mildly annoyed.

"Sometimes she's easier to talk to," Alonzo offered. "What kind of award was it?"

"Something meaningless," she answered, looking at him. "And I didn't win it. Anne Du Bignon did."

Alonzo risked a glance at her. "I don't understand."

"I didn't graduate from the program, Alonzo. Franklin Sargent didn't allow it. That award was a token, as meaningless as a pat on the head."

"I'm sorry."

"I'm not. It's a fitting swan song."

She looked at him in time to see the lopsided smile on his lips before he brought it under control.

"And you needn't worry anymore, Mr. Herndon. You'll be happy to know I left Anne Du Bignon on Fifty-Fifth Street."

Alonzo looked at her again. She was smiling. He chuckled and said, "Good riddance."

Adrienne saw in the distance the newly felled trees stacked on the edge of the roadway.

"Have you started without me?" she asked.

"We cleared the lot."

Alonzo pulled the car to a stop and helped Adrienne climb down from her seat.

"Hold your skirts up and watch where you step," he directed, taking her by the hand.

They walked to the middle of their property where Adrienne took it all in.

"Oh, Lonzo, look at the view across the city. It's lovely."

"I think the house should face this way," he told her, pointing toward the city skyline.

"Have you decided on a contractor?"

"No. I don't want one. We don't need one. This is our home, Addy. I want us to make all the choices. I want you to draw up the plan for the house of your dreams. You've been working on it for years. You've already made the sketches. Let's do this ourselves. Together."

Adrienne put her hands on her hips and scanned the surroundings. "I don't know; that's a tremendous undertaking."

"We can do it. I know we can. It'll be a lot of work," he told her, coming near and holding his hands out to her. "We've waited a long time for this. Let me build this house for you. I want to lay my hands on every square foot of it."

She slid her arms around him and said, "Thank you, Lonzo." She pointed toward the campus. "I think the front of the house should look this way." He followed the slope of the lush green grounds with his eyes, then smiled and nodded.

Louella and James Robert

MAY, 1920

16

Louella took the three flights of the medical staff stairway to the surgical floor at a dead run. Pushing through the double doors, she slowed her pace to a fast walk, rounded the corner, and slid in behind the reception desk.

Startled by her abrupt entrance, the nurse behind the desk asked, "Can I help you?"

"A patient was brought in sometime in the past hour. I was told she was taken to surgery. Fern Walker?"

"She's in surgery with Dr. Thompson."

"Where?" Louella asked adamantly.

"You're not going in there," the nurse ordered.

Louella paid no mind and headed down the hallway toward the operating rooms.

"Wait a minute!" The nurse called out, stepping from behind the desk. "Come here. I'll tell you what I know."

Louella walked back, crossed her arms, and waited.

"I was called down to bring her up. Pale as a ghost. Weak pulse. There's a big gash across her neck here," she said, indicating the location on herself. "She took a beating. It looked pretty bad."

"Is she your patient?" another nurse asked from behind the desk.

"Yes," Louella answered, unwilling to explain her connection to Fern in the moment.

"Do you know who the father is?"

"Fern's father? He's not around. And her mother's dead," Louella answered.

"No, I meant her baby's father," the nurse replied.

"Her baby?" Louella asked, confused.

"I thought you said she was your patient," the nurse responded. "She's pregnant, didn't you know?"

Dumbstruck, Louella could only shake her head.

"Almost full term too. No ideas about the father? And no family?"

Head shaking again, Louella's gaze wandered down the hallway. "No idea."

"You want to wait? I just brought up a pot of coffee from the kitchen," the nurse behind the counter offered.

Louella turned without answering and followed the nurse into the workroom behind the desk. She plopped down in a chair.

The nurse poured a cup of coffee and handed it to her. She watched Louella take an absentminded sip or two of the hot drink and then said, "She can't be more than sixteen. What's she doing here?"

Confounded by what she had just learned, it poured out. "Fifteen," Louella corrected. "She was born here. Her mother was my patient. She was pregnant with Fern when she was brought in." She closed her eyes and shook her head. "A little over fifteen years ago."

"And this girl, Fern, she still lives here?"

Louella nodded.

"She kept her here all those years?" the nurse asked, bewildered.

"She did. They didn't have anywhere to go." She saw the look of disbelief wash over the woman's face.

"How long have you been working here?" Louella asked her.

"Six years now."

And then wanting to make a point. "Then you know. These women that get brought here. The ones nobody wants. What are they supposed to do? They don't have anywhere to go. No money. No place to live."

The disbelief faded to resignation. "I don't know the answer to that. But I can't imagine raising a child here. Can you?" the nurse asked pointedly.

"Oh, the story gets worse," Louella added. "Nora, Fern's mother, worked on one of the children's wards. She got tuberculosis and died. That was about five years ago." The calculation of time added to Louella's anguish. "How could it have been that long?"

Neither one could answer that.

"She's in the post-surgery room if you want to see her," the nurse said, patting Louella on the shoulder to wake her and holding out a mask and head cover. "Clean up and put these on."

Louella shook off sleep and made her way to the nurses' lavatory.

"Come with me," the nurse said when she emerged.

"Can I see Dr. Thompson?" Louella asked. "We worked together a lot of years. Tell him it's Louella."

The nurse took her to Fern's bedside, then answered, "I'll go see if Dr. Thompson's still here."

Louella drew closer for a better look. Fern's face was swollen and bruised from a brutal beating and her neck wound was covered by a surgical dressing. She was just a child. Her condition made bare her youth and vulnerability. Louella pulled back the sheet and placed her hands around Fern's pregnant abdomen.

Judging what the nurse had said to be true, she asked the sleeping girl, "How did I miss this, Fern. Why didn't you come to me?"

"Louella?"

The doctor appeared at her side. "David. How is she?"

"She's not in good shape. She lost a lot of blood. I'm still not sure they'll make it. Do you know what happened to her?"

"She worked at the farm today. Supposed to meet me for supper. When she didn't show up, I got to asking around. Nobody remembered her coming back on the wagon. I got worried. Sent somebody out to look for her. Somebody attacked her is all I can figure."

"You know her then?"

"Yes. I've told you about her before. Fern and her mother Nora."

"It's been a while since we've seen each other, Louella."

"Nora was one of my first patients. She had Fern after she came here. I took care of Fern before and after Nora died."

"That's right. I remember now. You used to take her home with you sometimes. I'm sorry. I know you care about her," he said kindly. "The knife missed the carotid and the larynx, thank goodness. Nicked the outer jugular. I've cleaned out that neck wound and repaired what damage I could. We'll have to watch for infection. Those bruises on her face will heal, no broken bones there." He stepped closer. "I know this is hard to hear. Most of those physical injuries will heal with time. She put up a fight, that's for sure."

"What about the baby?"

"I'll have Dr. Walters take a look at her. He might want to deliver sooner rather than later. That's probably their best chance."

"Not Walters, David. Isn't there somebody else who could do it?" Louella asked.

"He's got experience in obstetrics. Not everybody around here does."

"Not him, David. You know what I'm talking about," Louella said, her fear and anger mingling.

"Louella. Those are just rumors. I don't know why you nurses spread talk like that."

"I'm not talking about rumors. I'm talking about what I know. And he's not the only one involved either. Old Dr. Albertson too."

"Rumors, Louella. Why don't you get some rest now, you must be exhausted," he said dismissively and patted her on the arm. "I'll stop by tomorrow." And then as almost an afterthought, "Maybe we can get together for dinner." As usual, it was a statement, not an invitation. Louella knew exactly what "dinner" meant.

Louella drew up a chair and sat down next to Fern's bed. She'd worked a fifteen-hour shift, missed supper, and couldn't remember when she last had some sleep. But this was Fern. She had made promises to look after her. Promised Nora. Promised she would not let Nora's fate be Fern's too. And now look at her. Louella hadn't thought about Nora for a while. She hadn't seen much of Fern the last few months either. Fern had always been invisible to most everyone else. She slipped in and out of the chaos that was daily life. Louella kept tabs on her through the staff's grapevine, but she hadn't seen her in months. That's why they had supper plans, to catch up. Louella remembered there was something about a boy last summer but couldn't really recall the details. She realized that was the last time she had a conversation with Fern.

During wartime and the influenza outbreak, they had been stretched thin with all the nurses and doctors leaving. Louella was one of the few who stayed. She had actually moved into the nurses' dormitory to better deal with the logistics of being on duty seven days a week. That long stretch of unending work had earned her a promotion to charge nurse. She still wasn't sure she liked the job. There was too much paperwork, and she didn't really like being in charge of other nurses. And though she still worked shifts, she didn't get to do much patient care. She missed that.

Louella put her hand on top of Fern's and made a promise to herself that she would not let anything bad happen to her if she could figure out a way to do it.

"Nurse. Nurse. Can you help me?"

Louella picked her head up from where it lay on the bed at Fern's side. "Nurse!"

Louella tried to focus. Someone was calling her.

"Here. I'm right here," a woman's voice demanded.

Louella finally connected the voice to the woman a couple of beds down from Fern. She was calling Louella, that was clear. "I'm sorry. I'm not on duty," Louella answered, groggy from sleep.

"Nobody's here, and my throat's dry as a creek bed in August. Could you get me some water?"

Louella scanned the room for the night nurse. Reluctantly she got up and approached the woman's bedside.

"And I need to pee."

"I'm not on duty."

"You're a nurse though."

"I am."

"Well I don't see any other ones around. Could I have some water?"

Wordlessly, Louella helped the woman use the bedpan, then found a water pitcher and brought it to her bedside.

After gulping down a cup full, the woman asked, "What's wrong with that doctor you was talking about? Dr. Walters?"

"What?"

"That Dr. Walters. He operated on me yesterday. What's wrong with him?"

"Nothing's wrong with him," Louella answered, realizing that the woman had listened in on her conversation.

"I heard you talking about him with that other doctor."

"He's a good doctor. What kind of surgery did you have?" Louella asked.

"He fixed me. Took care of a little problem, if you know what I mean, and fixed me for good," the woman answered.

Louella regarded the woman for a moment, nodded, and said, "Your nurse should be back soon."

Louella pulled the chair to the other side of Fern's bed so that the woman was behind her and made a mental note to watch what was said in the open room.

Louella was aware of the activity around her but had drowsed off until a hand on her shoulder and a familiar voice woke her.

"Did you sleep here?"

She looked up to find James Robert standing beside her. He handed her a cup of coffee.

"How's she doing?"

"I was afraid you hadn't gotten my message."

"I didn't till I got in last night. I had to see to some trouble downtown," James Robert answered, taking note of Fern's injuries. "You learned anything else about what might have happened?"

"No. You couldn't find out anything?"

"Nothing 'cept what you told me. She ain't woke up yet?"

"No. She was in surgery late." Louella stood and turned to James Robert. "Did you know that she's pregnant?"

"Good God, no," he said, dropping his head. "I was worried that could happen."

"Must have happened almost nine months ago," Louella told him, and seeing the look on his face, she had to ask, "Did you know anything about that?"

"I knew something was goin' on with her and Tom Ennis last year. Figured it was headed that way."

"Why didn't you tell me?"

"You were kind of busy, Sister."

"You should have told me, James Robert. Now here we are with another baby ready to be born here. You know how dangerous that is."

He shook his head. "What the hell are we gonna do about it, Louella?"

"David Thompson wants Dr. Walters to deliver the baby."

"When?"

"Soon. He's supposed to see her today."

Louella remembered she shouldn't be talking so freely with that big-eared patient nearby. She turned and saw her lying on her side, back turned, hopefully sleeping.

"Tom Ennis? Old Judge Ennis's son? Is that who you mean?" Louella asked.

"Yep. Don't you remember he had him brought here after he got home from the war? Tom and Fern. You never saw one without the other. Figures."

Louella put a hand on James Robert's arm. "That might be the answer."

"What might be?"

"The Ennis family. They might take the baby."

"What do you mean, take the baby? That's Fern's baby."

"Fern is no more than a child herself. She can't take care of a baby. And where would you have her do that anyway? Here? At the sanitarium? Another life just like Fern's?"

"What are you sayin' then, Louella? Give the baby to the Ennises?"

She glanced over at big ears again to make sure their conversation was private.

Turning back, she nodded. "Yes. That's what I'm saying."

It was late afternoon when James Robert pulled up in front of the Ennises house. He hoped the old man was home. He walked up to the front entrance, taking in the beautiful old house and the wide yard and thought about growing up in a place like that with room to run wild and all that money could buy. It would certainly be different from the life Fern had at the sanitarium and the life she could give that baby. Maybe Louella was on to something. He took the first step and the front door opened. The judge stepped out.

"Evenin', Judge."

"Deputy. What can I do for you?"

"I wonder if I might have a word with you, sir. It has to do with Tom."

The judge glanced back at the house, then said, "Let's take a walk out to the pond. I was headed that way."

James Robert wasn't sure how to start the conversation. The walk through the trees gave him some planning time.

"I know you came to see Tom right often when he was at the sanitarium last year."

"I should have brought him home instead," the judge said remorsefully.

"Did Tom ever tell you about a girl he met there? Fern?"

The judge turned his attention to James Robert. "I met Fern last fall. Is that what this is about? She wants some money?"

"No. It is about her, but it's not about money."

"She have that baby?"

James Robert was surprised that the old man knew.

"No, sir, not yet. She's in a bad way, though. She got attacked out at the farm. That baby's ready to be born. She's in no shape to care for it."

"Are you sure it's Tom's?"

"Yes, sir, I am. I've known Fern her whole life. I saw them together last year. They loved each other."

"How's that proof, Deputy?"

"I don't have any proof to give you. All I can tell you is I know Fern. That baby's Tom's."

"And what is it you want from me, young man?"

"I'm wondering if you and your wife might want that baby, sir. That baby needs a home. I think it should be your home. That's your grandbaby, Judge Ennis. I would swear to it."

The judge turned away and looked out over the pond. "We spent hours here, fishing this pond—Tom and me did. Damn that war. Took my boy, same as if it had killed him."

James Robert kicked at the dirt and waited.

"I'll have to think about this. And I'll have to talk with my wife."

The judge headed back and James Robert followed.

At the front of the house, the judge said, "Let me know when the baby comes. I'll want to see for myself when it does."

James Robert got in his truck and sat for a minute before starting it up.

"God Almighty. What am I doing?" he asked.

Louella had spent the day working out a plan while she worked at her desk. She cut the day short to head back to her room, get a shower, and change into something a little nicer than her uniform. She knew where she would find him at the end of the day, the doctors' lounge. It was a corner room in the administration building where doctors and nurses kept a well-stocked bar, so they could share a wind-down cocktail at the end of their shifts and make plans for later.

And there he was, the best dressed dandy in the corner, three young nurses hanging on his every word. She remembered being flattered by his attention when they first met, but was glad she had never said yes to his suggestions, especially when she learned what he did to earn some extra cash on the side. He hadn't invented selling babies, but he had certainly taken the trade to a new level. The sanitarium had a lot of problems. One of them was babies and what to do with them. Women came there already pregnant. Others got pregnant after they took up residence there. It was not a place to raise children. Louella knew that. So did Nora. But then there was Fern. Nora had been one of Louella's first patients. She had been working at the sanitarium for less than a week when they first met. Louella didn't really understand what all went on there when she decided to help Nora find a way to keep Fern. Nora had begged her and so she had begged Dr. Albertson to let Fern stay. Louella had flirted and promised more. Somehow, she avoided having to deliver, and then she had transferred to the children's ward and took Nora along as her assistant to remove herself from the situation.

Louella had been surprised to learn that there was money to be made selling babies to people who couldn't have their own and that the sanitarium was the perfect place to get one without going through the regular channels. People who were desperate enough were willing to pay for a baby, especially one whose birth had not been properly documented and assurance that no one would be coming for the baby later. A certificate of death and a burial marker in Cedar Lane took care of everything. At the Georgia State Sanitarium, they were able to bury their secrets deeper than most.

"Gin Rickey," Louella said to the nurse tending bar. "Make it strong."

Waiting for her drink, she turned her attention to Daniel Walters and waited for him to catch her looking. She held his gaze and tossed him an inviting smile.

Drink in hand, she crossed the room, pretending to head elsewhere when he called her name.

"Louella. Come over here. There's room for you."

He slid over and made a small space where she could squeeze in next to him.

"Where have you been, Dr. Walters? I haven't seen you in ages," she gushed.

"It's you who's been missing in action, Louella. I'm here most days about this time if you want to find me."

With the doctor's attention now focused on Louella, the other nurses lost interest and moved on to other more promising prospects.

"You aren't on the floors much anymore, Louella. Where've you been?"

"I have an office job now. Keeps me busy. I do a few shifts every week, but mostly boring stuff, schedules and records and such. How about you? What are you up to these days?"

"Seeing patients mostly."

"She leaned in a little closer and whispered in a sultry voice," You still in the baby business?"

He gave her a side-eyed look. "Delivering babies, you mean?"

She leaned in again with a playful shoulder shove. "You know what I mean, Daniel."

He crossed his arms defensively and smirked.

"I might have a connection for you if you are."

After a moment's pause, he loosened. "I'm listening."

"White girl. White father. She's in post-surgery. You might have heard about her already. David Thompson wanted you to see her."

"He told me about her. Said she wasn't in good shape. I didn't get to her today. I'll assess tomorrow. Make some choices."

"I know a family that's interested," Louella said in a quiet voice.

He turned to see her better. "I didn't think you approved of that, Louella. Changed your mind?"

"This is no place for a baby, Daniel. I know that."

"Is this family you have in mind, uh, well situated?"

Louella moved back in to close the gap between them. "You mean, do they have money? I'd say they're quite well situated."

"I'll come see her tomorrow. You want another drink?"

She nodded. He rose, then added, "Tell them five."

"Five?"

"The family. Tell them five hundred."

When the doctor returned to the cozy corner with the new drinks in hand, Louella was nowhere to be found.

Louella passed by the bed of the patient she called big ears on her way to Fern. She pulled a chair around to sit next to her and avoid looking at the woman who liked to listen in on other people's business. She ran a hand over Fern's forehead and leaned down to whisper to her.

"Fern. Fern, can you hear me?" There was no indication that she could. "I want to do what's right for you. I'll try to make the best decisions."

Louella sat down and pulled a thin blanket from her bag and lay it across her lap. Then she took a book from the bag and opened it to her bookmarked page.

"I remember how you used to like your mama to read to you. So, I thought I might read to you tonight," she said, not knowing whether Fern could hear her. Regardless, it gave Louella a way to pass the time.

"This book is called *Winesburg, Ohio*. It's a collection of stories, really. And the story I'm reading tonight is called "Departure." I hope you like it."

Sometime well after midnight, Louella rose from the depths of sleep, in response to a soft rubbing on her cheek. When she opened her eyes, she was surprised to see it was Fern, gently touching her face and watching her through her swollen lids. It instantly reminded Louella of the way Fern had touched Nora as she lay on her deathbed. Louella sat up slowly and took Fern's hand in her own.

"I'm so glad you're awake," Louella said softly. "I've been so worried about you."

Fern tried to speak but nothing came out. Alarm spread across her face.

"No, no, it's okay. You've had an injury to your neck: it's swollen, but you'll be able to talk again when it's healed more. The doctor took care of it. He said you'll be fine."

Fern nodded, but tears slid out of her eyes and down the sides of her face.

"You're all right, Fern. You'll be all right. I'm right here with you. I'll take care of you."

Remembering, Fern placed her hand on her abdomen and looked at Louella.

"The baby's all right. The doctor wants to deliver the baby soon, maybe even tomorrow. He says it's for the best. The best for both of you."

Fern started to shake her head slowly.

"He'll do it by caesarean. You'll be asleep. Everything will be all right," Louella said wondering if she should make such a promise.

Louella took her hand and held it tight until Fern's eyes began to close again. When she was sure Fern was sleeping, she laid her head down on the bed and cried.

Two days later, after another night spent at Fern's bedside, Louella was in her office when the door opened.

"Daniel," Louella stood up. "Come in. How'd it go?"

"The baby's fine. It's a boy. On the small side but healthy as can be. The patient came through just fine too. The caesarean was standard and the salpingectomy."

Louella put her hands on her desk to steady herself. "Salpingectomy? On Fern?"

"Standard procedure, Louella. That's what we do when we have evidence that a resident got pregnant at the sanitarium. It's for their own good."

"Why didn't you ask me first?" she demanded, her indignation flaring.

"Why would I ask you? It's standard procedure in obstetrics here. You're just a nurse. You had nothing to say in the matter," he answered arrogantly. "Anyway, make arrangements with the family. They can take the baby in three days. Have them come here to your office, and let me know when they show up. Payment in full. Cash only. Tell them to come prepared."

He left abruptly and left Louella standing at her desk, devastated.

Judge Ennis came to see the baby the next day. Louella met him outside the children's ward afterward. They sat on a bench in the shade of the pecan grove, and Louella told him about Nora and about Fern. The judge told Louella about Tom and about his wife and how her heart was broken when their son died. Together, they talked through what they thought would be best for the well-being of the child. And what Louella had decided was best for Fern. Judge Ennis said they would not take him if it meant Fern was going to want him back some day. He was not willing to risk that on account of his wife. Louella, for her part, explained that she was willing to take care of that on her end if the judge would help her bring an end to the black-market baby ring that had been operating out of the sanitarium for years. Louella had remembered that the judge had been a member of the state board commission that oversaw the sanitarium. Though he no longer had any authority in that regard, he was willing to help Louella shut down what he agreed was a vile and immoral practice. The more they talked, the more it became clear that the Ennises would need someone to care for the newborn. Judge Ennis asked Louella if she knew anyone who might be qualified and interested, and before she knew what she was doing, she said yes, she knew someone—and that someone was her.

On the afternoon of the third day after the baby was born, Dr. Daniel Walters opened the door to what had been Louella's office. Seated at the desk was Judge Elroy Ennis and by his side stood Deputy Sheriff James Robert Guthrie.

"Come in, Doctor. We've been waiting for you. Please have a seat." The judge indicated the chair across from the desk.

The doctor hesitated for a moment and then did as directed.

"I take it from the look on your face that I don't need to introduce myself. I'm here to collect my grandson. But I understand you're here to collect something else," the judge said.

"I don't know what that nurse told you, sir. I think there was a misunderstanding of some sort. You know how hysterical women can be."

"I don't imagine this has anything to do with hysterical women, Doctor. And if you want to keep that title, you'd better listen to what I have to say."

Walters gripped the arms of the chair, beads of perspiration appeared on his forehead.

"I was on the state commission of this hospital for ten years. I served in the Georgia Assembly for three terms. I was the mayor of Milledgeville at one time. And I still sit on the bench of a court that could with a clear conscience and a faithful heart sentence you to prison time for what you've been doing here."

The judge looked up at James Robert. "This officer of the law is here as my witness. And we will all three of us be party to this understanding."

He pushed a paper across the desk.

"I understand this is standard procedure in your business. You go ahead and sign this death certificate for the child born to Fern Walker. I'll see to it that this paperwork is filed here at the sanitarium."

He pushed another paper forward. "And then you sign this birth certificate for a baby boy born to Louella Guthrie with my son Tom, identified as the father. I'll be taking that with me."

Dr. Walters did what he was told and sat back in the chair.

"If you're waiting on your fee, well, there won't be one, Doctor. And just so you know how serious this business is, I plan to ask my former colleagues on the state commission to look into the allegations that doctors here are performing procedures on female patients without their consent and often without their knowledge. Oh, and I will mention that I have heard rumors of baby selling going on out here too. That should be enough to open an investigation. And it ought to be enough to keep you busy for a while. Too busy for all of these extracurricular activities."

The judge stood up. "We're finished here now. And if some cockeyed story about what happened here today gets out, well, you can imagine Deputy Guthrie's version and my version will be perfectly compatible. Good day, Doctor."

Louella, with the baby in her arms, met them outside the building. They walked together to where the judge and James Robert had left their cars. Louella went to the rear door of the judge's car and waited while he opened it for her. Mrs. Ennis reached out her arms. Louella handed the tiny bundle over to Tom's mother.

Louella climbed into James Robert's truck, already packed with her things. He climbed in and started it up.

"You sure about this, Louella?"

"Too late to question that now, James Robert."

"Did you see Fern?" he asked, suspecting he knew the answer.

Looking straight ahead she answered, "I haven't seen Fern since the night before that man birthed her baby and made her barren. Now I've had her son declared dead and left it to someone else to give her that news, when actually, I stole that baby and gave him away. If there is a God that understands I did what I thought was right, I hope he will make sure that I never have to see her again."

James Robert started up the engine. They followed the judge out the driveway.

Effie

APRIL, 1923

17

"Sallie. It's me. I'm coming in," Effie called as she opened the door. She caught sight of Sallie exactly where she thought she might, in the backyard.

"I hope you don't mind that I let myself in," Effie said, walking down the steps into the blooming paradise that was Sallie's sanctuary.

"No. I'm glad you did. I never would have heard you from back here," Sallie answered, pulling a bright red-and-white gingham cloth across a large table.

"That looks nice. New table?" Effie asked.

Sallie shook her head. "You know who talked me into this. She said since I liked to have company for dinner, and she had the backyard looking the best it ever had, that I needed to set a table out here so we could enjoy it. I bought the lumber. She made the table." Sallie stopped and surveyed Fern's handiwork. "Did a good job too."

"It's perfect," Effie agreed. "Speaking of Fern, where is she?"

"Oh, off doing whatever it is she does," Sallie said with a snort. She pointed to the multicolored flowers that sat along the kitchen steps. "Put those pots of violets on the table. Fern's got them blooming like I never could." Heading back toward the kitchen, she stopped and looked at Effie, "Glad you could make it."

"Me too. This seemed like the right place to be today," Effie said, following her back into the house. "I've never spent this day away from home."

At the sink, Sallie picked up a colander full of washed celery stalks and carrots.

"If you want to make yourself useful, throw on an apron and cut the celery and carrots for me. I want to put some vegetables on the table," Sallie told her. "I'm glad to spend it with you."

"The first couple of years after Mama died, we decided to make it a celebration day at home. Seemed more fitting," Effie recalled as she got busy with the celery.

A few quiet moments passed while Effie pulled herself back to the present and asked, "What's on the menu?"

"Picnic food. Roast beef sandwiches, cabbage slaw, butterscotch cake."

"That sounds wonderful. You must have been cooking for days."

"I had some help," Sallie said, slicing roast beef.

"What's this?" Effie asked, glancing at the book on the counter.

"I got that out for you," Sallie answered. "Will DuBois. You've read his books, I'm sure."

Effie stopped what she was doing to look at the title. "*Darkwate*r. I haven't read that one, actually."

"I chose it for the occasion. Seemed appropriate," Sallie said, getting back to her slicing.

"Which one, my visit or the anniversary of my mother's death?" Effie chided.

Without missing a slice, Sallie answered, "Both. They were great friends, you know, Addy and Will. Colleagues at the university and friends besides."

"He was always so serious. That's what I remember from his visits. Later, when I read some of his writings in school, I wondered about him. I wasn't always sure that he and my father got along very well."

"That sounds about right," Sallie offered.

Effie dressed quietly, hoping not to disturb the others still sleeping. She picked up the book Sallie had chosen for her and made her way to the kitchen where she put on a pot of coffee. Waiting for the stovetop percolator to finish its work, Effie stood at the door, looking out over the table and chairs, randomly scattered and thought about Sallie's motives for wanting her to read Will DuBois's book. She said she had chosen it for the occasion. One passage that Sallie had bookmarked for her included some DuBois storytelling set at an Atlanta home where he described being surrounded by "color in human flesh—brown that crimsoned readily; dim soft yellow that escaped description; cream-like duskiness that shadowed to rich tints of autumn leaves." That could have been her own home, Effie mused. She remembered gatherings that fit that perfectly. In the passage, DuBois recounted a conversation about train travel and another about going to the theater where he described the realities of life as he had experienced them in Boston and Atlanta. Effie wondered what Sallie had hoped would be illuminated by DuBois's words. She poured a cup of coffee and headed out to Fern's table, drew up a chair, and opened the book to the passage she had read the previous night. On her third read-through, the back door opened and Sallie emerged, coffee cup in hand, barefoot in her pale pink nightgown and matching robe.

"Still reading?" she asked, settling into a chair.

"Just the same thing over and over again," Effie admitted. "I'm not a sociologist like Will DuBois."

"I don't think you have to be to understand it." Sallie quoted from memory, "Pessimism is cowardice. The man who cannot frankly acknowledge the 'Jim Crow' car as a fact and yet live and hope is simply afraid either of himself or of the world."

Effie, her finger on the text looked at Sallie. "That's exactly what I was reading."

Sallie nodded and sipped, watching Effie over the top of her cup.

"So, what do you want me to understand from that, teacher?" Effie asked.

THE TRUTH TOGETHER

Sallie shook her head slowly. "That's not how this works. The teacher doesn't tell her students what to think about what they read. You know better than that."

"You think this is somehow connected to my mother, don't you?"

"And you aren't getting away with that either. There's no throwing this back at me, trying to figure out what I think. You're the reader. You're the one who's thinking this is somehow connected to Addy. You should be asking the questions, and you should be the one answering them."

Effie looked down at the text again. "Pessimism is cowardice," she read. "I'm thinking my mother was not a coward, and I don't imagine you thought she was either."

She looked at Sallie for confirmation. Sallie looked off into the garden, refusing to support or deny her student's unraveling of the riddle.

"And of all the train trips I ever took with my mother, we never rode Jim Crow," she continued. "I never thought about that much until I took the train by myself for the first time. You know when that was?"

Sallie turned back to Effie. "When?"

"When I came to Milledgeville last summer. I went to the station a few days before and bought a first-class ticket just to make sure I could. I put on a nice dress, went to the ticket window, and bought it. My hands were shaking. I felt sick at my stomach. I had to force myself not to bolt and run the minute I had it in my hand."

Effie closed the book and picked up her coffee. "Then I went back two days later and got on that train. Walked right in and sat down, praying to God I wouldn't be told to go to the Jim Crow car, wouldn't be humiliated in front of all those people."

"And everything worked out," Sallie stated the fact. "How did you feel about that?"

Effie smiled, recalling the moment on the train. "Relieved. Hopeful. I thought it was a sign that what I was doing was the right thing. Not just about the train ride, but coming here to the sanitarium."

"Hopeful," Sallie said. "Now that's a word I would say that I most often associate with Adrienne McNeil Herndon."

They smiled across their coffee.

"And for that matter, I would say with your father too. Their lives together and their lives apart were hopeful. Everything they accomplished, you and your brother are living proof of that."

Effie waited, knowing that Sallie needed to do some teaching, even if she had schooled her about figuring it out on her own.

"They were anything but cowards. They always chose hopefulness over pessimism. That's what I hope you understand. Your mother, when she went north and chose to be Anne DuBignon, that wasn't cowardly. That was pragmatic. She wanted something. Just like you. She wanted more than what she was able to have in Atlanta, and she decided the way to get it was to keep something about herself private. She was hopeful that she could find a way to rise above hatred and prejudice and get what she wanted in life. What she wanted was a career on the stage. And it had to be on the only stage that she thought mattered, in New York City. There was no other possibility. That was courageous. She tried to break free from what society and politics said she could be and get what she wanted. You have to understand that this had been Addy's dream for as long as she could remember."

"Do you really believe that, Sallie? That she was courageous? You don't think that she was ashamed of who she was, ashamed that she was colored, and so she decided to pretend to be something else?"

"No, child. I don't think that for a minute. She was hopeful, and she was willing to take risks and make sacrifices. She understood that the Jim Crow car was a fact of life, but she refused to accept that it would define her. Or her children. She chose to live and hope."

The screen door squeaked open, and Fern popped her head out. "I take it I'm on breakfast detail?"

"Late sleepers always are," Sallie answered.

"I don't quite understand that logic. But anyway, eggs and ham. Biscuits if I can find some. Ready in ten minutes." The door flapped shut.

Sallie turned back to Effie. "Never ashamed, your mama. Forever hopeful."

True to her word, Fern backed out the screen door ten minutes later, balancing steaming plates for the three of them. She dashed back in for the coffeepot and joined them at the table. Sharing food had always been a reverent undertaking for Sallie, and she had instilled a new habit in both Effie and Fern to behave likewise—at least when they sat at her table. After plates were emptied and fresh coffee poured, conversation resumed.

"So where were you last night?" Effie asked Fern.

"On a night-time reconnoiter."

"Any place in particular?" Effie inquired.

"I covered some ground," Fern responded, forever keeping her own counsel about how she spent her time, unwilling to expose herself to their judgement.

"Anything interesting?" Effie tried another tack.

"Nothing much," Fern hedged.

"I'm wondering if you're planning a career in detective work with all the snooping around you do. You're pretty good at it. Seem to enjoy it too," Effie chided her.

"Nope. Too much idle time in that kind of work. I like to occupy myself in a more meaningful way," Fern told them.

"Have you told Effie what you're thinking about doing?" Sallie put her on the spot.

"I didn't want to until we know something."

Effie looked from one to the other. "Is something in the works?"

Sallie raised her eyebrows at Fern, signaling that she would have to do the telling if it was to be told.

"I might want to go to nursing school," Fern said, looking everywhere but at Effie.

Now it was Effie's turn to raise her eyebrows. "I remember it wasn't too long ago that you thought you were better trained than most nurses anyway, including this one," Effie said, placing a hand to her chest.

Fern risked a sideways glance at Effie.

"Any ideas where you might go for your training?"

"That's a work in progress," Sallie answered for her. "She's had no formal schooling until now. Though I don't want her to get all full of herself when I say that she's a good student."

"Good? Just good?" Fern asked.

"Good is about the best you'll get from me. Always room for improvement." Sallie stood and gathered the dishes.

They watched Sallie disappear into the house and Fern asked, "You have to be back at the sanitarium this afternoon?"

"Yes. I'm supposed to work in the kitchen today," she said, reaching out and picking up a small clay pot of deep purple velvety blooms. "William's headed to Washington for some meetings about his research and asked me to oversee the attendants. They don't have much experience."

"I guess Albert still hasn't turned up?"

"Not since William confronted him about bringing whiskey into the ward and questioned him about Pearl."

"Too bad he scared him off. Now we might not find out what happened."

"I don't suppose you've learned anything about that prison work crew or what happened with Roselyn's companion?" Effie asked.

"No. The work site's quiet. I'm hoping construction might start back soon."

"So, you're thinking about going to nursing school? Seriously thinking about it?"

Fern nodded.

"I think that's a good choice, Fern," Effie ventured. "You'd make a great nurse."

"I'm ready for a change of scenery. There's nothing much left for me here. Not anything that I can call my own anyway," Fern declared.

"I've decided I'm going back to Atlanta in June myself. One year at the sanitarium is enough for me," Effie told her.

Fern nodded again. "I think that's a good choice, too, Effie."

Effie stepped off the train car and walked across the grounds toward her room. It was midday, the sky a brilliant sunlit blue and warm. Appreciating the fact that her time there was drawing to a close, she took a turn to take the long way around. The azaleas were a little past their prime, and the magnolia blossoms were not quite ready to open. The lush greenness of the landscape was such a contrast to all that happened in the confines of the grounds. Effie was pondering the disparity between the setting and the events that took place there when she found herself walking past Fern's old cottage. Two women were out on the front porch, one darning a sock, the other, trying to coax a decrepit-looking gray tabby cat to come up the steps with what looked like a chicken bone. Effie realized how empty the sanitarium had seemed since Fern had left. Knowing that she could see her at Sallie's every couple of weeks was better than not seeing her at all, but she missed being surprised by her random appearances. She felt as lonely as she had back in the summer when she had first arrived. It was one of several reasons that Effie had decided that another year's contract was not what she wanted. Her work on the ward was meaningful. She knew she was a comfort to the women that lived there, but the knowledge that their lives were not going to change much made it feel futile somehow. They were patients at a mental hospital. Many confined for an unspecified period of time. The state was stingy with money for the maintenance and care of the facility and the patients. Effie couldn't imagine spending her life there, and she was glad she had told Fern and Sallie that she was planning to leave. That made it more real somehow. Next, she'd have to tell her father and Norris. She wasn't sure how they would react, but she suspected that they would welcome her home. She knew how lucky she was to simply decide she was going back to Atlanta. She had family and she had a home. She had no idea what lay ahead. That would take some time to think through, and she knew having that time was something else she should be grateful for. Family, a place to live, that would sustain her while she decided what she wanted next. Fern couldn't count on a single one of those things. And yet, Effie felt envious of her somehow.

While she was musing about her good fortune, Effie passed by the construction site for the new nurses' dormitory and nursing school. She didn't get over to this part of the campus very often and was surprised to see a couple of men laying a brick sidewalk from the building, connecting it to the pathway she was walking along. She stopped for a moment and watched, wondering if Fern's hopes for construction to resume might not be in vain. She decided to keep an eye out, so she could report back to Fern. Though knowing Fern's tendency to do her reconnoiter, as she called it, Effie realized Fern would probably know what was happening before she did.

Just as she was turning away, the front door of the building opened and Creeper Albert walked through it, and if she wasn't mistaken, right behind him, the man they knew as Eddie. His appearance was distinctive. He was a tall, burly man with a barrel chest. Effie had seen him twice before on the same day. Once at the construction site, when he was yelling down at her from one of the top corner windows. The other, on Roselyn's front porch. On that day, he was dressed exactly as he was now, in a striped, steel-gray coverall. The only difference was that it was buttoned up tight and Roselyn was dead, not half naked and rubbing up against him like a cat in heat.

Effie clapped her hand over her mouth to stifle a yelp of surprise, turned, and with legs churning, walked away as fast as she dared. She wanted to run, but feared drawing attention to herself. She wasn't sure that they had seen her. Albert would certainly recognize her from the kitchen lab. Too afraid to look back, Effie headed straight to her building, ran down the hallway to her room, and fumbled with the key. Once inside she slammed the door shut, turned the lock, and leaned against it. After she realized no one was coming for her, she started pacing.

Effie tried to remember what William had told her about Albert. She couldn't recall the details, except that he had been mentally wounded by war, admitted as a patient several times, and was put to work at the sanitarium doing odd jobs. He'd been a cook in his past life, and when William asked for some kitchen workers to assist with his research, Albert showed up one day and had been with him ever since. William told her that Albert had disappeared from the sanitarium, though she wasn't sure how he knew that.

And what on earth was the connection between Albert and Eddie? Effie was certain that's who the other man was. She couldn't imagine why they would be together. From what Fern had told her, Eddie was one of the prison work crew foremen. She needed to get word to Fern as soon as she could. Then she reconsidered. What could Fern do? Were those the men connected to the attacks on Pearl and the other women who had disappeared? Were they dangerous? Effie had so much to figure out and no one to talk it over with. What a terrible time for William to be on a train to Washington.

Effie looked at her watch. She was supposed to be at the laboratory kitchen in five minutes. Somehow time had slipped away without her realizing. She changed out of her weekend clothes and pulled a uniform from a hanger in the closet, knowing she needed to present an authoritative appearance in order to get the new workers to follow her instructions.

William was depending on her to keep things running smoothly while he was away for the next few days. They had thought through most every scenario that could possibly cause problems, but they had not even considered the possibility of Albert showing up. Effie wondered if he had indeed actually left the sanitarium for a while, or if he simply had made himself scarce because William had confronted him. Regardless, Effie hoped that Albert wouldn't show up at the kitchen. He probably didn't know anything about William being away. And what business would he have at the kitchen anyway? Effie tried to apply reason to calm her fears that somehow Albert might have seen her outside the new nurses' building and that he might hold her responsible for his falling out with William at the kitchen lab. As she smoothed out her collar and put on her cap, she looked at herself in the tiny mirror she had placed on the wall.

"I'm not a coward, either, but I don't want to be naive," she said to her reflection. She gave a final nod, placed the leather strap with the key to the kitchen on it around her neck, and then as she was locking the door, had a thought. At the closet, she slipped her hand into the pocket of her jacket and pulled out the folded paper with the name of James Robert's contact at the police precinct. Best to keep it handy, she thought. She locked her room on the way out and headed for the laboratory.

Despite Effie's fears, everything went precisely according to plan. William's two new assistants were courteous and did exactly what she instructed. They prepared the food and the various supplements used in the nutrition experiments without incident. Everything had been properly measured and delivered on time to the women involved in the study. More heartening was that Albert had not come to the kitchen or jumped out of the bushes or anything else that Effie had conjured up in her imagination. Things went so smoothly that Effie had made it back to her ward in time to help serve supper to her women. And she had even had the chance to sit and chat with those gathered at the table over pork chops, cabbage, and cornbread. Bertie had taken over the tiresome task of measuring milk and yeast and recording data in the logbook. Even William had conceded that she was a proper taskmaster and statistician. Bertie took great pride in her new responsibilities, and Effie had more time to spend on her regular duties. Now, even those did not seem quite so daunting as they had a few months back. For one thing, the women were in better health than they had been since Effie had seen to it that they had proper food to eat. More and more, the women were able to leave the sick ward and return to other accommodations at the sanitarium. Though Effie wasn't sure that was the better outcome, since they were removed from the familiar environment of her ward and away from her care. But she knew she couldn't fix everything. For certain, with better health and fuller bellies, the mood in the ward was not as desperate as it had once been. She knew she needed to appreciate the positive outcomes she had helped achieve and not dwell on all that was left to be done.

When Effie had advised the nursing administration that she was not planning to renew her contract for a second year, they had immediately brought in a new young nurse. She had been trained at the Municipal Training School at Grady just like Effie. Though no one said it, Effie took it as validation that she had served well and that they hoped to replace her with someone as competent as she was. Effie watched the new nurse now from across the room. She was young and a little nervous. Though she had only been there for a little over a week, she seemed comfortable enough around the women of the ward. Now Effie just needed to gently hand over the women to her care.

"You got all that kitchen business taken care of?" Bertie asked as she pulled a chair up to the table.

"I did. The new workers did a good job," Effie answered.

"That's a good thing. Dr. William would get his dander up if they was slackin'," Bertie chuckled.

Effie smiled. "I'm sure he would. He's a little on the persnickety side, for sure."

"Pass me that cornbread, Ms. Effie."

Effie watched Bertie fix her plate. She was certainly the picture of health these days. Effie wondered when Bertie might be headed back to her own family. She knew that was the hoped-for outcome, but she wished their departures might coincide. She couldn't imagine the ward without her.

"Bertie, do you remember that night when Pearl left with those two men?"

Bertie frowned. "I wish I could forget it."

"You and Cora said that Albert was one of them. Have you remembered anything else about the other one?"

Bertie looked toward the door. "I don't think he came into the room. Stood back over next to the door. For sure I didn't see his face."

"Anything you noticed about him? Anything at all?"

Bertie looked back at the door for a minute and thought. Turning back to Effie, she said, "He was big. A big man. That's all I saw."

Effie nodded.

"Why you worryin' 'bout that?" Bertie asked.

"I wish I could forget too," Effie answered. "Wish we knew what happened to her is all." Remembering Pearl being lowered to the floor with her nightgown around her neck, she reached for her throat.

"Oh no!" Effie exclaimed, pulling the leather strap up, revealing the key to the kitchen. "I forgot to lock the kitchen when I left." She started to rise.

"I'll go do it," Bertie said, getting up.

"You finish your supper, Bertie, I'll go," Effie replied.

"Keep my supper safe," Bertie ordered, reaching for the key, slipping the cord around her neck. "I'll be right back."

After the attendants came to clear away the dishes, the women began passing in and out of the washroom for a last visit before bedtime. Effie got busy with night-time medical checks. The new nurse watched everything she did. How Effie wished that she had been able to observe rather than jump right in with both feet, as she had been expected to do when she first arrived back in June. Rather than regret that, she saw this as good teaching time and took care to treat the women with respect and kindness, hoping that would be a part of her legacy that the young nurse would continue. The checks complete, Effie stood at the desk, looking over her charts and realized she hadn't seen Bertie come back into the room. She walked down the row of beds to Bertie's spot. It was empty. Out on the portico several women stood, talking quietly among themselves, while the purple-shaded twilight engulfed the grounds.

"Anybody seen Bertie?" she asked them.

"Not since supper."

Effie walked with purpose through the ward, scanning the room from side to side. "She's not here," she said mostly to herself.

"I have to check on Bertie," she told the young nurse. "She went to the kitchen lab to lock up and hasn't made it back."

The lights were out when she got there. Effie stood outside in the shadows, wondering if she should go for help. Deciding that there was no time to waste, she balled up her fists and tested the door. It was unlocked and so she slowly opened it and stepped inside. The silence and the darkness settled over her. Effie took careful, soundless steps to reach the light switch on the far wall. Once there she waited and listened for any indication that she might not be alone. All was quiet. She flipped the switch and bathed the room in light. Effie breathed a sigh of relief that the kitchen was empty and walked through to see that everything was in order. Near the food pantry, she stopped. They never closed the door to the pantry. It was left open for their convenience. But now it was closed. Effie picked up a knife from the worktable, stepped closer to the pantry door and listened. Hardly breathing, she placed her hand on the doorknob, knife at the ready, and yanked it open.

No Bertie.

Fern

APRIL, 1923

18

Fern eased forward as much as she dared, hoping that in the shroud of foggy darkness James Robert would not sense her nearness. Unmoving and barely drawing a breath, she was no more than five feet away, hidden under the waxy green leaves of a magnolia, just outside the colored women's building where Effie worked. He was waiting for something or somebody. Fern figured it must be Effie. She wanted to be as close as she could to see and hear what happened next. He was nervous, walking back and forth, his head down, hat pulled low. Fern had been under the tree, going on two hours now, and she still had no clue what had happened. Her hunch was that something must have caused Effie to call for help. Fern had come unprepared for intrigue and was jumpy. All she had in her rucksack was a couple of oranges and a clay pot violet she was bringing to Effie. Scrounging around in the bottom of the bag while she waited, she had discovered that her pocketknife was missing. She couldn't remember when she used it last. She thought maybe she had left it in Sallie's backyard. The first sign that something was up was when Effie hurried toward the side entrance about an hour ago. While she stood there banging on the door, she kept glancing back as if worried that somebody was following her. Someone finally opened the door, Effie said something in a raised voice that she couldn't quite make out and disappeared inside. Then, James Robert showed up walked past where she was in hiding, went up the front steps, then came right back out a few minutes later. Now, Fern and James Robert were waiting, tension taunt as a wire from where she was beneath the tree to him, pacing the sidewalk. A few more minutes passed before Effie came out the side door, and James Robert hurried over to meet her. Fern was disappointed that they moved away from her hiding spot and that their voices were hushed, muted by the fog. They walked away in a direction that was certainly not toward the building where Effie lived. Rather than follow them and risk being discovered, Fern decided to head over to Effie's.

A while later Effie and James Robert materialized in the mist and talked for a few minutes more. When James Robert took his leave, Effie opened the door to her building. She spotted the violet left on the threshold and so wasn't startled when Fern closed the distance between them and slipped in behind her.

Once inside the safety of Effie's room, they both started in at once.

"What's going on?" Fern asked.

"Bertie's gone."

"Gone where?"

"She went over to William's lab to lock up. When I realized she hadn't come back, I got worried, went to look for her. She wasn't there. No one's seen her."

Fern stared.

"There's more." Effie unpinned her hat. "Alfred's back and guess who's with him?"

"Who?"

"Roselyn's Eddie. He's alive. I saw them outside the new nurses' building. I'm afraid they've done something to Bertie."

Fern tried to process all that Effie was saying. "I don't understand. They know each other?"

Effie, wide-eyed, nodded her head.

"What's the connection between those men?" Fern started pacing. "How does Roselyn fit into this? Obviously, Eddie was her lover or something. She was sure he was dead that night in the tunnel. Now here he is with Albert, who might have been the man who attacked me in the tunnel, killed Roselyn, and disappeared when he was questioned about Pearl. You think they took Bertie?"

"What else could it be?"

"Were they really after Bertie, or were they waiting for you?"

"How would I know?"

The sound of their quick breaths filled the space between them as they thought through what had happened.

"Why was James Robert here?" Fern asked.

"I asked him to come. He got here pretty quick."

"What did you tell him?"

"I told him about Bertie and about seeing Albert and Eddie."

"What did he say?"

"That he had no jurisdiction here. But he seemed concerned. Said he would try to find out anything he could about Bertie and see what he could learn about those men."

"How's that supposed to keep you safe?"

"I guess I'm on my own for that," Effie said, realizing that she actually was.

"Not on your own," Fern said adamantly.

"This could be dangerous, Fern."

"What are we supposed to do? Let them have Bertie? We've got to find her before she ends up like Pearl."

"She went there for me. I should have gone myself." Effie sat down on the bed. "I don't want anyone else to get hurt."

"We have one thing in our favor. We're smarter than they are. If we can come up with a plan to trap them, they won't be able to hurt anybody ever again."

"You're assuming they're the attackers," Effie added. "And if they are, they've gotten away with it before. You might think you're smarter, but they've been smart enough not to get caught."

"I think there're some signs that they're involved somehow, don't you? Why don't we go over what we know about the attacks and about Albert and Eddie and see what makes sense."

"And where will that get us?"

"And then we'll make a plan. Got any pencils and paper?"

"A plan for what?" Effie asked, going to the closet where she rummaged around on the shelf, pulling out a drawing pad and a box of pencils.

"Finding Bertie and how we're gonna put an end to this business," Fern said, resolute in her belief that they could outsmart two possible murderers.

Later that night, Fern moved stealthily along the side of the old brick laundry building where she had spent so much of the past few years. Looking at the old, crumbling façade, no one would understand what a haven it had been for Fern. Tonight, she was hoping that the old storage closet hadn't been cleaned out since she left in December. The treasure trove of disguises she squirreled away had served her well, and she was counting on being able to find everything she thought they would need to put her plan into action. The lights were out, and there was no indication that anybody was inside. Fern tested the door and as usual found it unlocked. Keys got lost or were forgotten and had mostly been dispensed with except where safety or privacy was a concern. Fern opened the door and let herself in. She made her way through the darkened room, around the sorting table to the short hallway. Once there she opened the closet door, reached up to the top shelf on the front left, and put her hand on a flashlight, right where she had left it. The one she had in her bag had burned out, and she was relieved to find a backup. She flicked it on, cast the light around. From the looks of it, nothing had been touched since she was last there. Below the bottom shelf Fern shoved a box aside, reached behind it and pulled another larger box free. Removing its top, she shined the light inside and smiled. Just as she had hoped. Just what she needed to put her plan in motion. After gathering a few more things she thought might be useful and stuffing them into her rucksack, she turned off the flashlight, slid it into the bag, and headed for the door. She paused in the doorway and gazed back at the dark interior for a last look.

Fern had lived at the sanitarium for enough years to know that a lot happened under the cover of darkness, but that the groundwork for those activities was usually laid during the light of day. She made it to Sallie's and back in record time and planned to spend the day scouting things out. First order of business was to see if she could find any signs of Bertie. She started at the new nurses' building. She wanted to have a look around, maybe catch sight of Eddie or Albert, see where they might lead her. The brick masons had left their work on the sidewalk unfinished. A pile of bricks nearby provided the perfect prop for pretending to complete the task. Fern, in a blue cotton work shirt and denim overalls, her hair covered by a blue corduroy flat cap, spent time moving the bricks over to the walkway. She hoped that no one would stop and wonder at work being done on a Sunday, when most everything went into slow motion. After a half hour and no sign of anyone at the work site, she walked the perimeter of the building and headed inside for a closer look. Other than the ordinary construction debris, there wasn't a clue.

Next, she was off to the open field near the old tunnel entrance where Roselyn and Eddie had disappeared that night and where Fern had eventually gone in to look for them. She hoped the tunnel was deserted, like the construction site, but she wanted to be sure before she ventured inside. A push reel lawn mower was standing against a tree, and Fern took it into the field as her cover as she kept a look out to see if anybody was making use of the tunnels for any reason. When another half hour had passed, and not a single person had appeared, Fern wheeled the mower over to the tunnel entrance, opened it and dragged the mower in behind her. The door closed with a bang. In an instant, she was plunged back into the cold reality of that December night, the discovery of Roselyn, and the excruciating concussion she had gotten in the bargain. She set the mower aside, pulled the flashlight and the knife from her rucksack, remembering how it had been her saving grace, and slipped it up her sleeve. Fern had avoided the tunnels. She had been warned against them early on. In that fateful experience inside the dark labyrinth, she felt something foul and malicious lurking inside. Not understanding why, the motivation to see this thing through was powerful enough to pull her back in.

Fern moved quickly, refusing to waste time or consider the dangers that could be skulking ahead. *It's about Bertie, most of all*, she reminded herself. She stopped for a minute where the tunnel turned and narrowed at the place where she remembered she had first found Roselyn hobbling on a likely broken ankle. Then steeling herself, pushed on, taking down cobwebs with one hand, directing a beam of light with the other. Further down, Fern came to the place where the tunnel widened and a series of short, wooden doors opened off the passageway to her left. Several of the doors stood partially open, only one was closed. Fern used her boot to push open the door to the first room. There was no sign of Bertie. What she did find was a low-ceilinged dingy room equipped with what looked like several old hospital mattresses separated from each other by cloth-covered divider screens that were filthy and torn. An examination of two other nearby rooms proved them to be identical to the first. She lifted the latch on the closed door to the last room and panned her light across the interior. Small wooden tables and chairs, rickety and time worn, were scattered throughout the space. Oil lamps sat atop the tables and a couple of medium-sized cupboards with padlocks were backed up against the rear of the room. Next to the cupboards, several dozen dull, gray metal beer mugs and whiskey glasses lined the shelves of a hutch. Fern stood pondering what possible explanation there might be for these clandestine bedrooms and bar room and only one thing made sense. Somebody was operating a business down here, and maybe somebody thought it was worth killing over.

Outside the rooms again, Fern wondered if this was a place people came to willingly, or was it a place where sometimes someone ended up there but didn't really want to? Maybe somebody like Pearl or Bertie. *Could that have happened to them? And what about Roselyn?* She and Effie had struggled to understand how Roselyn fit into a relationship between Eddie and Albert. Despite her last encounter with Roselyn and the remorse she felt about her death, Fern couldn't quite see her as a victim. They were all in the tunnel that night—Eddie, Roselyn, and Albert. These rooms were probably what had drawn them there. In the dank confines of the tunnel, the taunts

Roselyn had previously made, and then the things she had revealed that night, slowly came back to Fern. Fern thought about something Roselyn had said months before. A threat about something coming for her, something that she saw in her nightmares. Could this be what she meant by that? Was someone coming for her? Was this a place they might have taken her? And Roselyn told her that she had been in jail several times for prostitution. Fern looked at the doors to the filthy rooms. *Is that what this was—a business, operated by a prostitute and a man who lives outside the sanitarium with access to bootleg beer and whiskey?*

Fern had no proof that what she was considering might be the explanation for Pearl's and Roselyn's deaths, and Bertie's disappearance, but the discovery in the tunnel caused her to adjust her plans. Now she had a choice to make. *Which room would be most likely the one where they would take someone who really didn't want to be there? Somebody who might resist or call for help.* She chose the one farthest away from the barroom. She stepped inside and took from her bag some rope and a hammer and tucked them up under the filthy mattress in the far back corner.

Fern stood in the passageway. It was a risky plan, but she and Effie had agreed something had to be done, and they were the only ones they could think of who might be able to pull it off. She looked in both directions. There were other entrances; she just wasn't sure where. That was probably another important piece of information to have. If she and Effie were coming down here to take care of business, she needed to know where and how they might reach safety and where they might find other hiding spots along the way. Fern headed off into the darkness, away from the only entrance she knew, the knot in her gut pushing upward, she swallowed hard to shove it back down.

Fern found a bench with a straight sight line to the only door leading into the laboratory kitchen where Effie was working and took a seat. She wanted to think through her plans and more importantly keep an eye on that door. She'd had a productive day. She wasn't sure that Effie was really a target, but she wasn't taking any chances. It was overcast and the grounds were mostly deserted. She hadn't laid eyes on either of the two men. But it was Sunday after all. It was doubtful that Eddie would be around. Albert was another matter. If there was a plan to grab Effie, he might be watching to see what she was up to. If he somehow knew that William Tanner was away, he might be thinking this was the perfect time and place to make a move on her. Fern was not about to let that happen without being there to involve herself in his plans. She would watch for a while and decide on her next move.

Fern was exhausted and her mind wandered. That happened when she was tired and still. *It takes a patient person to sit here like this*, she thought. She wondered if that was something she had learned or just something a person was born with. Maybe it was a habit she had developed through her childhood. She had spent a lot of hours alone and waiting. There hadn't really been any timetables in her life dictating what she had to accomplish other than her daily work schedule and mealtime. The last few months living with Sallie hadn't changed much in that way. But the freedom she had experienced and what she had witnessed of other people's lives on the outside made her want something more. She was not completely sure what it was, but she was positive it was time to leave the sanitarium, leave Milledgeville, and leave the past behind. There were only a few things keeping her there for now. One was Effie. And come June, she was headed back to Atlanta. Another was that little boy at the Ennis place. There was something about him that she needed to know for sure. *Was it possible that he was her son?* It was one more thing that she had no proof of, but there was this nagging feeling that he was hers. And that meant that he was Tom's. But Tom was dead. And she had nothing. She didn't have a job, a family, or a place to live. And so far, she had no way to change any of those things. And that little boy, whether he belonged to her or not, did have those things. He had a family. He had a place to grow up safe and happy. But even with all of that, she remembered the one thing she did have in large measure when she was a young child. She had love. Her mother loved her. And Fern loved her back. No matter that Nora had been in almost exactly the same situation as Fern found herself now, she loved her child. And somehow, that was all that mattered. Fern hoped most of all for that little boy that someone loved him and loved him well. That's what she needed to know for sure.

And there was one more thing that she needed to do before she moved on. She needed to figure out what was happening to those poor defenseless women at the sanitarium. What had happened to Bertie? Was there a chance to save her? She had let her mind wander for too long and so she got back to it. Watching. Waiting. For the answer to reveal itself. It would require patience. Fern was sure that was one thing she had.

After several hours passed, Fern abandoned her perch and headed for the kitchen. Two steps from the door, movement in the bushes near the corner of the building caught her attention and slowed her movements. Careful not to react, but wanting to see if a person emerged, she stopped and patted down her pockets as if searching for something. The tactic paid off. Out of the corner of her eye, she could make out a person crouched behind the shrubbery, trying to remain unnoticed. Buying a bit more time, Fern scrounged around some more, pulled out an orange and held it to her nose. Someone was definitely hiding there. She opened the door, left it standing open behind her and walked over to Effie at the food preparation table.

Effie turned. "You must be Tom," she said, just as they had rehearsed. "Thanks for coming. Dr. Tanner is away and we need all the help we can get."

"Yes ma'am, what can I do to help?" Fern asked in a low, slow voice that threatened to make Effie laugh.

"Why don't you line those trays up on the counter there. We've got sixty-five meals to plate and deliver. These two gentlemen can show you what to do," she said, indicating the other kitchen workers.

"All right," Fern answered in the same voice.

Within the next hour, the work was done. Sixty-five trays of beef stew, green beans, and a slice of white bread were covered and stacked on rolling carts ready for delivery.

"Tom, we have to make our deliveries. We'll be back in about an hour. Go ahead and wash up those dishes, wipe down the counters. Have something to eat before you leave."

Fern nodded and held up a hand in a wave.

She wondered if Effie really meant for her to do the kitchen work and figured she might as well. She kept her eyes trained on the door while she scrubbed pots and returned utensils to the drawers and cupboards. When she was finished, she picked up the plate she had fixed for herself and sat down where she could keep an eye on the door. Taking the first bite, she realized how hungry she was and was soon distracted by the food. It wasn't until she heard the door close that she realized she wasn't alone. Fern quickly masked her alarm at being caught off guard and raised her eyes slowly.

"Hey," the man said as he walked across the room.

Fern stood and slowly stepped out from behind the table.

"You must be new here," the man with the eye patch said.

"What you want? This here's a lab," she said, her voice low and steady.

"I know. I work here. Used to anyways. I heard the doc left town. That true?"

"Don't know nothing 'bout that," Fern answered.

"You seen him?" the man prodded.

"Nope. Just that nurse that's runnin' things."

The man looked around the room, not wanting to be done yet.

"She say he was gone? Doc Tanner?"

"Seems like she said something 'bout that, don't remember what," she replied, playing slow and confused. "You want to wait for her, said she would be back right quick?"

"Nah. Don't got no business with her. It's him I'm wantin'."

Fern could tell he was lying as she watched him scanning the surroundings. She kept her eyes steady on him now. "All right then," she said smoothly.

"Yep," he said, turning for the door. "I'll catch him later." He eyed her again as he pulled the door closed behind him.

It was dark, and Fern couldn't be sure he wasn't watching her through the window, so she sat back down to her supper and went right on eating just in case. She wasn't sure, but thought that maybe he was checking to see that Tanner was gone and if Effie might at some point be alone in the kitchen and easy prey. The food had lost its appeal, but Fern kept at it until the door opened again, and Effie and the two attendants wheeled the carts and empty trays back into the room.

Fern stared at Effie until she had her attention, gave one slow nod, indicating that just as they had hoped, Albert had played his first card. Fern watched a case of the jitters take hold of Effie's features, and as she moved around the room kind of quick and jerky, Fern wondered if Effie could pull this off.

When Effie finally settled down enough to look at Fern again, Fern leaned her head toward the two men finishing the cleaning and then lifted her chin toward the door. Effie read the message well.

"You can go on now," she said, coming across the room. "We can finish up. See you in the morning. Don't forget your supper. She handed them their wrapped plates with a smile. "Thank you for all your help."

She saw them out and closed the door.

Fern walked over to the sink and stood there with the water running. Effie came to stand beside her. "He might be outside looking through the window, so let's just wash these dishes and lock up like you would on any other night. I don't think he's here for you. At least not this time. It's okay. I'm here," Fern told her, forever willing to be the courage others might lack.

"Who was it?" Effie asked quietly.

"Albert. Said he works here, or used to. Wanted to know about Tanner."

They worked without talking and got ready to go. At the door, Fern said loud enough for anyone who wanted to hear, "Let me walk you home, Miss Effie. It's pitch-black out here."

"Thank you, Tom. I would appreciate that."

They closed the door and locked it behind them and headed for Effie's building.

When they arrived, Fern made a show of saying good night and walked off into the darkness after Effie closed the door behind her. Fern slipped behind the building and into one of her favorite magnolia-leafed changing rooms. She stepped out of the coverall and pulled on a nurse's uniform, thinking how long it had been and how right it felt all at the same time. She folded the strap of the rucksack over and carried it like a nurse's bag as she walked back to the front of the building and let herself in. She wasn't sure the ruse was necessary, but they couldn't leave anything to chance. One mistake could be deadly.

When she knocked on her door, Effie opened it quickly and yanked her into the room.

"That was fast. How do you change like that?"

"Lots of practice," Fern answered, setting the bag down.

Effie stood with her hands on her hips, looking at Fern. "You know, I'm thinking that's really the right look for you."

Fern shook her head. "I don't know. We've got to get through this thing first."

Effie turned serious. "We will. Any sign of Bertie?"

Fern kicked off her shoes and plopped down on Effie's bed. "Not a clue. But I don't know. I saw some stuff today. Down in that tunnel." She blew out a breath. "This might be more dangerous than we thought. Somebody's got a blind pig down there."

Effie looked confused.

"You don't know what that is?" Fern asked her.

"Of course I know what it is. I grew up in Atlanta. I just can't believe there's one in a tunnel underneath all of this," she said, throwing up her arms.

"I could be wrong, but I think somehow it's somebody's business. Somebody must be making money off it. There's a barroom and there's rooms with beds. I think there's a brothel down there."

Effie looked unconvinced. "I thought you had never been anywhere but this sanitarium. How do you know so much about those kinds of things?"

Now it was Fern's turn to be the skeptic. "Oh come on. Think about it. I grew up here. You've seen what all goes on. I imagine I've seen as much as you have in Atlanta and probably more."

"Do you think all that's connected to the murders?" Effie asked, moving on.

"It's gonna sound crazy. But I think somebody might be taking women down there for prostitutes. Maybe some were willing. But probably not all. Like Pearl. Maybe Bertie. I don't imagine either one of them would have gone down there of their own free will."

"So, you think they forced women to go down there, sold them for sex, and then what?"

"Somehow things got out of hand. Maybe some tried to get away. Or maybe there was just evil down there. Bad people, doing bad things to other people."

"You think patients here paid money to somebody down there? You said you thought it was a business."

"I don't know, maybe," Fern said, drawing up her legs and wrapping her arms around them.

"Do patients have money?" Effie asked.

"Some do. There's a lot of people here that aren't patients, Effie. People who work here."

They were quiet for a few minutes and then Effie spoke again. "Well, what are we going to do now?"

Fern looked at Effie, and then with a huge sigh, put her head down on the tops of her knees.

"Don't you give up on me now," Effie said, stepping closer.

Fern raised her head and looked up. "I don't think we can do this. I don't want anything to happen that I can't control."

"Did you set things up down there, like we talked about?" Effie asked, taking charge.

Fern nodded.

"Then it's on. You said it before. We're the only ones these women have to keep them safe. And what about Bertie? If we have a chance to find her, we have to take it. There's nobody but us to help her. And besides, we have to do this while William's away. We couldn't do it with him here."

"It's too risky," Fern argued. "I've lived here my whole life. I've tried to fix things. Sometimes it's just not possible to make it all better. Some things are not fixable."

Effie stepped closer still to where Fern sat on the bed. "Somebody is killing defenseless women. We are the only ones who can help them. Nobody else cares. Let's take care of it right now before they hurt one more. I won't be able to live with myself if I don't try."

Fern looked at Effie, admiring the determination and courage she saw on her face but doubtful that she really understood the danger down in the tunnel.

"All right then," Fern answered.

Adrienne and Alonzo and Effie

MARCH, 1910

19

It was raining, and no matter that they were dressed in their fine clothes and Alonzo had to manage both of their bags, Adrienne insisted they get out of the taxicab and take the footbridge over Market Street on their way into Philadelphia's Broad Street Station. Clinging to Alonzo's arm, Adrienne began remembering weekend trips between New York City and Philadelphia. The memories flooded her thoughts. Had it really been two years since she had returned to Atlanta? The recollection of the sights and sounds of the busy city on Friday afternoons and the anxious anticipation to wrap her arms around the children brought a smile to her lips.

"Can we stop for just a minute?"

"Are you all right?" Alonzo asked, worry in his voice and in his eyes.

THE TRUTH TOGETHER

She nodded. "Just one more look."

When she was satisfied, they continued into the station where Adrienne sat down on a long wooden bench and waited while Alonzo secured reservations on the overnight train to Atlanta.

Alonzo returned and slid in next to her. "I got the last stateroom, all the way through to home."

"That's an extravagance, Mr. Herndon," she chided him.

"You're worth it, Mrs. Herndon," he responded, and for a moment the pallor of sadness that shrouded his features lifted away.

She couldn't resist reaching up to touch his cheek. He caught her hand and held it there.

"We could board now if you're ready," he told her.

Adrienne straightened and took a long, slow look around the cavernous station bustling with travelers.

Her eyes continued to roam as she said, "We've waited in a good deal of train stations in our lives, Lonzo. The prospect of the trip, whether we were coming or going, reuniting or parting, never felt quite like this."

She turned to look at him. "This is the last one for me. I want to savor it."

Alonzo opened his mouth to protest the morbidity of her words, thought better of it and simply nodded his acceptance of what she had spoken. They passed a mostly quiet half hour engulfed by the noisy excitement inside the terminal and then slowly made their way to board the train.

Alonzo settled Adrienne on the velvet-covered bench seat near the window of their stateroom and stepped out to have a word with the steward. During their visit to Philadelphia, she had only had a few moments alone. She hadn't minded much. She had made some promises to herself over the past few weeks, and one of them was that she would not dwell on regrets, but this one kept nagging at her. She was sorry to have spent so much time away from the people she loved. Alonzo was at the top of that list. She tried to summon up the urgency she had felt to do all of the things that took her away from him for long stretches of time that she thought were so critical to her very existence but she couldn't. Now she desperately wanted all of that time back.

Empty wishes, she thought as she pushed up from the chair, waited a moment for the dizziness to subside, and walked to the dressing table.

She removed her hat and leaned into the mirror for a closer look. Her complexion was lusterless and patchy gray. Her face, hollowed out, eyes rimmed by dark circles.

When Alonzo returned, Adrienne had changed into her dressing gown, loosened her hair, and brightened her cheeks and lips to a lively shade of pink.

"I thought you had left me here and boarded another train," she teased him. "Maybe found some young woman, looking for adventure with a dashing stranger."

Alonzo was struck by how young and healthy she suddenly appeared in the dim light of their room.

"Not a chance. I ordered some tea and arranged for our dinner to be brought in. Some champagne and oysters for later."

"That sounds nice. Come sit with me, so we can enjoy pulling out of the station together," she said, patting the space next to her. "And then, over tea, let's talk about the things we must. We'll dress for dinner and put all of our worries aside for the rest of the evening."

Alonzo lifted his eyebrows. "That sounds like a proposition."

"You're a smart man, Mr. Herndon."

By the time they pulled out of the train shed, the rain had stopped and the sun had slipped behind tall buildings. Adrienne and Alonzo, hands locked together, reveled in the golden halo that ringed the cityscape and reflected in the windows its warm light before everything beyond slid into darkness.

"Let me do it," Adrienne told Alonzo after the tea service was delivered. "I'm able to pour tea for my husband."

They sipped their tea and nibbled on the array of finger sandwiches and tiny sweets until Adrienne broke the silence.

"I heard everything the doctor said. I promise I did. And I'm not insinuating that he's wrong about my prognosis, but I feel better somehow. Maybe it's just knowing that all of this has a name, Addison's disease. And I am not after all, crazy, which I must tell you was my great fear."

"Have you thought about what you want to tell the children and Mattie?"

"I have. And I don't. I don't want to tell them that what I have is incurable. And I don't want to tell them anything that will make them sad."

"You don't want to prepare them?"

"Why would I want them to spend whatever time we have together, already planning for my death? They'll have plenty of time afterward to live with it."

Alonzo pursed his lips.

"I get to decide this, Lonzo. I get to decide what I want these months to be with the children."

Alonzo nodded. "All right then."

"Besides, they're so excited about finally being in the new house after all the delays. There's so much to do still, and I want to make it their home. With whatever time that I have, that's what I want more than anything. They'll need to feel settled in. The last few years have been so hard on them."

Adrienne put down her cup and studied Alonzo's face. "And you. You mustn't be so forlorn. I can't pull this off by myself. You have more than a supporting role here. One look at you, and anybody would think the world is coming to an end."

"Isn't it?" he asked, dropping his head.

Adrienne watched as tears slid down his face, trying to remember if she had ever in all their years together seen him hang his head and cry.

"Alonzo, you mustn't be so sad."

"No, Adrienne. That's one thing you don't get to decide. This is not some stage play," he said abruptly, startling both of them. "I am sad. I don't have to hide it from myself or from you. We've just gotten ready to live, and now you have to die. Our world. It is coming to an end."

He pulled his white cotton handkerchief from his pocket, removed his glasses, and wiped his face.

She sat quietly to allow him his grief.

"I'm so sorry," Adrienne whispered, putting her hand on his leg. "You're right. I can't tell you how to feel. But I can tell you what I hope."

Alonzo turned to face her, his eyes red and brimming.

"I hope you will go on living. And not just for the children, but for yourself. I know you'll be sad for a while. But then you must put sadness aside and find happiness again. You have a long life ahead of you yet, Lonzo.

Please don't spend it alone and brokenhearted. I want you to live a long and happy life, full of love and joy."

Adrienne reached up to touch his face. He took her hand and pressed a long kiss into it.

The next morning, an exquisite Sunday in early spring, the weary travelers took a taxicab home from Atlanta's Terminal station. The seasons seemed to have changed overnight. There were signs that an evening thunderstorm had washed away the urban grime as if in preparation for their arrival. Puddles of rain had pooled here and there on the streets; the air felt crisp and clean. As they drove past the familiar landmarks, despite the burden of their knowledge, the city charmed them. Church bells called the faithful to worship as they slipped through the streets of Atlanta. Early blooming tulips and dogwood trees, azalea blossoms waiting to burst set against the green foliage, and the cloudless blue sky lifted their spirits as they made their way toward University Place. The street along the edge of the Atlanta University campus that even before it had a name, felt more like theirs than any other place they had ever lived. On their approach to Bumstead Cottage, they were consumed by a rush of nostalgia as their old home of ten years came into view. Alonzo asked the driver to stop for a minute. Adrienne and Alonzo leaned forward to take a look at the place they had long called home. Since returning to the city two summers past, the family had been living in rooms at the university's dormitory. Adrienne's teaching and the children kept her busy. Alonzo was immersed in his thriving business empire of barber shops, real estate, and insurance. Somehow the two had made the time to design and build the home they had never had, and the effort had drawn them closer than they had been in years, both in physical proximity and through a deeper emotional bond. It had saved them, or at least, so it had seemed for a while.

In December they had moved into their beautiful new home set in the familiar landscape. Adrienne, already ill, had done her best to keep up appearances and join in the children's enthusiasm, until she couldn't and the search for answers had begun.

"Ready to go home?" Alonzo asked.

She smiled and nodded.

Adrienne waited outside the taxi, her eyes taking in every detail, while Alonzo gathered their bags and paid the fare. The painstaking process of designing and building the home that she and Alonzo had labored over for months gave her a deep sense of satisfaction that she had rarely known in her professional life. Somehow the children had not been alerted to their arrival and so they stood before the grand hilltop Beaux-Arts mansion, both not quite believing that it was theirs. Massive Corinthian columns framed the front of the perfectly symmetrical house that was finished with specially selected multicolored brick brought in from out of state. The flat-topped house was a masterpiece, inside and out, embodying the artistic flourishes of architecture from around the world, every detail from Adrienne's vision of the perfect home for their family. The rooftop terraces were intended to serve as open-air theaters for entertaining and performing, but as Adrienne saw them now, they stood empty and quiet and waiting somehow for the tragic drama that she knew would soon unfold within, regardless of what Alonzo might wish.

Effie crouched on her knees on the tufted stool that sat before Adrienne's kidney shaped, three-mirrored dressing table. She quietly picked up bottles, removed their tops, and sniffed the perfumes and liquids, careful not to make a sound that might disturb her sleeping mother. As she had seen Adrienne do countless times, she opened a jar of Dr. Fred Palmer's Skin Whitener, stuck two fingers in and rubbed the cool cream on her cheeks, turning her head from side to side, waiting for the result. A pot of rouge caught her eye, and she could not resist screwing open the top and drawing out a finger full of red paste that she applied liberally to her cheeks and lips. Effie slipped a sparkling necklace over her head and around her neck and watched its glittering reflection in each of the three mirrors. She picked up Adrienne's solid silver hairbrush and was busy drawing it through her thick, dark tresses when her mother giggled.

"Do you have some evening plans, Miss Effie?"

Effie glanced at her mother's reflection in the mirror, where she could see her propped up on white satin pillows in her sick bed and decided to play the role of entertainer as her mother often had when these roles were reversed.

"I'm due on stage at seven," she said in her best ten-year old's imitation of her mother's voice. "I can't disappoint the audience. They expect me to look my best."

Adrienne laughed again. "Come here to me and bring a washcloth with you." Adrienne pulled herself up with some effort, while Effie took a small cotton towel from the stack on the dresser and did as her mother commanded.

"Careful with those hands. I don't want that red rouge all over my bed covers," she said, reaching for the cloth and wrapping it around Effie's red-tinged fingers as she clamored up beside her.

"Let me have a look at you." Adrienne took hold of her chin and turned her face from side to side. "That's quite a blush you've given yourself, Miss Effie."

"Don't wipe it off. I'm ready for my performance," Effie said as she scrambled to stand up on the bed, jostling Adrienne and grabbing for her hands to gain her balance.

Bringing a hand dramatically to her chest and batting her eyes for full effect, Effie cleared her voice and said with perfect elocution in her Adrienne voice, "Do you not know that I am a woman?"

"Chin up, purse those lips," Adrienne directed, amused. "Fair Rosalind, I presume."

A single nod of Effie's head conceded that Adrienne had guessed correctly.

"I would cure you if you would but call me Rosalind," Effie continued.

"Oh my, what a brilliant understudy you are, young lady. I'll have to be careful that you don't take my place on the stage."

Overcome by her daughter's imitation, Adrienne reached up and pulled her down in a tight embrace.

"Careful of my makeup, Mama. Don't get it on you."

She pulled away, grabbed the towel, and scrubbed the rouge from her cheeks and lips.

Then, as she often had of late, Effie turned serious and somber.

"How are you feeling? Can I bring you something? I brought you some flowers. See?" she said, pointing her still pink finger toward the bedside table where a tall green glass vase held a clutch of red snapdragons.

THE TRUTH TOGETHER

"Those are lovely. Where did you find them?" Adrienne asked, kissing a finger and placing it on Effie's lips.

"In our old yard. They're your favorites. Remember? Will you come downstairs for supper?" Effie asked, hopeful.

"I'm not very hungry," Adrienne answered.

And just as suddenly Effie blurted, "Do you think you're going to die now?"

Barely two weeks had passed since Adrienne and Alonzo had returned from Philadelphia, and despite the positive prognosis they claimed to have gotten from their visit, her decline had been steady every day since. She bore it privately at first, but then could no longer pretend. Over the past week she had spent most of the time sleeping, and in the last two days, had found herself unable to summon the strength to get out of bed.

Effie, sensing something dire, had been reluctant to leave her side. Norris, sensing the same, could hardly stand to be in the room with her. Adrienne had dropped the charade. She no longer had the strength for it.

"I'm not ready yet," Adrienne answered as honestly as she could.

Effie looked straight into Adrienne's eyes, pondered the answer for a moment and judged it for its worth.

"Can you come to church tomorrow for the Easter play?' Effie asked, hoping to give Adrienne a reason to get out of bed.

"Are you ready, my dear Rosalind, for that performance?"

"I am. Let me put on my new dress and I'll show you," Effie answered, sliding from the bed and hurrying across the room.

"And send Norrie in to me, please. I haven't seen him today," Adrienne added.

At the doorway Effie nodded. "Wait there, Mama," she instructed, worried that Adrienne might not.

Effie walked determinedly to Norris's room and pushed open the door without knocking as he constantly reminded her to do. He wasn't there. Knowing that he liked to spend time up on the rooftop, where he and their father were working on a garden, she headed up the stairs and stepped out into the early evening light. She wasn't disappointed. She found them huddled in the corner with the planters and the seedlings they had started back in January. Alonzo had promised to create a beautiful blooming paradise for Adrienne's "summer season" as they had christened the plans for the dramatic events she hoped to stage for family and friends. Norris wanted to grow some vegetables and so among the peonies and the dahlias, the alyssum and the begonias, there were pole beans and squashes, collards and cucumbers.

Dressed in their overalls and matching straw hats, they were on their knees and elbows-deep in a large tub of soil and manure, mixing away to their heart's content. Effie wrinkled her nose and held it closed with her fingers as she drew near the farmers.

"That smells so bad, Papa. Why do we have to have this on the top of our house?"

Alonzo peered over the top of his glasses. "I promised your mother a garden. To grow, these plants need fertilizer," he answered, delighted to be using his farming skills.

"Mama wants to see you, Norris. But you'd better get a bath first," she said, still holding her nose.

"I'm busy," Norris answered brusquely without looking at her.

"She asked for you. You should go," Effie told him sternly.

Norris kept his head down and continued mixing.

"Papa?" Effie pleaded.

"We'll be in, in a bit," Alonzo answered, dismissing her.

Effie crossed her arms and stood there for a moment. "You'll be sorry," she warned as she headed back into the house.

Fretting about Norris, Effie stripped down to her underclothes in the bathroom and gave her hands and face a good scrub. In her large corner room, she stood before the cheval full-length dressing mirror her mother had insisted was a necessity for every young girl's practice of good posture, carriage, and facial expressions, and tried on several happy and sad faces that she thought would be useful over the coming days. From her dressing table, a smaller replica of Adrienne's, she took her own silver brush and pulled it through her hair. The rhythm of the brushing reminded her of how her mother always tenderly brushed it for her. Effie closed her eyes and for a moment was able to pretend that Adrienne's hand, and not her own, moved gently through her hair over and over again.

Effie opened the wardrobe where the new dress her mother had brought her from Philadelphia was ironed and waiting for Easter Sunday. She took the pale blue two-tiered, hand-embroidered dress from the clothes hanger, unbuttoned several of the small buttons along its back, and stepped into it. Pulling the dress up over her shoulders and adjusting it the best she could, she stood once again before the mirror. Effie smoothed out the pin tuck folds below the wide belt that encircled the dropped waist and ran her hands along the silk ribbon threaded through the embroidery that framed the square neck of the dress. She placed a matching pale blue satin bow just to the side of the crown of her head and slid on her small white gloves. She practiced the happy faces a few more times and then picked up the half sheet of paper that held her handwritten Bible verse for tomorrow's service. Once again at the mirror, Effie read the words to herself several times over and then folded the paper, holding it discreetly in her gloved hands. She repeated the verse until she was certain it was perfect, even for an audience as particular as her mother.

By the time Effie returned to Adrienne's bedside, her mother was sleeping deeply. Effie observed her for a few moments and then went to the window seat and settled in. She watched the gathering darkness, closed her eyes, and drifted into a peaceful slumber.

The sound of sobbing woke her. Effie sat bolt upright on the window seat and threw off the blanket someone had covered her with as she lay sleeping. Then she realized that the crying was coming from Norris, sitting at Adrienne's side, wrapped in her arms as she tried to comfort him. The lamplight softly framed them both, and when Effie was able to take her eyes from them, she saw her papa and her grandmother in the matching rose-colored wingback armchairs and knew for certain that her fears had not yet overtaken them. Papa had his glasses on, his shirt sleeves were rolled up and he was reading. Big Mama, as she and Norris still liked to call her, had her sewing basket in her lap and was replacing a button on one of her favorite house dresses.

"Ready for bed?" Alonzo asked her.

"I'll take her," Mattie said, putting her sewing aside and getting a better look at Effie, added, "I'll want that dress for ironing. I thought I had already done that, but from the looks of you, it needs doing again."

"Come here." Alonzo lay his book aside and opened his arms to receive her.

"Rubbing sleep from her eyes and still getting her bearings, Effie headed toward him. He reached up, gently removed the bow from her hair, handed it to Mattie, and gathered Effie into his arms. She wrapped her arms tightly around his neck.

"I'm right here, baby girl," he whispered in her ear. "I'm right here."

She held tight for as long as she needed and then kissed him on the cheek. "I'm right here, too, Papa," she whispered to him and then climbed down and took her grandmother's hand.

As she passed her mother and Norris, Adrienne, still holding him tight, caught her eye for a moment and mouthed the words "I love you."

Effie kissed her finger and held it up for mother to see.

"Come on, sleeping beauty. Time to get up," Norris announced, already dressed in his new Easter suit.

"No, it's dark, Norrie," she said, sleepyheaded and then coming to herself, "Is it Mama?"

"Mama's fine. Come on, there's a surprise. Get your dress on and come up to the roof. Hurry, Effie," he said, switching the overhead light on.

Effie closed her eyes against the brightness and struggled out of her warm blankets. Squinting against the light, she found her freshly ironed dress lying across the foot of her bed, slipped it over her head, combed her hair, and set her bow. She pulled on her white lace top socks and black leather Mary Janes, checked herself all around in the mirror, and opened the door. Strangers in the hallway were quietly heading up the stairs to the roof. Some of them, Adrienne's students from the university, smiled and waved. One or two carried instruments and hymnals Effie knew from church.

Mattie emerged from her room at the end of the hallway dressed in her Easter finery.

"Happy Easter, baby," she said quietly, holding out her hand. "Come on, let's go up."

Out on the rooftop, the sun had not yet risen, yet the rooftop was glowing with lantern light and candles. Pots of Easter lilies, gardenias, and daffodils filled the space with their soft colors and sweet fragrance. The dining chairs had been arranged in rows facing the east, and on blankets sat people who Effie knew as friends of her parents. A table full of food baskets sat in one corner, while the students with their hymnals and instruments had gathered along the edge of the patio.

"What is this?" Effie asked her grandmother.

"Easter sunrise service," Mattie answered, her voice wobbly with emotion. "For your mama. And for us." She smiled down at Effie. "Are you ready with your Bible verse?"

"I didn't bring it," Effie answered, alarmed. "I didn't know I needed it."

"Don't you know it?" Mattie admonished.

Effie nodded. "I think so. I hope I don't forget."

"Let's go sit down," her grandmother directed.

"I want to stand next to the door," Effie told her. "To see Mama's face."

"I'll save you a seat." Mattie headed through the crowd, stopping along the way to wish everyone a happy Easter.

Effie stood near the door and waited. Norris slipped in beside her. He lay his hand on her shoulder, and Effie reached up to hold it there.

When everyone was settled and quiet, Effie and Norris watched as their father rose up the staircase with their mother in his arms. Adrienne was in her nightclothes and white silk dressing gown, her feet bare. The children could see the confused look on her face and heard her asking Alonzo question after question. Alonzo kept quiet.

When they cleared the doorway, she saw them. "Well, look at you. Aren't you lovely?"

"Look, Mama," Effie said, pointing to the rooftop gathering. "This is for you."

Adrienne looked over the crowd and the lanterns and the flowers and a hint of the sun peeking up over the city beyond.

"Let me down, Alonzo. I want to walk. I can do it if you help me."

He put her down gently. Norris took her left arm and tucked it into his own as Alonzo took the other. With Effie following behind them, they made their way to the front row of chairs. After they seated themselves, the choral group, with their accompanying instruments began to play and sing "Christ the Lord is Risen Today."

The sun continued its assent as the choir and the small congregation sang. When it was fully above the horizon and everyone was silent, Effie stood and walked to Adrienne. Facing her with folded hands, she looked into her mother's eyes.

Effie recited from memory with perfect delivery, "As they entered the tomb, they saw a young man dressed in a white robe sitting on the right side, and they were alarmed. 'Don't be alarmed,' he said. 'You are looking for Jesus the Nazarene, who was crucified. He has risen! He is not here. See the place where they laid him. But go, tell his disciples and Peter. He is going ahead of you into Galilee. There you will see him, just as he told you.' Hear the word of the Lord from the Holy Gospel of Mark, chapter sixteen, verses five through seven."

If the flowers bloomed that summer or the vegetables ripened and fell from the vines, Effie never knew. A little more than a week after Easter, Adrienne died in her sleep, and the door to the rooftop portico remained closed and locked.

Nora and Fern

MAY, 1913

20

Charlie was small for his age. At eight years old, he stood about three inches shorter than Fern, who was seven. His bluish-tinged skin was so pale as to appear transparent. Curls black as midnight covered his small head. His big dark eyes slanted slightly upward and were framed with deep, dark circles, and his cheeks sometimes flamed scarlet, just like Nora's. What she had learned about Charlie was that he was dropped off at the sanitarium two years ago. The old woman who left him said he was a deaf mute, and his mother had gone to Texas with her new man and promised to come for him when she could. The mother had never shown up, and the old woman said she couldn't do for him anymore. When Nora washed his face and arms with a cloth at night, she thought of how much he reminded her of a frail bird. As she secured his overnight diaper and slipped a clean gown over his head, she sang as many verses of "Froggie Went a-Courtin'" as she could get through. Charlie didn't speak, but by the third verse he would hum the melody as she said the words. She knew she shouldn't do it, but she couldn't resist giving him a kiss on the forehead every night and whispering softly in his ear, "I love you, Charlie boy." He always smiled when she said that. After she pulled the top of his enclosed bed down and latched it, she walked away, turned back and waved. That was a part of their nightly routine too. He was always watching when she did. He waved back, lay down and went to sleep.

Lillie was a year and a half. Her golden hair had been shorn close to her head after a bout of lice. She couldn't sit up on her own and had just recently learned to roll over. She had some trouble holding her head up, and Nora thought the more she was upright instead of lying down in the bed, the better chance there was that she might get stronger. For months, Nora had spent a good part of the day carrying Lillie on her hip as she tended to the other children's needs, until the day that Fern asked if she could hold her and she found herself a willing and capable new assistant. It was a good thing too. Nora was worn out most days by early afternoon, and if she didn't get to sit down for a spell, she could hardly make it through. Nora opened Lillie's bed and reached in to pull the little girl from her blankets for a diaper change. Lillie had trouble swallowing food and so got milk three times each day. Nora sat down in the rocker in the corner of the big, lamp-lit, whitewashed room and gave the little girl her bottle, grateful for the chance to sit for a few minutes. She closed her eyes and leaned her head back against the chair, remembering Fern at that age and how nighttime feeding was one of the things she loved most about being a mother. The quiet and the darkness and the warm, sweet smell of the baby, the sounds of suckling and swallowing assured her that her baby would grow and be there for her to love for another day. That memory was one of her favorites to let play out in her head when she felt sad or scared about the future.

Nora opened her eyes just as Louella pushed through the double doors at the end of the ward. She headed in Nora's direction. It was all Louella's doing that Nora got to work and live in the special children's ward. Louella was the head nurse on that floor and specifically asked for Nora to be her helper. It was all her doing, too, that she and Fern were able to clean out an old storage closet in the back corner and turn it into their one-room home. It wasn't much, but it was better than most had there.

"It looks like you worked your magic. I wonder how long it will last," Louella offered.   All of their other patients, who were not sick but whose conditions had led to their families giving them over to the sanitarium for care, were sleeping peacefully. Her eyes lit on Lillie. "You want me to take her?"

Nora marveled at the tranquil face of the little girl sleeping in her arms. "She looks like she doesn't have a care in the world when she's like this," she said as she shifted to lift Lillie into Louella's arms.

Louella answered, "When they're sleeping, they all do." Then turned her attention to Nora. "You look exhausted. Why don't you get some rest? I'm pulling the night shift tonight. I can handle whatever comes up out here."

Nora hoisted herself from the chair. "Thanks. I'll do that," was all she could muster before walking slowly to the hallway lavatory to wash up before heading off to bed.

In the washroom a coughing fit overwhelmed her. She braced her hands on either side of the sink and coughed so hard that tears ran down her face. When Nora opened her eyes, the pink foamy spittle speckled across the white porcelain bowl struck her like an arrow. Once she got her breathing and crying under control, she rinsed the basin and scrubbed it with the cleanser stored on the high shelf. Nora knew she couldn't keep her illness secret for much longer. Louella most certainly already suspected.

Nora finished up and headed back to her room, her sanctuary with Fern, who was the reason she had to keep to herself about her condition. She had no idea what would become of Fern. Thinking about it broke Nora's heart. She didn't know how long she might have before it became obvious that she had tuberculosis, but in the meantime, she wanted to spend every minute of it with Fern. Maybe this was just another low spell.   Maybe she would get better again. All of those thoughts tumbled through her head as she opened the door to her room and found Fern entwined in the white cotton sheets in the middle of the narrow bed. Nora closed the door softly behind her, relieved to put the day behind her too. She soundlessly took off her clothes and pulled her nightgown on over her head. Sitting on the end of the bed, she watched Fern sleeping. Like the young patients in the big room, peacefulness and vulnerability seemed tucked in beside her in her slumber. A tumble of auburn curls framed her head in a wreath. Her long arms and legs reminded Nora of Harry, and she wondered if Fern would grow to be tall like him. Her breathing was deep and even. Her face untroubled. Nora knew she should move Fern to her little pallet on the floor, but she wasn't sure she had the strength to lift her. Sometimes she was overcome by the thought that Fern might catch her sickness, but weariness and sadness made her less vigilant and so she wrapped herself around her little girl. Holding her close and feeling her warmth, Nora fell into a deep sleep.

"Mama. Mama, can we read my book, Mama?" Nora opened one eye to a wide-eyed Fern standing next to her with a book in her hands. When Nora forgot to turn off the lamp, Fern often rose in the middle of the night and finding that she had her mother to herself wanted to curl up beside her and read. It was such a luxurious treat, Nora, despite her weariness, treasured those moments with Fern. Louella had brought several books for the curious little girl, and Nora was amazed by how much she loved to read. *The Wonderful Wizard of Oz* and *The Ransom of Red Chief* were two of her favorites, and they had read through both several times. Nora roused herself and made room for Fern. They snuggled in under the blankets, and in their hearts and minds, left the closet room in the children's ward and floated up above the dense pine forests of middle Georgia on a magical adventure together. Tonight, it was all about *Five Children and It*. Nora understood why Fern liked it so much. She did, too, and they often spent time looking for a sand fairy like the one in the book that would make all of their wishes come true. It was a fantastic tale about children out on their own, making mischief, dealing with adversity, and solving all their problems without the grown-ups ever knowing what was going on. Everything always turned out right for the children. When she asked Fern what she would wish for if they found a mystical wish-granting beast, what she wanted most was always something for the other children. She wished that Charlie could talk or that Lillie could crawl or that she would get a pair of silver shoes and they could all skip down a yellow brick road to an enchanted place like Oz.

"Read now," Fern demanded and lay her head against Nora's shoulder.

When Nora opened her eyes, it was morning. The sound of the children clamoring for attention streamed in through the open door of their room. Fern wasn't next to her nor on the pallet on the floor. Nora pulled herself from bed, weary and dizzy-headed, her chest heavy and achy. Looking across the children's room, she spotted Fern, already dressed for the day, on her knees next to Charlie's bed. Nora sat back down, already weary before she started her custodial duties. Each time a cough welled up, she tried to suppress it. When she was finally able to stand again, she dressed slowly and walked unsteadily into the main room. Louella was nowhere to be seen. That wasn't unusual, but Nora needed a hand this morning to get the children up and fed.

On a good day, Nora got about her business before the children were fully awake. A quick turn around the room told her who was in the most desperate condition requiring a bath or an immediate diaper change. Those that were able were dressed and brought to the table in the center of the room to await breakfast. The rest would have to be fed individually after they were cleaned and comforted. Nora thought about her work as having a houseful of babies and small children, twelve of them if she counted Fern, whose well-being depended entirely on her. Most days the work was completely exhausting, but Louella had chosen her helper well. Nora remained calm and made the children her priority, lavishing as much attention and love on each one of them that she had time for, tending to their needs and taming them with kindness.

"Listen to Charlie, Mama," Fern said excitedly when Nora made her way to them and opened the top of his bed.

"Charlie, what's my name?" Fern asked him, pointing at herself. "Charlie, look at me."

Charlie only had eyes for Nora when she was near. Not even Fern commanded more attention. Nora opened the door of the bed, and Charlie climbed out, immediately wrapping his arms around her.

"My Charlie boy," Nora said weakly.

"Charlie, look at me. What's my name?" Fern implored.

Reluctantly, Charlie pulled his eyes from Nora and turned to Fern.

"What's my name, Charlie?"

"Fern," he blurted and smiled.

Fern clapped and Charlie joined in.

When Nora bent down to pull Charlie's day clothes from the small chest at the foot of his bed, the room began to spin. She braced herself against the chest and tried to take in some deep breaths. A coughing fit doubled her over. She was vaguely aware that children were crying, as she tried desperately to fill her lungs with air. A whimpering Charlie clung tightly to her skirt. Fern was calling, "Mama, Mama," when she collapsed on the floor.

Two kitchen custodians bringing the children's breakfast found Nora on the floor, barely conscious and whispering Fern's name, her apron spattered in pink. They had just gotten her back to her bed when Louella walked in.

"What's going on in here?" she asked over the voices of the wailing children.

"We found her like this," one of the men answered.

"Go get me some help for these children. I'll see to her. Close the door behind you," she told them as they left the room. Spotting a pitcher on a table in the corner of the tiny room, Louella poured some water in a cup, then wet a washcloth and rung it out. At Nora's bedside, she gently wiped her face.

"Nora, what happened?" she asked quietly, handing Nora the water to drink. "Why didn't you tell me how bad it was?"

Nora took a few sips and when finally able to focus on Louella, whispered, "Fern. Where's Fern? Is she okay?"

"I'm sure she's fine. She's out there with the children. When did you get this sick? Why didn't you tell me?"

Nora slowly shook her head. "Don't let them take Fern away." Tears seeped from her eyes.

"We need to take care of you. Don't worry about Fern. I'll make sure she's okay. Let's just worry about you first," Louella said, cooling Nora's face with the wet cloth.

"Is it tuberculosis?" Nora finally said the dreaded word aloud.

Louella nodded. "It looks that way. We'll need to do some tests to know for sure. How long has this been going on?"

"Off and on for a while," Nora answered vaguely.

"For how long, Nora?"

"Probably since last summer," she answered, closing her eyes.

"Why didn't you tell me? I could have helped you."

"I didn't think much about it at first. Thought it was just a bad cold. Then I got scared. Scared for Fern. Scared you might figure it out."

Louella turned away. "You're skin and bones. I've heard that cough. I should have said something."

"It's not your fault. I was afraid to tell you."

A knock on the door ended their conversation. Louella rose and opened the door to one of the young nursing students called to the ward to help. Louella stepped out of Nora's room.

"Is everything under control out here?"

"The patient ledger isn't where it's supposed to be. How many patients should we have in this room?" the girl asked nervously.

"Eleven patients and the daughter of my aide, so twelve children total."

The girl glanced around. "Some seem to be missing."

Louella walked into the ward room and counted. "Do we know who?"

"I can show you the empty beds. Here and over there," she said, pointing.

"What's your name?" Louella asked.

"I'm Vallie."

"Did you happen to see a red-haired girl?"

"No, ma'am, I haven't."

"Charlie, a little mongoloid boy, and Lillie. She has cerebral paralysis. I think those are the missing children," Louella told her.

"Where could they have gone?" Nurse Vallie asked.

"I suspect that Fern, that's the red-haired girl, took them somewhere. In all the commotion, they're probably scared."

"What should we do?" Vallie asked, alarmed.

"Find them," Louella answered.

It's just like Sunday, Fern told herself. On Sundays the nursing school students spent time in the wards, practicing being nurses, so the children didn't need Nora as much. That was a day when she and her mother grabbed a blanket, stopped by the kitchen for some biscuits and ham, and found the perfect spot out on the grounds where they lolled around in the sunshine for an hour or two. That was Fern's favorite thing to do. Sometimes they would sing, or Nora would make up a story. They played school and house. Nora pointed out the different birds and called them by name. She explained the weather and the changing of the seasons. The worst part was when they had to go back inside.

In the chaos of her mother's collapse, that's all Fern could think of. The world outside. If she could get outside, everything would be okay. Charlie and Lillie would stop screaming. Nothing bad would happen to her mama if Fern waited for her on the blanket under the tree. Fern thought for a few minutes about everything they might need for a day outdoors. The men from the kitchen who brought in breakfast got busy with her mama and forgot all about what they were supposed to be doing. After Louella came in and closed the door to their room and the men left, Fern went right to work. She got Charlie dressed and found some shoes for both of them. She had no problem getting what she needed from the breakfast cart. Biscuits with ham and Lillie's morning bottle were sitting right on top. She picked up two spoons from the cart, too, thinking they might be useful. She took the blanket from Charlie's bed and then grabbed the baby-sized ones she found in Lillie's.

A couple of diapers from the clean laundry cart made for good food wraps. She piled everything together in the center of Charlie's blanket and made it into a bundle, like her mama always did when they were going outside. She slipped the long ends of the blanket around Charlie's shoulders and tied them in front so he could carry it on his back. Then, she picked up a crying Lillie from her bed. At the doorway she grabbed the two hats the kitchen men had left on the coat pegs and put one on herself and the other on Charlie. They walked right out the doors and down the stairs without anyone taking any notice.

Charlie kept close to Fern, so close she had to be careful not to tangle up their legs and fall down. They crossed the south lawn where the newly cut grass prickled against her ankles. Lillie had cried herself to sleep, and Fern's arms were trembling from the weight of her. Fern hummed the frog song because she didn't know all the words, but it seemed to keep Charlie happy anyway. He hummed along with her as they walked. When they reached a stand of pines where the wild azaleas were particularly thick and colorful, Fern decided they had gone far enough. She laid the sleeping Lillie down on the grass. After she got the bundle free from Charlie, she set about making a nice place for them. Fern spread out the blanket so they could all enjoy the bright sunshine. Lillie still drowsing, let out a contented sigh when Fern moved her to the soft pile of blankets.

"Let's build a straw house," Fern said to Charlie. "I'll show you how." Fern went to the edge of the pine forest and began scraping together an armload of pine straw while Charlie watched.

"Now you do this," she instructed, walking back to the clearing near the blanket where she made straight-lined piles of straw. "These are the walls. Then you leave a space like this for a window and for the doors. Now let's get some more." They scampered back to the pine trees and both began scooping together as much pine straw as they could carry to build their straw house around the blanket. When they finished, Fern put her hands on her hips and surveyed their handiwork.

"This can be my room," Fern told Charlie. "And this one next to it is yours." She walked through the imaginary door. "And here's the kitchen where we make our food," she said about the space where Lillie was lying in the blanket jumble. Having coaxed Charlie to sit down, she unwrapped a biscuit for him and then gave Lillie her bottle. When the bottle was mostly empty, she sat Lillie up and held her on her lap while she ate. They gobbled down their biscuits in familiar silence, listening to the wind blow through the tops of the pines and the squawking of some very noisy crows.

"Do you want to go outside to look for a Sammy? We can make some wishes if we find one," Fern said, grabbing the two spoons and hoisting Lillie to her hip.

Charlie just looked at her. She handed him a spoon, and he put it in his mouth.

"No, not that," she told him, stepping through the imaginary door. "Dig with it." And she showed him how to dig a hole to look for a sand fairy.

Louella was relieved that Nora slept most of the day. She hadn't had to tell her that Fern and the others were missing. When her brother, James Robert—who was now a sheriff's deputy—came to give her a ride home from work, she explained why she couldn't leave, and he joined the search for the lost children. Though married with a family of his own, he still had a soft spot for Nora and Fern.

Louella reluctantly opened the door to peek in at Nora late in the afternoon and found her sitting on the side of the bed.

"How're you feeling?" she asked.

Nora nodded slowly. "A little more rested, I think. Could I have some water?"

Louella got the pitcher and poured Nora a drink.

"Could you bring Fern in? She must be worried. I'm surprised you could keep her out of here all day."

Louella paused a moment too long before answering, "Why don't we wait until tomorrow and let you get your strength up."

"I want to see her now. See that she's all right."

Nora read the worried look on Louella's face.

"Where's Fern?" she asked, getting up from the bed.

"You shouldn't be out of bed. Here, let me help you."

"I want Fern, Louella," she answered, her voice rising. "Where is she?"

"Sit down," Louella ordered in a firm voice. "Sit down and I'll tell you. I'm sure she's fine."

She took Nora by the arms and forced her back down on the bed, sitting beside her to keep her there.

"This morning in all the commotion, Fern left the building. No, sit still now," she countered Nora's attempt to get up. "She has Charlie and Lillie. The grounds are being searched. A lot of people are out looking for them. Even James Robert. You know she'll go right to him when she hears his voice."

Nora covered her face with her hands. "What have I done to that poor child?"

"How can you even think this is something you've done? You're sick. You can't help that."

NORA AND FERN

"I kept her here because I was selfish. I couldn't face giving her up."

"And who were you going to give her to? Not that no account husband of yours. And you said you wrote to your family but never heard a word from them."

"What am I going to do for her now that I'm sick? What kind of life will she have after I'm gone?"

"Listen to yourself, Nora, you're not a whiner. First of all, you're not going anywhere. We can help you get better, stronger again. The best place for Fern is with the person who loves her and that's you," Louella offered, putting her arm around Nora and pulling her close. "And besides, one thing about that girl that we both know—and we have both known her since the day she was born—not one single day in all those seven years have I seen her scared or worried. She's as cool as a cucumber and smart as a fox."

The hole was a disappointment. They didn't find a Sammy, and their hands were filthy from digging. Lillie cried for a long time, and Fern tried to change her diaper, but her hands were so dirty she made more of a mess than when she started. She pinned a clean diaper on her and threw the other one into the woods, but Lillie was kind of muddy from Fern's hands and she didn't smell very good. Fern tried to teach Charlie some more words, but they were both too tired and thirsty and finally Fern decided it was time to head back. She packed up their things and tied the bundle on Charlie's back. By the time she got everything together, both Lillie and Charlie were crying. Charlie's face and arms were red and hot to the touch, and Lillie's complaints were too many to list.

Fern picked up Lillie, and with Charlie bumping up against her as they walked, they began the trek back home. Fern sang silly rhyming words to the frog song to try and calm Charlie. After they had been walking for a while, she stopped and looked around in all directions. It was getting dark and nothing looked familiar. Charlie's humming had turned to whimpering, and Lille was so heavy Fern had to put her down in the grass for a few minutes while she tried to figure out which way to go. And then above Charlie's whimper and Lillie's fussing, Fern heard someone calling her name.

"Let's go, Charlie!" She snatched Lillie from the ground and grabbed Charlie's hand.

Louella had marshalled all the forces of the student nurses by the time James Robert walked through the door with the children in tow. Every child in the room had their own caretaker. The uniform gave him an air of authority, and when he handed off Lillie and Charlie and asked that they be taken straight away for a warm bath and served a good supper, the young nurses asked no questions and went right to work. He took Fern to the washroom and ordered her to do a good handwashing, and then he cleaned up her face as best he could. She needed a bath, too, but he knew there was a more important next stop.

"Your mama's sick. You already knew that, though, didn't you?" he asked as he wiped the dirt from her face.

Fern nodded. "Is she gonna die?"

"Everybody dies at some point, Fern. But with some rest and Louella taking care of her, she's got a good chance to get better. Maybe you ought to come stay with me for a while," James Robert offered.

"No. I'm not leaving Mama," Fern answered, jutting her chin out so he would know she meant it.

"I thought that was what you'd say. Let's go see how she's doin' tonight. She'll be happy to see your face, even dirty," he said, tweaking her nose.

"Come in," Nora said, rising from her bed when James Robert knocked on the door.

He poked his head in and said in his best deputy sheriff's voice, "Thought you might want to give this red-headed vagabond a talkin' to, ma'am."

Fern pushed past him and wrapped herself around her mother's frail body.

"Thank you, James Robert. And don't leave yet. I want to talk to you about something," she said over the top of Fern.

He nodded and closed the door to give them some privacy.

Nora sat down on the bed so she could see Fern face-to-face. "You scared me near to death. Why did you leave like that?"

"They were scared. 'Specially Charlie. He loves you more than anybody. And nobody but you holds Lillie," Fern answered.

"Those children need special care, Fern."

"I gave it to 'em. Me and Charlie ate biscuits. I gave Lillie her milk. I changed her diaper. We played outside."

"You can't just take them away like that. I know you help me all the time, but I'm responsible for those children who can't take care of themselves."

"You're sick, Mama. I was helping you."

"And you weren't scared at all about me being sick?"

Fern shook her head. "People were taking care of you. I was taking care of Charlie and Lillie."

"I know you were trying to help me, Fern. But you can't take the children outside. It could be dangerous for them. And for you."

"I won't do it again. But I took care of them. I did everything that had to be done."

"You're too young to be taking care of everybody. You still need taking care of, too, Fern. That's what I'm supposed to do, take care of you."

"You do, Mama. You do take the best care of me," Fern said, wrapping her arms around Nora's neck.

They comforted each other for a few minutes more before Nora drew back and said, "You smell pretty bad. Can you get a bath by yourself?"

Fern nodded and picked up a towel and her pajamas before she went to the door where she said, "I won't ever leave you again."

Nora smiled but did not make the same promise. "Would you tell James Robert to come see me?"

"I need you to do something for me, James Robert. I hope you won't mind too much."

"Whatever I can do to help you, Nora. You know that."

"I need to make some plans for Fern, in case something happens to me. Now, don't start saying it's too early for that because it's way past time," she said as he lowered his head. "It's mine to take care of, and I aim to do it."

"You've told me that before, Nora."

"My family lives right outside of Social Circle. At least the last I knew of 'em they did. My mama never answered any of the letters I sent, so I don't know what might have happened, but I need to know if they might be willing to take Fern."

"I can find out for you if they're still there. All I have to do is call the sheriff over there to find out."

"I would be so grateful for that," she answered.

"And what if they're not there anymore or not willin'? Have you thought about that?"

"I'm not that far along yet. Let me do this one step at a time."

"Yes, ma'am," he said, stepping forward and kissing her on the forehead.

"You might not do that. I've probably got tuberculosis," she told him.

"And I've probably kissed worse, Nora. Take care of yourself now. I'll let you know what I find out."

Ten days later, Nora's Mantoux skin test showed positive for tuberculosis. On the same day, James Robert stopped by to tell her what he had found out about her family.

"Hey, Nora, he said when he opened the door to her room, where she sat in a rocking chair next to the bed with a book in her lap. "I went over to see about your kin. Took a drive over to Social Circle myself rather than call somebody." He sat down on the edge of the bed, turning his hat around in his hands. "News ain't good."

"I'm ready for it," she answered.

"Your daddy died in '09. Your mama, well, she passed last month."

Nora closed her eyes, leaned her head back, and started rocking.

"You've got a brother still there, but I didn't get to see him. There's a cousin or two, but that farmland is pretty much useless. Nobody knew much about your sisters, said they thought a couple of 'em were out west somewhere with their families."

Nora kept rocking.

"Nobody knew nothin' about you, though. Didn't know about no letters. Never knew you was here at the sanitarium or that you were still alive. Said your mama thought you died a while back over in Eatonton. Your cousin said she heard tell that your husband, Harry, wrote your mama a letter and told her that."

Nora rocked a minute more before opening her eyes. She looked at James Robert and said, "I wish I'd served him a heapin' plate full of them grits."

Effie and Fern

MAY, 1923

21

Fern hoped she made the right choice. Of the two entrances to the tunnels she had found, the one nearest the new nurses' building seemed the best hidden and the most approachable. Most likely, convenient for Eddie and Albert to access from the work site and a clandestine way to bring unsuspecting victims down to the underground flophouse for illicit purposes. Disguised in the baggy denim overalls with useful pockets, she sauntered around for a good part of the day, pausing under trees and on benches, hoping to be noticed and considered part of the landscape. When dusk settled in, she thought about Effie and hoped that she could keep her safe as their scheme to expose the vicious perpetrators played out. Too much thinking time led her to doubt the conclusions she had made about Albert, Eddie, and the underground tunnels. The more she went over it in her head, the more outlandish it seemed. With the approaching darkness and the idea of Effie offering herself up as a mousetrap, she was having a harder time keeping her cool. It could be hours yet before there were any signs that the frame-up they devised was in motion. Maybe she should have been more earnest about talking Effie out of it. They were both anxious to unravel the mystery of the attacks, but was the risk too great? And what about Bertie? The longer it took to find her, the possibility for a happy ending slipped further away.

Effie folded the yellow Western Union telegram and put it in her pocket. The new lab attendants were eyeing her, checking her reaction to whatever news she had received.

The news was unexpected. William had been told he would not be returning to the sanitarium. Instead, he would be staying in Washington and documenting his research findings for an important presentation about the early results of the yeast protocol. The results were looking promising. After years of painstaking work, they were making progress toward finding the answers to solve the mystery of pellagra. He had asked Effie to close down the lab as soon as she was able and said that his boss, Dr. Goldberger, would be coming in late May to make decisions about the continuation of their work with the female patients.

Effie wasn't sure how she felt about that. She hoped that even after she left in June, somehow her women would continue to benefit from being included in the nutrition research. She couldn't get distracted by the news. She was saddened, though, about the work coming to an end and even more so about the likelihood that hunger and malnutrition would seep back into her ward.

"Let's clean up as much as we can before we deliver," she told her helpers. She didn't want to lose the time advantage she had worked to gain so that she could get rid of the workers early and get ready for whatever might happen if Albert showed up.

The kitchen was mostly tidy when they left with their tray carts. Effie did her best to keep her eyes from wandering to the spot where Fern had spotted Albert lurking in the bushes. She had meant to talk loudly about letting her workers leave early and explaining that she would finish the cleanup alone, but the news from William had rattled her. That along with her worries about Bertie. No matter what she might have accomplished during her time in the ward with her women, Pearl was dead and Bertie was missing. Effie was responsible for them and she had let them down. If there was a chance to find Bertie and save her, she was ready to risk everything to make that happen. And Roselyn. She hadn't been Effie's patient, but her unexplained and largely ignored murder deserved attention. Effie tried to loosen the extra layer she was wearing under her nurse's uniform discreetly but only accomplished to relocate where she felt the pinch. Fern was counting on her. But more importantly, she was counting on herself. Walking across the grounds, pushing their carts, Effie realized how much that mattered to her. Over the months she had spent at the sanitarium, there hadn't been any tangible confirmation by any person of authority that she was doing a good job or even doing what was expected. Frustrated at first by the lack of scrutiny and oversight, she thought it was as much to do with her skin color as with anything else. Nobody really knew what to do with her. There were hundreds of colored patients, but until recently, only one colored nurse. Never had she felt the insulating distinction society put on her race in the way she had here. That had not been a significant part of her life in Atlanta. Her family's monied position protected her from reality, and she understood now what a privileged life she had led. Despite the overwhelming workload, the confinement and isolation of her existence at the sanitarium had turned her attention to herself. Not in a selfish way but in a way that she believed allowed her to learn to rely on herself instead of others. She had spent a great deal of reflective time the last few months, much of it done on the stage in the Big Hall. She hadn't come to any world-altering understandings, but she realized that she spent far too much time doing things to please others, to win praise and recognition of the people around her. She had been running away from that when she left Atlanta. Effie had always measured herself by how much she satisfied others' expectations, not her own. She promised that from this time forward, she would make decisions about her future based on what she wanted and how she decided to spend her life. Right now, she hoped the routine of supper deliveries would calm her nerves and take her mind off the closing down of the research, the tight under layer she was wearing, and her future so she could get back to what needed her attention.

What needed her attention could be summed up with one word. Bertie. Effie tugged herself back to the moment, sensing that Bertie's life and perhaps even her own depended on it.

It was fully dark, the air thick and hazy gray with fog. So far, Fern's night watch at the tunnel had revealed a somewhat steady stream of subjects slinking through the entrance, none of whom she thought was Albert or Eddie. As she rose from the bench and stepped closer to the hidden passage, she knew her previous assessment of the depth of her patience was way overblown. Something was pulling her into the underground burrow and she decided to go with her gut instead of remaining true to the plan.

Fern stashed her flashlight in a pocket. A faint yellow glow illuminated the brick interior. The light was a good sign that visitors to the blind pig entered this way. She wondered if she had miscalculated that those being brought in against their will would pass through here, too, unless they were subdued in some way. Fern adjusted her hat and pulled at the collar of her work shirt to better conceal her face. The tunnel itself was empty. She walked slowly to avoid making noise. Arriving at the barroom, she heard voices mingled with the flickering light flowing out around the edges of the wooden door. She knocked rather than let herself in.

The door was cracked open, while the man checked her over.

"Fifty cents," he barked and held out his hand.

Fern pulled a fifty-cent piece from her bib pocket and forked it over.

The door jerked open. Stepping inside, she found herself face-to-face with Albert. His sweaty stench and beery breath flashed the image of a rock coming down hard on her head, and she lowered her eyes as she passed him.

Fern made her way to a place where she could sit with her back to the wall and keep watch on the door. She laid her arms on the table and leaned in, her head cast down. Her hat and the dim interior gave cover for her roving eyes as she took in the setting and the patrons. Albert shuffled over, plunked a beer mug in front of her, turned his back, and walked away. He ambled to the far table in the back corner, where a big man in a green work coat sat hunched over his drink, head down, hat pulled low. Albert leaned in, said something. The man reached into his pants pocket, pulled out a wad of dollar bills and pushed them across the table. Albert thumbed through them, stuffed them into his own pocket, and headed for the door. Fern wondered what the man had just bought.

Effie left the door open and switched on every light in the room. She moved about the kitchen, humming to contain her foreboding. She wondered if she should make some preparations for the morning, remembered that William had asked her to close the kitchen and then again admonished herself for the distraction.

"Focus," she said as she came out of the pantry. She headed for the sink, just as Albert walked through the door, closing it behind him. He took his hat off at first and held it in his twitchy hands, turning it round. Effie froze where she stood.

"Dr. Tanner's not here."

He didn't answer but put his hat back on his head and took a step forward.

"I'm closing down the kitchen. The research is ending," she said to buy time.

Albert took a handkerchief from his pocket, wiped it across his face.

"I could help you," he mumbled.

"There's not much to do," she lied.

Cutting his eyes around the room, he said, "I left my jacket in the pantry."

"I don't think I've seen it," Effie responded.

"Up on the top shelf. I'll get it." He made a move for the closet.

His quick gesture was enough to make her take her eyes off of him for a second as she turned to the pantry. Just as he passed her, she stepped sideways and bumped into his arm. A small brown vile clattered to the floor, spilling its contents at her feet. They watched the liquid spread and then looked at each other.

"Where's Bertie?" Effie blurted.

Albert stepped into the pantry. She reached out to him to steady herself. He pinned her arms and lifted the handkerchief to her face. They struggled briefly before they fell to the floor. Time passed, but she had no idea how much. From her chloroform haze, Effie heard the door open and saw Albert's accomplice Eddie striding toward her.

Fern was afraid she had made a terrible blunder planting herself underground while Effie might be in trouble up above. Albert hadn't come back. Eddie had never shown up at all. Contemplating her next move, she lifted her head to see the green jacket man at the back corner, staring her down. Unnerved, Fern stood abruptly, upending her still full beer mug and drawing eyes from around the room. She righted the empty stein, left it on the table, and walked as coolly as she could for the door.

Despite her cold sweat and goosebumps, she wasn't leaving until she had looked for Bertie and confirmed the purpose of the other rooms. Fern slowly pushed open the door to the room farthest removed from the bar, where she had earlier stashed some supplies. Things she now realized were not in any way useful to the events of the evening. In the back corner, beyond the dingy divider, the filthy mattress was plainly occupied. She drew close enough to make sure it wasn't Bertie. She had proof of what the room was used for, but not of anything else she suspected about a clandestine business that involved vulnerable captive residents of the sanitarium.

After a few uncomfortable moments inside the room, Fern returned to the hallway. Then, she darted in and out of the other spaces. Bertie was not to be found. She headed out the way she had come in. Just as she stepped out, a hand clamped across her mouth, a strong arm grabbed her around the waist, lifting her off the ground. She struggled, but was no match for her captor.

He moved her quickly around the construction site nearby, and when they reached the rear of the building, spoke firmly and calmly into her ear.

"Fern. I'm gonna take my hand off your mouth now and put you down."

The sound of the voice ended her struggling, and when he did what he said he would, she rounded on him.

"What were you doing down there, James Robert?" she hissed.

"What the hell kind of question is that, Fern? I'm a damn officer of the law. What were you doing down there? I told you to stay the hell away from this place." His voice conveyed his anger.

Flustered, Fern replied, "We have to go. We have to get to Effie. She's in trouble. I know it."

She turned to run, he reached out and grabbed for her again.

"Don't call attention to yourself. Let's walk. We're exposed out here and I'm not armed."

"She's supposed to be in the kitchen lab. At least that's where I hope she is," Fern said just above a whisper.

She tried to match her strides to his.

"What did you pay that man for?" she asked him, searching for his face in the dark.

"God almighty, Fern. Were you and Effie runnin' some hustle on that man Albert?"

Fern realized how stupid she had been. "We thought we could handle it. Nobody was doing anything to find Bertie or figure out what was going on out here. Women disappearing. Getting murdered."

"I've been doing something about it. I've been out here most nights since December."

They looked at each other as they walked.

"I haven't seen you," Fern told him.

"I've seen you," James Robert fired back. "You're not a detective, Fern. You hide in the same places. You're predictable."

She was stung by his observation.

"What were you up to tonight?" he asked her again, still hurrying across the open green space of the grounds.

Fern shook her head. "We thought Albert and Eddie were out to get Effie. Thought maybe that's what they were after when they took Bertie. We decided to make it easy."

The kitchen lab in sight, they slowed to check on their surroundings.

"Why did you pay him?" Fern asked again.

They had stopped outside the building, looking for any sign of danger nearby.

James Robert looked straight at Fern. "I paid him to bring me a girl."

Fern stared at him, confounded. "Is that how you knew Roselyn?"

"It wasn't like that, Fern. I had to catch Albert in the act to prove what's been happening to these girls out here."

Still subdued by the chloroform, Effie lay helpless on the pantry floor. Both men had taken up weapons and towered above her. Eddie held a butcher knife and Albert clutched a meat cleaver. Effie couldn't understand why they had turned on each other.

"You botched the whole deal again, you worthless rummy," Eddie snarled. "I'm done with cleanin' up your screwups."

"I'm done with it," Albert growled. "It's you with blood on your hands."

"You are nothin' but a liability to me now, same as her," Eddie taunted.

Albert raised the cleaver and lunged for Eddie. His legs got tangled up with Effie, and as he fell, the cleaver clanged to the floor.

On his back now beside her, Albert raised his hands and pleaded. "Let me go, man, I'll clear out."

Eddie dropped to his knees. "Like hell you will," he mumbled and plunged the knife into Albert's chest.

The door to the darkened building was closed. James Robert told Fern to wait, but when he couldn't find the light switch, she went in to help.

The light did not immediately answer all of their questions. Effie was not there. There was no sign of a disturbance. Remembering what Effie had said about the pantry door drew Fern's attention to the fact that it was closed. She pointed to it and then put her finger to her lips to caution James Robert. He headed toward it with Fern on his heels. Trying to see around him, she stepped to his right. Her foot hit something that rolled. They looked down to see a small, brown bottle roll out into the open. James Robert pulled out his handkerchief and picked it up. He brought it to his nose and then wrapped the bottle in his handkerchief and put it in his jacket pocket.

At the pantry door, he listened, then slowly opened it. A dark purplish pool of recently spilled blood spread out beneath the man crumpled on the floor, the hilt of a large carving knife squarely planted in his chest. Though James Robert knew his condition before checking, he bent down to feel for Albert's pulse.

When he stood, he turned and said, "I need to get to a phone and call the state police. You're coming with me."

Fern could only nod.

She couldn't move a muscle. The space small and cramped. Yet there was movement, vibration. It was a vehicle of some kind, the ride bumpy and fast. Her head was pounding. Opening her eyes was painful. She was dizzy and needed air. Trying to gather a breath, she felt the tightness of the contraption she had wrapped around herself and cursed the ridiculous idea that she would have been able to get out of the straitjacket and put it on Albert in order to subdue him. Albert was dead. She was absolutely certain of that. The recollection of the sickening sound of the butcher knife being plunged into his chest brought bile to her mouth.

Effie tried taking small bites of air and was finally able to open her eyes. Pitch darkness. With her arms and legs bunched up around her, she realized she was inside some kind of container. Trying to make sense of her surroundings, Effie pried an arm loose. The interior of the box was wooden and rough, she could feel the slats. Some type of barrel, a whiskey barrel maybe. With her hand free and barely space to move, she lifted an arm and felt around the top of the enclosure. *Could she nudge it open?* Effie worked to bring her other arm up, balled her hands into fists, gave a push and then another. The top slid free. Effie drew in the most delicious lung full of air she had ever tasted. The noise was deafening. The ride jarring. Overhead the trees were thick. She caught glimpses of the starlit sky through their branches. Effie inhaled. The sudden jolt upended her. The barrel crashed down and rolled. Effie braced her hands against the sides, swiftly descending, rolling, lurching, and for a moment, seemingly suspended and then landed with a jarring thud. The noise of the motor running receded, sputtered, and ended.

Birds twittered. Effie peered out into the dove-gray early dawn light that silhouetted the pine forest and hilly terrain. How long had she been there, in her wooden shelter in the piney woods? Effie pulled herself free, assessed her pain and the surroundings. Her left shoulder numb, bruised and battered.

Her elbow swollen, throbbing. Standing on wobbly legs and a tender right ankle, she looked around. The path left by the truck was clear. Tree branches broken and hanging, tire treads visible across the straw-littered clay. At the bottom of the decline she could make out the shape of it, crashed into a tree, near the water's edge, the stake bed truck that brought her there. Up at the top, she realized was where they had left the road, purposefully or not, she had no way of knowing. Remembering that she had been a captive of whomever was driving that wreck below, Effie slid behind a tree and watched shapes gain their form as more light filtered through. Then she saw him, sprawled there near where the truck rested along the riverbank.

Effie crept closer, using the trees for cover. He hadn't moved since she began her approach. If he was breathing at all, it was shallow, undetectable. It was Eddie. She knew that now. His big, hulking frame and the striped coveralls. If he was only sleeping, Effie didn't want to wake him. If he was uninjured, she knew she wouldn't outrun him, her ankle screaming with every step. Effie patted her side pocket. It was still there. She pulled the cloth-wrapped bottle of chloroform free. It was miraculously intact. She recalled seeing a similar one rolling across the floor of the kitchen. She had been afraid that she had dropped it. But it had been Albert's. It was all too easy to get your hands on the tools of the trade at the sanitarium, and she obviously wasn't the only one who had armed themselves with it for last night's misadventures.

Effie lay the bottle and the cloth at the base of the tree. Sensing no movement from Eddie, she unbuttoned her uniform, stepped out of it, and lay it on the ground. She unwrapped the long sleeves of the oversized straitjacket she had swaddled herself in the day before and thanked her lucky stars that she had gotten the biggest one she could find. If she could only get it on him and secure it properly.

Effie dressed quickly and began her final approach. About five feet from her patient, she stood and watched for signs of life and then signs of waking. He was breathing but still out cold. She hoped the chloroform would do the job quickly. Effie lay the jacket on the ground nearby. She picked up the brown bottle and carefully removed the top. She didn't want to risk being overcome by it again and knew once she poured it, she would have to move fast. Keeping her eye on Eddie, she poured the liquid onto the cloth in haste, held her breath and screwed the top on tight, jammed the bottle back into her pocket.

Now or never, she told herself. Effie took three big steps and leapt atop the sleeping giant, pinning his arms with her knees. His eyes flew open as she pressed the cloth over his nose and mouth. She squeezed her legs tightly, cinching him to the ground, his left arm fighting, his right arm useless, his eyes wide and menacing.

"This is for Bertie and Pearl," Effie snarled, digging her nails into his face."

After what seemed like forever to Effie, the man stopped struggling. His eyes rolled up in his head, his left arm flopped to the ground. Effie sat atop him for a while longer, just to be certain he could cause her no harm. Satisfied, she got the straitjacket. She'd never put one on a patient before, but she was grateful for all the practice she had rolling and cleaning and dressing the women on her ward. She trussed him up as tightly as she could with limited function in her arm.

Not knowing how long he might be out and what he might be capable of when he woke, Effie mapped out her next move. Thinking the truck might be a source of useful tools, she made her way to it and wrenched open the door. There on the floorboard, beneath the steering wheel, was a pistol and a silver flask. She reached in to retrieve them. From beneath the steering wheel, she saw it, dangling from the gear lever. The brown leather strap with the kitchen lab key that she had placed around Bertie's neck. Effie slipped it off the stick, closed her fist around it, and drew it over her head. She kept her hand on the key and limped back to where Eddie lay, out cold on the ground.

She kicked him with her good foot and screamed, "What have you done with her?"

Back at the truck, she picked up the flask, shook it, and screwed off the top. It was whiskey. She wiped off the mouthpiece, took a swig, and slipped it into her pocket. Eyeing the weapon, she remembered those shooting lessons her father had enjoyed so much every time they went out into the country, near the old farm where he had grown up. She and Norris had hated it. Effie picked up the weapon, checked that it was loaded. She found a long branch to help better maneuver on her bad ankle and headed over to sit in the shade of a nearby tree.

Effie knew the next step was to climb her way back to the road, but she didn't want to leave until she had some answers.

It was peaceful by the river. Sunlight twinkling like stars on the water, the wind rushing through the tops of the pines, birds warbling and trilling. Effie's eyes heavy with exhaustion, closed momentarily until rustling and cursing brought her back.

He was near the water's edge, fuming and flailing. Effie struggled to her feet and hobbled a few steps nearer.

She pointed the gun and called out, "You fall in that river, I'm not comin' after you."

He rolled to his side to see her.

"Get me out of this damn thing," he demanded.

Effie shook her head. "That's not happening."

"My arm's broke. Ain't that enough?"

Effie snorted and took another step. "Not nearly. Not for what you've done."

"What do you mean, what I done?"

"What were you planning on doing to me? Why did you put me in that barrel, take me off in that truck?" she asked, waving the gun at the wreck.

"You were just gonna get what you asked for," he sneered.

Effie aimed and fired at the front tire, making her mark.

"What the hell, you little whore!" Eddie yelled.

She drew a bead on the rear tire and took it out with the second shot.

She turned, taking another step toward him.

"Where's Bertie? What have you done with her? What made you think you could take those women, sell them, and kill them, like they were livestock?"

"Easy pickins' at that hellhole. Nobody cared about them girls. They was trash," he sneered. "Good for one thing."

Effie cocked the pistol again and took aim at the man. "You best start talkin', mister. I don't mind at all if I shoot your fool head off."

"That colored gal we snatched from your kitchen? That's who you're all worked up about?"

"Her name is Bertie," Effie proclaimed, holding the gun steady. "Say it, Bertie."

Eddie sneered. "She was a fast movin' little cooze. Got away from me that one did."

On her front porch, Sallie, holding a white enamel bowl of pecans in her lap for cracking and picking, saw how tightly Fern held to the arm of the swing, her face blank.

Fern kept the swing in motion, pushing off with both her bare feet every time they touched down.

"He told you he'd let us know as soon as he learns something," Sallie told her, keeping her eyes on her work.

"It'll be dark in a couple of hours. I should have kept looking," Fern answered.

"You planning to walk all over the county?"

Fern pursed her lips.

Sallie stopped working and took ahold of the rim of the bowl with both hands. She looked at Fern. "You think I did right by her, telling him not to call her family yet?"

Fern sighed and looked at Sallie. "What would he have told them if he had? That she's missing? That we're not even sure what's happened to her?"

Sallie went back to cracking. "I just want to do the right thing is all." She turned in time to see Fern rising from the swing. She let her eyes follow Fern's. A police truck had rounded the corner and was pulling up, out front of Sallie's.

Fern was standing on the bottom step when James Robert climbed out.

"They found Effie. She's banged up but she's okay," he said, walking toward them.

"Bertie?" Fern asked.

"Not yet. Still lookin'."

Fern sat down hard on the front step and covered her face with her hands.

"Let me get us some tea, Sheriff. Come have a seat," Sallie said, heading into the house.

James Robert stood above where Fern sat—exhausted, relieved, emotions bubbling over.

He reached down to pull her to her feet. "Come on now, she's all right. State police took her to the hospital. Might have a broken arm. A banged-up ankle, too, but she's okay."

Fern made her way back to the swing, not able to talk yet. James Robert sat down beside her.

"Thank you, Miss Davis," James Robert said, standing and taking a tall glass of ice tea.

Fern waved it off.

"What can you tell us, Sheriff?" Sallie asked, taking her seat.

"Couple of boys out fishin', came down the river in their boat. Saw the truck sittin' almost in the water. They pulled up to see what was what and found Eddie Johnson, propped up in the shade of the truck bed."

He looked at Fern and chuckled. "Said he was done up like a pig for the spit, in a straitjacket, a bullet in his leg."

Fern smiled and shook her head.

"One of 'em stayed there with Eddie, the other one climbed up to the road, found Effie, sitting alongside it. They flagged down a car. Got the state police out there about two hours ago."

Sallie spoke first, "She put him in a straitjacket? What was she doing with a straitjacket?"

James Robert took a long pull of his tea before he answered. "Had it on under her uniform."

He turned to look at Fern. She was still smiling. She stood up, grabbed a glass of tea, and perched herself on the porch rail.

"I'm guessing that was your idea?"

Fern shook her head. "No. Effie has to own that one." She smiled. "I wish I could have seen that."

"Can we go see her?" Sallie asked.

"Yes, ma'am. I came to give you a ride over there in my truck."

Sallie glanced at the police truck and noticed all the neighbors standing out on their front porches, watching.

"I'll be explaining this for weeks to come," she said, rising from her chair.

"Everybody on the street will be talking about all the white folks over at Miss Sallie's, the sheriff taking Miss Sallie off to jail, who knows what all." She reached for the door. "At least let me put on some respectable clothes before you put me in that truck, Sheriff. And maybe we could ride by your office so I can call Effie's family, if you've a mind to."

"We can do that," James Robert answered and turned to wave at the neighbors.

A little after midnight, Effie opened her eyes for the first time since coming out of surgery to set her broken arm. Her throat was dry, and when she turned to look for a nurse, she saw Fern dozing under a blanket in a chair next to her bed.

"Hey," she croaked. Fern didn't stir.

The night attendant walking past saw her and stopped to check. "I bet you need some water," she said quietly, picking up a pitcher and cup from the bedside table. She poured a cup full and then brought the paper straw to Effie's lips. Effie sipped the soothing liquid and then nodded that she had enough.

"Look who's awake," Fern said, standing at her bedside.

Effie turned and smiled.

"You need anything else, let me know," the attendant said, looking from one of them to the other.

When she walked away, Fern said quietly, "She didn't want to let me stay here. Said it was the colored ward. I asked her if she minded that I was white. She left me alone after that."

Effie rolled her eyes, then remembered. "Did they find Bertie?"

Fern stepped closer and placed her hand lightly on Effie's bandaged arm. "Yes. You won't believe where. At her mama's, down in Brunswick. She went home. I don't know how she got there."

"Thank the Lord," Effie uttered.

"I heard you went for a barrel roll. I've always wanted to do that."

Effie snorted. "Well don't invite me when you go. It's not as much fun as it sounds."

"You could have broken your neck," Fern said, serious again.

"Well, I didn't exactly go willingly," Effie answered.

"Sallie called your family. Your father's in Florida. But I guess you knew that. Norris wanted to come right down. Sallie told him to wait and hear from you what you wanted him to do."

Effie nodded.

"I really don't know what to say, Effie. I'm so sorry I got you into all this," Fern said, their eyes meeting.

Effie looked confused. "Got me into this? I was responsible for Bertie. You didn't get me into this. You tried to talk me out of it.

"Not hard enough," Fern replied.

"It's not your fault that it turned out this way, Fern," Effie told her. "We cooked this up together, remember? I wanted to find Bertie and catch the culprits just as much as you did."

"Yeah, but I used you as the bait. You shouldn't blame yourself for Bertie."

"I offered," Effie countered and closed her eyes. "And I am to blame for Bertie's fate."

"You tired?" Fern asked.

"Bone weary," Effie answered softly.

Fern watched her for a moment as her breathing slowed and deepened.

"Hey, Effie," Fern said, tapping her hand lightly.

Effie's eyes fluttered open.

"Did you really wear a straitjacket out there?"

Effie smiled and nodded.

"And then what did you do? Take it off and put it on him?"

Effie nodded again.

"And that bullet in his leg?

"I put it there," Effie answered. "I didn't like the way he was talking about Bertie."

"I would have paid good money to see that," Fern said.

Effie smiled and drifted off to sleep.

Fern pulled her chair up a little closer. She watched her friend for a few minutes more. Tears filled her eyes and spilled over, streaming down her face.

"I almost lost you," Fern whispered. "Thank God you're safe."

She lay her head back and pulled the blanket up to her nose, drew her legs up in the chair and closed her eyes.

Effie and Alonzo and Fern

JUNE, 1923

22

Grateful to be back in the ward after several weeks of wasted time, the pain in Effie's elbow made her wince. Not really wasted, she decided. She had to recover from her injuries, but there were so few days left now before her year-long stint at the sanitarium came to an end. Already in the time she had been away from them, her women seemed to have drawn in on themselves somehow. The hopefulness she had about their well-being was dimming. It was her first day back, and the breakfast trays with their grits, cornbread, and syrup seemed to mock her and the belief that she had somehow had some lasting impact, made some transformative and permanent difference in their lives. Some seemed happy to see her, glad that she was all right. But they knew she was a short-timer now. They had already turned themselves over to her replacement. Effie knew that would make her departure easier on them, but she was troubled by the thought that her time among them had been inconsequential. She saw them now, many out on the portico—sitting, watching, waiting. The sadness she felt in leaving threatened to overwhelm her and surprised her in its depth.

"Hey, Miss Effie," Cora said, wheeling in a cart of freshly laundered bedding. "I'm sure glad to see you doin' all right."

Effie smiled. "Let me help you with that, Cora."

"You cain't put no sheets on them beds with that hurt arm."

"Yes, I can," Effie answered, feisty.

They started in on the first bed in the first row, pulling sheets and replacing them with fresh ones.

"I was waitin' to get some time with you to hear what all happened. Just heard bits and pieces is all," Cora prodded.

"It was pretty awful, I'll tell you that much," Effie answered, a little reluctant to dredge up the story again.

"Heard tell them men was runnin' a whorehouse and a juke joint down in them tunnels," Cora said, waiting for confirmation.

"Somethin' like that."

"Was they the ones done that to Pearl, took Bertie?"

Effie nodded.

"Praise God Bertie's safe and home with her mama." Cora went on, "That big man, he killed that Albert?"

"He did." Effie tried to tuck under the corner of the sheet with one arm, Cora following behind her fixed it the right way.

"I heard they was all in it together, them men and that other woman they killed, that one named Rose."

"Roselyn," Effie corrected. "Yes, that's what he told the police. He claimed the brothel was her idea, but she was gettin' too bossy, talkin' too much, tellin' too many people 'bout what they were up to."

"That's cause to split somebody down the middle?"

"We can't understand why people do the things they do."

"Why'd they put her on Fern's porch? You know anything 'bout that?"

Effie shook her head. "The police said they were probably tryin' to scare Fern off, keep her from comin' back into the tunnel."

"And why did he kill that creeper? I thought they was in on it together."

"He was a violent and angry man. He thought Albert had made a mess of things. Said he was the one caused it all to come crashing down when he decided to come for me."

"That's pure wickedness, that is."

"Yes, it is, Cora. Let's just hope it's over now," Effie said, picking up another sheet and fumbling with it, trying to spread it out.

"You goin' after them men, that's what saved Bertie," Cora declared.

"I'm glad she's safe," Effie answered.

"I won't never forget it, what you done, nobody will," Cora told her.

The door to the ward opened, and a nurse's aide walked in.

"Nurse Herndon?" she started. Everyone knew who she was now.

"Yes?"

"There's somebody waiting to see you at the laboratory kitchen."

"Thank you." Turning to Cora, she asked, "Can you finish this without me?"

"I reckon I can manage," cutting her eyes, Cora answered slyly.

Spread before her on the small kitchen table were a composition book for note taking, a fistful of sharpened pencils, and the *New Essentials of Biology Presented in Problems*, a gift from Sallie. Fern recently finished the section on vertebrate animals and had moved on to man. The day's lesson, to compare man to a frog. On first look, Fern had thought that was pretty simple, but the reading seemed a bit more dense. The discussion was about the human body as a machine. Just thinking about the structure and function of human legs compared to frog legs required a different frame of reference than anything else in Fern's life. After taking a sip of coffee, she chuckled and muttered, "I like this" and started sketching a frog leg in her notebook, carefully labelling the flexor and extensor muscles.

"Fern," Sallie called from the screen door. "My arms are full. Come let me in."

Fern hurried to help Sallie with her schoolbag and some groceries.

"Got something in the mail from Ludie Andrews today," Sallie told her. "Let's see what she says."

Fern deposited the groceries on the countertop, then sat back down at the table and waited while Sallie ripped open the envelope and unfolded the letter they had both been anxious to receive. She tried to read Sallie's face as her eyes darted back and forth across the paper, but as usual, she remained willfully inscrutable.

Sallie looked over the top of the letter at Fern, watched her for a minute without her realizing it and then said, "Looks like Miss Effie's not the only one headed to Atlanta."

Fern stood up quickly. "What did she say?"

Sallie skimmed over the letter. "Says she'll meet with you, talk over your plans. If she thinks you're serious about your studies, she'll introduce you to Miss Annie Feebeck. She's in charge of nursing education at the Grady Hospital. You'll have an interview with her."

"And then what?"

Sallie looked at her again. "Then you're a student at the Grady School of Nursing."

Fern shot straight into the air. "Yes!" she cried out. Just as suddenly, she came back down to earth and her face sagged. "Does it cost money?"

"It does. But there're ways to make do. One thing at a time, Fern. You go to Atlanta. Show them how smart and hardworking you are. After they say yes, we'll figure out the rest."

Fern stood, looking across the room at Sallie. "Thank you, Sallie. None of this could have happened without you."

Sallie's face broke into one of her rare and beautiful smiles. "I like helping young folks. And you best not be thanking me yet. You have a long road ahead of you."

"Hello," Effie called out at the doorway of the kitchen lab.

A tall, dark-haired man wearing gold-framed pince-nez glasses just like her father's, poked his head out of the pantry.

It was the first time Effie had been back after having to walk through the events of the fateful night with the state police.

The man came forward, extending his hand and smiling.

"I'm Joseph Goldberger. You must be Miss Herndon."

Effie shook his hand. "Yes. How do you do, Dr. Goldberger?"

"I'm well, thank you, and after hearing about what you've been through, I'm glad to see you looking so well yourself." He pointed toward two stools at the prep counter. "Could we have a seat for a moment?"

Effie looked around, uncomfortable in her surroundings, the site of recent mayhem and murder.

"Or maybe you would prefer we go outside? Of course you would. Why don't you show me a more suitable place where we can talk for a few minutes?"

Once outside she pointed. "Right over here, in the shade."

They sat down on the bench.

"I haven't been down here in a while," he said, looking around. "This has always been my favorite time of year in the South."

He turned to Effie. "William Tanner has spoken so highly of you, Miss Herndon. I wanted to thank you for the interest you've taken in our research here and all the progress you contributed to."

"I appreciated the opportunity to learn more about it and to see the impact of your theories about nutrition on my patients with my own eyes," Effie said earnestly.

"Yes. It's been an astounding journey. I think we're on our way to identifying the pellagra preventative," he acknowledged.

"It's a shame the research is being shut down," Effie offered.

He gave her a quizzical look. "Where did you get that idea? We're not closing down the research."

"I'm so glad to hear that."

"I'm here to get things back on track. I brought William to Washington to do some analysis. That kind of work is impossible to accomplish in the field. I've been stuck in the lab far too long. I needed to get back down here, roll my sleeves up, and do the real work," Dr. Goldberger explained.

"I thought the experiments were ending," Effie added.

"Oh no. This new yeast protocol shows so much promise. We'll be continuing it for another year, at least. That's what I wanted to talk with you about. I understand your one-year term at the sanitarium is ending and you're heading back to Atlanta."

"Yes," she answered, somewhat regrettably.

"I need an assistant, Miss Herndon. And I believe you're uniquely qualified to take on that job."

Effie was dumbfounded.

"You don't have to give me an answer today. Take some time and think about it. The Hygienic Laboratory needs dedicated nurses like you to help us connect with our patients, continue our work to solve the problems of epidemic diseases."

"I really don't know what to say. It's a great compliment that you would make such an offer. I'll need to think about it."

"Good. I'm glad. I would expect you to think it over. Please understand, though, that I'm talking about a career in public health, well beyond this research at the sanitarium. If you're interested, I want you to come to Washington, get a good understanding of what we do, then head out to do some field work. It will mean some travel."

"I would like that. I'll give it some serious thought."

He rose and extended his hand. Effie stood and took it. Even though he towered over her by a good half foot, she looked him straight in the eye and said, "Thank you, Dr. Goldberger."

***

Fern sat on the bench across the street from the sheriff's office. James Robert's police truck was missing from its usual spot and so she thought it was safe to assume he wasn't inside. After Norris had come for Effie, and they had said their goodbyes, she had made her way over to see if she could catch James Robert on his lunch break. They had a couple more things to talk about, and she wanted to tell him about Atlanta.

Over the past two months, she had spent a good bit of time out at the Ennis place. She hadn't gotten up the courage to reveal herself to Mr. Ennis or to engage the little boy that was the spitting image of Tom, but she had watched them. Around noon each day, Judge Ennis drove up, went inside. From along the tree line, Fern followed as they emerged from the back side of the house. They wandered around through the garden, sometimes made their way down to the fishpond, picked up stones, and threw them into the water. Or the old man pulled the little boy around in his wagon. Their lunch was brought outside on a big silver tray, spread on the table under the shade of a large oak tree. The two of them ate together. The man gently preparing bites of food for the boy. Afterward, on a blanket, spread across a sheltered patch of grass, they lay down with a book. The little boy—his head on the man's shoulder, listening, pointing—asking for more. More often than not, they both fell asleep. Those tender, tranquil moments soothed Fern and yet left her grieving for lost things, forfeited time, irrecoverable kinship.

Fern wasn't sure what she wanted from James Robert, or if he even knew the answer to that question that had welled up to the point of bursting, but she knew she absolutely had to ask. She had no intentions beyond that moment of knowing. She simply had no other choice but to know for sure if somehow, by some tangled ruse, that little boy was her son.

James Robert wheeled his truck right up to the front of the police station. Fern loped across the street to meet him.

"Hey. Got time for lunch, Sheriff?"

"Bout to head that way."

Fern walked into the diner ahead of him.

From behind the counter, Wanda called, "Hey, Fern. Sheriff. The usual? Burger for you, Fern, egg sandwich, James Robert?"

After they slid into the booth, James Robert couldn't let it pass. "I see you and Wanda got chummy."

"Yep. She knows lots of stuff 'bout lots of people," Fern jabbed back.

James Robert folded his hands on the table in front of him. "You doin' all right?"

"I am. I wanted to let you know that I'm goin' to Atlanta. I might be goin' to nursing school if everything works out."

"That's great news, Fern. When did all this happen?"

"It's been in the works for a while now. Sallie's been helping. I'm gonna stay at Effie's until I get everything worked out."

A little surprised by the arrangements, James Robert kept it to himself. "You want me to drive you up there?"

"No. I'm taking the train," Fern answered.

"When you leavin?"

"Next week, Monday morning."

"You sure this is what you want, Fern?"

She nodded. "It's exactly what I want."

Wanda put their ice-cold Cokes in front of them. "Did I hear you say you're leavin?"

Fern looked up with a smile. "That's right. It's time for me to do something with myself."

"Atlanta? You sure 'bout that?" Wanda questioned.

"For now," Fern answered. Wanda turned back to the counter, muttering something about why anybody would want to go to that big, nasty city.

"Did you find out anything else about Albert and Eddie? Were they the ones that attacked me a few years back?" Fern asked.

"My buddy at the state police said Albert wasn't around here back then. Eddie's been working over at the State Prison Farm for a while. He was running work crews all over the county the last couple of years. He used them prisoners for his own purposes. Pimped out women. Had a couple of stills back in the woods by the river, close to where he wrecked his truck that night. He was takin' bootleg whiskey to all kinds of joints. The tunnel was just one of 'em. He met up with Roselyn at the sanitarium and they got friendly. He let her in on it. Roselyn picked out the girls they took down there. Albert snatched 'em if they weren't willin'."

"Just another horror story from my childhood home," Fern offered.

"Pretty much," he answered. "No way of knowin' if it was him that attacked you."

They sipped and waited for what was next. Fern, the bolder of the two, got to it first.

"We've talked about a lot the last few weeks." She looked him in the eye. "We've avoided one subject."

James Robert dropped his head.

"You didn't want to tell, and I didn't want to know the truth," she told him. "But I'm ready now, and the only thing I'm expecting from you is that. Tell me the truth. No reason not to."

Wanda came back with their plates. "Y'all good now?"

"Thanks, Wanda," James Robert answered, giving her his best smile. She left satisfied for the moment.

He looked at Fern. "What you want to know, Fern?"

"I've been out to the Ennis place."

"I figured you would," he said, hands gripping the edge of the table, his egg sandwich cooling.

"Is that little boy mine?"

James Robert shook his head, blew out a puff of air. "That little boy belongs to Judge Ennis."

Fern drained her Coke, looked hard at him for another minute, and asked again. "Is he the baby I gave birth to?"

"There ain't no record that connects that boy to you, Fern. He belongs to Judge Ennis. He adopted him, legal."

Fern crossed her arms. "And how did he come to do that, James Robert? Your sister, Louella? Did she do this?"

He started by nodding his head in an almost imperceptible way. "Her and me, Fern. We both did it."

Fern had to look away from him then and waited for more.

"We did it for you. We did it for Nora. Couldn't see you raisin' a baby at that place. I promised Nora I would make sure you didn't end up like her. Louella, too, we promised her we would see to it."

"Why? Why did they tell me he died? I thought all this time that he was somewhere out there in Cedar Lane. Why couldn't you have just told me that Ennis might want him? I mighta said yes to that, James Robert. Why didn't anybody ask me?" Fern didn't even try to keep her voice down.

"That was all we could agree to, Fern. Ennis didn't want you comin' after that baby someday. I promised him you wouldn't. Tellin' you he died. We thought that was the only way."

"That wasn't yours to take care of," Fern told him.

Wanda was back at the table. "I can heat that up," she said, reaching for their untouched plates.

"Don't bother," Fern said, rising. "I lost my appetite." She gave James Robert one last look and turned for the door.

Effie settled into the far corner of the rooftop terrace of her family home, the morning sun already warm. Despite being so close to the ever-expanding city, it was a space protected from the chaos of the outside world. Norris had done his best to keep the garden alive. Now she wanted to make it the refuge her mother had dreamed of. She flipped the page of her drawing pad and began sketching a master plan. The door to the stairwell squeaked and her father peeked through the opening.

"Papa! When did you arrive? I wasn't sure you were coming today." She hurried to meet him, and he scooped her into his arms. She stood on tiptoe to latch her arms around his neck.

"Thank the good Lord, girl. I'm so glad to get my arms around you." He held her out so he could see her, gave her a quick appraisal, and drew her back in.

"Did Norris come for you at the station?"

"No. I didn't want to interrupt his work. Decided to get on the overnight and get up here early. I couldn't wait any longer to see you."

"I'm so glad you came," Effie said, taking him by the hand and walking him back to the sitting area in the corner.

"What are you up to?" he asked, noting the drawing pad.

"I thought it was time for a resurrection," she told him, looking around. "Mama wanted this to be a grand garden—fit for parties, dramas, reading. I aim to bring it back to life."

"She did have grand ideas." Alonzo smiled and looked around.

"And how about you? Are you all right? You gave me a scare, Effie." He took off his glasses, pulled out his handkerchief, and started wiping them down.

"I'm fine, Papa. I'm glad to be home. I hope you can stay for a while."

"I'll be here for a few days. Got some business to tend to. I want to see that you're doing all right," he said, putting his glasses back on and looking at her again. "You look good. I'll say that."

She chuckled. "I am. I'm better. I was scared though," she told him, reaching for his hand again.

"You want to talk about it?" he asked her.

"Not yet. Maybe later."

"I heard you've got a friend coming to stay for a while. Somebody you met at the sanitarium."

"Fern. She'll be here tomorrow. I think you'll like her. I hope she'll get to go to the Grady nursing school. Sallie and Mrs. Andrews have been sorting it all out."

Alonzo snorted out a chuckle. "Those women know how to fix things, all right. Took you off to the sanitarium for a year before I even knew what was happening."

Effie smiled. "You knew, Papa, even if you want to pretend otherwise."

He turned to her. "I reckon I did."

"You know when you showed up at Sallie's back in September, I thought you had come to get me and bring me home."

Alonzo snorted. "You know better. I would never do that."

"I don't know, Papa. You like to be the boss of things."

"That I do. But I've never gotten in the way of what you wanted for yourself. I've treated you the way your mama would have expected me to. I let her decide for herself what she needed. I want you to do the same for yourself."

"I know. You always support me, Papa. I really do appreciate that. And I really appreciate that you let me make my own choices."

"I was glad though that Sallie Davis was there to help you when you needed her."

"Yes. She was so gracious to me and to Fern. I'm so glad I got to know her. She's a kind, good person."

"She is. And she was a good friend to your mama," Alonzo offered, looking out over the rooftop.

"We talked about her a lot," Effie offered.

He nodded.

"I guess there's a lot I never knew about her. I didn't understand the things she struggled over," Effie admitted.

"It's not for children to know everything about their parents, Effie. Just like you have your own private hopes and dreams. Your mama and I did too," Alonzo explained wistfully.

"Do you think she was happy, Papa?" Effie watched her father consider the question before he answered.

"She was happy," he answered thoughtfully. "But like so many, she had unfulfilled dreams and they haunted her."

Alonzo turned to face her. "That she felt that way had nothing to do with us, Effie. She loved us all with her whole heart."

"Did you ever feel forsaken by her, Papa?" Effie asked, hoping she hadn't gone too far.

Alonzo chuckled. "That's a word that Addy would use. And I would probably have to ask her to explain it to me."

"I'm serious, Papa. Did you feel abandoned or repudiated?"

Alonzo chuckled again. "She would be proud to hear you askin' with those fancy words. But no, Effie, she never abandoned me or rejected what I am or who I became."

"I'm glad to hear that. I was worried," she said, moving her hand to his arm.

"Worried about what, child?" Alonzo asked gently.

"I can't explain it, Papa. I just didn't want you to have been hurt by her doing the things she did, wanting a different life."

"You mean, her wanting to have a life free from limitations? To not have to worry for her children and their safety and their futures? Crossing that color line, because she was able?"

She nodded.

"I worried about your mother's safety in a world with so much hate. I worried that she would get hurt. I was afraid she would be defeated, destroyed by it. But I had underestimated her. She was bold, Effie. And she held on to hope, every single day."

Effie smiled. "That's what Sallie said about her. That she was hopeful."

She put her head on his shoulder. He leaned in and planted a kiss on her forehead.

"Bold and hopeful. I'd say you turned out just like her," Alonzo said, wrapping his arm around her. "Now tell me about your plans. What's next, Effie Herndon?"

Effie laughed. "Oh, Papa, I don't think you're ready for that news yet."

"Well it couldn't be any worse than what you've just come through, could it?"

"No. It couldn't," Effie answered. "Dr. Goldberger has asked me to come to work for the Public Health Service."

"Oh my," Alonzo responded.

"In Washington," she added and smiled.

"Are you going?" her father asked.

"I would be foolish not to, Papa."

"Yes" was all he answered.

Fern and Sallie stood on the platform, waiting for the conductor to signal for boarding.

"Thank you for the trunk, Sallie. And the clothes."

They were having a hard time making eye contact, trying hard to hold in their feelings.

"I can send you more if need be," Sallie told her.

"I'm sure this is plenty," Fern answered, looking down, hunting for words. "I don't really know how to tell you how much I appreciate everything you've done for me."

"Don't get me started. I'm out in public. I can't let anybody see me shedding tears over you."

Fern smiled.

The ticket man came toward them, carrying a leather case. "Good morning, Miss Davis," he said, dipping his head. "I think this is for you, miss," he addressed Fern. "The sheriff asked me to give it to you."

"Thank you," Fern answered a little surprised, taking the case from him.

"All aboard," the conductor called.

Fern turned to Sallie and smiled. "No cryin' now, Miss Davis. I won't disappoint you." She wrapped her arms around Sallie and hugged her tight. "I'll have to come visit and check up on that garden, make sure you're taking care of things," she said as she turned toward the train.

"I was growing things a long time before you came along," Sallie said as she watched her go and lifted her hand in farewell.

Fern grabbed the handrail and stepped aboard the train just before it pulled away from the platform and left the small city of Milledgeville behind.

Fern took the leather case from the unoccupied seat next to her. She placed it on her lap and clicked open the latches. The box top was lined with a brown, silky fabric, some ink spots visible here and there. The interior seemed made for writing implements, divided into seven sections, some covered with velvet. One of the compartments held a stack of envelopes, letters she thought. In another, a slimmer envelope with her name on it. She picked it up, slid the single sheet of pale-yellow writing paper from it. It was a short note. Only a couple of lines. *"Dear Fern, these papers belonged to your mother. Some seem to be letters that were never sent. I took them from the files at the sanitarium. I know she would want you to have them."* The note was signed simply, *"Louella."*

There were some scraps of paper with Bible verses recorded on them. A few others were writings vaguely familiar. She assumed she had penned those herself. They were sweet little notes to her mother, in the shaky scrawl of a child learning to write. They said the things that children said, "I love you, Mama. I hope you love me too." "Will you play with me today?" "Can we go outside?" Treasures only a mother would keep.

She picked up the stack of letters and counted them. There were twelve. They were all addressed to the same person, Mrs. Elisha Herndon. How strange, Fern thought, that her mother would be writing letters to a person named Herndon. She opened the first letter and then the next. She saw that they were dated and decided to open all of them, arrange them first to last, before she read.

Fern tried to help with the dishes after supper, but Norris insisted he and his housekeeper could take care of them. She walked through the rooms of the main floor, taking in the details. Fern knew nothing about architecture, but learning that Effie's mother had designed and decorated the entire home herself made it even more remarkable. Fern had never been inside a palace, she had only seen them in books, but she felt certain, many of the rooms were inspired by those found in those grand places.

In the living room, where she was looking at the mural that lined the frieze just beneath the ceiling, Alonzo caught up with her. He came and stood beside her as she examined the paintings.

"I'm guessing this tells a story," Fern offered.

"It does," he replied. "My story." He turned to Fern. "I reckon Effie hasn't told you about my life, how I started out."

"No. She hasn't," Fern answered, looking back to the mural. "Did you grow up on a farm?"

Alonzo chuckled. "I did. That first picture there, of the pyramids and the great sphinx of Giza in Egypt. That represents our African roots. In that next picture, that woman you see there, chopping the firewood. That's my mama. She was a slave. I was born into slavery myself. That's me there, carrying the wood to the house. Next, that's me working the farm."

He turned to look at Fern again. "I don't seem to be working too hard. Heart's not in it." He smiled. "Working for the man, can't make nothin' of yourself. Not until you head out on your own, make your own way. That next picture," he said, pointing. "You recognize that. That's this house. That's the life I made for my family, by working hard."

"But you don't even live here anymore. You built this beautiful house, and you moved to Florida. That's what Effie said."

"This was always Addy's house more than mine. I made the money to build it. She dreamed it up and made it a home for the children. When Norris took over the business, I was able to get away from Atlanta, move to Florida. Life's slower there. I live in an orange grove. Can you imagine that?"

Fern's face lit up. "In an orange grove? That sounds like heaven."

"Near enough." Alonzo smiled.

"And that last picture, what's it about?"

"That's my old granddaddy, Carter Herndon. He's the one that owned that land, there, called Herndonville. His son, he fathered me. And he owned me."

Alonzo turned his attention to Fern. He watched her over the top of his glasses while she took in what he had told her. It took a few minutes before she spoke.

"You were a slave. Fathered by your master?"

He nodded.

She studied the paintings in silence.

"You said Herndonville." She pointed to the images. "That's where you grew up?"

"I sure did," Alonzo answered, folding his arms, looking back at his life story laid out across the wall.

"Your family, the Herndon family, that was their land?" Fern said, piecing it together.

"Still is, some of 'em still live there," he added, nodding. "Black folks and white."

Fern stood, arms at her sides, slowly shaking her head. "I thought there was some strange coincidence when I saw that."

"When you saw what?" Alonzo asked her.

"That name. Herndon. When I saw that name on a letter my mama wrote to her mama. She lived in Herndonville. Her name was Mrs. Elisha Herndon."

Now it was Alonzo's turn to be muddled. "Mrs. Elisha Herndon? That's Martha. Martha was your mama's mama? And your mama was?"

"Nora. Nora Walker," Fern said. "Nora Herndon Walker," Fern pronounced each name slowly while shaking her head.

It took a minute to sink in. "Wait here. I'll show you." She ran up the stairs to where Norris had taken her bags. In an instant she was back, walking across the living room with the stack of letters.

"I had never seen these before until today. Someone who took care of my mother at the sanitarium had them. She gave them to me before I left Milledgeville."

She handed the letters to Alonzo. He went to the writing table, turned on the reading lamp, unfolded the yellowed paper, and held it beneath the lamplight to make out the faded handwriting. "Mrs. Elisha Herndon, Herndonville, Georgia," he read. Then he shook his head. He looked up at Fern again and back to the letter and chuckled. "Well, I'll be damned."

"Norris, Effie, get in here," he boomed. "Get in here now." And he started laughing, then uncontrollably laughing.

Effie and Norris came through the doorway and stopped short, not knowing what to make of their father's hysteria. They looked from Fern to Alonzo and back again.

"Somebody want to tell us what's going on?" Norris asked.

Alonzo tried to get ahold of himself. By now Fern had caught the laughing sickness too. Alonzo draped his arm around her shoulder, and she held on to him around the waist. Neither one could speak yet. When they finally got themselves together, Alonzo handed her his handkerchief. She wiped her face and handed it back. He dabbed his eyes.

"If you two have gotten yourselves under control now, why don't you tell us what's going on?" Effie told them, crossing her arms.

"Effie, Norris. I'd like to introduce you to Miss Fern Walker. I don't know who her daddy is." This made them both erupt in laughter again. Effie put her hands on her hips.   Norris smiled at his father's mirth.

"But her mama, was my niece, Nora Herndon, the daughter of my half-brother Elisha Herndon and his wife Martha."

Effie's mouth dropped open.

"This girl's family," Alonzo said, looking down at Fern.

"Good Lord of mercy," Norris said. And the laughing started all over again. When they finally pulled themselves together, they tried to make sense of the discovery.

"Who's up for a little drive tomorrow?" Alonzo asked them. He rubbed his hands together, a gesture his children knew as a sign of excited anticipation. "I think we need to take Fern to Herndonville for a little visit."

Later that evening over second helpings of fresh apple cake made from Big Mama's recipe, Effie and Fern sat across from each other at the kitchen table.

Fern chewed and kept her eyes on Effie.

Effie looked up from her cake. "What?"

Fern shook her head. "I was just wondering. Do you think somehow blood just recognizes blood? Drawn to it, somehow?"

"What does that mean?" Effie asked, picking up the crumbs from her plate with a finger and putting them in her mouth.

"I don't know. Don't you find it strange that we would meet up in Milledgeville at a sanitarium, do all the things that we did and then find out we're kin?"

Effie hunted down some more crumbs and said, "It is a strange tale. That's for sure."

Fern chuckled. "I think it's more than strange. I think it's something else. I don't know. Isn't there a word for something like that when something happens that just seems so?" Fern lifted her palms, unable to come up with the word so Effie helped.

"Perfect?" Effie offered.

"That's not the word I was trying to come up with." Fern dropped her hands. "Is that how you see it?"

Effie folded her arms on the table. "That's how I see it."

Fern considered it for a minute and then said, "Well, all right then."

Through the sun-drenched summer, Effie, Fern, and Norris spent their evenings in the garden paradise. When the sun trekked to the western sky and the hammers grew quiet along University Place, their light-hearted voices and lively laughter mingling with the delicate perfume of the flourishing oasis, bubbled over the edge of the rooftop terrace, and drifted down the street. Boxwoods and hydrangeas, hostas, and lavender. Verdant green, dusty peach, soft pink. A riot of ever-changing color, as flowers blossomed and faded and others burst into bloom. Snapdragons and dahlias, asters and irises, vibrant red, pearl-white, periwinkle-blue, contrasting and harmonizing, shifting and changing. A soft breeze rustled the leaves. Waterdrops glistened in the afternoon glow, catching and holding the colors of the rainbow for the briefest of moments, only to fade with the dusk.

Acknowledgements

On an August night in 2019, in my living room with family members, I read aloud the first two chapters of *The Truth Together*. I trusted my familiarity with those assembled enough to believe that I would know by the looks on their faces and sounds of their voices if they were just indulging my fantasy about writing an historical novel or if maybe there was a slender chance that I could pull this off. Their reactions encouraged me to continue and by May the first draft was complete. Then the real work began.

I am so grateful to my family, Rodger, Hillary, Haley, Nick and Kirsten, you all listened to me tell this story long before I put it down on paper and offered unending support throughout the process. Mike and Julie, Laura, Katie and Meredith, I appreciate your encouragement and enthusiasm, you kept me going. And, my sister Karen who read the manuscript so many times that she could quote it verbatim. Thank you, sister. You listened for many hours. We talked it through for many more. Your insight and love made this possible.

Thank you to Tamara Hollingsworth and Kelley Kirkland, my first non-familial readers, both teachers and lovers of the written word, for your critical but gentle feedback and encouragement.

The story took shape and polished form through the careful editing of Rosanna Chiofalo Aponte and Alyssa Matesic.

The History Quill team of beta readers assembled by Andrew Noakes led me to believe that I was on the right track. Their feedback pushed me to the finish line.

And, the design work of Laura Boyle made the work real and absolutely worth the journey.

Book writing is after all a collaborative art form. I am so grateful to have had such an incredible team to bring this story to life.

When 2019 began, I had already resolved to write a story that year. In keeping with writing what you know, I knew I wanted to write a Georgia story. More than just a time period, I wanted to write about the experiences of people that focused on their resilience, hard work, and overcoming obstacles. I wanted to write about families and their love for each other. And I wanted to write about people who because of their gender, their skin color, their poverty, or their inability to simply cope with life, haven't been acknowledged or appreciated. This is when I stumbled on the Herndon family of Atlanta and Social Circle. The story was not an uncommon one, in that Alonzo, was born enslaved and his master was also his biological father. But his story became an extraordinary one when Alonzo left his childhood home, learned to be a barber, moved to Atlanta, and then became a business owner, eventually becoming so successful that he was regarded as one of the wealthiest Black men in America. But the story got even better. Adrienne McNeil Herndon, Alonzo's wife, was a woman of ambition, intellect and determination to have the life she dreamed about. She became a Shakespearean actress and noteworthy teacher of elocution at Atlanta University. Her ambition was to become a star on the stages of New York and Boston. She was

ACKNOWLEDGEMENTS

unwilling to let the obstacles of the Jim Crow South stand in her way, and so created a stage persona for herself, Anne DuBignon, a creole from South Carolina. But Adrienne never gained the success that she longed for. Many believe this was likely because her true identity became known.

The Truth Together is a work of fiction. Though some of the events that take place in the book did actually happen, the experiences of those events by members of the Herndon family, both the real-life family members and those that are a product of my imagination, are completely fictional. In my research about the real-life Herndons, Atlanta in the early 20th century, the pellagra epidemic in the south, Central State Hospital in Milledgeville, Sallie Ellis Davis, and Ludie Clay Andrews, I came across many invaluable sources. To those authors and their painstaking work, I owe a large debt of gratitude. I hope that readers of this book who want to learn about the historical inspirations for this story will seek them out and uncover the real truths of the lives and events fictitiously portrayed here. Here are but a few,

The Herndons: An Atlanta Family, by Carol Merritt, 2002. The definitive work on the Alonzo Herndon family.

Negrophobia: A Race Riot in Atlanta, 1906, Mark Bauerlain, 2002.

"Gone to Milledgeville: Northeast Georgia Women and the Georgia Sanitarium, 1886-1936," Laurie Jane Varner's dissertation, 2011.

But for the Grace of God: The Inside Story of the World's Largest Insane Asylum, Peter G. Cranford, 1953.

The Butterfly Caste: A Social History of Pellegra in the South, by Elizabeth Etheridge, 1972.

"Politics and Pellegra: The Epidemic of Pellegra in the U.S. in the Early Twentieth Century," by Alred Jay Bollet, M.D., 1992.

"Shakespeare in Black and White: Atlanta: 1916," by Justin Shaw, *Atlanta Studies*, February, 2017.

The writings of W.E.B. DuBois. Particularly "Of Beauty and Death," where DuBois describes the realities of the Jim Crow era and the humiliation of travelling by train for people of color.

The reports submitted by the trustees of the Georgia Sanitarium to the Georgia Legislature each year, detailing what was happening there, including the numbers of patients according to diagnosis, an update on construction projects, the colony farm crop yields and the pellagra research conducted by U.S. Public Health Service.

The website, Georgia Women of Achievement for information on Ludie Clay Andrews and Sallie Ellis Davis.

In the end, all of the mistakes in my book I own completely.

Made in United States
Orlando, FL
13 May 2024